FRUITLESS BODIES
ANNOTATED

A COLLECTION BY

J.D. BUFFINGTON

FRUITLESS BODIES: ANNOTATED: A Collection by J.D. Buffington

Contents

Introduction

Included in this collection of fiction are previously published pieces and self-published titles. From the first short story in a small press 'zine in 1997 to single pieces I put out on my own. My first collection as an independent author was PUNCH/PANTS: A Collection of Words, which is recollected here. This is my own set of the good, the bad, and the ugly. Here is an eclectic assortment of horror, science fiction, thriller, and the one time I wrote a western script. I share these stories to keep them alive, I still cherish every word I have put down, even if all I received were contributor copies. In this recollection of my original self-published collection, the short stories I published piecemeal. These are stories I tried to sell, some receiving praise, but not acceptance. The industry is a hard one to crack and the number of voices seeking that same acceptance is innumerable. The taste for genre fiction ebbs and flows with the economy and social movements. Publications rise and fall. Ultimately, there are stories in a lot of people that a lot more will never hear. Still, we commit ourselves to the void. This presentation will be organized chronologically, to show my growth and development. There will be gaps in time, it isn't *everything* I wrote from 1997 onward. The gaps were not always empty, but what I produced remains unfinished or abandoned to this day. But I did lose my drive in the wake of my mother's passing. I still knew I was a writer, I had a grand design that I thought about more than wrote, and I still struggle with getting my butt in the chair—it took time to start again, and collecting these stories is a part of that. Sometimes our growth is in fits and starts.

Gratitude

Authors Candace Nola, Steve Stred, and Alan Baxter are inspirations for this venture. Thank you for the confidence you express in the world.

To the 'zine editors who believed in a kid. And to an old friend who showed me what to expect and how to take it in stride. I hope you're still out there surfing, Dennis McDade!

And of course, for my mother, Irene, always.

A federal court room in this old piece of shit space station? Ha! That's a joke. Agile couldn't believe that they wouldn't hold the trial on Earth or Mars. Secondly, they knew a Story Teller was in the hearings as a witness, what she just went through was pointless. No, she corrected, it was a mental evaluation. It was just to make sure she hadn't gone nuts after seeing the body of Colonel Rupert. He was the unfortunate recipient of a system shock.

It was horrible, they didn't think it could happen, they'd always been cautious and avoided them at all costs, but...Mars base thought they could get the Colonel through before the next shock. They didn't. Agile remembered it more clearly than she did getting up this morning.

It was early, something around 0200, Mars said they had to send the Colonel over immediately, he was demanding he be sent right then. Agile, the attending receiver operator, told them to hold him for five minutes, a shock was coming. She didn't know what a shock was; she was just told that a Gate shouldn't be used before or after a shock for two minutes. The Colonel was adamant.

They began the procedures as quickly as possible. When they sent him through, they didn't think anything would happen. They shot him off about a minute and 59.9 seconds before the shock. One would think that's enough time, it wasn't. The Colonel was going through the beam and seeing all the normal sights, then saw one he hadn't heard of from other people.

It was a giant bubble of light, just sitting there right in front of him. He didn't have motor skills so he couldn't dodge it. He went straight in and straight out, didn't feel a thing. That is until he slipped into the receiving pad.

Agile was watching with sweat threatening to burst from her forehead. The image slowly began to fade in; she let out a sigh when Colonel Rupert looked fine. The translucent image looked to her and smiled. It took about 15 seconds to rebuild a body. The smile began to fade. As his body drew closer to being again solid, it was apparent he wasn't going to come out the same.

His body came out and he stumbled forward, screaming. Agile tried to calm him down but he just kept screaming. He kept screaming to the very end, his body began to bloat, and blood seeped from his nose, ears, and mouth. He looked up to Agile and screamed at peak level, then exploded. It was an explosion with a load "pop," pieces of him splattered onto the walls and blood covered the entire room. There was a central mess and Agile was standing in it. Covered in blood and trying to figure out what had happened, she contacted Mars Base.

"Um, guys, I got, uh, something really wrong here."

"Well, Agile, you're going to have to figure it out yourself. We sent off the Colonel and then we got some kind of back fire. There was a loud hum and blood came gushing out of our Gate. Got any answers?"

Agile tried to figure out what would cause that, and then came up with an answer. "Yeah. One question first: Did it happen one minute and 59.9 seconds after you sent him off?" She was looking at the Gate clock. An answer came back after Mars Base looked at their clock.

"Yes. How'd you know?"

"The Colonel showed up here at that time, started screaming and, well, uh, blew up."

"What d'you mean 'blew up?' Was he pissed?"

"Quite to the contrary, he literally blew up. His body, or what's left of it anyway, is all over the receiving room. He came out, started to bloat, and then exploded. I think he hit the shock. To tell you the truth, I didn't know it was that deadly. The whole ordeal must have happened inside the wave, you got blood, and I got an echo of the body."

"The shock is when the Gate hiccups. To tell the honest to whoever truth, I didn't know the shock could do that either. I'll contact my superiors, you do the same."

"Roger. You might want to call a custodian too. I know I'll need to."

The other operator chuckled, and communication was cut. This was serious, what other hidden dangers could there be inside the Gate wave?

This was the whole reason hearings were being held on this God forsaken space station. It was a relay between Earth and Mars, but also served as a military installment, which is why the Colonel wanted to come here. The station wasn't named, but was called several things, mainly Relay.

She turned and walked down the corridor. Lights were sparse for such a large place, which made it seem a little bit too gloomy. This place seemed like it should be a spawning ground for evil, with that Gate here, it was possible. Agile had been reading a book by a man from the twentieth century, it was originally seen as fiction, but with the recent building of the Gates, it seemed possible.

"The Applications of Inter-dimensional Travel as Written by James Tanner Thomas Jr. of the 20th Century." Yeah, it was a long title, but this guy was prophetic as Hell. He wrote that over 200 billion different dimensions can be attributed to one single grown person. Every thought someone thinks could have been different, thus a different outcome, each time a new universe is born based on that small outcome. With an infinite number of races and thinking beings, that would be a mind-boggling amount of possible dimensions.

If Gates existed in other dimensions, which they would almost have to, something from those dimensions could get through to here. Relay was the main Gate station, it had over thirty different units, both receiving and outgoing, and some were two ways. Although this had been the very first bad event to happen, it opened some people's eyes.

Especially Agile's. She didn't want to think about it too hard; it could easily upset anyone thinking about the possibility of a hostile environment corrupting this one. So, she walked down the metallic halls not making a sound, and hearing none as well.

*   *   *

That evening she had dreams, too many dreams to remember, but one stood out. It was extremely realistic, almost like she watched it from a documentary. She herself had never slipped, only listened to people's stories. In this dream she was forced to slip because the station was failing and critical to blow up at any time. Why everything was failing was beyond her until she stepped onto the pad. When she started to dematerialize, it was bright red instead of the blue everyone had explained.

When she slipped, she saw a whole number of energies passing around and through her. They must have been others going into the Gates at Relay. When she finally came into the other place there was a countless number of what looked like soldiers. They were all mutilated and appeared to be dead; although once she came through, they all began to attack her. She was killed but could still see. The soldiers kept beating her body until she woke up to the sight of the Story Teller's face.

Story Tellers aren't the most attractive people; they have very flat faces with no hair. Agile jumped at the sight of it.

"He! What the Hell do you think you're doing? You scared the shit outta me!"

"Sorry to have awoken you, but I see no feces; I did not scare you that much. A great trouble has arisen; someone else has just died due to the Gate."

"Who?"

"The Judge over the trial. She wished to sleep in her own bed. For some reason unknown to the technicians, she never showed up on the other side."

"How do you know she's dead? She's just missing."

"Her body exploded when the machine began the transfer. No one saw it, but one millionth of a second before transfer, her body shook, and blood sprayed into the air. It was teleported, no evidence can be found."

"Shit. Have the technicians changed the receiving coordinates?"

"Not to my knowledge."

Agile cringed at the thought of her dream coming true. She stood out of bed, when she noticed the Story Teller was staring at her, she ordered it to turn around while she dressed. It obeyed with reluctance. Story Tellers really saw no use in clothes; their skin was thick enough to protect them. Humans could adapt such a cover if they let themselves evolve, but they would have to stop with the clothing.

Agile reached the Gate room with the Story Teller close behind. "Have you changed the destination coordinates?"

"No, ma'am."

"Activate the Gate; I'm going to find out what happened."

"Right after someone died? I don't think so. I'm sorry, but I can't allow anyone to go through the Gate."

"I have a wave rider implanted in my arm. With it, I can travel through the waves and beams; I can even change the coordinates while inside..."

"I'm well aware of a wave rider. Had I known, I am sorry."

"Thank you. After all is said and done, you may be commended."

"Thank you, ma'am."

Agile stepped onto the pad, she feared the worst, but hoped that she would just end up on Earth. She pressed on the little button under her wrist and it glowed red.

"You have twenty minutes until the next shock. Good luck."

"Thanks." I may need it, she thought.

When the electric tingle ran over her body, she couldn't help but smile at the feeling. Then she saw the waves and beams, they were all mixed and tied together. No wonder the judge was torn up, her pattern couldn't fit through the beams.

Fortunately, it was all a soft blue, no creatures were around, and everything seemed okay. She started looking around; trying to find what could have messed up the Gate. Upon investigating, she found that there were a lot more beams than there were gates. *Hmm*, she thought.

Thinking about entering, it occurred to her that she might just end up inside another base or Mars. But one caught her attention, it was bright and massive, many of the other beams seemed to be stuck to its sides. She touched it trying to get a look inside. Nothing was going through. With her wave rider she could walk through as if it was a tunnel, but she instead let the flow take her.

She could see the exit coming up and halted her progress. This looked like it may be the Gate to God. The tunnels width went to infinite points; she couldn't see the edges anymore. Taking her chances, she entered the massive opening.

On the other side was not God, in fact there was nothing. It was just a big dark room; the only bit of light came from the sides of the Gate. "Geez, Relay's more attractive than this."

She stepped forward and found that the floor was slippery. Sometimes, Gates would get cold from lack of use; this would create lots of condensation that would leak onto the floor. Kneeling down to feel the floor, she noted this was no condensation, it was too thick. Mud? She walked further forward and a light from high above showed what she was standing in. Colonel Rupert's remains.

Only they weren't all over the place, it was like he'd been shot, with a big gun, but shot. But he had shot too, what appeared to be another human was lying in the corner, still alive.

"What happened?" she asked of it.

It didn't respond.

"Are you okay?"

This time it moaned and shifted its weight. She could tell it was looking at her, what little light was in here caught the glint of its eyes. It slowly got up and stumbled to her. Once in full light, Agile screamed in terror, this thing shouldn't even be alive.

The glint was not eyes, but the absence of such. It screamed back, only this scream was nowhere near human. It raised a rifle (that was the closest thing Agile could compare it to) and pulled the trigger.

She cringed expecting white hot pain to rip through her. When she opened her eyes, she saw that the creature was just as surprised. Remembering the Colonel's side arm, she dropped into his body, grabbed hold of the small .45 and fired three rounds into the creatures head.

It made a grunt, as if it didn't understand what had happened, and then fell face first with a loud resounding thud. This place had to be Hell; where else could such a thing be alive?

Agile quickly came to the realization that she was lying on a dead body. She jumped faster than she thought was possible. She sighed and wiped her forehead, looked around and wondered where the control booth was for the Gate. Finding no doors, her best bet was to hot wire the Gate to get out of here.

She began working; this thing looked as though the only use it got was through hot wiring. The inside was slightly different than what she was used to, but following ware marks, she got it started up and heard that magnificent hum.

Stepping onto the pad she expected to just go straight into the beams, her wave rider should have stopped all motion inside a beam. Instead, she ended up in another place just like before. But the Story Teller was there, so were the two technicians. Everything was dark, and the Gate was again the only source of light.

"He? What happened?" She asked.

The Story Teller stepped towards her. "You are alive? We thought you had been caught by the shock. What happened to you?"

"What do you mean; I couldn't have been gone longer than 10 minutes. I did find out something that could be potentially dangerous to us, though. We have to shut down all the Gates on Relay, Mars, and Earth."

"The embassy may not like that, ma'am." Said one of the technicians.

"I hate to pull rank, but I am the commanding Gate operator, my orders go above the High Council's if I say something is wrong. Shut down all the Gates on Relay, I'll inform Mars and Earth."

"Yes, ma'am."

Agile left the room with the Story Teller still on her tail. "How did you survive through the shock?" It asked.

"What d'you mean?"

"You were gone for more than 30 minutes."

Agile stopped and turned towards the Story Teller. "That's more than twice as much time as how long I was in there. Wait, perhaps time went faster there...no, must be inside the beam. I'm sorry, if I was gone that long then that's how long it was."

The Story Teller tried to comprehend her remarks, "What do you mean, 'there?'"

Agile began to walk again. "It was another place, just like here, only I was attacked by a *zombie* or something. The Colonel's body was there as well. I think I'm beginning to figure everything out."

"How so?"

"You know what a shock is?"

"It is the point in a peak of energy usage for the Gates when it must discharge excess energy."

"Exactly. What would happen if something interrupted that?"

The Story Teller didn't answer.

"Well, to tell you the truth, I wouldn't know in your case either. Once another energy hits a shock, the shock is disrupted and must find a different path. But shocks follow every beam so they can't find another path, unless they shove into another path. Since shocks go off at the exact same time on every Gate everywhere, when the Colonel disrupted one, he threw everything out of whack.

"While I was inside the beams, they were all tied around a central beam, this beam was huge. Once one shock hit another, it must have caused a chain reaction, forming a giant beam. This beam leads somewhere else, another dimension I mean."

"So, when Rupert hit the shock, he opened a portal to another plain of existence?"

"Yes, that's it right on the nose..."

The Story Teller looked down the bridge of its nose, not understanding the comment.

"One problem. If we still want to use the Gates, we're going to have to fix and rearrange the beams and close that one. I don't know how we go about doing that, but if we were to somehow get one of those creatures here, it would not be a pretty sight."

Agile didn't want to go back into the beams; she didn't want anyone to go there. It was not safe that place she had been. Even if it was a one room world with just that demon, imagine what else could be out there. She didn't want to; her main priority was to have all the Gates shut down.

*   *   *

"I had told the judge they weren't safe at the hearings. Teleportation is not meant to exist. Eventually, something like this was going to happen, or someone was going to use them as a weapon. After the things I have seen, they would be a weapon of unlimited power. All that I ask is that you completely shut down all the Gates until we figure out what all this means."

"Madam Agile," the portly man said from her view screen. "What you are asking is ridiculous. Yes, the two occurrences that happened at your base are not very pleasant, and it is fine that you wish to shut down Relay's Gate power, I support you completely. But to shut down all Gate activity? That would anger a great many people. I am sorry, I can't comply."

Agile hated to use her title to get what she wanted, but it was apparent that this 'Secretary of Peace,' wasn't going to lose money to save lives. "Then Mr. Secretary, I must order you to shut down all Gate activity and power."

"On what grounds?"

"In my recent studies, I have found that it is unsafe to slip, that is, to use the Gates. If you continue to allow the Gates to operate you will be putting many lives in danger, possibly fatal danger. If you do not answer to my orders, I will be forced to contact your superiors and inform them of your inability to do so. I will also advise them to study your behaviors toward superior officers of the opposite sex. In essence, I will ruin you if you do not 'comply.' If you look in your book of regulations or whatever, you will see that I have every right to do so, this is not blackmail, but a threat upon your position."

"Yes ma'am. I will consult with the operating Gate conductors—"

"NO!! You will give a direct order to have all Gates shut down! Comprende?"

"Yes."

And the view screen changed to the insignia of the Coalition of Planets. She didn't know if it would work, but after such a threat, if he didn't, he must want to quit his job. She next called the Ambassador of Mars, but didn't have to fight at all, in fact, once he was apprised of the situation, he quickly ordered all Gates to be shut down immediately. Hopefully that would end all this.

The next step was to begin studies of what happened. This was easier said than done. She didn't want any person to enter the beams, whether they had a wave rider or not. She sent probes in to collect data, but every time one came through, it was always messed up in some way. Components would be missing, or new components would be *added*. Sometimes they wouldn't get one back at all. On one occasion, three came back.

18

She finally broke down and sent wave riders into the beams. Once they slipped, they recorded anything unusual, which was everything. No wave riders were lost fortunately, but they did enter the other dimension Agile spoke of. The two bodies were found and brought back for study. The body of the Colonel was laid to rest with a proper burial. The zombie creature was studied and dissected.

In almost all properties, it was human. They could not identify it with a sex group, but it was called he for its massive size. It appeared that this creature, wherever it came from, was artificially gestated. It appeared that there were no sex organs, nor were there ever. The eyes that Agile thought had been ripped out were torn, but still there. It had small black marble sized eyes. Teeth were sparse and it had no tongue. The vocal cords were huge, which explained its loud howl. Otherwise the creature was completely human.

The gun was of extreme interest. It had been jammed, the only thing that saved Agile's life, but there was plenty of ammunition. It ran off of little pellets. Once it was operating, the gun would shoot the ammo at near light speeds. Once they hit a solid surface, they would explode, or even sometimes melt. It was speculated that the gun was based on the particle accelerator. Very ingenious.

The wave riders never encountered another one of these creatures, but Agile always told them to be careful. Agile then worked up the courage to enter again. Once she did, she could see that the disuse of the beams was allowing them to go back to normal. She witnessed a couple shocks work their ways through the beams. Each time a shock would come through; the beams would ripple and fix themselves. Apparently, the beams had an AI; shocks would wait for each other and cooperate to fix the beams.

The giant one was still open though. Agile organized a party and entered it to try and solve the mystery of why that Gate was there, and why the Colonel and the creature were there as well.

It was still the same, a small dark room with only the Gate. When you would walk so far forward, a light would come on. They found the walls, but no doors or seals could be felt. The next best thing they could think of was to blast the wall open.

They armed a charge and stood behind the Gate; once it blew, they heard a hissing noise. After the smoke and dust cleared, they emerged from hiding and saw that there was a door. It was a blast activated door, probably would have opened from a gunshot. When they stepped through, they saw an entirely different world. A vast open plain spread before them. The sky was a deep purple with several clouds drifting. In the distance, a building could be seen, from the look of it, it appeared to be a fortification. When they started towards it, they noticed several of those zombie like creatures pacing its walls.

They looked back at where they had come from and saw a rather large building in itself. The door had again slid shut, but they could see a pattern difference where the door was. Some of the creatures spotted them from above, and began scaling the walls, screaming and wailing all the way down. They began to hear gun fire and realized, this was not a safe place. Agile shot the door and rushed in. She ordered for a bomb to be placed on the Gate to ensure that none of those would be able to get through.

The team got through, but unfortunately, so did some of the monsters. Once the explosion went off it sent a super shock through the beams. The light blue turned to a red, and many of the beams collapsed. Agile got back to her base so that she could shut down the Gate to make sure that no creatures would get to her world.

She was wrong, some had already seeped their way onto Earth. When she arrived on Relay, the station had gone critical. Agile felt an uncanny deja vu but couldn't place it in all the hectic running around. She asked what made the station fail and was answered with a question she felt automatic guilt for.

"About 18 of the Gates exploded at one time; they were all pretty close to the core and did lots of damage, now we gotta get out of here."

She reluctantly stepped onto the pad and turned on her wave rider. When she slipped, everything was red. All the beams were actually straight and lots of activity was going on. She tried to find her way to Earth on different beams but got picked up by one with a flow too great to withstand.

When she entered the new world, she was surrounded by those zombie creatures. It now occurred to her she had prophesied this event. Readying herself for death, she saw that it was not her who was dying. A whole army was being killed by the Gate she was standing on. Once the fire war had stopped, she stepped off the Gate to see what happened.

"You guys left me behind! Fortunately, I had this, those things hate fire. Some of them are good, though. They said this is the only Gate on their world, that's why it was so heavily guarded."

Agile knew something was wrong, no one brought fire weapons, no one was left behind, the whole Gate was destroyed, but whoever this was, saved her ass.

"Thanks, sorry to have left you behind like that. I really owe you my life."

"Don't think nothin' of it; I was rather enjoying blasting them away. You guys did the right thing retreating though, don't worry about it. Now let's get the hell outta here."

She agreed, and then realized...this was Colonel Rupert! What the hell is going on here? She tried to get the Gate up and running, but it had been damaged by the weapons those creatures had. While working, the idea came to her that Rupert had been the cause of this, why shouldn't he be the end of it, this was obviously a different dimension just like the one she'd been to. Only this was the one where Rupert stayed alive. It all made sense now. Every possibility or chance something different could have happened; a whole new universe was made.

It was all being proved to her, right in her face. But something happened between Rupert and the Gate to cause this.

"What do you remember about transferring from Mars?" Agile asked.

He looked at her and tried to come up with the words. There was no easy way to explain it. "I just remember seeing this giant blue ball. I passed through it, and saw this giant tunnel spread out before me. I couldn't control where I was going, so I just followed through. When I came out, I was standing on this Gate, there was some kind of guard, after it tried to attack, and I emptied my side arm on it. This here," he said lifting the gun, "was what it had. So I took it and sat here. Then you all showed up, we looked around outside, monsters started attacking, you all went through the Gate while I covered you, and then the Gate got shot. Now here you are. Can you fix it?"

It was the shock, when Rupert hit it, he opened up all the Gates in the *multi*-verse. Ending up here, he stayed alive, and was possibly the best hope they had. She had fixed it but was waiting for a shock to come through; she was going to send him back into it. It just might work.

*   *   *

"In Star Trek it worked great, all you had to do was say, 'Beam me up, Scotty!' Worked fine, if there was a problem; it could be attributed to the pattern buffers and fixed within one episode. No one ever died due to a transporter malfunction.

"But that was a science fiction fantasy, what we have here is the truth, unfortunately it isn't very pretty. 'Gates,' as we call them, are the closest thing to teleporting we have. You stand on the pad, the computer reads each and every single molecule of your being, remembers where each one was, and shoots you through a radio signal. Works just like a phone.

"People have said that slipping, oh, excuse me, slipping is the term we use for teleporting. Anyway, slipping is like jumping into a warm pool that has nothing but lights on the bottom. Everything is wavy and subtle, you can't breathe but you don't need to. We can slip up to 50 million miles away, which at times allows us to go to Mars. When people slip that far, it passes in about two minutes, fortunately, it has been proven that no accidents can occur if the Gate is used properly.

"The only cautions I can give you: do not, ever, *ever*, send someone through a shock. It has been documented in computer models that another energy passing through a shock, can force it out of the way, thus causing chaos." Agile told her class.

"But Ms. Sedek wasn't there something like an incident like that fifty years ago?" One of her students asked.

She took in a long breath; she didn't want to have to remember it. "Yes, but that is for another time. Class, this evening, for those of you who are on operator training, General Rupert will assist in the beam aligning and show you how to bypass a shock if you're in dire need to slip someone. Have a nice day."

She sat in the large observatory long after her class had left. The question the student had asked was asked of her every year. And every year she choked up with bitter disgust of that time.

Agile had saved the entire Gate network, helped in the cleaning out of the demons. She even was commended and raised in rank. Where she could have just sent Rupert through and taken a chance of those creatures coming back, she took the chance of killing him again. It was something about then Colonel Rupert, the second time he passed through the shock everything reverted back to normal. The beam that had caused so much trouble had been collapsed.

When they had gotten back, Agile and Rupert seemed to be the only ones left on Relay. The last words of the Story Teller told them that they had been attacked by several strange things, some had looked human, but some looked completely monstrous. Rupert still had his gun, so they went about exterminating them. The spawn of that universe weren't very bright, so they were easy to kill. Earth had a similar problem, but with the army, their trouble makers were put out rather quickly.

Right now, Agile and Rupert are on a Mars based space station. Tower, nearly a century old, was rumored to be haunted by a creature from Mars. It was the first station out of Earth orbit, so it was natural that anyone on it would make up stories. Rupert had made a good point upon coming here though.

If all that happened with the Gates did happen, who's to say one of those things didn't find its way to Tower through a rip in one of the beams? It was too scary to think about.

ST

THE DEMON
Written 1996
Abunái November 1997
Portland, OR
Editor, Jeffrey Deboo

Another suggestion from my growing relationship with Dennis McDade acting as my mentor, this admittedly indelicate attempt at demons and dark fantasy captured the interest of Jeffrey Deboo at Abunái. He had read GATE in Ultimate Unknown and said he would have accepted it as well. These editors and producers read each other! This one read me and complimented my work! I really felt good about this acceptance, even though, dear reader, I think it's one of my weaker pieces here. I don't want to be dishonest, this was me playing with concepts and somehow that got published. Or maybe I should reevaluate that? This is me playing with concepts and it got published. I had an initial idea, I had an ending. What could have been an intriguing middle be damned. This is transformation and betrayal—no plot for you!

The mage stood spellbound. He really hadn't expected the enchantment to work. Yet, the far wall of his small laboratory rippled and seemingly melted away to produce a void. Instead of the other side being the dreary forest the mage knew, a fog of dust infested a sweltering plane below an alien star. But the mage knew what this world was.

He had opened a portal that led to the place most commonly known as Hell. Screams of hatred and pain escaped the ever-opening hole. Hell is not an attractive land. It burns red, and creatures of all shapes roam, searching for the greatest delicacy among the undead. Souls.

Burning craters seemed to be the source of the screams; the mage believed that souls were tortured in these pits. The mage soon realized that if he did not close the portal, he could easily end up in such a pit. Not to mention the two worlds could merge.

He frantically whipped through the putrid pages of his book, bound in human flesh, looking for a spell to close the door. As he thumbed through the pages, something on the other side of the portal noticed the ever-growing portal in its world. From the darkness it inspected the gaping hole with its long talon-like fingers and sniffed the air with its wet, convoluted snout. Finding the smell pungent, it began to retreat. The mage noticed the creature and screamed in terror.

Hearing his screams, the demon was again interested in the other side of the portal. Rearing its reptilian head towards the opening, it stared at the fear-stricken man. The demon knew what this quivering thing was. It was a hu-man. Mind you, not just a soul, but a living body. The demon, which was now apparent to the mage as being a female, stepped into the planet beyond hers. The world of *living* humans.

The mage began to babble spells as the demon drew closer, finally remembering the spell to close the portal.

"Fkt esk porter non woe!" He screamed over and over again.

The gate seemed to be closing and the demon knew. Looking back, she saw that it was now too small for her to fit. Her face saddened, long pointed ears drooping, but the expression changed quickly. She snarled and again faced the mage. She exposed her blood stained teeth and made a low rumbling growl that made the room shake, and the mage with it. She thrust her claws outward, widened her jaws, and emitted a hideous screech as she seemed to fly across the room.

The man screamed and ducked. The demon smashed into the wall behind the mage with such force that sunlight bled in through the cracks in the heavy timbers. He screamed in horror at the demon that was now shaking off the impact. Fighting his panic, he made a wild dash for the door. She sensed the sudden movement, flipped her tail, and the hu-man ran no more, nor would he ever. His legs folded under him with his fall, although not in a normal fashion. Pouncing on his collapsed body she abruptly broke his neck with a hideous crack. He never had time to scream.

Looking at the wall from which she had entered, now completely closed, the realization of her entrapment set in. She made a garbled noise in the direction of the dead man, probably a curse or swear. Looking back to where the mage had been standing when she first saw him, she approached the work table and began rummaging through his materials.

Coming across an urn, she shook it, knocking the lid loose. A careful sniff of its contents produced a burning sensation, in turn causing a sneeze. A billowing cloud of purple dust around her head seized her nose again. She looked at the urn; one eyebrow lifted in wonder, and then threw it over her shoulder.

Finally, she came upon what she was looking for, the book of spells and enchantments the mage had been studying. She flipped through it and recited the invocation to again open the portal.

"Gok on mow inn ther fi u dis an." She said aloud.

A serpentine hiss began to escape the wall where the portal once dilated. A wraithlike vision appeared from the other side. It gingerly floated through the tiny opening hole, much like steam. It then began to take shape, but not physically. It was still a ghost in the greatest sense of the word, naked, like her, but male. Its translucent skin seemed to shimmer, red and orange; its eyes glowing a blinding white. Horns weighed the creatures head greatly. It looked at her as she trembled and spoke in English with a low rumbling voice.

"Daughter, you have entered the world known as Urth. You have disobeyed the rules set forth to every demon by myself: 'No entrance to the world of living flesh is allowed without great purpose.' I cannot let you come back to our home; you must stay here until I grant thee permission."

"But, father...why?" asked she. There was no reply.

The creature disappeared in a smoky fireball. She quivered and sighed. The ground beneath her feet began to tremble and break. Her eyes widened with fear, what could possibly make solid ground rumble?

"In your stay, you will look as a hu-man." The voice said again from all around her.

From the cracked ground, heat, blood, light of great intensity, and flesh, began to unravel and cover her body. She screamed as it grafted to her body and twisted her form. Tail ripped from her back, she howled in pain as it lay on the floor flailing like a fish out of water.

The skin boiling up from the ground ripped and contorted her form. She was in the agony of those souls in the craters of her world.

As the pain slowly subsided, she was reminded of her home, the living fleshes that crawled along the grounds, looking for something, anything to consume. It occurred to her, that this new flesh covering her was most likely one of those that lived in her world.

She gazed upon her new form and was disgusted. These fat filled breasts with light pink nipples. Smooth cream-white skin, completely unattractive and less durable than scales, soft to the touch of these short fingers that lacked talons. She then paced around the room, examined again where the passage had been, as if to make sure it was really gone. She saw out of the corner of her eye, another hu-man.

She stood still; knowing that she looked hu-man might help with not being detected by this other being. She turned to it slowly, and saw that it was a female, just as naked as she. She cocked her head, and so did the other female, the other female seem to mimic her every movement.

She was angered with this other creature and grabbed a stone from the floor and threw it at her, this female still mimicked her, but soon shattered into several pieces. The realization set in that it was a looking device. She felt a hot wave course through her face. Embarrassment.

She looked at herself in the bits remaining on the wall. Her hind and back looked odd without a tail, the legs weren't quite as disgusting, and at least she would be able to run. She began to explore the orifices of her body, she laughed slightly when she probed her new nose.

She slipped her fingers through the moist opening between her legs. Strange, she'd never felt anything like this. She would have to figure it out later.

Though in its entirety, the body was revolting, it would have to do. After all, she was going to be on this plane of existence for quite a while. She knew that these hu-mans had a problem with being seen naked, she didn't, but she *looked* hu-man. So, she had to act like one, at least for now.

Still unaccustomed to the new body she was in; she walked to the lifeless corpse and donned its robe after much struggling to remove it from the body. It was somewhat big, it draped both her and the floor, but, she figured, it would have to do. She stepped to the opening in the wall that she had created when she smashed into it. She looked through and saw her second living creature. It was small, had a big hairy tail, powerful hind legs, and small weak forelegs that were holding some sort of food. That's what she wanted, food. The creature sitting outside would do nicely.

It was now that she experienced her first dilemma. How to get out there. She growled in confusion. From the looks of it, there was no way out. She pleaded for her father's advice.

"Father," said she, surprised by the higher pitch of the voice. It sounded whiny, another thing that disgusted her. "Father, how do I leave this place?"

No reply. *Great*, she thought. Now she was trapped, a small cell with nothing to eat.

Wait, she thought again.

There was something to eat. The hu-man in the corner. She remembered the first hu-man *soul* she had consumed. It was sweet, but she was warned never to eat a hu-man *body*. They were tough and bland. But in this situation, taste did not matter to her; it was food that she craved.

On the body the minute she thought of it, she quickly rolled it over on to its back so that its fleshy stomach was exposed. She tried to bite down into it. Nothing happened. No rush of blood, no taste of meat.

It then dawned on her, these were the teeth of a hu-man, and flat, meant to eat leaves, and *exposed* meat. Somehow, she needed to expose this body's innards, break the skin, something, so that she could eat.

She looked around the room for something sharp, she rummaged through the mage's table again, and she found the cap to the urn she had sniffed earlier. Though not as efficient as talons or fangs, it did have a sharp edge and pointed handle. She quickly turned and jumped across the room to the body. Upon landing she thrust the cap into the body's stomach. The lid burrowed through the skin with ease. She turned it and cut a slit through the soft flesh of the stomach. Blood oozed through the wound and onto her hands she sucked it from her fingers.

Reaching into the wound, the blood and organs felt delectably warm to her touch, she grabbed something inside the body and pulled. It was difficult at first, but eventually the cartilage and muscle let loose, and she held a mass of dark, wet, and meat. She did not know what it was, but that did not stop her from biting down into it. It was far from bland, but more...exquisite.

Licking the blood from her lips and hands, she took another bite and heard a noise from behind her. Turning to the sound, she saw there was another hu-man, who had come through an opening in the wall. These hu-mans must know extreme magic spells and enchantments. Looking at her, the other hu-man covered its mouth and stumbled backwards, throes of fear racking its body. She grabbed the urn from beside her, spilling the dust contents, and lunged at the other hu-man.

It finally did scream, but the scream was ultimately stopped when the urn collapsed this new being's skull. The body fell limp. She let loose of the unconscious creature, the body made a dull thud as it struck the ground. Returning to the mound of entrails she had been eating, she picked it up and sunk her jaws into it.

As she chewed, she walked back to the opening in the wall. It was not magic that had produced the opening, but a separate, movable, portion of the wall. A kind of door, blending with the wall, which is why she could not find the way out.

She looked outside at this new world, smiled, and took another bite of meat as she stepped through the threshold. A world teeming with hu-mans. Off to her left there seemed to be yet another.

She slowly sneaked up behind it, a male, judging by its size. The hu-man never knew what had happened. None of these hu-mans would know what happened.

*　　*　　*

Nearly a thousand years after her arrival in the world Urth, the demon had figured out her great purpose. It was destined she would be here. She was dubbed "collector" by her father and lord who appeared every fifty years. She reaped the souls of men.

But her purpose was drawing to a close; her father was due at any time now. He promised her return with his next visit.

She had never left the land she first set foot on, even with the discovery of new lands. Purchased nearly six hundred years ago, she owned the land she was thus born human. She built and rebuilt houses on the same plot where the mage once lived, and now sat in the den of her most recent.

She stared in awe as the rock wall began to hiss and creek, the father was returning. She had mastered all the human emotions and now showed the emotion of glee as she watched the portal open in the wall.

What she did not see on the other side of the portal was something she never could have expected. The father stood at the head of Hell's greatest military. The souls gathered by the collector. He intended on letting them get their last justice, by destroying the one who introduced them to their current state. The demon, through all her years, never suspected that she would be betrayed, by the ultimate betrayer.

Her face was obliterated before the smile ever left it.

THW

J.D. Buffington

TOWER

Written 1996

The Ultimate Unknown, Summer and Fall 1998
Streamwood, IL
Editor, David D Combs

The sequel to GATE, this was my first time having an editor ask for some touch-ups before accepting. Thinking back on this piece now, here in the 2020's, I'm trying to envision Democratic Socialism, and it gets accused of being fancier Nazis. But the "New Reich" is really just a government of "what if we really had equal rights?" I wrote this immediately after GATE, I was still 16; yes, this is still a violent video game short story, but I'm doing more world-building here, and expressing my personal opinion through it. The name doesn't denote the villain, the actions do. Again, this story owes inspiration to Star Trek, for inspiring a culturally diverse crew and a world trying to get closer to Roddenberry's vision of Starfleet. Herein also lies my first foray into time travel antics, a trope I desperately love to explore. This story sits in a different, more utopian future, but the underlying current that a ruined world of their own making is where these demons come from, and wants to break in and wreck their world. These are still themes I play with.

In 2142, a new German Reich was born, the fourth in Earth's history. Some feared that this Reich would be no better than the Third Reich of almost 200 years before. In fact, this "New Reich" was marked against by opposing politicians as being nothing more than "dressed-up Nazi's." Unfortunately, the name stuck. But they soon proved when they came to power that the people of Germany were accepting them, and they proved they were far different than any other Reich before them.

Still socialists, the New Reich seemed to give the same old view of Communism: absolutely no freedom from the state. This wasn't correct. The New Reich formed themselves to be more of a "...what if the USA was still the same, only there truly was equal rights," as Gries

Eberhardt, founder of the New Reich, had put it. The only thing that was similar between the different Nazi parties was their names.

For Otto Fein, the year 2146 was both a godsend and a nightmare. Otto worked for the New Reich as a renowned medical figure. He was a doctor in Bonn before the New Reich rose, he was one of those that hated the idea of a new Nazi party rising. He was scared that it would raise much turmoil among German people and the other countries. He also hated the idea of losing his high pay so that more "unfortunate" people could get medical care. He was selfish, and realized it, but he had grown used to the amount of money he received annually due to his career.

When the party did come to power, he never lost his pay, in fact it was raised. All hospitals were deemed government property and all workers in the medical profession were re-designated as government workers. But before anything like that happened, he had to register with the new party. He had no reason to go and do it, plenty of hospitals in the world would have accepted him and paid him equally as much. None the less, he became part of the New Reich before they even became the outstanding power.

But in early that same year, he was told that he would represent the German community and serve as Chief Medical Officer of the Martian Delegation on a newly built space station outside Mars orbit. This station was named Tower and was a "wait" station. No one was on the structure when it was finally completed. Tower spun at exactly Earth's velocity, but over an extended amount of time, it would slow to Mars gravity.

Otto was honored that the Reich chose him to represent Germany in the newly formed Mars Delegation, but he was hurt that he would never reach the same status he was given for Mars here on Earth. But deep down in him was that childhood wish to traverse the planets. He *was* extremely excited that he was going to Mars.

The departure date seemed so far away. On the 5th of April, he was to report to the Embassy of Space Travel (EST), when he arrived, he would go through a two week training course to ready him for space travel. When the date finally did come, he had studied everything he could get his hands on, the two weeks flew by like a breeze. The next step was the actual trip to Tower.

During his training, though, he met some of the other people he would be sharing the Tower with. Engo and Yemen Thurman, Swedish twins, they were seismologists who entered their profession from being models after they experienced a small earthquake in Kyoto, Japan. Charles Sinaka, a Chinese Microbiologist, whom Otto had immediately become friends with. York Shire, an American computer analyst who had it in him that he was better than anyone else at his profession. York seemed at first to be the one who might cause trouble, but after a private meeting with Olga Thompson a burly Russian woman who was also an analyst, he was fairly quiet for the rest of the two weeks. Apparently, she proved to him that he was not the best.

The other members that would accompany them were being trained in a base in southern Florida, where NASA had once operated before becoming the EST right after putting the first people on Mars. There were twenty people all together on that original mission, they were to form a colony instead of coming back. They had succeeded, and now, a little more than a hundred years later, there were two colonies with around 200 people. That long ago, many people thought that the colonists had no chance. But the colonists proved otherwise, and they also made some serious breakthroughs. They proved that Martian soil could support Earthling plants. They had even started terra-forming the geodesic domes they had constructed.

One of the missions for the teams that were going to Tower was to bring new supplies to the colonies. York supposedly had relatives there, although they were *extremely* distant cousins. Otto, along with the others, was anxious to meet the Martian people, to see if living on a different planet affected their way of life.

All and all, this mission had many glories. The group going to Mars was dubbed by the evening news as the Terra-Formists, their main mission was to do as their name implied. While the group was prepared for Mars gravity (a luxury the original colonists did not have), factory-like machines would be sent to the colonists to start a global warming process. The process would not harm the environment, after years of working and melting the polar ice caps, the new oceans and lakes would begin to clean the skies by way of evaporation and rain. With water would come plants supplied by the colonists and Terra-Formists, with that would be oxygen. With time, a period of probably centuries, the entire Martian surface would be green and blue.

But that was a long time away, and none of the colonists living there now, and none of the Terra-Formists going would see more than a small pond near the north.

But the entire team going was excited that they would be written in history as the pioneering Terra-Formists of Mars.

*   *   *

"All hands ready for docking with Mars Station 001-A." The mechanical voice said over the intercom.

Otto and the Thurman twins along with York were all in the same room looking at the Tower station with Mars in the immediate distance.

As they buckled into their seats, Engo said, "Isn't it beautiful?"

"I don't know that it's beautiful, Engo, but it is awe inspiring." York commented.

Otto nodded in agreement as he gazed on. "Just think," he said. "In six months, we'll be on it, assisting the colonists."

An even better sight came with his quiet. Sol, the sun, came into the window. Deimos, one of Mars' double moons, caught the light cutting a path of darkness, Tower, just outside the window, did the same. Windows on Tower caught the suns light as well, making it shimmer in the cold void. After a moment, Mars' other moon, Phobos, drifted into the shadow of Deimos.

"A double eclipse. Amazing." Yemen whispered.

"You think they made it to where we would see this?" York asked to no one in particular.

After a few moments the show was over, and Tower had taken over the window's view. They felt a slight bump and heard a hiss from somewhere inside the large ship.

A total of sixteen people were sent on the voyage. Two groups of five and Otto's group of six. Tower was a large station and could easily accommodate over two hundred people. These sixteen could live in separate rooms and never see another person for weeks.

But the three groups were assigned sections, and would live in halls together, each with their own generously large quarters. Tower seemed dark and lonely when all the people unloaded. Only the low power lights and the sun lit the hanger they had entered. A very large window graced the far wall, giving them a spectacular sight of Mars and Sol. The two moons had all but become invisible again.

"Welcome to Mars Station 001-A; Tower." A pleasant feminine voice said from the walls. "For the next six months this base will slow to Mars gravity, it is now spinning at Earth gravity which explains your ease and comfort. During your stay you may use all of the Tower's resources at your disposal. The Tower offers a wide variety of entertainment and activities to pass time in your stay, along with large databases to learn more about Mars in each of your individual fields.

"Many of you may have brought software that you wish to use here on the station. We welcome you to do so, Tower has several yottabytes of free memory at your disposal—"

The computer droned on, at first it was nice to hear the voice after hearing that monotonous droll the ship put out. But even this voice got tiring. Otto grabbed his bags and stepped over to an elevator with a carry-borg at his side lugging his heavier bags.

"Name?" the same female voice said.

"Chief Medical Officer, Otto Fein."

After only half a moment the doors slid open, and he stepped in. The doors were about to slip shut when Charles hollered for the door. When he stepped in the computer asked for his name.

"Sinaka."

The computer acknowledged with a beep and continued with its original order. In less than a minute, the doors slid open to reveal another large room. Several Windows lined the walls, but on a different level, and with the turn of the station, the view was different, here the stars could be seen.

"I'm only a microbiologist, but before we came here, I memorized star patterns," Charles said. Shortly thereafter, the sun crept into view. "There," he said pointing out one of the windows. "That's Earth. Right next to the sun."

Otto stepped up next to Charles, he looked down the length of Sinaka's arm and saw a faint blue speck behind the glare of the sun. "Amazing. I never thought that in my lifetime I would see the Earth like this. It makes you think about what's over there, and how much you didn't do." He said.

"Yes, but think about the things you did do." Charles said. "I mean, especially you. You had a great part in helping the New Reich help other people. You must be a hero to your people."

Otto smiled inwardly. He had done a great deal for his people and government. He only hoped that he could do the same for the Martian people on the planet that was now coming into view. What looked like canals and dry lake beds lined the surface of the arid planet. Centuries earlier astronomers formed theories that other life had tried to irrigate the planet. Then during the late twentieth century, a great discovery was made.

From photographs of the surface of Mars, what appeared to be an ancient civilization with architecture beyond Human comprehension appeared. The "Mars Face," as it was called, was the subject of debate for many years until that last NASA mission to put Humans on Mars. When we finally did study it, we found no proof of civilization, just a freak of nature. It has been documented in nature on Earth that the Human face has appeared in rocks, plants, almost anything that can be shaped by the elements. This was the largest by far.

Otto wanted to see that face, he wanted to see all Mars had to offer. But that wouldn't be for another six months. Half a year away.

By now, though, the twins, York, and Olga had made their way to the room as well. Charles greeted them while Otto watched the rusty world float completely into view and out. "Home." He mumbled in a whisper.

"What?" Said Engo.

"Huh? Oh, nothing." Otto lied. "Did you know that that tiny blue star is Earth?"

"Where?" She asked.

"Right there, in that open area." He said pointing.

"What are you talking about, that's Venus, Otto. That's Earth." York said pointing to a faint blue speck towards the top of the window. "Here, I'll show you." He stepped up to the window and touched it where the star he called Earth was.

Two crossed lines centered on to the area and flashed. The circle that had formed around the designated area enlarged and pulled the image forward and filled the window. A small blue and white orb with hints of brown turned slowly on the window.

"Had you stayed and listened to the computer's greeting, you would have heard that these 'windows' are actually computer screens. There's not a single window on this place. They were too worried about meteorites smacking them. So, if you press onto a star it magnifies it 60 times. If you push it again...like so...it magnifies it again." The screen flashed again and enlarged the planet to fill almost the entire window, which was roughly 2 meters square.

York was right, this was Earth. Clouds and continents could now be seen with clarity. From behind it the moon slowly came from hiding behind the ocean planet. He touched it again, and the screen went back to its original view.

"I hope you can tell a heart from a stomach better than you can tell the Earth from Venus." York said with a laugh.

Otto blushed slightly at his ignorance and his sudden emotion for home while seeing a planet that was nowhere near it. "Ah, but that is where you are wrong, my friend." Otto retorted with a smile. "I am a medical doctor, not a surgeon."

"Then would you be so kind to give me something for *my* stomach. Even with artificial gravity, I hate being in space." Said the immense Olga.

"Feeling sick, eh?" Otto said with concern.

She nodded and he put the back of his hand to her head. She was slightly warm. Olga had complained of a little nausea before they had even taken flight from Earth. Perhaps she was suffering from too much excitement. He rummaged through his smallest bag and pulled out a small compression gun. He put it to her arm and pulled the small trigger. The drug inside was forced through her skin at such a speed that she could not feel it.

"You should be better soon. If you're still queasy later, please tell me." Otto said.

"Da, I will." She said with a thanks.

For the next two weeks, all the people on the station had found appropriate living quarters, explored their section, and even some of the others. Each section was designed to fit each group's needs. Entertainment was not difficult to find at all, just the windows were fun to play with. York had it half right, the windows would magnify at different ranges for how far away an object was. The magnifying capabilities were astonishing, the trio of stars called Alpha Cintauri could be seen with ease and clarity. Even stars and planets up to eleven light years away could be seen.

Other activities included a kind of virtual reality room. Using a complex set of lights, mirrors and particle distributors, the square half kilometer room gave a real to life experience with substance. With 82 pre-designed programs and a programmable feature to create new ones, gave the visitors countless hours of entertainment. There were six of these Holographic Environment Rooms (HER's), two to a sector. They began to get so much attention that reservations and schedules had to be made.

It was these rooms that started Otto's nightmare, as well as the other people on the station.

*　　*　　*

Otto sat at the base of a tree having a talk with Emil Adolph von Behring, a 19th century bacteriologist who helped in the discovery of the process of immunization.

"So, I said to Kitasato," Emil said. "'Inject the damn monkey with the tetanus. We'll see what happens later!' I will never forget the look on his face when we saw that the monkey had become immune."

Otto laughed at the story. "I had always thought it was a little more serious than that. Kitasato Shiasaburo was always dull from what I read as a child."

"Do not always believe what you read. Kitasato was very bright, had a great sense of humor. He was one of the first people I thanked when I was awarded the first Nobel Prize in medicine. Which reminds me, how far has medicine come in the 22nd century?"

Otto began to explain that without Behring's discovery, medicine would most likely still be archaic. But before he had really gotten into his explanation, he noticed Emil was fidgeting. He, Otto, looked at him and noticed that the body was rippling like water.

"Mein Gott," said Otto. "Computer, freeze program."

The computer acknowledged with a beep. The rippling persisted, the only thing that told Otto that the computer had obeyed was that a bird had stopped in midair.

"Computer, remove character Emil Adolph von Behring."

A sound of sizzling air came from the ripple as the computer tried to remove the image. "A malfunction has disturbed the computer's ability to remove certain objects or characters from the program. It is advised that you terminate the entire program and suspend use of this Holographic Environment Room for a five hour period so that the computer can run a self-diagnostic and attempt to repair the malfunctioning routine." The computer voice said from hidden speakers.

"Then terminate program." Otto said.

The same sizzling sound came as the computer tried to comply. Finally, with a bit of struggle, the room turned again silver with tubes running in several directions. The ripple was gone, but a strong smell of ozone was all around the area it had been.

Otto had no idea as to what had just happened. There were two people he knew right off hand that he could ask, and it would be wise to ask the both of them, and to see if they could actually do something about it. As he recalled, York had set his quarters rather close to the HER.

"Computer," Otto said. It acknowledged. "Locate York Shire and patch a communications link."

"Yes?" York had said after a moment.

"Um, I need you to come to HER 2-1. I'm not sure, but I think the computer may have a problem, and I have no idea where to start on fixing it." Otto said sheepishly. He was scared that it might have been something he did to the computer.

York had complied and was in the room moments later. "What happened?"

Otto searched for words. "Well, I was running my historical figure program when one of the characters started glitching out."

York said, "Computer, define any...oddities that may have occurred within the last run program."

After a moment, the computer said, "There were no oddities present."

"Then where did the odor of ozone come from?" Otto asked more to himself than to York or the computer.

"Odor?" York asked. "Computer, what are the current levels of ozone gas in relation to standard levels?"

"Three percent above normal."

"Where did that extra three percent originate?"

Again, there was a silence followed with an answer. "The origin of the high levels of ozone gas is unknown. Would you like for the computer to conduct an investigation?"

"Yes." York said.

With that, York and Otto left. York to conduct his own investigation, and Otto to take it easy. But before they both went on their separate ways, York instructed Otto to contact him if at any moment the computer or any other programs showed similar quirks.

Otto agreed and went directly to his quarters and asked for the computer to link into the HER's mainframe. Once it did his window showed a diagnostic of all parts in the HER, which seemed to be operating fine.

"Computer, did the investigation of the ozone gas bring any results?"

"Yes. The origins were found to be a part of the program being used, integrated with an atmospheric anomaly."

"What? How could the program integrate with the atmosphere, and what was the anomaly?" Otto was getting far over his head, much more and he would be completely lost on what he was talking about. But curiosity drove him forward.

"The anomaly was that of time displacement, much like that of the end result of lightning when the air must refill an emptied area—"

"Time displacement?" Otto interrupted. "Lightning doesn't stop time. What are you talking about? Explain terminology and verify accuracy, please."

The computer did not respond, instead, Otto's window began to ripple much like the image of Emil had. Instead of asking for the computer to shut down the program, he told it to record the events with all sensors and called for York to come to his quarters.

The screen looked to crinkle and warp as the ripple grew larger. Eventually a hole began to open in the center of the screen. Through it Otto could see an entire dimension of tunnels and similar ripple effects. Beams of free moving particles shot through the tunnels at a rapid pace. Sometimes a giant shock wave would shoot through. The environment was a deep blue with bright white highlights. As Otto watched, a particle beam like the others started to appear in the distance and was headed straight for the opening in Otto's room. "Computer, terminate program."

York stepped in as Otto had made the command. It was the same thing that York would have tried, but still yet, he made a small curse for Otto doing something so blind.

"Cannot comply, a system error has occurred, repeat your order in fifteen minutes." The computer said.

"No, not fifteen minutes! Shut the damn thing off *right now*! Use as much power as it takes, I don't care if you have to shut down the station, just *end program*!"

"Computer!" York yelled from behind. Now there was a slight sound coming through like wind. It was just loud enough for it to be difficult to hear. Otto whirled to see York standing there, wide eyed with disbelief.

"Ignore last command made by Otto Fein. Instead, began Earth viewing field, magnify by 120."

It beeped.

The entire wall, which had almost been engulfed by the scene, was as normal as any other wall in the universe.

"What was that?" Otto asked. York only turned and left the room in a hurry. So, Otto, without really thinking anything of it, asked the question again of the computer.

"Please specify what should be explained."

"The 'atmospheric anomaly' that just tried to eat my room."

"The atmospheric anomaly was the same as found in the Holographic Environment Room."

Just what I thought, it probably has something to do with holographic emitters, probably the same thing York is thinking I bet he went there. He thought. The only thing he could think of to do now was to follow York.

*   *   *

His room was dark after he left, so he never saw the mass of...*something*...laying in the corner of his room. A small glassy eye twitched with the closing of the door, then the other slowly rolled to match its twin. It gurgled some noise, writhed, then stood on two tiny legs hidden under its oval-shaped, armored back. Four tentacles, which looked like massive dead snakes, began to slither up off the floor.

It looked around with its tiny head, then rose up to over two meters high with its tentacles. This creature was definitely from somewhere else. It seemed to glide forward, then up the wall. Once it reached the ceiling, it ripped a hole through the paneling, and crawled in.

*   *   *

Otto only had an idea of what York was thinking, he wasn't even sure that York was headed for the HER at all. What Otto had thought to himself was that the holographic programs throughout the station were infected. What better place to test that theory than in the Holographic Environment Room's. But he was soon diverted from his original course when he saw a figure down the corridor.

Olga, woozy from something unknown, came stumbling towards him.

"Little one?" she said. "What was that flash?"

Otto tried to figure what she was speaking of but had no idea. "What flash?"

"That one that just happened. I was watching a letter tape from my nephew in Bulgaria, then the screen went blank, the room got bright and, well...I was waking up."

Yemen, too, came stumbling down the hall, only in time to hear the end of Olga's explanation, and told a similar story. "We were walking down the hall, and when the door opened to the HER when we had already walked by, we looked back. There was this blue light and we looked in, there was this giant hole in the wall. Engo stepped up to get a better look.

"That's when there was this flash. Only when we woke up, we were still in the HER. There was this little black thing running from one wall to the other. Next thing I know, we're laying in the hall." She pointed back to where her sister was slumped against the wall.

"Is she okay?" Yemen asked for Engo.

Otto looked at Engo and determined that she had fallen asleep. When he tried to pick her up, she awoke with a scream. She almost crawled up the wall when she saw the other people.

"What is it?" Olga said after holding her down.

She eventually settled down and looked into Olga's eyes.

"Is it gone?" Engo said.

"Is what gone?" asked Otto.

"The thing...the thing that attacked us."

"I don't remember anything attacking us." Said Yemen.

Suddenly there was a loud explosion from down the hall. All four of them jumped when it sounded and ran in its general direction. Halfway there they saw York shivering in a fetal position. He kept mumbling about something, kept calling whatever it was "It."

Otto looked him over, tried to pull him back to being awake, but he just kept mumbling. "Well, York is beyond help, he's gone into shock for some reason. I can't do anything for him with what I have on me. He won't come out of this for at least an hour or two." He said. "Help me get him to the Medic Office. At least there he can rest."

Mainly it was Olga who carried him. But the office wasn't too far so she didn't mind. "Apparently that flash was the appearance of a visitor. We now have two counts of 'it.' Now we just have to find Charles and contact the other habitation rings. Who knows where that *thing* could be." Said Engo.

"Agreed. We have to stop what's doing this." Said Olga.

Otto attended to York while Olga and the twins tried to find Charles. Moments later, over the intercom, in a very quiet voice, Yemen ordered Otto to come to the Second Habitat Ring. Curious, He told York he would be back, but York didn't respond, he just whimpered.

When Otto entered the giant greeting room they had first entered on the Tower, he was flabbergasted. The giant window was completely destroyed, the computer repeated itself several times when it tried to tell him that he had reached the second ring.

He stepped out and saw several small electric fires and a couple of bodies from the second team. Upon inspection, those murdered had been killed in a very peculiar manner. Their eyes and bowels were pulled from their bodies with surgical precision and very little loss of blood from neighboring organs. But with this was some symbol scratched onto the victims chest. One that surprised Otto and disturbed him greatly was a swastika, the Nazi symbol that had been stolen from other cultures.

Otto was even more sickened when he noticed that the recipient of the bent cross was Jewish. He was the only one to have two symbols on him, the second was etched on his face. An up-side-down cross. Whoever, or *whatever*, had done this was sick and cunning.

Otto couldn't help but to wonder if all this had to do with what he had done in his own room.

"Over here!" said a memorable voice. It was Charles Sinaka, he was apparently okay. "Otto, we need your help," Charles said rushing to Otto's side. "This man over here, he only speaks German, and the translators are down. He was almost killed by that, that...thing, before we got here."

Otto knelt down before the man. The symbol of a pentagram was on his chest, but there were no other wounds. Otto began speaking and the old German man on the floor listened intently. Then the man began to speak, looking periodically around the room and to the other people.

"He says that everyone was doing something or minding his business when there was this great white flash." Otto translated. "He awoke to see a great beast rivaling even dragons sitting on his chest. It had four long black tails that each had a barb on the end. It was poised to rip into his stomach before it noticed he was awake.

"The creature quickly jumped off his chest and ran off into the dark corner...over there." Otto said pointing toward a blacked out room. He again spoke to the man and gave him a sedative to calm his nerves. The man smiled and laid his head back down. Otto then instructed Olga and the Thurman twins to stay with the man, "I asked him if he knew any Russian or Swedish, he knows barley a little Russian, and speaks fluently in Swedish."

"I wish we had known that from the start." Said Yemen.

"I told you to try," said Engo.

Otto glared at them and they immediately quieted. "Now is not the time for argument. York mumbled something about tentacles, and these bodies here are evidence to prove that something is here. We have to find it and stop it."

Charles knew what Otto wanted to do and followed him. "How many dead?" he asked.

"Three. The old man, his name is Hein, will probably die tonight. He had suffered a heart attack, he was lucky to have survived that. I don't have any idea where the fifth member of their team is, but this ring is big, they could be anywhere."

*   *   *

In the same black corner, the creature pulled its lips back in a mock smile. This was going to be too easy, and there was too little prey for there to be any amusement. But still yet, it knew of these creatures that stood so tall and on only two legs. It had met one, had almost killed it, had felt a surge of something from its emotion center. That one creature it had met was here, different from all its relative creatures out in that large area.

The creature writhed and slid up the wall, the only thing it had to do was find a way out of the dark area it was now.

*　*　*

"But you're not looking for the fifth member, are you?" Charles continued.

"No. The third ring is home to the military, if they've been attacked and couldn't hold off that creature both York and Hein explained..."

"Then we don't stand a chance."

"That's where you're wrong. Everything that lives, can die."

Charles thought about how perfect that sounded. Apparently, if this was a motion picture, Otto would be the hero. But this was real life, or so thought Charles. For the entire time the Human race had been in space, even if it was in their own solar system, they have never met an alien species. To meet only this one, presuming it was *only* one, and finding you couldn't defend yourself, sounded way too much like fiction.

The thought cleared from his mind when the elevator arrived. The doors slid open and there on the back wall was a man. He was severely mutilated, his legs had been ripped off at the hips, his bowels, like the others, had been perfectly removed. Instead of just his eyes, the entire head was removed, leaving only a crude bloody stump.

The arms had been stretched out and tied with electrical wires from the ceiling of the compartment. Sparks fell also from the ceiling. Both Otto and Charles looked up to see an enormous hole had been ripped out. Standing above the opening was a black face without eyes or nose, just completely smooth. Invisibly thin lips pulled back to show blood stained teeth that appeared to shine like metal. A snarl resembling cats fighting escaped the creature.

It hissed with a high whistling note that seemed to reverberate in the creature's throat. It pulled back and jumped straight up, four long tendrils caught the light of falling sparks as it ascended.

"Are you absolutely positive you want to go to the third ring?" asked Charles.

Otto only looked at him. "I think there's another elevator on the opposite side."

Charles sighed and shook his head. *Please*, he prayed, *whatever you are, kill me quick and with mercy.* He then followed Otto to the other side.

Here was a completely different scene. Everything was normal, nothing was broken or torn up. Charles and Otto surmised that the person in the elevator was the fifth member of the second ring, so no one was to be found. When they got to the elevator, it was perfectly normal.

They had a smooth ride, the creature evidently hadn't made it here. When the doors opened to reveal the large customary room, one would think it was normal, if they were in Hell.

The room was barely lit by controlled fires. The floor was lined with the peoples' missing innards, the entire pattern was a pentagram. Whatever this creature was, it knew everything about Earth's dark religions. The smell was almost unbearable, and at one point was for Charles, when he vomited just outside of the intestine ring. Otto found a storage compartment with a flashlight and a hand gun.

He shined the light at the walls, then at the floor, and back at the walls.

"What is it?" Charles asked, wiping his mouth.

"Each way the star points, there's a dead body on the wall. I don't know how they're being held up, but four of them are placed in a flipped cross. That one," he pointed with his flashlight. "Is placed with his legs and arms pulled to form another star. I think there's a ring of blood around him."

"How can you stay so calm, Otto, there's dead bodies all over the place with guts on the floor."

"You forget, I'm a doctor. I can stand the sight and smell, but the image and the method make me more scared than you'll ever know."

With that they heard a horrible hiss from high above. Otto quickly darted the flashlight from point to point trying to find it. Suddenly he came onto it. It reeled back from the light but stayed where they could see it. Otto aimed the gun and shot. There was a loud growl, and the creature was again quickly out of sight.

"What the hell is that thing?" Charles asked rhetorically. He knew Otto couldn't answer.

"You're almost right." Said a voice from behind them. Otto almost fell trying to turn and aim the gun. "Whoa, there. I'm on *your* side, no need for the gun. Allow me to introduce myself, I am William Rupert, I just managed to survive the attack by that thing. Hid in a closet I did."

The man walked to a compartment that had been torn half way open as the perplexed Otto and Charles watched on.

"Here!" said the man. He handed both men a large gun that strapped to their shoulders and swiveled like a pendulum. "You know how to work these?"

"'Just point, click, and shit,' as my dad used to say." Said Charles with a broad smile. He now knew that this was indeed a real man bent on killing that creature.

Rupert laughed as he checked the ammo on his gun, then on the other two. "Between us three, we could kill about 40 dozen of those creatures. But from what I've noticed, these things are very wily, can sneak up behind you when you think they're in front of you."

"How do you know all this?" asked Otto.

"I watched it." Rupert said. "I am in the army you know. I have to survey the enemy at all times and make sure I don't get my butt fried in the process. Now, to kill this damn thing, I'm assuming, is going to be difficult. The four tentacles are both weapons and defense. They give the illusion that they're much bigger than they really are.

"The body is no bigger than your head, so try to aim for what looks like the center of the tails."

"Why not just keep shooting until it stops?" Charles asked.

"That's a great idea, but there's only one problem. They move quick enough to dodge bullets, they can actually see them coming. Ready?"

Otto and Charles again looked at each other with wonder. This Rupert fellow was either really brave or really stupid; they hoped it was the former.

Each gun had a pair of night vision goggles that also showed an image as to where the gun was being aimed. The three of them ran in a straight line, all looking around, looking for tell-tale signs of where the monster could be. Rupert advised that with their guns they could scare the creature and not be attacked, so they should split up, one person to a ring. Otto got the second ring, Charles the first, and Rupert stayed in the third ring. Each man got an additional side arm...just in case.

Otto's first place to go was the room where he had left the others. He was scared that he would find them mutilated like the other people he had seen. He was surprised to find that the body in the elevator was gone, blood was smeared all over where it had been, and where it had been dragged. He looked up with his gun aimed at the hole, there was nothing.

When he walked down the corridor to the main room, he was thankful for the goggles, otherwise he wouldn't be able to see where he was going. He came into a very bright room, then pulled off his goggles. Olga was sitting back against the far wall, asleep from what Otto could tell. The twins and the man, Hein, were having a conversation in Swedish.

Olga nodded her head and opened her eyes to see Otto standing there with a giant gun hanging at his side. Every time Otto moved the gun would stay in the same spot, not even swaying. At first Olga thought she was hallucinating, but when Otto noticed that he had been spotted, he walked over.

"So, you're real," she said with a smile. "It'd been so long since we tried to contact you—"

Otto interrupted, "Tried to contact me? When?"

"I don't know, about 15 minutes ago. Apparently, we're up against something big..." she said pointing to the gun.

"No, not really, these are just our only chance. The thing's super small. A guy we met in the military ring said he watched it as it killed his partners. Said his name was Rupert, I was somewhat curious as to who he really was and why he didn't help his dying comrades. I checked for his records in every file, but there weren't any." Otto explained. "He's down in the military ring, he sent me here, and Charles to our ring. On the way up, I told Charles to check on York, if he's all right, we could definitely use the help. I'm not sure, but we might have ourselves a killer with some little killing machine on his side."

After talking with Olga for a while, Otto let her go back to sleep, then talked with the twins and Hein. Hein had slept from the time he received the sedative but had awakened over 10 minutes ago. The twins said they heard some weird scratching noises beyond the wall.

Otto went to check on it, the creature had been there and had done extensive damage to the wall, had almost gotten through too. But it wasn't there anymore, Otto checked the entire office, but he couldn't tell where the creature had gone.

When he turned to leave, he didn't notice the four tentacles slither off the wall and toward the ceiling. They slowly moved a ceiling panel and pulled the small creature up through the panel hole. It slid back the board and dashed off, making not a sound.

"There wasn't anything there, but the entire station is basically wrecked so it could have been anything." Otto reassured, not mentioning the markings.

He swung around with the gun making a *whoosh* as it followed him when he heard a crash behind him. It was Charles pushing a piece of metal away, on the opposite side of the gun was York. He was standing on his own but still had a hand on Charles shoulder to steady himself.

"What's this about a monster and an unknown soldier?" York tried to say with a smile.

"How are you?" Otto asked.

"I'm not dead anyway. Where's this Colonel Rupert at?"

"He's on the third ring, didn't Charles tell you?"

"We checked," said Charles. "He wasn't there, and we know he isn't on the first ring."

"I'm right here!" Rupert said from high above.

"Dammit! You just like scaring the crap out of people, don't you?" yelled Charles.

"I don't do it intentionally, I assure you. I know where that thing is, he went back to the third ring, he's begun some kind of process. Let's go, we have a better chance if we all shoot at it. Bring him." Rupert said pointing to York.

*   *   *

The four of them stood there looking upon the putrid mess spread out across the floor, nothing much was happening right now, but the overall feel of the place was enough to scare the hell out of all of them. But Otto scared the hell out of them by charging his gun and aiming it at Rupert.

"Who are you?" Otto asked.

"Colonel William Rupert. I thought I explained all of this..." he fidgeted.

Otto shook his head and looked down. "No. You know your way around this place, you know a lot about that weird creature, and there isn't one damned record of your being even alive. I just thought I'd go ahead and clear some things up, so I'm assuming that you have caused the trouble here, and you're one of those idiots who was against sending more people to Mars."

"No," Rupert slumped, taking his hand away from the gun. "This whole thing is too far gone. We've gotten deep into this, and you were bound to find out when this battle was won." He fidgeted, looking for words.

The creature screamed from above and darted through the group of people. An unarmed York yelped and ducked behind Otto, although the brunt of the attack seemed to be on Rupert himself. It stopped in front of him, snarled, grabbed him with two of the tentacles and dragged him off. All of them, including Rupert, were too shocked to actually react. Rupert did scream eventually, more out of surprise than fear. The whole incident took place in less than two seconds.

There were snarls and pounds and grunts and sounds, but no discernible way to tell who was winning. Finally, there was an electric hum of the gun charging, then a shot, and a loud scream.

"Which one died?" Charles asked.

All of them were silent as they looked into the dark Rupert had been dragged into. There was a solid thump as though something rolled over something else. Then a slight dragging noise, and the appearance of Rupert, covered in black blood and chunks of shell. "I won."

"So that's it?" Otto continued from his original insinuation. "You're about to explain to us your whole presence, then the creature attacks you, you make us think you're a hero, and we let you off. Not so easy, I should think. Who are you?" Otto pointed the gun again.

"Come on, Otto, the creature's dead, what more do you want?" York asked.

"No," Rupert defended. "He's right, you should know. My name is William Rupert, but the reason there's no file of my existence is because there is none, won't be for quite some time. See, where that creature came from, so did I, in a sense.

"I'm from the...uh," he paused, clearly lost. "The future?"

Otto mumbled a curse of disbelief. The others didn't know what to think.

"In my time...we have what can be easily called teleporters. I myself was involved in an accident, well, counting this, two accidents. Something in the Gateway mainframe messed up, and I ended up on a version of Earth that was totally run over by Satanism, rather than Christianity. With that came a lot of genetic experiments from what I could figure, and that thing was made. A woman came in for me and tried to save me from getting killed there, but I ended up here, in the past, with one of those creatures--"

A crackling explosion ripped through the air as Rupert tried to explain. In a way he was almost thankful that it occurred. It was clear they weren't taking him seriously. They all looked to the far wall, the same blue anomaly that had occurred in Otto's room was there.

The ripple was emanating from the man who was placed in a pentagram pose. Four arcs of blue electric light shot from the chests of the men in up-side-down crosses to a skull in the small hands of another creature. When this one looked up, it bared it's silver teeth with a snarl that couldn't be heard by the men due to the wind escaping the portal.

"I knew it, another one. That was why it was moving so fast, there were two of the bastards!" Rupert exclaimed.

He killed the first one because he was in such close proximity, and that one wasn't as smart. It was younger, didn't know what was going on, but this one...

This one knew how it had gotten here, and how to get home. It never wanted to be here in the first place, the damned human brought it here, all it wanted to do was open the same rip in time that had brought it here so that it could get home. This one was smart. And it was going to leave the human here.

"We have to stop it, and I know enough about how particle beams work that I can return everything back to normal for you people, but you have to trust me!" Rupert yelled over the wind.

The others looked to each other. If Rupert was going to kill them, he probably would have done it by now...right? It didn't matter, York had already stepped forward to be with Rupert. Charles crept forward, too. That left Otto standing there, with a gun pointed on possibly their only hope.

Otto blinked as if something hit his eye, rubbed his head, then swung the gun towards the creature and looked at Rupert. "So, you say to aim at the middle of the tentacles?"

Rupert smiled and nodded. They only had a limited time, so he had to explain quick. "York, as soon as the creature has moved away from the skull, smash it into four pieces. This is where it gets difficult," with that was a rumbling roar from the ripple. "When the skull has been smashed, the arcs will transfer to a particular piece, make sure that you throw an arc into a different body, otherwise you'll speed up the process. Understand?"

"Yeah, but I'm still weak, it might take a while."

"We'll hold off the monster, just make sure you don't put the arcs to their origin."

Otto sighed, and took the first shot, the other two started blasting away at the creature until it was far enough away from the skull to allow York to get in.

"Go, now!" Rupert yelled over the fire.

He ran out to the skull that was sitting in the pentagram shape at the center of the star. When he reached down to pick up the skull, the arcs shocked him severely. The creature, jumping from wall to ceiling to wall to floor again, was erratic, and wasn't hit at all, but when it saw York, it became even more erratic.

York forced himself up and grabbed the skull in spite of the arcs. He held it high above his head and brought it barreling down. When it struck the ground, the skull smashed into four perfect segments. Amused, York almost didn't pick up the pieces.

The little creature was full blown pissed when it saw what York had done. Despite the sound of a full-fledged cat fight with gun fire in the middle, York managed to figure out which piece went to which arc. Then placed them on the ground. He figured that if he went ahead and crossed the beams across the room, it would do the best job.

He crossed the beams into an "X" and watched as the arcs grew in intensity. Everyone was mesmerized, even the creature stopped jumping around. But soon it realized what had been done. Otto was the first to notice and began firing his gun again. The other two fired as well. The creature was beginning to get tired, but about that same time, all three of the gunmen ran out of ammunition. The creature looked at them and made a face that looked like a smile.

It stood up on all four tentacles and leaped toward York. Remembering his side arm, Otto quickly aimed and fired, grazing the creatures back. It fell in mid-flight and shook its head. It looked around and disappeared. Without anyone seeing it, the camouflaged monster darted toward the portal.

"Dammit, I forgot, they can mimic surroundings, bastard's probably already gone!" Rupert yelled.

It was at that moment that Rupert noticed the color variance when the creature went from gray to blue. He pushed a small button on the side of his gun and a magazine case fell to the ground. He grabbed another off the shoulder harness and popped it in.

Otto was already ahead of him and was blindly aiming toward the ripple's center. When he fired there was a crunching sound and a spray of blood that seemed to turn the entire portal red. There was a thump of meat hitting the ground and a slight puddle of blood. The creature slowly turned black as the men approached it.

"Nice shot." Rupert said. He looked to the small gun in Otto's hand, then to the monstrosity hanging from his own side. "I guess size really doesn't matter." Rupert quipped.

The tentacles slightly slithered before it finally died. All and all it wasn't that hard to kill. "Now what?" asked Otto referring to the portal.

"I go home. As soon as I pass through the portal throw the creature into the center of that X. York, you did a good job. It was nice meeting you all, sorry about the casualties." Said Rupert.

York sat down, wondering how one could go on after something like that. They watched as Rupert disarmed and walked into the ripple. After a couple minutes, when they were sure Rupert was gone, Otto picked up the creature.

Quietly, Otto said. "I wish I could study this thing, but..."

He stood directly underneath the center of the crossed beams and looked at it, then to the creature. He then looked to the others and wondered if any of this was real. He again looked at the X.

"Go ahead." Said York with a nod.

Otto sighed and thrust it upward. In a loud crackle and roaring noise, the arcs disappeared, and the ripple collapsed into itself. The creature was nowhere to be seen, nor were the bodies on the wall, or the innards on the floor. It appeared that everything had been reverted to normal.

"Do you think he might have known this would happen, and that was why he didn't care?" Charles asked.

"No telling." Otto responded.

Otto and Charles dropped their guns and turned to see five very stunned people staring at them. York turned and tried to explain but couldn't find any words. "Yep. It looks like everything is back to normal." He finally said.

ST

DEADWORLD

Written 1997
PUNCH/PANTS, October 2012
These three short stories poured out one after the other. Dennis McDade had faith in these stories, but I couldn't find a home for them, as they're a set. Too big a piece from someone with no cachet, maybe. Or maybe a bit too dour? Here comes the grief horror, long before I knew what that was. A teenager starting to face mortality, wondering if there is anything beyond life? This story deals with loss, assault, and suicide, years before what would happen in my own life—losing my mother after a falling out. Then there's the third act of this three part series which connects to the world of my attempt at a comic book, and related to other stories set in my fictional version of Grand Marais, Minnesota.

THE DARK ERA

Bryan Vladimir woke with a start to face the first light. A clap of thunder pulled him from the half sleep he had been dwindling in. A dream he knew he had, but not what about, slowly left his mind as he wiped the tired from his eyes. The window let silver light filter through rain streaked shadows. It was one of the first rains of the season, light rain that wasn't anything to the hurricane season approaching.

He knew when he moved to Eastern Florida, he was subjecting himself to such conditions, this wasn't anything compared to Minnesota. Florida was much warmer, a lot more wet and dangerous, but at least the winter didn't ruin standard living. He threw off his sheet and slid to the side of his bed letting his feet fall to the floor. His routine, one of about two weeks now, began again as it did every morning.

Bryan looked to the little stand next to his bed, the same things always there: Lamp, phone, clock, book, and a framed photograph of his ex-girlfriend, also of two weeks. Her name was Joanne Woodward; she'd left him for he had a drinking problem, another thing he'd lost in that same two week span. Not a drop, he'd been dry...but with giving up drinking, he couldn't write anymore either.

But those two things had given him his ability. His love for her and the odd clearness of being drunk gave him the needed edge to write the fiction that kept him a step above poverty. The job that kept him alive in the meantime was the sanitation department, but he only worked once a week for an entire day, so for the most part, he sat at home and sulked.

With his morning routine, he picked up the phone, dialed the first six digits to Joanne's number, then sat there until the young lady on the other end would say: "Your number cannot be completed as dialed—" and he would hang up the receiver, give a great sigh, then pick it up again and dial his best friend, Michael Gray...a co-worker and the only saving grace keeping Bryan from insanity.

The phone rang, rang...and rang. Odd, Mike usually answered on the second ring. Hmmm, he must have been in the shower. Bryan set the phone down onto its cradle and stepped onto the plush carpet. It was warm, almost damp because of the humidity coming in through the attic fans in his small house.

Actually, a shower sounded pretty good right now. Living in Florida made one feel a little sticky almost all the time. He flipped on the TV in the front room out of habit, but jumped as the sound of hissing erupted into the quiet sound of rain drops on windows. He looked to it, cursed it, and then changed the channel. Nothing but static on each channel. The rain must have *been* a storm and blown out the cable. He hit the remote's power button and proceeded to strip as he readied for a shower.

It was cold and taking a long time to warm up. Seems that everything was running odd this morning. Finally, the water did get hot, but just as he started to enjoy the warmth...he heard a faint ringing. Mike most likely. He could call back. But what if it was Joanne? He half fell/ran out of the shower stall and grabbed at the phone.

"Hello?" he asked trying to stifle excitement.

"Bryan? Hey! What's up?" Mike asked oddly.

Bryan sighed and responded. "Nothing...taking a shower. How goes it?"

"Oh, well as can be expected. We still on for coffee?"

"As usual. But you didn't hafta call...why would I not be there?"

"Oh...forgot...you're in the area that went out 'cause of the storm. Bry, I hate to be the bearer of bad tidings..."

Bryan suddenly went flush. On only one other occasion had Mike called him "Bry," when they were at the funeral of Bryan's mother, and he had tried to console him.

"...Joanne died last night."

It was just as he thought. Bryan dropped the phone to the floor and went into a shudder of sobs. Mike, on the other end, could hear the muffled crying and slowly hung up. Bryan could hear the double click, and knew that an annoying "beep, beep" would burst into the air soon. He didn't care. By the time the sound alarmed he was too deep into his emotions to notice.

*   *   *

Bryan then realized he was in bed right next to a very alive Joanne, twirling his downy chest hairs between her fingers.

"You moaned," she said plainly.

"After a night like that I would worry over the man who didn't," he returned.

"No, silly," she laughed. "In your sleep. Did you have a nightmare?"

He moved his eyes around, as if searching for where the dream could have gone.

"Yeah...I had a nightmare. Bad one. But it's over now"

"Want to talk about it?"

"Not really, but you are a dream analyst...and it would probably do me good to get it out anyway."

She nodded as he tried to come up with words to explain his dream.

"Well, it started with me waking up in the morning...a week day I think...it was late so I guess I wasn't working that day. Details...I know how you love 'em. The first scary part was that you weren't there, and I had it in my mind that we hadn't been seeing each other for over a couple of weeks. Something about my *drinking habits* was in there. I was near obsession, dialing the first six numbers of where you were staying then hanging up.

"Anyway, I tried to call Mike, but he didn't answer. So, I went to take a shower...like I always do, I turned on the TV. There had been a storm that knocked out the cable so there was nothing but static on every channel. I turned it off and went to the shower. It took a while for the water to warm up, but when it did...Mike called. I thought it might be you, so I made my way to the phone. Wasn't you, as is obvious, but Mike called to tell me that you had been killed. I went into hysterics and fell down crying. Then here I am. Anything?" He finished.

"Not one damn thing. I mean...all of the images mean something and I'm sure you've heard it all before...but in that fashion order and context...not one damn thing can I get from it. Guess maybe you're worried about losing me. I don't think you need to...," she said rolling on top of him.

He eagerly accepted her insinuation and pulled her tight as he found her lips with his. He always kissed with his eyes closed; just something he did, felt weird to kiss looking at the side of someone's eye and head. But this time he opened his eyes and couldn't explain why for the life of him. Just behind Joanne's neck was the image of some*one* standing there. He pulled away from her and looked to where the figure stood.

She opened her eyes wistfully and asked, "What?"

The figure was there...obvious, but somewhat blurry. A fuzzy thing standing there in a world of clearness. She looked back to where he was, staring then back into his face. "What?" she asked again.

Holding out a distorted hand, the figure beckoned him. Bryan blinked and shook his head. The image was gone. He looked back to her face. "Did you see that?"

"Well...for the third time...what?"

"Never mind. More better things to attend to." And he kissed her again.

They continued into the throes of passion but very small, very minute was a nagging sensation at the back of his brain. Curiosity as to what that was. Were his eyes playing tricks? Was he still half asleep? Was he - oops. Passion's done for now.

Bryan had woken up before he was really done with sleeping...so after Joanne had left to clean herself up, he let himself drift back into sleep. There, the image of, of...whatever that was...plagued him. It continued to beckon inside his closed eyes. Tossing around in the bed, he tried to remove the image from his head. He squeezed his eyes tighter hoping that he would be able to close already closed eyes. Then...despite the odd images floating around...he fell into sleep.

*   *   *

"Our top story this evening comes on a tragic note. A tanker truck lost control on slippery roads today after the storm had dwindled resulting in a seven car pileup that left a total of five people dead and several others critically injured. Notably was the death of a local fiction writer's fiancée.

"Joanne Woodward, originally set to marry Bryan Vladimir, died instantly say-"

Bryan thumbed the "off" button on his television remote. "No way they'll mention my best friend died, though. Hell, if they did the media would just have a bigger heyday." He mumbled to no one. He had fixed himself into this situation of not caring whether or not anyone lived. It was the only way he could cope with the fact that the woman he loved and the man he had been friends with his entire life were dead and gone.

Course, the empty bottle of J.D. next to him might also explain his odd behavior for the situation. "No... I don't have a drinking problem. That was just a dream within a dream," he thought aloud over the subject. But it was such a wonderful dream. She was alive, his friend was alive...and all anything else was a dream. But this was the real world; everything else was just a dream. He could feel and move here. He could think and feel sorry for himself. Here it was real. This morning his fiancée and best friend died, he fell asleep in his own tears...dreamed that only one of them was dead, then woke up within a dream where no one had died. Now he was back here where the two people he cared most about were *both* dead.

Another bout of tears welled up in his raw and tired eyes. He fingered the lip of the bottle next to him, looked to it, watched as it blurred with the coming tears, screamed with fear, hate, and anger, and then launched it across the room where it smashed against the wall. Shards of glass clattered to the floor and the remaining liquid in the bottle streamed down the wall light amber. But Bryan didn't care. He was too strong to care, and the tears weren't really there. It was all just a dream, and he knew that he would wake up here in just a few minutes and he would be lying next to Joanne.

*　　*　　*

He did wake up. But it wasn't next to Joanne; he wasn't even in his own bed. In fact, he had no idea as to *where* he was. Outside. That had to be it, but it was very dark. He couldn't see, really couldn't hear either. There was just that thick feeling like when you take a hard hit to the head. Maybe that was it. He had gone outside in a drunken stupor, fell, and hit his head. Yes, all he needed to do now was open his eyes, find his bearings, and go back into his own home so he could actually sleep in bed. He knew that this time it was real.

Dream from a dream.

He did open his eyes...still dark. He shook his head and rubbed his eyes. Blind.

NO

What the hell was that?

WHEN ARE YOU GOING TO FIGURE THIS OUT

Good question. Bryan shook his head again and went about trying to find where the hell he was. The ground, or what passed for it anyway, was way too cool. Somewhat metallic and it bent under pressure.

GET UP

YOU'RE NOT A BABY

"Who the hell are you?" Bryan managed to vocalize, although, it came out weak and sheepish.

I BELIEVE THE QUESTION IS

WHO THE HELL ARE YOU

He scoffed. This right here must be a dream, he thought.

AGAIN WITH THE DREAM THEORY

ALWAYS YOU HUMANS TRY AND GIVE EXPLANATION

Now Bryan's attention was intense and focused. It still was a dream...he was sure of that...but one that responded and gave insinuations.

NOT INSINUATIONS

TRUTH

"I'm really tired of this. I think I'm just gonna wake up now and get this over with. Nothing more than a dream. Just my mind trying to screw with me."

WRITERS ARE EVEN WORSE

YOU HAVE GREAT MINDS THAT CAN GIVE YOU FAME

BUT YOU BLAME EVERYTHING ON THEM

YOUR MIND DID NOTHING TO YOU

THIS IS NOTHING MORE THAN THE TRUTH

WHEN ARE YOU GOING TO REALIZE THAT

Bryan tried to ignore the voice, but it was always there. It simply was, and there was no way of getting away from it. It was the ground and the darkness and inside him.

"I'm waking up now."

* * *

Bryan Vladimir woke with a start to face the first light. A clap of thunder pulled him from the half sleep he had been dwindling in. A dream he knew he had, but not what about, slowly left his mind as he wiped the tired from his eyes. The window let silver light filter through rain streaked shadows. It was one of the first rains of the season, light rain that wasn't anything to the hurricane season approaching.

He knew when he moved to Eastern Florida, he was subjecting himself to such conditions, this wasn't anything compared to Minnesota. Florida was much warmer, a lot more wet and dangerous, but at least the winter didn't ruin standard living. He threw off his sheet and slid to the side of his bed letting his feet fall to the floor. His routine, one of about two weeks now, began again as it did every morning.

Bryan looked to the little stand next to his bed, the same things always there: Lamp, phone, clock, book, and a framed photograph of his ex-girlfriend, also of two weeks. Her name was Joanne Woodward; she'd left him for he had a drinking problem, another thing he'd lost in that same two week span. Not a drop, he'd been dry...but with giving up drinking, he couldn't write anymore either.

Those two things had given him his ability. His love for her and the odd clearness of being drunk gave him the needed edge to write the fiction that kept him a step above poverty. The job that kept him alive in the meantime was the sanitation department, but he only worked once a week for an entire day, so for the most part, he sat at home and sulked.

With his morning routine, he picked up the phone, dialed the first six digits to Joanne's number, and then sat there until the young lady on the other end would say: "Your number cannot be completed as dialed—" and he would hang up the receiver.

Wait a second. This was awfully familiar. The phone hung in one hand, his other hand hovering over the number pad as he tried to figure out exactly what was going on.

"This is whacked." He said.

Putting the receiver to his head, Bryan took a chance and dialed the entire number. Maybe this was the real world...the only way to tell, was to see if Joanne was alive. To see if she was still mad at him. The phone rang once, twice, three times. No answer. Dropping the receiver, Bryan grabbed his face. He didn't know if he wanted to cry or curse. He could hear the rhythmic sound of the ringing...then a double click. His face brightened and he grabbed the now quiet earpiece.

"Hello?"

WHEN ARE YOU GOING TO LEARN

He was more scared than surprised by the voice. First off, he wasn't expecting it, second, it was the loudest thing he had ever heard going right into his ear.

"What are you...some kind of demon...Satan?" Bryan stuttered, into the mouthpiece.

IF ONLY IT WERE THAT EASY

ONE DAY YOU HUMANS WILL LEARN THAT YOUR AFTERLIVES ARE NOTHING MORE THAN STORIES

A sudden cold rushed across his neck. It reminded him of Joanne. When she would blow on the nape of his neck when he was in-between sleep and the waking world. The rush here was slightly colder...but just as erotic.

YOU KNOW THAT IF YOU JUST ADMIT IT

YOU CAN SEE HER AGAIN

YOU JUST HAVE TO GIVE UP ON THIS WORLD

"I'd still like to know what the hell you are."

THEN LOOK AT ME

As Bryan had assumed, the thing was in his room. It was a female, and about the same size as the person who had beckoned him in the dream-within-the-dream...hell, he couldn't remember. It was the same person is all he knew.

"So... what are you?" Bryan looked down, trying without success to find words that didn't sound stupid. He couldn't think of anything better than, "death?"

The woman laughed. Now the image was clearer of what she looked like, young, no older than 16. She was a little taller than five and a half feet tall. Still wearing the same brown shroud.

"No... I'm not death. More a messenger of someone's death. Actually, this is out of my league," she *said*, as opposed to shouting mentally.

"So, I'm dead?"

She nodded. "Have been for quite some time, too. We tried something new...but it didn't work, and you apparently forgot how to get home."

"I'm dead?"

"Humans," she scoffed under her breath. "Yes...you are dead. It is time for you to go into the next level of death. You must go into the *Dark Era*."

Bryan looked up, his face clouded with confusion. A million questions loomed in his eyes, the woman searched for one to answer, finally finding one that was actually worth answering.

"Yes...we chose you for our experiment. We found that when Humans die, they go into this same denial, usually for about two to four of your years. We wanted to try and set up a program when you died that you wouldn't know that you died. We were slowly going to integrate the *Dark Era*, a time in death when you change from Human to energy, then go into *Outer Darkness* where you can again go into a state of living where you will continue in any fashion you wish.

"It didn't work. You just wanted to stay here. Once you had been here for about seventeen years...real memories started leaking in. You died in a car accident with your fiancée and best friend-"

"I'm dead?"

WILL YOU PLEASE SHUT UP

Bryan jumped. "I'm not dead. I'm just dreaming."

BELIEVE WHAT YOU WILL

* * *

"Hey there, Mike, ready for coffee?" Bryan asked over the telephone, oblivious to the dreams.

OUTER DARKNESS

There is a certain thing that can be said for ignorance: it *is* bliss. Bryan woke the next morning without a worry in the world. All his friends were there, even Joanne and Mike. He even managed to forget all that had happened in those weird dreams as he was taking his shower. Joanne had helped somewhat in *that* process. Here it was; all back to normal.

After showering, he called good-old-always-there-never-been-dead Mike Gray.

They scheduled to have coffee at their usual corner diner; one straight out of the old Bogart films. Bryan kissed Joanne on the cheek as he tried to leave, but she grabbed his head and kissed him much deeper than she had before.

"What was that?" he asked.

Joanne blushed and shuffled her feet. "Do I hafta have a reason?"

He laughed and shook his head.

She giggled and shifted her weight.

He didn't want to leave, especially after an event like that. But he had promised Mike, and Joanne knew they always had coffee before they went off to work. She sighed, sensing his turmoil, and shoved him out the door.

"Go...have coffee. I'll see you this afternoon."

Bryan laughed again and was on his way. As he got in the car, he looked up to wave good-bye. She wasn't there. He blinked a few times, started the car, looked back and there she was waving like usual. She must have stepped away for a moment, he thought. He waved and pulled out of the drive. Damn it was a beautiful day.

Bryan got to Mike's house and waited for a moment before honking his horn. Mike usually heard the car pull up, but today he didn't. Bryan saw the curtain move as Mike looked to see who it was. He came sauntering out the door and down to the car.

"Early, aren't we?" Mike asked.

Bryan looked to his watch. "*Man*! I didn't know I was *that* early." He was a solid hour ahead of his normal schedule. He could clearly remember it being a different time when he left. "Well, care to join me for coffee an hour earlier than usual?" he said sheepishly.

"Sure, but I have to finish some stuff, come on in." Mike said.

Bryan turned off the car and walked after Mike. When they stepped in, Mike said something, but Bryan didn't hear it too well. Saying "huh" didn't seem worth it, so he repressed the normal impulse to say it. Taking a seat on the couch near the window, Bryan watched as Mike went down the hall to his bedroom. There was silence for a while, broken every so often by the sound of a drawer sliding in a dresser.

Bryan yawned and closed his eyes. He heard a muffled sound from the other room, thought it might be Mike saying something, and walked back to see. Mike wasn't there. Okay, this was getting weird. Flashes of the dreams from before edged their way into his head. He tried to shake free of them, but they persisted. At one point he thought he felt the presence of the same girl that had spoken to him.

"What are you doing?" Mike asked from behind his friend

Bryan spun around at the sound of the voice. "Jesus, man, don't scare me like that..."

"You okay?"

Bryan nodded and asked if Mike was ready.

"Yep...anxious to leave?" he said with a laugh.

"Kind of." Bryan returned. "I guess I didn't get as good a night of sleep as I thought, I figure the coffee might clear my head."

"I keep telling you: If you stay up all night with that little girl of yours, you're gonna go nuts!"

Both laughed, but Bryan more so because he was uneasy.

*　　*　　*

That morning, Bryan woke up somewhat stressed, who wouldn't after such a wicked night of dreams? But everything was as normal as could be. He woke up and there was Joanne. She wasn't dead, they weren't broke-up, so everything was fine. Right? Bryan thought so.

He went out for coffee like he did all the time, only he was out when usually he was asleep. Maybe he was just running early this morning. Mike seemed to be just fine too. So, Bryan wasn't concerned, why should he have been? Then why did he feel worried? Mike didn't say a word in the five minute ride to the diner. Maybe that was it; Mike usually spoke all the time.

Arriving at the diner, both walked in. At the counter are two cups of coffee, as if it were known the two of them were coming. No one, no one but the two of them. No counter attendants, no customers, nobody. Just the two of them, and Mike was okay with this. He walked right to the counter, snatched a newspaper from a table on his way, sat, sipped deeply of his coffee, and opened the sports section. It took

Mike a moment to notice that Bryan hadn't sat down. "Bry, what the hell is wrong with you this morning?"

Bryan just let his jaw hang. This was all too weird. How come Mike wasn't privy to this? Or how come Bryan wasn't privy to the calm Mike was experiencing?

He thought himself a fool just standing there not making a sound, despite the fact this was all too baffling. He sat next to Mike and began to say something when he pulled it back in. Resting his head in his hands, Bryan stared at the black liquid in the little white cup. Steam wafted into his face. It was a warm comfortable smell that urged him to grab the cup and gulp its contents. He shuddered and reached for the cup.

When he looked up...there stood the usual red-haired geeky kid who usually gave him his coffee. He let out a solitary laugh and looked to his side. All the normal people. All of them. All of them except Mike.

"Now what the hell is going on? Where the hell are you, you little bitch!" Bryan let out.

The kid looked to him. "Huh?"

"Where's the guy who was sitting right next to me?"

"What guy?"

"The guy who sits next to me every damned time I come in here for coffee!"

"I'm sorry, I guess I don't understand. More coffee?"

"NO!" he yelled slamming his cup to the counter. The coffee splashing onto his hand was very cold, but Bryan didn't take notice. "I want to know what the hell is going on and when this crap is going to end! What? Am I in a coma stuck in one eternal nightmare that I just *can't* get out of?"

"Not until you decide to get with the program," a female voice said from next to him.

He looked to her, and realized there was no one in the booths or tables behind her. He felt that everything had been sucked out of the world, he and her were the only ones left.

"We are, if you want to think of it that way," she said.

She was wearing an average white shirt and blue jeans. She had her own cup of coffee resting on the table between her small hands. Still, she looked like an adolescent. Still, she seemed to be such a calming influence yet so frustrating at the same time. Always reading his mind and telling him exactly what he didn't want to hear.

"So, I'm just stuck in this damned dream...forever...?" he said, realizing from the first encounter, asking obvious questions was almost like pulling teeth.

"I'm dead?"
WILL YOU PLEASE SHUT UP
Bryan jumped. "I'm not dead. I'm just dreaming."
BELIEVE WHAT YOU WILL

"No...as I once said, you're dead. You need to go into *Outer Darkness*. There, all your questions about what happened will be answered."

Bryan sat back. There was another cup of coffee, this time hot, steaming hot. He thought, *Maybe she read my mind for good reason this time*. Taking a long careful sip, he bowed his head as he prepared himself to listen to the girl try and explain.

"I know it's difficult. I don't blame you for fearing what's on the other side. It's not the same existence you're used to. Hell, when you get right down to it, *this* world isn't what you're used to. The dates and times are never the same. You thought you were on time this morning to pick up your friend, but you were an hour early. You don't remember it, but yesterday you were in your teens, when you had your first sexual experience. Right in the middle of intercourse, the girl disappeared, and you became very scared. I came in trying to explain to you, you need to go to the other side.

"Tomorrow, you'll be an infant, the next day an adult again. But you'll never be the same age each day. You've been here too long, and the world can't support you. You need to go to the other side. *Outer Darkness*. The *literal* Purgatory."

Bryan sipped his coffee again and said, "Can you prove something to me?"

"Anything," the girl said.
"Take me home...?"
AS YOU WISH

*   *   *

He was sitting on the floor, right next to an unkempt bed. The girl stood across the room, somber as usual. He shook his head and began to laugh. Soon it became nothing more than ragged sobs on the side of his bed.

"So...," he said through the gasps. "I'm really dead? No doubt about it? 100% accurate news I'm receiving here? I'm dead?"

YES

"Can you now explain something to me?"

I WILL TELL WHAT I CAN TELL

"What is this place? Before I leave, I'd like to know where I've been."

THIS IS THE DARK ERA

HERE IS WHERE WE SET UP A TRANSITION WORLD WHERE THE HUMAN CAN REST OUT ALL THE ENERGY THEY DID NOT SPEND WHILE ALIVE

IT IS HERE THAT AN AGENT IS SENT TO EXPLAIN THAT THE PERSON IS DEAD AND THAT THEY MUST MOVE ON

I AM YOUR AGENT

BUT YOU HAVE ALWAYS REFUSED TO BELIEVE THAT YOU ARE DEAD

THE LAST TIME WE MET AND YOU COMMITTED ME TO MEMORY

YOU WERE DEAD FOR OVER 15 YEARS

THAT IS THE MAXIMUM LENGTH A HUMAN SHOULD SPEND IN THE DARK ERA

YOU HAVE NOW BEEN HERE FOR OVER 3.28 MILLION YEARS

WE THINK IT IS TIME YOU COME TO BE WITH ALL THOSE WHOM YOU LIVED WITH

THEY HAVE REQUESTED THAT I BRING YOU

EVEN IF BY FORCE

Bryan laughed and looked up again. "You know, I'm actually starting to believe that now. I mean, what could be worse than seeing all your friends or even people you don't know just disappear? Wouldn't that have to be death?"

THIS IS WHAT YOU MADE IT TO BE

"So, you've said."

YOU STILL DON'T UNDERSTAND

"No."

THEN LOOK AT IT THIS WAY

YOU ARE A CRUEL JOKE MADE BY GOD

AN ADAM WITHOUT AN EVE

A WORLD ALL TO YOURSELF

WHERE EVERYONE THAT IS

EXISTS BECAUSE YOU IMAGINE THEM TO BE THERE

ONLY THERE IS NO GOD

JUST AN AFTERLIFE

That was easier to understand. Bryan was simply the guinea pig in some weird experiment being performed by god-*like* creatures. All he had to do was accept that they had control over him and give up control of his life.

THAT IS NOTHING LIKE WHAT I EXPLAINED

"Isn't it though?" Bryan shook his head as he stared at the girl. "What happens when I pass over? This *Outer Darkness* place sounds pretty creepy. Course, so does this *Dark Era* I'm living in. I guess that means that if I go forward, it couldn't get any worse, right?"

AS I HAVE SAID

THIS IS STILL UP TO YOUR ACCEPTING IT

"What if I just don't want to handle with it anymore? What if I want to go to the next level but still want to live as well?"

THIS IS UP TO ACCEPTING

NOT WANTING

THAT IS WHY YOU HAVE BEEN HERE FOR MORE THAN 3 MILLION YEARS

YOU WILL NOT ACCEPT THE SIMPLE FACT THAT YOU ARE--

"--Dead. It makes more sense now than it did before. I don't appreciate the fact that who- or whatever you work for decided to screw with me so that they could better other people. I guess now I know how the mouse feels. Once I'm free I don't want to leave the cage." He shook his head. "How?"

ACCEPT IT

"That's it...no ritual or prayer or anything?"

THIS IS UP TO ACCEPTING

"Then I want to go. I want to accept."

The figure of the girl was blurred by a new batch of tears welling up in his raw eyes. He had been crying through the entire conversation, but now he was going into something he didn't understand. He was accepting a fact that no human should ever have to accept.

"I am dead." He said easily.

He sighed and whispered it again. A small image and feel of the last scenes to *The Wizard of Oz* crept into his head.

"There's no place like home," he mocked in a whimper.

*   *   *

At first there was only darkness. He felt that he had been here before, once before. Everything around him was black, yet he felt that he was seeing better than he had ever seen before. When he rolled to his side, it felt like wet grass and mud beneath him. It gave bend to his weight but was firm enough to hold him steady.

The *ground*, or whatever it was, felt metallic and cool despite the grass and mud masking it. Yes, he had been here once before. Long ago, when he was still young, in the eyes of the dead. He had almost accepted it once, but was scared away by an untimely, thundering voice. He could have had all this over with so long ago.

SO

That was weird. It wasn't the girl's voice, it was his own. He could see and feel the words. Just like when the girl spoke, only now he was talking, but there were no words, no actual audio to accompany the words. They were just there.

72

"And so, they shall be." The girl's voice said from a distance.

WHY DO YOU NOT SPEAK LIKE ME

"Because having two of those kinds of voices in your head, even if one is your own, can cause complications. Besides, you're never going to *hear* again after this. Only feel. I figured you would appreciate the actual sound of one last voice."

WHAT HAPPENS NOW

He could feel her thinking. What was this? It was as if he were everywhere and everything.

"You are now. Just wait; *they* will come when they think you have accepted it."

I HAVE ACCEPTED

HAVE I NOT

"It is up to your accepting."

THEN I ACCEPT

With that, what can only be discerned as a far wall, opened and there was a world looking almost exactly like the one he just left. In the doorway stood the figure of a female, the same girl that had attempted to escort him from the *Dark Era* into *Outer Darkness*. From behind her came the figure of Joanne. She seemed much older now, much more developed. Joanne put her hand on the shoulder of the girl, and then looked into the darkness occupied by Bryan.

"Bryan," Joanne said. "It's good to have you here. I want you to meet someone that came along after you died in your accident." She nudged the girl forward.

"Hello, dad."

A FINAL PLACE

Death comes to us all. The greatest achievement in life is death. There is nothing to fear in death. All of life's questions can only be answered in death. No matter who you are, what you look like, how you act, where you work, what you do, we all have three things in common: We all live, we all bleed, we all die.

All of this, and it would seem that there is no reason for living if, after so long, we only die, and no one remembers us and we no longer make an impact. Death, no matter who you are or how you think, is frightening. You may not be afraid of being dead, you know it will happen, but the act of dying is the part that gets people.

So, I designed this. Take the person as he or she dies, put them into their better memories, take out the entire event that led to their death, and let them continue to live, giving subtle hints that they are dead. Putting in their head the dreams and events that unfold in their *afterlife*. After so long, it became a little easier to control, kind of hard making the dead believe they are dead. You can only make it to this place, this *Final Place* if you accept that you are dead and are willing to learn the ways of the dead.

I've been around a long time, long before death was feared. Only the pain of death. Those who were hunted down, the animals accept death before they are even dead, releasing the pain as their still living carcasses are devoured. Animals are so much easier to let in here.

Spirit, you ask? No, no, I've never seen one of those. There is an essence to you all, all you living things. It's called your mind, as I sit here thumping my own incorporeal head as though you could see me. But like I said, I've been around a lot longer than you thinking-kind.

Created, designed, instilled and implicated. Am I God? Hardly. That's something else I have no concept of. For a long time, a *very* long time, you thinking-kind didn't have any concept of religion. That came along for an odd reason. Some people think that's what makes them Human. Among my kind, the Ancients as we are called by some consider the term Human as a swear, a curse upon someone. To be Human is to be jaded and conceded. There is only one thing in humanity that anyone might envy. That is your ability to *love*. Too bad love is so hard to find among any of you.

Designed for battles and conflict. So, love doesn't really have a place among you. But this is my own opinion, I keep drifting.

When you die, and forgive me for telling you, but this is the *truth*, that's all that happens. No fancy lights or tunnels. No dead family or friends to greet you. You just sit there, your mind the only thing left. Thinking in that place your body ends up, even as it turns to earth, that is where your mind remains. You can't see or feel, taste or hear. Just think.

I don't like that too much, after so many billion years it gets boring, and you just stop thinking. There's nothing left to figure out. You answer all your own questions, become super intelligent and further any studies you had in Life, because here in death your mind is brought back to full. And your subconscious mind is revealed to you in full. You just get to think forever and ever. Boring right? *Exactly*!

So, I created something that wasn't so boring. I made a world for the mind. A place it can roam forever with other minds, mingling. You almost think as one with it all, but at least here you can live as you did when you were in a body. As I said, I find your best memory and allow you to live in it for a while. Basically I put your incorporeal body into a pleasant dream. Now, you begin to realize you are dreaming if strange things happen right?

And the whole atmosphere becomes kind of gray and cloudy and the thickness of your head gets to you. Not so hard to accept once you realize. And it's not as scary as you might think. I've seen people accept a day after they're dead, and some about a year. But never as long as one of them.

He can be considered my first. And his dream began to plague him. He swore it *was* a dream. Didn't want to accept he was really dead. Oh, poor Bryan Vladimir. There are stages to this thing that I have created. The first, the *Dark Era*, comes right after I have set up their "dream." Now, somehow, Bryan got stuck here. It took me a long time to set up his dream. But when finally I did, he wouldn't take the signals and symbols correctly. Always "woke-up" from some dream.

He managed to manipulate it all. Then he managed to get stuck between the *Dark Era* and *Outer Darkness*, the second phase. In *Outer Darkness*, everything is explained to them. Usually by family, they seem to take it better that way. And for some reason they keep seeing it as going to Heaven. That's when I go in, even though the family has explained it to them that this isn't an afterlife but a community of the dead, a Necropolis, they still want to believe they have paid for their sins and gone to Heaven.

"Not true." I used to tell them. "This is a place that I created..."

"So, you are God?" They would say, a hint of fear in their voices.

I could only laugh in their faces. I didn't do it to intimidate them, but merely because I found it amusing. "No, far from God am I. My name is Bolj. A friend to Death you might say. I helped create this place, so in essence I am *a* god, but not *the* God. You, as it has been explained, are dead."

They would smile.

"You have gone through a transitional phase where you are more willing to accept this fact. And seeing as you are here, you have accepted that you are dead."

"Rather reluctantly." Bryan finally told me.

"Yes, you took some time to finally get around to it."

"Thank you for sending my daughter to me."

"It was the only way I saw fit." And it was the truth.

What other way to get him to accept than to prove to him that there were parts to him he didn't know? His daughter, Jesse, conceived only weeks before his death. He had had no idea. When Joanne told him this, he couldn't speak. He only stared like a dumbfounded idiot.

I laughed silently at him from behind the scenes. I could see that in all this *fighting* he did to keep himself safe from the truth, we would soon have this conversation I had with him now. To explain the *Final Place*.

"So that was the *Dark Era*?" he asked.

"Yes, Bryan. Perhaps you would like a better explanation than your daughter gave? Or perhaps you would like to learn of your daughter alone?"

"Actually, I would like to learn everything, but right now, I would like to know what I was going through."

Always the analyst. That's what I love about writers, they'd rather learn the facts before they go anywhere near "good news."

"The *Dark Era*. When you die, you enter a kind of limbo, a syndrome of R.E.M. for the dead, so to speak. *Dark Era* clouds your mind, concealing the truth, for that period of time, hence the name of the place. It is there that you will be given subtle signs you are dead—" Never before had I been interrupted.

"Great, great, all the technicalities, but I want to know how, not why."

A smirk crawled across my face. The same smirk I wear every time I think of Bryan.

"Okay, *how*. I am one of a great race that spans the entire universe. Dead from the time we were born, but in essence, we were never born and never died. We have just been, forever. I am an Ancient. Bolj."

I offered my hand. How he saw me I have no idea, the Ancients have an ability to allow whoever sees us, see us as they wish. But nonetheless, he took the thing and shook firmly.

"So, Bolj, the *Dark Era*, *Outer Darkness*, however many other places I have to go through..."

"Yes," I began. "The *Dark Era*, as I explained is a large dream that will tell you, when you are ready, that you are dead. Once that happens, the way to *Outer Darkness* is opened. You follow me so far?"

"Not really. Why can't you just come up to the recently dead and say: 'Hey, you're dead, welcome!'"

An image flashed in Bryan's head.

"So, I'm dead?"

She nodded. "Have been for quite some time, too. We tried something new...but it didn't work, and you apparently forgot how to get home."

"I'm dead?"

"Humans," she scoffed under her breath. "Yes...you are dead. It is time for you to go into the next level of death. You must go into the Dark Era*."*

"Ah, but right there it says that the *next* level of death is the *Dark Era*. So where was I?"

"First off, I wanted you to observe the point that just 'saying so' won't work. Secondly, the *Dark Era* is where you are revealed. A little phase where the dream dissipates. As I said, you were in a limbo where the dream was set up, but you never let it complete. Once you finally began to accept, you had entered the *Dark Era*. Once you did accept, you got here. *Outer Darkness*."

"Okay, so what is this?"

"This, my dear Bryan, is where you meet me."

"So why is it called *Outer Darkness*?"

"You still have a lot of questions, correct?"

Bryan grunted under his breath and folded his arms.

I could only laugh. It was so amusing that he wasn't going to go too far without the answers he wanted.

"Bryan, there is one more place beyond this, but no questions or requirements there. Once you are satisfied here, you go to a *Final Place*."

"That name seems too obvious. Not as sinister as the other two, but fitting, I guess."

I laughed again. "No, not quite as elaborate, I admit it. But what better name for such a thing? So, Bryan. Ask away, you are *in Outer Darkness*."

"How did I die?"

"Simple, in a car accident. You, your fiancée, and best friend were all on your way to the hospital because Joanne had been cramping rather badly. Going across an intersection in the roads, the driver's side of your vehicle was rammed, and you died instantly, which made it easy for me. The less you know of your death at the time of the death, the easier you slip into that limbo."

"And seeing as I never *saw* it myself, I automatically assumed I was still alive, therefore I never slipped into the *Dark Era*."

"Exactly." For a brief moment it was just the two of us standing there nodding. I broke the silence. "After you died, an ambulance took the others to the hospital; that was where it was found that Joanne was pregnant, that being the cause of her cramps. Now, just so you know, the baby was fine and suffered none from the accident."

"And one other thing on that matter. Did Mike end up *caring* for Joanne?"

"Yes, but not in the way you are thinking. They never engaged in any sexual acts, not even so much as a kiss. To tell the truth, Joanne never kissed or engaged after you were gone. Mike just became a constant companion, her best friend. He was, however, a father-figure to Jesse."

"I know, how did Jesse die so young?"

"Yes."

"Jesse wasn't careless, but someone else was. At a party, as she slept, someone took what wasn't theirs. This someone had taken a great many and was also taken by great many others. Along the line somewhere, the boy contracted A.I.D.S., you do know of that?"

Bryan nodded.

"It was not her fault, and she never knew she was raped until she found out she had contracted the syndrome. She was very smart in her life and deduced the obvious on her own. But she was also one of the lucky ones. Even though she was very young, and it has been seen that the A.I.D.S. virus can be suppressed for many years, Jesse didn't want that. Her own body produced a special product that killed her. Self-suicide, if you will."

Bryan still only nodded.

I put my hand to his shoulder, realizing that these kinds of thing aren't easy for anyone to hear, even with the fore knowledge that you and all the others involved are dead as well. It still is hard to hear that kind of thing.

"Joanne," he managed to put forth.

"She died at a young age, too. Near 50. She just couldn't handle it anymore, not having the ones she loved. First, she lost you, then her...*your* daughter. Mike just wasn't enough to keep her. It was a mental death at first, and then she just passed away in her sleep."

"All of this pain and hurt because I died?"

"Not really, it's not fair to put all the blame on yourself. And you should see the good in the bad at all times. You have accepted you are dead, Bryan. You have the answers you have always wanted, and even though they are gruesome, at least you now know."

It was at that point Joanne and Jesse stepped closer towards him. They had been watching the entire time as I spoke to him. Remembering when they had underwent the same thing. They both wanted to be with him right then, they were finally a family again.

I, Bolj, have no place in the way of Love. It's the one thing the Ancients respect and admire about you humans.

I nodded to them, and they both came forward, taking him into their arms. He began to weep softly. Never had he known the girl, but he wanted so much to hold her right then. Just as he did. This was his blood before him. And next to him was the love that had brought the girl into the world.

They began talking on their own; they could answer any other questions he had. Rather personal questions. But sometimes it's better to hear it from someone you don't know. That way you remain composed.

I stepped away from the three, I had no place there. I merely opened the way to their *Final Place*, a world in which they lived as a happy family for all eternity. But right now? I still have others to attend to. Great thing about being an Ancient, so many people enter *Outer Darkness* at the same time, I can talk to all of them. Bryan was special, though. He was the first. For you humans I speak to, all in the same time that Bryan first reaches my *Dark Era*, these realms are all very young.

Now I'm not saying go and die just so you can see it. If I say anything to you, it's stay alive as long as you can. Like I said, Ancients admire that one aspect about you. Maybe that's why I liked Bryan so much as well. He had so much love, and that was possibly the only thing that took him out of the limbo.

"Welcome to your *Final Place*," I had said to them.

Bryan looked at me through wet eyes. "Say, think I'll ever get to see you again, Bolj?"

"Any time, Bryan. The pleasure would be mine." I smiled.

Not often anyone wants to see me again.

Love. The only thing the Ancients respect and admire in humans.

THW

J.D. Buffington

DARK HANDS

Written 1998
Mausoleum: Mortis es Veritus, October 1998
Albuquerque, NM
Editor, Crow Ravenscar

This story, of my old 'zine published pieces, I still like. It also takes place in Grand Marais, and starts building the town and world. This piece even earned the right to be paired with original artwork in Mausoleum. There's no one likable here, everyone is terrible, and that was always the intent. Its also one of my few attempts at placing a story around a holiday, Halloween as incidental set dressing.

His was a strange, erotic, power. Not everyone could convey their emotions through their hands. Oh, sure, some people can do a lot with their hands, musicians are proof of that. But just how many people do you know can make a woman fall in love with him just by his touching her bare skin? A mere touch at most and he could do anything he wanted with someone. Female *and* male.

Francis Deangelo. First off, the guy's Italian and good looking; sharp, clean, a nice dresser, he could probably get away with half the things he does with his looks and attitude alone, but why would he with a power like his? Yes, Francis has one of those weird "gifts" you hear about people having. I bet if he wanted to, he could even heal people with those hands, even be a second Jesus Christ if he wanted to. But Francis never wanted fame. He just liked using his ability for when he might need it. But sometimes it just got in the way.

If an emotion ever got too strong in Francis? It was conveyed through those hands, causing that same emotion to form in the person or thing lucky enough to be touched by him. I hated seeing him fight. Just kept making the other people (if he was winning the fight that is) stronger and stronger, thus making the fight a losing battle. Never seen him win a fist fight, he's really only beating himself up in those.

Me? I was touched by him a long time ago. Changed my life forever. Seeing as I don't have a life any longer. Humph, no, I'm not dead and talking to you from the grave. Sheesh, not everything you read in the tabloids is true, just a few of the cases. But I am...

immortal? Actually, I'm not sure, just that I don't really bleed anymore, don't age, don't eat...hell I don't even need to take a piss or crap anymore. But I hang out with Francis a lot. I at least look normal. Not like I'm rotting away.

So, before I get any further with Francis, may as well tell you who I am. My name? Can't remember, but he calls me Jay all the time. When we were kids, he had that power. But he never used it for anything serious. He'd make dogs all of a sudden go bark at trees, or he'd make a teacher fall asleep in school so we could all cut class. Just pranks. I was always with him. I can't remember how many times he touched me, but I didn't care, he wasn't doing anything to me, nothing ever felt wrong when he would.

But he was slowly pulling the life from me. I'm still alive mind you, I can still think and go around, I still talk to people in bars when he's playing around. I even got laid the other night, and I tell you what, having my own little ability to control what comes out of me when...I'm sure you get the idea.

I kept growing up, grew up faster because my age was being accelerated. I had no idea, neither did Francis. We just screwed around like any kids would. Then I had to move away and didn't see him for a while. So, I started living life normal again, although I was about five years older than everyone physically. I didn't care.

Francis went on and discovered other things he could do with his hands. Found he could get what he wanted just by thinking it as he touched somebody. But it never occurred to him that if he wasn't thinking on anything specific thing when his hands came into contact with flesh, he was actually just pulling the life out of it. A neutral thing that happened, never knew until I came back, and he shook my hand, happy to see me, I was suddenly filled with the same elation he had. Shaking hands...sometimes you do it a little longer than you realize, a conversation ensues, and you forget you're holding this other guys hand.

"Man, if only you could stay alive forever," he said to me.

Damn when the thought went through his head. Then from there down his arm into his hand and to his fingers and right into me. You would think...or well, if this sort of thing was a normal occurrence...that just having a thought wouldn't do much. Maybe make me agree with him more. But all those years of life he was absorbing from me, and all those other people, no telling how many stolen years were in those hands.

I couldn't feel it, it's not like it was an instant thing. Not until I realized I was a little sluggish more often than not. Sleeping felt so damn good and getting up was just hell. But if I touched Francis' hand? I was back again. Until it started to wear off and my body was ready to die.

Kept putting years back into me that he took from others. I came to him about it once. Said: "Francis, I think there's something to your power there."

He said: "One hell of a power, yeah, I tell you—"

"No stories now, Francis," I said. "I have a problem and I think you caused it. Those hands, every time I touch them, I feel a lot better, more *alive* if you will. The only problem? I think that's what it is."

So now every morning when he wakes up, he comes in and touches my chest, waking me up from death. My body won't decay, there's still years in it, but getting up is the hard thing. I don't know how much he puts in or takes out, but it's kinda like I'm his chore now. He says he doesn't care, just as long as I don't end up sleeping somewhere he can't reach me. I'll laugh, saying: "Yeah, they come to you saying: 'do you know this guy who died last night but seems to have been dead a couple years?'"

He'll laugh in return.

Mmm, damn this is good schnapps. Warm. Glad the nerves still work in this old body. Can't remember how old I am, can't remember my name. Can't remember my parents. Don't remember anything about a brother I supposedly had. Only remember Francis and those hands. They are why I exist. And I don't have a problem with that, like I said, I'm kinda in a good place being half dead here.

But back to why I'm even telling you any of this. Those things are dark. Very evil. He's started turning out more menacing products with them. I hated having to kill a woman. He sucked so much life out of her when she fell asleep in his arms. He didn't mean for it to happen, how can you? After you explode into a woman you just get that weird calm feeling, like you can fall asleep or something...you're not thinking: *Oh, where are my hands right now?*

But Francis has to, and it's bad when he forgets. She fell asleep, he fell asleep, and then she woke up in the middle of the night, some twenty years aged. Very obvious for someone who was only twenty to begin with. Screaming and wailing. He tried to grab her, but the fear in him for her, what he was going to do...it all went into her. I came in, awakened from the noise and saw what was going on.

Even though I hated doing it, it was, like, natural for me. That's why I hated it. Because it was so easy. I grabbed a baseball bat from Francis' closet.

Ah, thank God for alcohol.

Francis is a little more careful now, when he feels that tired feeling in his head, he makes it to where he really wants to go away, then touches the girls he's with. They leave almost instantly. Better for them, they've probably lost a year or so of life that evening.

I hate to say it, like I said, for reasons that these thoughts come to me so naturally, but I've been coming up with a way to save Francis and anybody else. I know that lady's life still haunts him. He has bad dreams, when I'm staying up watching Skin-a-max I can hear him trying to get out of the nightmares. But I've been coming up with this plan.

Taking his life, I couldn't do. That's not natural, and the thoughts on those lines hurt, so at least I'm still caring of my friend. Just like he's caring of me...so I guess that explains the pang of guilt within me. He's keeping me alive (or something akin to that anyway) and here I am thinking in these ways.

"Francis!" I yelled to him from down the bar.

Looking to me he said, "Yo!"

I smiled at him, I know I probably look drunk, but how can you be drunk if your blood is thick and congealed anyway? Maybe that's why these thoughts are coming to me. For the first time in a long while I'm drunk? Doesn't matter, this will be for the better. Saving a lot of people, I am.

I leaned into him, not stumbling, and whispered: "Not tonight, bud, don't take any home."

"You got that same bad feeling too, huh? Something's got me as well. Sure, let's get out of here."

That same bad feeling, sure. Damn, this is just getting harder and harder to follow through with. But I have to.

We get home and he throws off his jacket, always it lands right there in that chair, and always I throw it on the floor and fall asleep in that chair, so the sun comes in on my body every morning from the big windows. He comes up and touches my chest from underneath my shirt and I get this tingly feeling like blood is rushing back into me. Brings me back to life every morning. I wonder what not waking up is going to be like tomorrow. I wonder how long it'll be before I'm found, or he tries to explain anything.

Last night, while he pumped into some tart, I left the apartment with some cash and went down to a hardware store that stayed open late, 'cause, you know...have to fix the sink at three in the morning when it starts to leak. An ax, nothing special, it's sharp enough I assume.

Yeah, last night, pretty close to Halloween, it was only about fifteen minutes till midnight. All the decorations of zombies and skeletons and all I could think of was how that's all I was. Then, inside the store, a little cardboard cut-out of a dismembered hand. I could only smile.

The blunt side was definitely dull enough to knock his ass out when I clocked him with it. He only grunted and went straight to the floor, his keys sliding from his hand and across the wood. I wonder; could he take life from non-living things? Those keys sure are rusted for how little time he's been living here. Or maybe it's just the light.

We live on the bottom floor, so I'm not too worried about the neighbors hearing. Even if they do it won't matter, I'll be done before help gets here. I just hope that he stays knocked out here, as I'm putting his hands together. Just like he's diving or something, diving into a great big hole of trouble. I'm doing him a favor really, he'll thank me in the long run, if he ever gets to come to my grave; or ever *chooses* to.

Lifting the ax above my head so I can get enough strength into one swing, so I don't have to try again, I think back on my *life*. It's not been so bad, I had some fun, watched my best friend have fun. Lots of sex and a lot of jokes. Just too bad when you see someone get twisted. Did I forget to mention that?

That girl is still alive in the back room. Her head all beat in. He liked her body. She can't speak anymore; I bashed in her throat, too, with one of my blows. All I wanted to do was save her, but apparently our definitions conflicted. I just hope she's in a similar situation as I am; that if he isn't able to work, she just won't wake up. I told her about it, once while Francis was asleep. I think she liked the idea.

So, I bring down the ax and there's this hideous crunch. I can feel the ax hit bone and tear through. Maybe having muscles so tight from atrophy has made them stronger. Both hands fell to their sides. A little bit of ragged flesh holding them on. He's not awake; I hope I didn't kill the bastard. Although now, killing him doesn't seem so bad.

But I've seen people without hands before; they seem to get along just fine. Maybe Francis will get one of those nifty little hooks for each of his stumps...I'd like to see that. Kicking the two hands away from his wrists, making sure that they stay away and hopefully get too screwed up to fix, I drop the ax to the floor and go sit in my chair. Just so tired, that little action right there took a lot from me.

I flip on the TV and see its reflection in the pooling blood. I guess now, seeing as I'm yawning, and also seeing as the girl hasn't been touched for a while, hopefully she's asleep, I should call 911. Can't just let my friend die.

"911 Emergency, please state the nature of the emergency...?" nice voice, gonna miss hearing those kinds of things.

"I just cut off my friend's hands with an ax. I live--" so I went on and the lady said an ambulance and police car would be there soon. Definitely would be great to see the looks on their faces. Late night Halloween and here you have two long dead people and a guy with his hands cut off and the dead guy's prints all over the place. Definitely a worthy case of such a special holiday.

I'll be asleep then. Just have to shut my eyes and fall asleep to the bustle of trick-or-treaters outside. One last time I wonder, what finally staying asleep is going to be like?

THW

PAIN

Written 1998
PUNCH/PANTS, October 2012

Sometimes I think about these guys and want to bring them back. I'm playing in Christian mythology again, a version of the War in Heaven. While not in Grand Marais, these characters would definitely crossover given the chance. I wanted to build to a twist, and then I twisted again. It was going to be a straight murder mystery, but I couldn't help it. Adding a little dollop of weirdness on the end felt natural for me.

"I was born in the Year of our Lord nineteen hundred and forty-seven. I was born in a blessed house of God to a doctor who also was a man of the cloth. I was raised in the House of our Lord and the Lord Jehovah is within my heart. The Prophet and son of God, Jesus Christ of Nazarene is within my spirit. I live by the Good Book and worship and give all I have to offer in the name of my Lord and Father. I am also a messenger of the word of God.

"Through my life I have known nothing but the divine glory of God and His court of angels. Never once has the way of Satan and his rebel band of dark angels ever tempted me. The ways of the flesh and the filth of the corrupt have never entered my personal domain. I sin but once a year on the Protestant holiday of Thanksgiving, adopted by the Christian calendar and the US Government under the One and Powerful God. Even then, it is only a sin of minor importance, gluttony. Very easy to purge, but still yet it is a sin that I must deal with in my own way.

"But I am man of God. And as the hand of God guides me, so has He guided me here to this place below the only home I have ever known, in the Holiest of places this area knows. It is my crypt; it is my hole of purity to purge sins of sinners, a Purgatory on Earth to allow me to do God's will on Earth.

"I am the Deliverer of Pain," the voice finally subsided. The young man, tied to a table tried to see where it might come from, but the combination of complete darkness and swollen eyes from severe blows to his head kept him from seeing anyone or -thing.

"You have committed a sin unforgivable by any, Chris, even by God Himself. It is my duty to point this out to you and tell you why you must pay. Taking the innocence of a child? Rape! You took from that girl something that she can never re-attain; you plucked her of the only flower that ever would blossom within her, plucked before its time. So, you have been brought to here, so that you may pay in the only possibly correct way.

"An eye for an eye, my son. It is God's will; may He have mercy upon your soul in its eternal damnation with the dark Lord Lucifer."

It was then the boy, Chris, knew part of his discomfort, he wasn't tied down on his back, but bent over the edge of a table. His eyes managed to open slightly wider in the agonizing surprise of that swollen member entering his nether region. As it pumped into him and he tried to scream past the rubber ball in his mouth, he could feel the other's body press closer into him and whisper into his ear.

"I am the Proliferator of Pain. You are to know the pain of that girl, trifold, this is merely to prepare you for the eternal pain you will suffer in Hell."

With the last words, spittle went into his ear as the man growled and hissed in his morbid pleasure. Not shortly after, the boy passed out, more out of fear than the pain of the alien object within him.

What seemed only an instant he was awake again. His anus throbbed and burned from the torture, and he could only think of if and when it might happen again. But as he came slowly to, he could hear something muffled, or was that his head still swimming? A hard sudden smack across his face drove his mind to quick working order. There were lights now, but not many, some across the room on a work bench. But the main source came from above.

Still the voice was only muffled, and the image of the man was too blurry to tell whom it could be. Chris tried to look around, but his head was grabbed and shoved into some iron apparatus that held his head in position to look down upon his own body. He was naked, bloody, beaten severely.

A snarl louder than anything he had ever heard came to his ears. "Do you hear me?"

Chris gasped. There was no other response he could think of or dare even try to utter.

The man laughed. "Do you feel that you have paid for your crimes against humanity, Chris? Go ahead, nod or shake your head."

Chris tested his mobility and felt that the bones in his neck were very near breaking, but slowly he nodded. Instead of the taunt he expected, he saw a knee ram up between his legs smashing into his already battered genitals. He tried to scream but only choked on the ball in his mouth. He could feel bile trying to make its way from his stomach, but he knew if he threw up now, he would more than likely drown.

"I am the Apex of Pain, Chris, sending you into the damnable land you so belong within. But no long journey is complete without a correct sending off."

Tears streamed and dripped off of Chris's face, spattering to the bloody floor.

"So how should it be done? You raped, you were raped, but it is just too simply known that he who commits a crime shall do it again if released back into society. So how should it be done?"

A small shutter wracked Chris's body in the restraints holding him to stand. The pain between his legs was far from gone, but at least it was dull now instead of stinging.

"Answer something, it's a simple question really, would you rather die slowly or quickly?"

Chris mumbled something unrecognizable.

"Oh good, for a second there I thought you were going to say quickly."

A silver glint flew across Chris's vision and a small red line streaked across his lower belly. He gasped and watched as a hot spray flew from the visage of his stomach and coils upon coils of intestine fell from him. A searing burning pain filled his mid-section, and he convulsed horribly in his restraints.

"Enjoy your stay in the anus of the universe; enjoy Hell." The man said walking out and barely leaving the door open.

The pain made Chris shake violently until his neck snapped free of the harness. Falling to the floor, his intestines smeared out across the floor and under his body. He tried to scream but taking in the breath was far more painful than just lying there. Feeling all of his essence drain from him, the light of the door seemed to fade and melt away. But something was at his cheek, somehow drawing his attention.

The feeling crawled from the side of his face to his nose where he turned his battered eyes to. There, on the tip of his nose, squirming and inching to some open wound, a solitary maggot.

*   *   *

"God Dammit all to Hell! What is this…four in two weeks?" Inspector Ferguson yelled.

"Yeah, this is the fourth. But what kind of connection do you see?" Inspector Grey, a rookie, came back.

"None from the obvious! All severely mutilated and beaten and all so close in time?"

Grey only nodded.

"Then there's this little thing else that connects all of them, or the other three so far, but I'm willing to bet it's the same for this guy. They go to the same church and are involved in it beyond regular attendance."

"So, someone in the church?"

"Possibly, but it could be some messed-up freak who decided to take out worshippers. But if this guy went to the same church, I want everything on everyone. We already have the father's information, but I'm willing to bet again that there's someone we don't know about right off hand."

Grey shuffled and looked at the body again. "I can get on it without anyone knowing right now if you wanted, Ferguson."

"You could," and he turned away from the body.

Grey nodded solemnly and stepped back, turned, and headed out of the alley. Toward the edge of the buildings, a throng of onlookers had gathered to see what might lie in the alley. Police barricades had been set up and uniforms themselves had to hold back the masses.

One in particular, who wasn't too outward, but still caught Grey's attention, was a man of the cloth uttering a small prayer with his eyes closed, mumbled something else, looked toward the alley and said: "May God have mercy on your soul," and stepped away into the crowd.

Grey shook his head in wonder at how someone could be that strong in a world so tormenting. But we all need leaders.

He stepped into his car, started it up, and slowly pushed his way through the foliage of massed bodies, all hot and stinking with anticipation, their hideous slack jaws drooling for blood and gore. Certainly, a crime by Grey's standards, one worthy of a few punishments.

And these damn photographers, he thought. *All wanting a shot at the latest victim. What I wouldn't give to take shots of their bodies.*

Traffic was light for a rainy Sunday morning, church was in session, but that only explained about two percent of the traffic. With a city full of atheists, undecided, and opportunists, this must be Hell and Grey was already dead.

He shook the feelings from him; he was just shaken by the sight of that young man. He had seen victims of sodomy before, but this poor guy, literally, had been ripped a new ass hole. Beaten so severely, they were lucky to find that his thumb had half a fingerprint left so that they might be able to identify him, assuming that he had ever been fingerprinted. But here? Almost everyone had been more than once.

Upon making it to the station house, the rain had strengthened. Today was not a good day and wasn't going to get any better. Not with a case like this.

Inside, removing his coat and throwing it towards a chair, he sat at his desk and switched on his computer, hoping that the local database might have something on that church that Ferguson had mentioned the previous victims were associated with. His fingers flew over the keyboard, entering commands and bringing up other files from only weeks passed.

First Minister's Catholic Church.

So, this was the place? Bizarre name, foreboding, but it was worth a shot at looking into. The current proprietor was also the Father to the church; Jonathan Philitetese. The picture of him on the screen reminded him of someone, someone he had only seen recently. The priest at the crime scene? It could certainly be worth looking into further.

He had the current screen printed, just a photo I.D. with a few tidbits of information. He would have to investigate further to find anything else that might point to any kind of connection. He was going purely on a hunch right about now.

* * *

"If only the dead could speak," Ferguson mumbled as he crouched over the body bag holding the body of one Chris Fernandez. "*'Oh but, Inspector, I can, and if you let me out of this bag, I'll tell you everything.'*

"I wish." he finished.

"Sir, can we take the body now?" a paramedic spoke from behind.

"Yes, yes, take it away," and he waved his hand.

Ferguson stood up, moaning slowly with the ache in his knees. "I hate this rain."

"What, Sir?" an officer inquired from the far side of the alley.

"The rain," he pointed to the sky. "Makes my knees hurt. Thing about getting too old, you start to agree with Danny Glover."

The other officer laughed lightly and stepped away, but not towards the squad cars, but further down the alley. Ferguson, only slightly curious, followed the officer back into the alley.

"Officer?" Ferguson called out.

There was a quick shuffling of feet at the sound.

"Oh, shit, I don't want to do this today." He said with a groan as he sped up.

When he came to the corner, where the body had been, he could see the officer running to the end of the alley. Ferguson smiled slightly, there was no ladder to climb over a brick wall between the buildings.

"Freeze!" he said, putting his hand to his gun.

The other officer whirled almost effortlessly from full stride, pulled a gun, and fired at Ferguson. Ferguson only barely ducked back behind the wall before the bullet hissed passed him. But the officer had managed to do the whole thing in one running turn and was back on his way to the end of the alley.

"I don't know where the Hell you think you're going *officer*, but it ain't far from here!" Ferguson yelled from behind the wall.

The man stopped, presumably in front of the wall. "Where I'm going you can't follow, Inspector. I would suggest you let this one be buried under more important cases like you've been doing. He deserved to die. Let God do His work, Sir."

There was the sound of a door opening then coming shut. Ferguson peeped his head around the corner carefully and there was nothing there. No officer, no door, no sign of any kind of escape. Nothing but a wet and cold alley where some kid's body had been dumped. But things started to click in his mind, why this alley to dispose of a body? How this alley. The only people to come here would be the sanitation department, so very few would see it, there's only the front entrance. Or so it would seem. Ferguson went back into the alley and investigated the walls, nothing. He swore he had heard a door.

No time for it now. Especially if he found the door, what would he do? Go in after him? The guy had almost killed him for Christ's sake, if not *for* Christ's sake. What the hell was that comment supposed to mean anyway?

"God's work, eh?" he mumbled.

Ferguson's cell phone rang out into the silent air, making him jump slightly and sigh in embarrassment. "Ferguson," he said.

"Inspector, that Chris kid? I found a connection between him, the others, and this First Minister's Catholic Church. Especially with one Jonathan Philitetese." Grey said.

"Hmm?"

"They, the victims, were all in Philitetese's youth group at the church. He presided over only one class, the others were held by some volunteers and parents. Mean anything?"

"Phil's a sick bastard?"

"Probably. But I was more asking *you*..."

"Oh, well, only one way to find out."

"Inspector? You okay, sir? Sound winded..."

"I'm fine thanks, I'll see you at the church, we have a few hours left before the end of the day, and maybe we can get a few things figured out."

"Sure thing, sir, meet you there. You do know where it is?"

Ferguson looked up to see the main steeple of the church Grey was talking about. Looked at the wall, back to the church, smiled slightly, and: "Just a hop, skip and a jump away, Grey. See you there."

"All right, Sir." And Grey hung up.

He looked back to the computer and decided he would pull up a few more records on Philitetese before he would take leave to the church. He pulled up a state birth record and hospital birth record. A small window on the computer noted that a third record was in possession of the police department with the same or similar information as the two showing documents.

Grey was about to ignore the document before he noticed that the two visible records had a slight variation. The one from state had the birth date and time as January 1, 1947; 12:59a.m. The hospital has January 1, 1947; 1:18a.m. He pulled up the third record: January 1, 1947; 1:32a.m.

Three different times for one person? Nothing was similar, it wasn't like someone misjudged a 4 for a 9, and these were completely different times. A "new year's" baby, but which time was correct? Grey shook his head; he had seen some screwed up files in his life, no reason to let this bother him, not now. All he had to do was ask Philitetese a couple questions, maybe even slip in the mishap of his birth certificate, if he didn't know, and then Grey would just pass it off as some dimwitted clerical error.

He grabbed a printed copy of all three different certificates, his coat and I.D. and was gone back out into the rain. After a long monotonous drive through the traffic of a *speedway*, Grey reached the First Minister's Catholic Church and parked next to Inspector Ferguson's car.

Walking into the church and hanging his wet overcoat on an older-than-him brass coat hanger, Grey could see that Ferguson and Philitetese had already begun a conversation on the odd occurrences in the alley behind the church.

Ferguson looked up. "Ah, here he is."

Philitetese, dressed in the normal attire of a minister, but still somehow making Grey feel uneasy instead of comforted, smiled as he looked up himself from the edge of the pulpit.

Grey nodded, somewhat stuttered: "How do you do?"

In a soothing but overly deep and raspy voice, not by nature but almost as if he had been yelling excessively, Philitetese said: "Good, I thank you. And how does our abode find you?"

Ferguson stood and excused himself to a restroom as Grey sat down. As he walked toward the front entrance of the congregation room he could hear Grey open with his normal line of questioning to someone already questioned: "I know you've already answered all of this by now, but..." his voice trailed off with distance.

Ferguson followed the directions of a small black and white sign pointing down the hall towards a restroom. Upon relieving himself and exiting, he saw the open door of a janitor's closet. Not much by usual standards, someone probably half-minded when they went to shut it, but it was the awful smell coming from it that caught Ferguson's attention. Unless it was long dirty mopping water, what could cause the putrid smell of something dead?

Investigation by curiosity. Ferguson hoped to himself he was more human than cat at this point and also hoped no one would come along, but as far as he could tell, Philitetese was the only person here.

"Inspector Ferguson?" a raspy voice called lightly from next to him.

It made him jump and gasp. He looked with surprised anger toward the speaker. Very much to his surprise again it was Philitetese. He must have taken a side exit from the original room.

"Is Grey done with his questions?" Ferguson managed to put forward finally.

"Oh no, sir, I'm merely giving myself a needed break. Even the Lord's disciples have to pee, you know." And he slightly laughed.

Ferguson nervously chuckled along with him. But was quick to shake off his encounter and head back to Grey to find if they had any story variations. Yet Grey was not alone. There sat Philitetese and Grey, laughing at some snide remark that *this* minister had just made. He looked down the hall toward where he had just seen Philitetese, but nothing and no one was there. Even staring for an extended period of time showed no second Philitetese. But the closet was closed now.

"Ahem, Inspector Grey?" Ferguson called softly.

Grey looked up, and then back to Philitetese who nodded, and Grey was up and with Ferguson.

"Did you find anything on this guy, like maybe a twin brother or something?" Ferguson said, still looking down the hall.

It was only then that everything started to click in Grey's mind. He said not a word, only kept calm and handed Ferguson the folded-up copies of birth certificates and walked back to Philitetese, resuming in a small laugh and commenting on some "good joke."

Ferguson leaned his back against the wall so that the two couldn't watch him as he tried to quietly unfold the papers. He was quick to notice the different birth times. Folding the paper back and shoving it into his pocket, he began to walk back toward the closet when he heard Grey say: "I noticed what looked like a clerical error on your birth certificate when I was looking up some information on you..."

I could damn you or thank you... this could either buy us time or the farm. Ferguson thought as he went back down the hall.

Now hoping that this time he could pull off being a cat, Ferguson went about his original investigation as quietly and secretively as he could. Although, he couldn't shake the feeling of being watched in some way. He opened the closet door. Now, either he was astounded that there was nothing there in the way of clues, or that there was nothing there in the way of cleaning materials. But the smell was definitely there.

He looked all over the closet, no bar to hang coats, no shelf to put boxes on, just an empty sunken door frame really, until he noticed a molding that was only on the floor of the back part of the closet. Curious he pushed his foot against it, watched it depress, then swing open a crack with an even more devastating smell assailing him.

The light of an old hanging lamp, or one hanging very far away seemed to be the only light coming through the hidden door. Ferguson dare not use his personal flashlight; he had to go trying to conceal himself completely.

"Oh, a strange story which I barely remember really. When I was born, my mother gave me up for adoption immediately, never even giving me a name. The hospital, unaware and completely unprepared for such a thing, hastily tried to fill out the certificates. This was before they started using carbon paper of course, so each one needed to be filled out by hand. Unfortunately, instead of asking what time I was born, they looked at the clock each time they came to the question of date and time. Otherwise, how could I be born at three different times?" Philitetese laughed.

It was only barely muffled but Ferguson could hear him and Grey perfectly through the wall here. So that's how the other Philitetese knew names. As he descended the old stairs, careful to keep his feet on the supports rather than the actual step, the sound drowned out and it became dead quiet, not to mention cold.

At the bottom of the stairs, he could see the light blue haze of a brighter light from behind a wall. Scared out of his wits at this point, fearing that the other Philitetese would be down here, he peeked around the corner and could see the other minister cleaning off a marble table with leather straps and harnesses wound through and attached to it. Cleaning off blood, bile, and God only knows what else. Ferguson was able to manage his stomach and was back up the stairs as quietly as before; but definitely quicker than before.

He changed his demeanor before stepping back in with Grey and one of the Philitetese's. "Just curious here, really, I should keep my nose to myself, but you know, I *am* an investigator, if not by hire then by nature. Anyway, I noticed something of an odd smell when I came out of the bathroom. I know for sure I didn't cause such a reek," he laughed to himself, trying to keep humor about him. "But it seemed to come from the empty closet across the hall from the bathroom. Any idea what that might be, Mr. Philitetese?"

But no answer ever came to him. Ferguson could hear the *whoosh* of something very heavy being swung, and then there was a dull warm pain at the back of his head, then darkness.

Grey bolted to his feet and was quick to draw his gun at the twin of Philitetese holding the coat rack he had hung his own jacket on. "What the *Hell* is going on here?" he blurted looking back to the first minister. *Well, that explains the name of the church, it's his and his brother is his henchman.* He thought. Then more and more began to click through his mind. "There's a third of you isn't there?"

And from behind the altar at the front of the room: "Yes. He, our eldest, is the Deliverer," the third Philitetese pointed to the one Ferguson and Grey had been speaking to. "That," pointing to the second, "is the Proliferator."

"And who are you, the Violator?" Grey remarked, sweeping his gun toward the first Philitetese.

"This is not some comic book, Inspector! I am the Apex of Pain. Now, we have nothing against you, Inspector Grey. You are free to leave without ever mentioning this place again in your life, but your fellow investigator has committed a crime against us by trespassing into our inner sanctum. He will be duly dealt with." Apex said.

"So why do you all have the same name?" Grey pressed.

The first Philitetese, the Deliverer, said: "As I told you, given up at birth, but such a small practice hospital was nowhere near prepared for a woman to give up triplets, we were all given different names, that was the error, the times are correct. You only found a few of our certificates; we've done well to keep it down to seeming as there is only one of us."

"But why?"

"How else could we perform our duty to the Lord without police involvement?" the Proliferator said.

Too much confusion and Grey's gun had managed to waiver its way to his side. The Deliverer swung hard and connected with the side of Grey's face, knocking him out.

Waking, very groggy and thickheaded, Ferguson could only see a little bit of light through hazy eyes.

"Nice to see you joining us, Inspector. Did you enjoy your nap?" the deep voice of one of the Philitetese's said.

Ferguson didn't pay much attention; he was more interested in what was poking him in the side rather than what some crazy minister had to say or rant about. When he tried to look down, he felt that his head was held in place. The marble table.

"You unfortunately took leave before we made our introductions to your partner, Inspector Grey. I, am the Deliverer of Pain." The voice came again.

Ferguson heard, but still wasn't paying attention. Not until he saw the glint of a chest splitter.

"Trespassing is caused by a multitude of things." A farther away voice said. Possibly another Philitetese.

"But yours was caused by curiosity." A third Philitetese?

Ferguson, although his interest in the voices became stronger, was still rapt on what was jabbing his side.

"And curiosity is a thing of the heart." The first one said.

Followed by: "So the heart must be dealt with."

Then: "And such a case must be driven to the Apex at the beginning."

The tool used to crack open rips in heart surgeries was passed from hand to hand until the face of John Philitetese, or at least one of him anyway, came into clear view.

"Yes, but the heart can be a masterful thing if it's in touch with the mind." Ferguson blurted as he finally realized what was at his side.

Philitetese, the one who had said "Apex," cocked his head slightly.

"And I'm double jointed." Ferguson said casually as his thumb seemed to dislocate and fold into the palm of his hand. All in one motion, he slipped the folded mass of fingers through the leather strap holding his wrists. He popped his thumb back into place, grabbed his gun which had been stuck in his side, and shot this Philitetese straight between the eyes, blowing a large and clear hole out the back of his head.

Blood and bits of flesh, brain and skull exploded into the back of the room with the loud crack of the gun firing. The other Philitetese's stared in shock and fear as the body of Apex fell to the rotten floor. Ferguson trained his gun on the both of them and slipped his head out of the harness with the new mobility he gained with freeing his arm.

"Now, I'm just guessing, but it seems that the three of you had a little thing going on down here reminiscent of torture...?" Ferguson said, hanging out from the upright table.

Both of them still stared in fear without saying or uttering anything. Until one of them lurched forward, a large blade bursting through his chest. Blood poured out his mouth as he coughed slightly, turned his head and saw the beaten Grey standing behind him.

"It really hurt when you punched me, you son of a bitch." Grey mumbled as that Philitetese fell to the ground, only grunting as the light in his eyes faded with oncoming death.

"And as for you," Grey continued, "the Proliferator, seeing as your name would dictate that you like long drawn-out things, we may as well keep you alive. We'll go ahead and prolong the agony of your existence without your brothers. And if you were lucky, you might get a death sentence."

"You're really corny, you know that, Grey?" Ferguson said.

"You saw what I did to him," he pointed to the ground, "for punching me."

"*Point* taken, I'll shut up. But could you let me out of this thing?"

Grey found handcuffs in Ferguson's pocket and locked the last Philitetese around a pipe on the wall. Then let Ferguson down from the table.

"That was certainly a day worth living." Ferguson quipped.

"It'll be one hell of thing to explain for the reports and cases."

The other Philitetese, astounded that they talked so casually, "What are you two doing? You kill my brothers then pass it off as just an unusual day?"

Grey took off his coat, hunched over and growled deep like a wild cat. Bright white feathery wings erupted from his back and spread out across the room, then folded back into a rested position. He stood, slightly leaning forward with the weight of the wings.

Ferguson, upon stepping down off the table, performed a similar act.

Philitetese began to whimper and quiver in complete fear and surprise.

Ferguson stepped forward, his wings swaying with the steps. "God gave you or your brothers no purpose. You acted against Him and your kind. So, we were sent by Him to stop your blasphemy."

"You...you're...Angels?" Philitetese mumbled.

Grey came forward now, all light disappearing from Philitetese's face as the two inspectors crowded him. "Yeah, but the Bible made us out the wrong way. We're not exactly calm, cool and collected."

"Neither is God." Ferguson said, pointing his gun at Philitetese.

THW

SUICIDE KING:
LAST RANT OF A DRUNKEN DEMON

Written 2001

PUNCH/PANTS, October 2012

Another Grand Marais tale, and one that connects to my novel, IN TGE HOUSE OF IN BETWEEN. A couple of characters even appear in the novel. This could be considered backstory for the novel, and also my version of the War in Heaven. This piece is another one also filled with deplorable characters. The main character is a villain, who he's hunting is a villain, who creates the situation isn't friendly, even if they're also a villain on the "same side." I initially began writing this story working a temp job during the U.S. election, finishing maybe around the time W was sworn in. Losing my mother in 2001, the way I did, made this feel unfairly poignant, much like DEADWORLD. It made writing more difficult, a reaction I still deal with.

"Show me your true form."

"Eh? Oh; crawling black skin and glowing eyes, horns and talons, yes? Perhaps you expect me to spit fire or breathe some noxious gas that hypnotizes children? No, I'm sorry, I have dark brown eyes and auburn hair, fair Caucasian skin and a slightly crooked overbite from a fight I had when I was younger."

"Then what the hell are you?"

"I'm *not* a monster, I am…a *demon*. Monsters exist, yes, in ways you wouldn't expect or even dare to fathom. I am in legion with a few monsters, but demons, overall, are fairly normal looking individuals."

I can't believe I'm having this discussion yet again. He probably thinks I'm shitting him, putting him on because he's drunk, play a few parlor tricks and anyone believes anything. But get a few drinks in me and I'll tell you the history of the two Angelic Wars, the fall of Satanail and the hidden government established by terran based Angels in over two billion galaxies across the universe. I'm not the best at keeping secrets, torture me and I'll tell you the six degrees of Kevin Bacon.

"So really prove to me that you're a demon. You've got to have some powers…"

"I already told you your own life story and we've never met."

"Maybe you work for the CIA or somethin'."

That's a new one. "Alright, how's about I show someone their deepest darkest fear right in the middle of the bar, and I'll walk you through what they're seeing?"

"Really, you can do that?"

"I'm a demon… Pick someone."

"Do me!"

So typical of humans. "Trust me, the last thing I want is you to start a bar fight or try to murder me after I scare the holy living shit out of you. Pick someone *else*."

"Hmm, how about that big guy playin' pool? He doesn't look like he'd be scared of anything."

I have to laugh. He thinks, genuinely thinks he's stumped me. "Everyone's afraid of something." I close my eyes, reaching out to the burly man. He's a typical biker kind of guy, bald with a graying beard, leather jacket, very well built. He does look like it'd take a lot to startle him, but I'm going to make him afraid. I'm going to prove to this drunk that I'm some spawn of another realm. But demons, we don't usually work like this, me however, it's how I get by.

"His mother was found dead in her house, seemingly neglected, when he was very young. Possibly the reason he's conditioned himself this way. Problem is, *Harold White* thinks he's the whole reason his mother died, he lived with his father across town and his mother had always been a nervous wreck, but still, he loved her very much and visited her as often as he could. His main fear is that his mother will haunt him, even after all these years, he's afraid her spirit will find some way to torment him and gain some sort of personal vengeance against him."

"He's afraid of his own mother?"

"Shut up. When he goes to make his next shot, I'm going to whisper like his mother into his ear."

Sure enough, the drunk was thrilled. As Harold the Biker bent slightly over, taking aim at the cue ball, I whispered. He shot up immediately.

"Whoa…"

Harold shakes his head. He looks a little disoriented but shakes his head again and goes to make the shot again. Timing is key here; I have to get the look of horror to coincide with his final stroke so that he'll make a big reaction that'll get the entire bar's attention. Only Harold can see this, the apparition of his mother standing at the corner pocket, staring at him with decaying eyes.

"You did this to me…" I whisper. The drunk's own face is a little terrified as I say it and Harold screams and rips the top of the table with his stick.

Harold is stumbling back, his whole body paper white. He utters some unintelligible thing and makes for the door, I laugh, turning on my bar stool to take another drink. Everyone is staring in the direction of Harold but me. I do this all the time. I've done it for hire; I've done it for pleasure. Most of the time the two go hand in hand. Give a demo, gain an offer, and get a job. I get paid a high amount for my services and I move on until I need more cash. I'm pretty much the homeless person of demon society.

The drunk sits quietly, uncomfortable for a little while. He's sobered up a bit, but still *wants* to believe all this was some trick. He looks at me finally, a little weary, "How'd you do that?"

I smile, "It's *magic*."

"Well, I gotta get home. It was fun meeting you," he offers me his hand, I take it firmly. "What's your name again?"

"I didn't tell you…and I don't have one." I say shaking my head.

He tries to smile but only bares his teeth in some slur of a facial expression. He'll remember me but won't want to.

The bartender laughs as the guy leaves hurriedly. "Of course, you have a name." He says to me.

I look at him and smile. "Oh, beautiful Lucifer, why dost thou light shine upon me?"

"Because I got stuck on one of these rocks just like you."

"Give me vodka," I say closing my eyes and shaking my head.

"Sure, you can handle it?"

"Of course, I'm a *demon*." Elaborate, overacted, there is no glory in living a horror lifestyle. He was an angel of the Lord, fallen in the Great War in tail of the most beautiful of all angels. Lucifer chose a side, I was born into it, and then, when I couldn't hold my liquor, they threw me out into the universe to roam.

He scratches his head, wipes off his hands with a towel, grabs another towel and cleans a glass for me. "Why'd they put you on Earth?" he asks me.

"It's where I fell. They kind of just cast me aside, no assignment, just stay out of trouble."

"I thought demons were designed to make trouble…"

"Sure, when it's focused and established. Me? I ran rampant, getting drunk and coming just this close to blowing one of the biggest operations of the campaign."

"You still could, you know, it doesn't seem right to leave you be on a backwater planet, you can still wreak havoc, even if this is a small place."

He pours me the drink. I slide it to me, nursing it at first, then downing the whole thing, I point at the glass as I swallow the last of it. "Look around you Lucy, everyone here thinks that *you're* Satanail himself, and if you came out and even proved beyond a shadow of a doubt who you were and what was going on, would any of them believe you?"

"Point taken." He nods. He pours one more glass, "That's your last, demon. You have a place to stay?"

"A traitor offering me a place to stay? Or do you wish to just toy around with someone who could give you half a challenge?"

"That hurts."

I down the second glass. "I hope it does." I leer at him. My eyes are cold, but glassy, he knows I'm just venting, and I know I'm treading dangerous water talking to a General like this. "Sorry, Lucy, let me pay my tab and I'll be on…"

"Forget it. Out here I don't see too much of the War so when a soldier, even one on leave, comes through, I'm happy to cover his charges. You picked a good place to rest it out."

"I like the name."

Grand Marais, Minnesota, a lost town little town often jokingly referred to by its inhabitants as *Malaise*. Grand Marais is where people go when their souls are dying, it's one big graveyard and only special people have plots. They just haven't died yet. The whole place is gray, they might have picked a good place to send me, but Lucy there, the Angel of light, the morning star, picked the most dismal and contradictory place to call home. He's been holding that bar for quite a few years now.

Outside, my drunken friend and Harold are arguing. Apparently, Harold noticed the odd smirk on my friend's face as he stumbled out the door only moments ago. Harold has a gun, but I pay him no mind. Though, he expects my respect for he sees me and his temper flares even more.

"Is this your magician friend, *Jimmy*?" he blurts out, scared, angry and drunk.

Jimmy seems to fit this little man; he looks and sounds like a rat. Jimmy the Rat. Where's Cagney when you need him?

"Yes, I am a magician and any further questions *about* me can be directed *at* me." I say, raising a hand as if in an offering gesture. Though really, I'm preparing to stop this whole incident.

Harold does as I expect, as you probably expect. Drunk he can't control his rage and swings the pistol my way firing lazily. The bullet misses far off to my left and spatters concrete from the side of a wall. His next shot, however, is dead on for where any human heart would be. Technically, and only for technical reasons, my heart is there as well, but far different. That's not what I'm talking about, though.

Harold and Jimmy both are staring hard as if to try and determine whether or not what they're looking at is real. My hand is held in front of my chest in that motion you offer naughty children, as these two are, obviously. At the end of my index finger spins and whistles the bullet intended to shatter my chest. Demons are like flies, only as big as humans, we see everything that comes at us in slow-motion, so it takes a few swats before you can hit us. But then, unlike a fly, we'll get back up. Eventually.

There's a little bit of smoke where it hit my finger (the continuous spinning is just another trick, entertain the primitives, you know?), not to say bullets don't hurt, this is about as bad as any flaming pit you can imagine. That's why Hell is impressed with Earth. You're one of the few species who have created weapons solely for destruction rather than defense. I reach my other fingers forward and pluck the bullet from its standing point.

"Harold, I just have one question…"

He doesn't answer, I didn't want him to.

"Did you really think you could shoot me?"

This time he won't answer, but I reach out with my mind in curiosity. I want to know what he's feeling, what he's thinking…

"Jesus Fucking Christ!" Jimmy. Oh, how delicately that was put, but Harold couldn't agree more.

I manipulate the bullet in my hand, put it between my index and thumb as though I was to flip a coin. I bring it to my ear, making a clicking noise with my tongue and the roof of my mouth. Both of them are stupefied, how tense simple movements can make someone; I extend my arm, pointing right at Harold.

I can only smile. "Bang."

I flick the bullet faster than sound can follow and Harold's heart explodes in his chest. The resulting carnage of his chest spatters Jimmy's face and the exiting bullet demolishes Harold's spine so that he falls at an odd, almost sickening, angle. But I've seen far worse.

Jimmy pisses his pants. He can't handle this anymore, he wants to run, but like the urine from his penis, the life in his legs is fleeting.

"What?" I ask of him. Then I realize that he _is_ only human, such weak creatures despite their destructive capabilities. I point at the dead body of Harold. "That?"

I blow a raspberry. My hand, still pointing, blossoms into a full palm spread, an aura of light surrounds it and air crackles like miniature thunder blasts. The aura brightens and holds for a moment then lashes out at Harold, ripping into him and sewing his being back together. Harold's body falls limp, but air is travelling through his lungs again.

Jimmy still can't move, but stares in wonder as the bully shifts a bit, starts, and then stands very quickly seeming disoriented. He looks at me, then at Jimmy, and "How the hell did I get out here?"

I answer. "You passed out inside, we brought you out for some air, a bit smoky in there for someone unconscious."

He nods, thinking he remembers feeling weak, though really, I'm only feeding it to him. There's still blood and a bullet on the ground beneath him, but he pays it no attention.

Then, a voice behind me seems to steal all the air from around us. "Perhaps you boys should call it a night."

Both of them are terrified, but I recognize it. I turn to confirm my notions and see only a crawling darkness with torn and dirty wings flaring. The essence of the thing, the very lack of color seemed to spread and distort everything around it, as though these things of the living world, including the atmosphere itself wanted desperately to be as far away as possible from this creature. I can only smile at the Fallen Angel Lucifer, once the Morning Star, as he reveals *his* true form.

Once so beautiful, I think to myself.

Jimmy scurries, stumbles then bolts down the street, surprising even himself. The last thoughts I hear from him are *God, please tell me this is a dream!*

I laugh, only barely audible.

Harold is a bit more stubborn. He thinks he's seeing things and tries to rub out whatever this thing is in his eyes. Lucifer flows forward, doesn't move mind you, but roils forth, like a column of oil rolling through the air. The wings stretch farther then snap down, creating a gust of wind so cold that even I have to admit a bit of chill. But now, almost literally frozen, Harold manages a blink.

The words almost fall from Lucifer's...mouth. His speech is dripping, pure vile essence that grabs hold of Harold's mind and forces him to pay attention. "This is nightmare," Lucifer begins. "A dream world from which you will awake tomorrow, but you shall *always* remember me..."

A hand forms extending a finger that graces the bully's cheek. To him it feels like a cold, dead slug dragging across his skin, its flesh somehow oozing onto,_*into* his. He wants to scream, throw-up, cry, move, and do *anything* to get this over with. And suddenly it is as Harold's body finally responds and runs in the opposite direction Jimmy took.

The hideous thing rolls around to face me, but before actually facing me, takes shape into the blonde-haired blue-eyed man who owns Lucy's Dynamo Bay. It overlooks a very large shipping bay on Lake Superior that is often called the Whale Tail, almost reminds me of some ponds back home. "Causing trouble?"

"Just a little, nothing I would let them remember."

"I was hoping I might be able to catch you before you disappeared. I have a favor to ask…"

I mull this over. What could a fallen seraph want with me, a lowly demon?

"Actually, not so much a favor, but, say…an *offer*."

"What kind of offer?" never take candy from strangers, children.

"A way back home."

A chill runs down my spine. I feel a roar bubble in my stomach, or is that bile? I whisper, hiss, "Don't fuck with me, Lucifer."

"I appreciate your enthusiasm," he smiles, but it quickly becomes a frown, and the venom that fills it burns my own skin. "But do watch your tongue."

I shake my head. "How? *How* can you offer something like that?"

"I may be on hiatus, but that doesn't lessen my pull. You do something for me, and I pay you for the deed."

I ponder it, what could possibly warrant a ticket home? "What's this *something*?"

"You've probably taken more difficult tasks from humans…"

"Go on."

"There is a law enforcement individual who wishes to shut down my bar by exposing some of its more profiting aspects."

"Breaking the law, are we?"

"I need him gone and no follow up investigation. This cannot be associated with me, nor can it come back to me."

"Sounds serious. You could just pick up and take off with no effort…what's so important about this bar?"

It's Lucifer's turn to shake his head. I know he doesn't need or have to explain reason, but, "Call it personal."

"Okay, why me?"

"I don't have time for it," (He's lying to me, but I can't say so) "And I need someone to focus their entire attention to the situation. Find all the people involved and dispense of them as well."

A girl comes running down the street, she's very determined to be somewhere. Lucifer flashes a bright and warm smile at her as she comes closer, "Good evening, Rena."

"Hey, Lucy." She says disinterested.

He watches her turn a corner at the end of the block, I look directly at him. "And leave no possible witnesses."

"Hmm, *yes*. You already know all of this. His name is Cooper Townsmen," he reaches out a finger and touches my forehead; everything I need to know is forced into my brain. "I expect thorough results."

I turn to walk away, soaking in what I have just learned. It's an odd way to be given your briefing but it is by far the most efficient. I've got several options to choose from in how to complete my task, but the main task is to make it perfect. No chance anyone would even want to touch this case, and I begin to see where each of the options points, and I begin to smile.

"Do you really know me?" I ask of Lucifer.

Backlit by a streetlamp, he is beautiful, and I can still see his smile back to me. "By reputation."

I shake my head and laugh. This is going to happen soon, I have to meet Mr. Townsmen, and I have a feeling I know where I can find him at this late hour.

Walking through these streets, I realize that if there was ever a place to begin Armageddon, Grand Marais is perfect. It's like a road between worlds, as though this is the gate to everywhere, but no one knows about it. Lucifer is here, Satanail knows about it, he dropped me here. Sometimes I wonder if this is all some plan and I'm a part in it and now, at this point in time, it's coming to some sort of head. Well, at least for me. But I shouldn't be thinking about things like this, I have a mission to fulfill.

At three o'clock in the morning, even a cop will sleep. He's a daytime worker, so this is a good place to study. Eyes are the window to the soul is what you humans say, dreams are the material your soul is made of. But right now, it's just random movements, nothing major, his brain processing the day's information and creating the new creases of memory.

"Wake up..." I whisper.

His eyes bolt open and he shifts in bed. I get to see what he looks like. Slightly overweight balding but how his hair is messed now; it looks like he brushes his hair forward to cover it.

"Look at me."

He's groggy, his brain is screaming both to look just to see and not to for fear of what it will be. He does though, through half closed eyes, but they come just as wide as when he woke. He doesn't want to believe it, a thing all black, oily, smoky, eyes burning white.

"Now dream."

His eyes shut almost as though feinting. And I watch for a moment more, droplets of sweat appearing like dew. I smile, though you wouldn't know it. My eyes grow more intense, concentrating, his body spasms and the girl in the bed shifts, moving from him. Too young to be a wife, she's probably too young to even be seen with this man. I give a nod to the good side just so I can fuck this man a little harder. The seed planted in her will make her quit whoring, she may not become reputable, and she may start this career again, but this man especially, will keep her from it. A very special nightmare that will stay with her for a very long time.

"I'll see you soon, Captain Townsmen."

He wakes just as soon as I leave, a slug in the shape of a man moving slowly from his window. What was this, all a dream? What did I eat? Do I want to go back to sleep...

In the alley behind his downtown apartment, I finish a hidden bottle of whiskey I stole from a homeless person. It's cheap and definitely no cognac, but the bite is something else. 'Course, this may be because of the blood mixed in with it. I spit a little on the ground and scrape it out in a design. Some days from now I will kill Townsmen, this is how it works, he will have nightmares so severe that he will consider professional help, but by then it will be too late. He's already seen me, that was half a mistake, he might recognize me if I hang around too much. But then again, it might be fun.

I sit cross-legged and stare at the symbol, it begins to smolder, and the smell of alcohol fills my nostrils. I take another heavy hit and savor the flavor, but this one isn't for me, it sprays from my mouth in a vapor cloud that raises straight up in a wisp of heat. I lay my head back just a bit, only for my protection, the cloud becomes a ball of fire and I smile that sick demented smile only a murderer could understand. My skin crawls at it, all the tiny hairs recoiling in miniature explosive deaths.

In his dream he awakes terribly, something shook him, but as he looks at the whore, she's covered in something. He reaches to his nightstand to flip on the light but feels something on his arm, his other hand reaching; he's not quite quick enough before his skin bursts open spewing a hundred million maggots and flies. The fire of his own pain gives him sight enough to see that what was crawling on the girl was the same, though they had devoured all her flesh and now it lay sagging and tearing away by the separation of decay. He tries to run but only slams himself into the wall, his skin pulling off onto the wall, insects of death flopping like fat fingers reaching through him.

A scream, though not his, wakes him. His hands have become like vices on the girl's neck, but then he realizes yet again he has no control of his hands and that they only tighten as his eyes open. He screams in return, both in anger and in fear and this is the final little thing. I'm finally pushed out and lying on the street.

This is where I encounter a problem. Being cocky and trying to perform this right behind the building and only a block, no less, from the poor bum I released from his personal prison, has made me a nuisance to somebody. The cops stand over me, wondering what language I'm cursing in, trust me, it's no Latin. I'll be put into some cell with a few other winos that I'll have to dispatch and then whatever guards. Why can't I move my legs?

*　*　*

As I come to, I can smell something foul, that putrid acid tingle in my nostrils that can only be bile. Whether it's mine or that of one of the humans in here is what I can't discern. I'm still weak, probably the only time I could ever be mugged, which means I should bring myself out of this funk quickly. I hear someone rousing as I begin to stir.

"Look everybody," the voice is slurred, but not from drink. He's missing teeth, too many redneck fights. "The little bastard is waking up."

I try to bring my head around to look at him, but I feel as though someone has put a vice on me and my body won't respond the right way.

"Thinks he can just come in here and try to kick our asses or somethin'."

What have I done?

His hand basically fits around my neck as he picks me up. My eyes shift into focus, and I can see the loose teeth are recent; his mouth is caked with dry blood. Why doesn't anyone stop this? Then I realize this burly oaf is a police official. I am not in the drunk tank but sitting in some small office with six giants watching over me. This must have been bad.

"Excuse me officer," I manage to choke. "But it's a little hard to breathe this way."

I half smile/grimace, it's painful but nothing I can't stand.

"Fuck you, you little fucker!"

The others sort of laugh at this. I join in on the fun. "Great vocabulary, you dirty swine."

The other cops "ooo" to this, but I'm leading them. It's all a game now and I have home advantage. The burly officer tightens his grip.

"You'd better watch you're fuckin' mouth, prick."

I look around a bit; tighten my own grip on the five other men, no chance in this failing. I have a mission to fulfill, and no witnesses.

"I say…you…should swallow…your tongue."

He looks at me quizzically. Not the response he was looking for or the reaction he ever expected. His own tongue fights his mouth, like some terrible worm burrowing through his throat. His throat convulses, pulling it down and choking him. It is one of the strongest muscles in your body, if it wants down there, it's gonna go. His eyes roll up and turn a pastel pink color as he begins to asphyxiate, the other men are laughing. The man's grip has tightened on my neck almost to the point of shattering bone, but I have no need for charades now. They'll all be dead in a moment and no evidence pointing toward me.

Behind me, all the men are laughing as they pull their guns from holsters. The choking man grows suddenly fragile and lets me go; I drift slowly to the floor, turning to watch. They bring the guns to their chins, still watching, and their eyes dumb as rabbits. I smile at them all.

"Funny, isn't it?"

A spray of blood fills the room, a symphony of gunshot and the visual display of fragmented skull, brain and flesh. The final drumbeat of them all hitting the floor, I am the Suicide King.

Outside, the air feels cold, it's always cold here, but now, there's a very certain chill to the air. I take a quick look around and everything is hazy. That giant bastard must have actually suffocated this body because I feel a little sick. I know what can cure that, but I have a hard time deciding if I should pay another visit to the Captain or Captain Morgan. Withdrawal screams its passion.

* * *

In the old life, I was a demon, a shapeshifter given assignments on a million different worlds that had been taken over or were under Armageddon. I was born of earth and blood and given life by the greatest angel to have ever graced Heaven, but like him, I had weaknesses. We all had them; usually it was of the mind but mine was of will, which could be an attribute of the mind, but addictions are so hard to place.

* * *

As I sat at the bar, laughing about how I had just destroyed several men by shear thought alone, I never even thought of whom I was telling the story to. They were dumbfounded. Was I telling the truth or was this some drunken rant? Both of course, but they had a hard time telling, too absurd to be real, too realistic to be a lie, too false to be believable. Then I was yanked hard from my stool at the bar, my feet hitting the ground, I could only giggle.

The man waved his hand, all the people listening to my story suddenly confused. Their confusion would last until I was dragged away, out of the bar so I could have a good stern talking-to.

That same chill was in the air, only now, it emanated from *him*. "Just what the fuck do you think you're doing?"

I could only laugh. "If this is such an easy task, why not do it yourself?"

"It's not a matter of if I can do it myself, but that you might find the key to your prison. I offer you survival and you damn your own chances!"

"Damn? *Damn*! Damn, damn, damn! I'm a fucking demon, Lucy, I was born *damned*. What can they possibly do to me I can't handle?"

He shoves me harder into the wall, brick actually cracking under the pressure. "Listen here you peon,"

I spit in his face.

His hand lashes up, breaking my neck. His arms go into furry, scratching and tearing at my flesh, breaking bones, my back snaps as he pounds me into the ground. Fortunately, the alcohol manages to dull the pain, I can focus on other things while he vents.

Why don't you do this yourself, Lucy? What are you hoping to achieve by being a saint for me?

He reels at the telepathy, not expecting it. He shakes it off, a snarl crossing his breath. *Why must you ask questions of a superior? I have given you an assignment and all you can do is botch things. You only have a few more days; otherwise, I do far worse things than mangle you.*

I think you've torn away my jaw. I try to make movement, but I'm too deep into coma. My demonic gifts repairing and stitching all his dealings. But he is gone before I can offer any sort of apology, I do realize that I have gone astray and only made a complicated matter worse. Ah, fuck it. I can do this on my own, who cares if he kills me? Where am I gonna go? Hell?

Someone wanders down the alley as I begin to gain control of my body, but *before* I'm completely healed. This could make things downright difficult, he says something, and then mutters some cry of shock as I turn to face him. There is absolute horror stealing all color from his skin, he'll faint if he doesn't breathe. I try to smile in amusement, but I realize that I have no lower lip, no jawbone for that matter, to smile with. This *could* make a human uneasy.

"Wh-what are you?" he squeaks.

Something else... I whisper into his head.

He drops to the ground, almost lifeless. I hear the splash of water as he hits and take a curiosity as to what Lucifer has done to me. As the ripples fade, I can see that by no means am I even remotely human. My shoulder is dislocated and my clavicle broken, giving my left side an almost freakish difference to the other. My jaw is completely missing and part of my upper lip torn away, a part of my scalp has been torn loose, exposing my cranial cap. Eyes bloodshot from pressure, I look back down the alley wondering if anyone will come check on this monkey.

I root through his pockets finding a cell phone, looking it and him over I decide there's an opportunity awaiting me here. I lift him to a sitting position and punch a hole in the back of his head, grabbing onto his brain, no worries, he doesn't feel a thing. With my other hand I dial nine-eleven, then holding the phone to his head, listening through his brain.

"Nine-One-One Emergency, what is the nature of the emergency, please?"

There's just been a fight behind, uh... I look up and around.

"...Behind Harrington's Billiards." I continue in his voice. The woman on the other end hears this only as a normal call, if she saw the exchange she would surely be scarred for life. Ah, telepathy.

*   *   *

This mission was handed down to me by Satanail himself. "I have heard of your excellence in dealing with secret assassination. A skill that has even earned you a name, yes?"

I cower in the way a girl cowers before being raped by the most popular guy in school.

"Yes, the Suicide King. You have a way of using psychology over a course of time, making everyone involved believe it was in the cards... Very tricky. I have a very special task for you, my child."

No, the fear was more like that of an abused child, as he slid his arm around my shoulder, walking and talking.

*　*　*

The paramedics, ambulance drivers, police and onlookers all could not see me. I had healed myself almost completely by now, but I still hid in my own shadow, sneaking aboard the ambulance that would take me to my next destination. Stitching the man's head was no problem and roughing him up a bit was only for pleasure. The paramedics only saw the result of a street brawl.

The secret is to make sure no one touches you and having a little mind control helps. I sat near the rear doors, waiting, hoping I wouldn't experience any difficulties. Something was poking my hip, I tried to ignore it thinking it was only a not-yet-healed bruise, but my ever-present flask filled with God only knows what sort of cocktail, dug into me, beckoning me. But Lucifer was right, I couldn't continue screwing around. I had to set a goal and achieve it, and in so doing, complete my *mission*.

Entering the hospital was no problem, making my way around to medical records was something else entirely. I could make present people not see me, but if I was to be snuck up on by some unwitting doctor, I'd have to explain myself. And right now, I feel just a little belligerent, especially after having to wait for three goddamn hours for some RN to enter the room I needed.

I fumbled my way around a computer until I finally found Capt. Townsmen's records. A fairly healthy man. "But there's gotta be something here... Ah, yes, this will do nicely."

Walking out is no problem. No one even cares, if I was in there, then I must have been doing something important. A nurse does something of a double take but decides whatever she was headed for is more important than a stranger.

With the knowledge of allergic reactions and certain cocktails I know of myself, I can make this man become the most watched person in all of Grand Marais.

*　　*　　*

Captain Cooper Townsmen is a desk jockey. He hits the streets every once in a while, does some rough and tumble *cop* work, but he prefers the comforts of a closed environment. I try to expound on this by bringing myself close to him, making him think that I'm just another brown-noser rookie hoping to gain a role model. I'm betting he's so arrogant he'll take a shine to that kind of attention.

I cautiously set a cup of coffee on his desk. "Good day, Captain." I say with the biggest shit-eating grin I can possibly muster.

He looks up from his file; I surmise that this is the case that Lucifer is worried about. Looks like some grisly murders and bodies dumped into Dragon Lake. Lucifer doesn't care, it can't be really penned to him, but he does have easy access to the lake and the victims are, *were*, all frequents to the bar.

"Can I help you?" he says in an overly high-pitched voice for his size. Nasal, geeky, the little fat kid you beat up after school when your brothers hogged the Atari. I'm revolted but keep my stature.

"No, no, only offering you a cup of coffee. I-I noticed yours was nearly empty."

He looks at the nearly full cup of his own. I laugh nervously.

He looks back at me, a twinge of humor. His voice is now booming, much stronger than before. "And what's your name, son?"

"Stanley Kurtin, just-just a beat-cop. I just graduated…" I know nothing of how they work. I stole a uniform from a locker and now I'm trying to fool a Captain.

He laughs too loud, embarrassingly loud. "Well, Kurtin, you're not going to get too far kissing ass around here," he lowers his voice finally. "But thanks for the coffee anyway,"

He lifts the cup and takes a long careful sip. I smile, more devious now. He *loves* me. Soon he'll shit his pants at the sight of me. I step back, turn and walk away, looking slightly over my shoulder, hoping the effects are short in coming.

*   *   *

Though made by the very bile of Hell's earth, I had acquired weakness to certain substances. My first encounter was actually by accident, blending with locals in an attempt to move in close to a rogue Heavenly creature that dwelled on an island in the middle of a swamp. The waters of the swamp were used in a drink they poured at every dinner.

On the planet Jurii, I found the substance again, already an addict to the effects it produced for my mind and body. Here it was an item sold by market vendors in large leather sacks, I drank two, slightly worrying my fellow demon escorts. Satanail had produced an assignment that would vastly change the direction of the war, clenching a hold on a large once heavily guarded galaxy that we had managed to weasel our ways into controlling.

The environment demanded stealth and a speedy delivery. An ambassador had been secretly dealing with Angels, despite this is supposed to be a war held in secrecy that no living creature could fathom. He was supplying weaponry and what we could only surmise as *gadgets* that detected Outer Plain essence. With him dead, the Angels could no longer have contact with the planet, and we could make our move, Armageddon, our procurement of a planet.

*   *   *

Jimmy the Rat is a police officer, and he recognizes me. I have both a hard time believing it and wondering how I ever could have missed it. He doesn't want to speak to me, but he has a good mind to say something to someone, a Rat to the end. I smile and make him look at me again, his fear subsiding, as he now no longer recognizes me. But nightmares are something personal, something to cherish in privacy, and he still can't shake the feeling that he has seen me before.

If anyone can fuck this up more than I can, it will be that man. I have half a mind to kill him without a second thought, but the other half of my mind is singing circus music and I'm waiting for the results of my second major move on the captain.

And so, it comes, crashing into reality. In today's society there is a drug for everything, from being too sad to being like the captain, just too mad. He takes a sort of "downer" for his condition, but I have laced this ass-kissing coffee offering with the opposite drug, hoping for an over-reaction to the hallucinogenic also in the coffee. I have no idea what he sees but it has made him overturn his desk and go crashing to the floor himself. Several police officers come to his aid, though it seems more likely they are in need of assistance as Captain Townsmen is currently in the middle of an adrenaline-fueled *trip*. I raise my head in curiosity, masking laughter with concern and yammering out "W-What's going on?"

Jimbo has come back down the hall to witness the onslaught as well; he stares in disbelief, looking back at me, still remembering only slightly what I did to the oaf in the bar. He lets out a quivering sigh and rushes to become one with the melee.

"Ah, yes," I say to myself. "Now he'll be checked out by doctors and psychologists."

A man not exactly close to me hears my personal conversation. "What'd you say?"

I look at the floor in front of the toppled desk, a light tan spread of coffee smearing across the floor as five men now gain control of the captain. "Shouldn't happen to a better man."

The man is confused but wonder brings his eyes back to the fight. Several men have blood on them, though it's actually just from one man who the captain managed to break his nose. Now I let doctors do the work, making him believe it's something wrong with his head and he should take a few days off, rest, vacation, take his mind off of work for at least a while. This is my process.

For years, centuries actually, people from all planets believe that life can only exist in their environment. This is because *they* exist here and obviously, life is working out just fine. Earth however has a very wide variety of life, from the abundant "air" breathing creatures of the land and some ocean waters to those creatures that have created filters to absorb the nutrients to be supplied to the brain straight from that water. Then there are those creatures that actually live underground or near completely different environmental standards of volcanic vents or even within landlocked glacier ices. To believe that one's planet is unique is fair; to think that you are the only life bearing planet is absurd. I carry within me diseases from almost every living creature; it is part of my arsenal in the continuing effort to gain control of the universe.

The hallucinogenic in Townsmen's coffee is actually one part of the genetic makeup of a worm that attacks the visual cortex of the brain. It just so happens that Human stomach acid is the other part. Combined (and over the next few days) that worm will be born and will make its way into his head. Once there, he will not be able to fathom what is real and what is only vision, this will make him a raving lunatic, at which point he will be locked away for observation. I will make my final visit to the Captain of the Grand Marais Police Department at that time. Now, however, it is time for drink.

*   *   *

My escort felt that it was necessary to just end it and not get too involved with my "process." Angels were known to frequent the area in their dealings with the Padi Oolithium. The Padi also had guards who used these *devices* that could snoop out Other Plainers. I, on the other hand, was very intent on following through with the dramatic display I was hired for.

Wasted, I failed to protect myself when entering an open field that was the entrance to the Padi's private residence. My escorts were doing their job in gathering information on the Padi's local hangouts and dining areas and who was close to him and who could be turned against him. I was caught immediately.

The Angels were of a rogue unit, three on a vigilante *ambush* mission actually waiting for a bone-headed demon to slip up. Invisible to Angels, I thought I could just walk in and do it. But just one curse word as I tripped on a stone in the courtyard and the Angels knew I was demon. They held me, asked me what I was doing, but belligerent to a fault, I could only spit in their faces, cursing them and their lord and all they stood for.

The actual plan was that after the Padi was dead and the Angels pulled anchor, Armageddon could be brought on, giving us control over one of the most technologically advanced planets in that particular galaxy. The Angels didn't know this, nor did they notice my escort taking stances outside to snipe them. The mission, of course, was aborted.

The few seconds it takes to make the transitional journey from the Universe to Hell felt as though an eternity and I was sober by the time the black skies and rocky earth replaced the Padi's courtyard.

*   *   *

I of course go to Lucy's Dynamo Bay in hopes of seeing Lucifer to report on my mission. But behind the bar was not the Angel Lucifer but a slightly overweight red-haired man who hadn't shaved in a few days.

"Hey d'ere, chap, Lucy said I might expect you." He says after making eye contact with me.

"…and who might you be?" I ask, painfully sober. He pulls out a bottle of Everclear with a note attached to it and I slink towards the bar. There are only a few stragglers here during the day, poor alcoholic saps that have lost or are losing their jobs.

"You might be sayin', oh, just a friend o' th' family." He smiles too big, his eyes squinting and wrinkles stretching out across his cheeks.

"A monster?" I take the note; it's scrawled out in hieroglyphics, and a very ancient text I haven't seen in millennia.

"Me a mon'ser? Nah! Just a bartender, I watch the place when Lucy's gone, and I take care of his regulars. He said to listen to anything you had to say…" and he winked, his eye blanking out a blackish color just before he did it.

"A monster."

The note is hard to read at first, but after I manage through the first couple of lines, it's just like getting back on a bicycle.

"Dear, *King*, it has been reported to me that you are making a very significant breakthrough in your punishment on Earth and are actually clearing a small path for others like you in the town you have taken residence. I must say, I am surprised and ecstatic at this news and eagerly await judging you again in a possible reinstatement to the True Gardens."

The note is not signed, but there is only one who called Hell the *True Gardens*. I begin to shiver a little, my hands trembling as I reach for the bottle of clear liquid.

"Good news?" the redheaded thing asks me.

My eyes roll to meet his, but there is no coherent message conveyed there. He smiles that same too big toothy grin at me and chuckles before walking off to get someone's drink order. I look to the end of the bar and recognize the man as the surly individual I terrified only nights ago.

There's a small drinking glass next to the bottle and I spill a little trying to hold both the glass and bottle steady in pouring. I take a big deep breath and bring the glass close to my face, my hand almost uncontrollably shaking now, pursing my lips I prepare for that burn and fire down my throat.

But I never taste it, never know what it was like to take my last drink, don't know that I've spilled it in my crotch and have absolutely no clue who just pistol-whipped me.

*   *   *

As I come to, it's like before, there're voices, shadows, a bad smell, though I can't tell from where, and I can't feel a goddamned thing. I'm completely numb but my mind is racing, screaming at me in all the different languages I've spoken over a thousand billion lifetimes, all saying to get out. But I can't move or is it that I *can't* move? I'm bound somehow, but I can't feel the ropes, nor can I tell if I can break them.

I start babbling, then cursing, then screaming in a hundred different tongues all at the same time and I lose cohesion. My "true form" as Jimmy wanted to see bursts its way into Earth through my mouth screaming. Black, teeth pointed in all directions, there's no skin, only this tarry liquid material held together by bits of bone and viscera and just as suddenly as it comes screaming out, I come crashing back to reality.

I can tell my face has been beaten, for one of my eyes is swollen shut. I look around, the three men are stupefied, horrified even, at what they have just seen. One of them is Jimmy himself.

I roll my head around to look at them in general. "Oh, I didn't mean to scare you."

Jimmy manages to blurt something that isn't really a word. "J-just a trick! He's messing with our heads again!"

Again? "May I ask what I'm being held for?"

They stay quiet for a long time before it registers that I have just asked a legitimate question. One of them tries his vocal cords but chokes at the words. Another actually manages it. "Suspect in murder, brutality, menace to society, impersonating an officer; among other things."

"And what proof do you have?" I ask boldly.

Jimmy holds up a tape. "I thought I saw you in here this morning and what with the odd suicides yesterday I thought I'd do a little *detective* work."

"Hope you didn't hurt yourself." I say.

One of them glares hard at me, an "I dare you" type look. I only smile slightly before returning my own gaze back to Jimmy starting up the tape. It's of the police who apprehended me in the alley, they're all laughing with blank stares on their faces as the leader convulses, then, in unison they shoot out their own brains. Wow, that looks pretty good on tape; maybe I should start recording more of my stuff. But on the tape, I'm nowhere to be seen.

"I don't see the point…" I begin, but Jimmy interrupts.

"I may not know how you did it, but just seconds after this, you…" he fast-forwards the tape a little to take up slack in his editing. "*You* are caught coming out of that room."

And, sure enough, it's me. Drunk and walking the curvy dance of someone who's lost balance. I even look at the camera and smile. What was I thinking? I should have done something better than *smile*.

"Even if I was in the room, it's obvious I didn't kill them, you just proved that!"

Jimmy is relentless; he wants to explain this somehow. "Another one of your tricks, *smoke and mirrors*, or something, but I saw what you did at Lucy's Dynamo and that's proof enough for *me*." He's dead serious.

"So, what do you plan to do?"

It's one of the other men that speak this time. They've composed themselves very well after seeing the flesh of Hell. Admirable. "We intend to hold you until we can have you properly tried and convicted."

I have nothing better to do. I wanted to watch the captain spiral downward, but it's still a few days or so before my final move.

*   *   *

When we reached Hell, I was told to "wait here."

"Here" was an open field, flat and rocky with sway grasses, the earth was red and black while the sky burned in oily smokes. To me it was the most serene place I could be, anyone else, one of you Humans or some such other race, would probably find it vile and depressing. But I felt very at ease, if Satanail wished to have me slain, I could think of no more satisfying a place.

When he did come to me, to pass his judgment, I think it was more painful to see the disappointment in his eyes; that I had let him down after he had thought so highly of me; I had let my *father* down. He didn't beat me or curse me or cast me into some torturous plain of existence. He pointed off in a direction, bowing his head.

"You have cost me more than I can afford."

When I turned, it was no longer the serene field, but a vast and bright blue sky that I could barely hold my eyes open to. I stood on the shore of a lake, looking out onto it, behind me was an older extension of a cemetery, it was all somehow fitting.

*　　*　　*

When I came to this time, I was no longer in the same room, but I was still bound. A nurse was there, and she had awoken me to give me more drugs. I babbled to her in my own tongue, though not even making sense to myself. In the back of my mind I waited, my body was under the control of the drugs, but soon I would be loosed.

It's amazing what these people can do to you in just a couple of days. The drugs alone possibly make these people worse off than they were. A solution, but not necessarily the answer. I drool a lot now, my body's a mess, and as I've said I'm incoherent. But that's just on the outside. They can control the shell but all it takes is for me to move forward. The nurse drops her keys just as she tries to shut the door, seemingly an accident, and she has no reason to look back in the room as she shuts the door and locks it. I stand behind her, smiling, wiping my face.

I follow her, unnoticed, down the hall, waiting patiently outside each room until she comes upon Cooper Townsmen. She opens the door and that's where it stops. He looks up, his face terrified, but he doesn't know of what, just expecting something bad to happen. I adjust myself, making myself presentable and slink around the nurse into his room. He screams like a maniac, though the worm is inactive at the moment. What he sees is the truth, what I am, how I was born, what Jimmy only barely saw before I made him gauge out his own eyes.

Captain Townsmen sees a thing made of dirt, bone, broken flesh and spikes of jagged rocks. There's the smell of blood and bile and no discernible eyes, though I'm looking directly at him. What looks like possibly a leg and foot reaches out and grabs him by his throat, dragging him up the padded wall. He smells shit, but for the life of him he doesn't think it's what's grabbing him. He gurgles like a baby, and I laugh at this, though he doesn't recognize the sound. I open my lower jaw, pointed teeth in no discernible order seeming to grow up and sharper.

"Captain Cooper Townsmen, you are about to die, but I want you to know why, and how."

I lower my hand and stand up straight on what really are my legs, standing with only a foot left between my head and the ceiling. Townsmen stays stuck to the wall, defying gravity.

"You see, I'm a hired assassin in a war that you actually know about, and in part, worship certain individuals involved in it. Though, as I can tell from your expression now, you have no want in this knowledge, so I'll make it quick. You are not insane; rest assured that your death comes at the hands of a well-trained and very persuasive psychologist. The visions, and some of the nightmares, you have experienced over the past couple days are a result of a parasite who is bent on making sure you die.

"I won't go into any major details, but let's just say that there's an alien in your head, whose defense for the many is to sacrifice its own life by slowly eating away the brain of its victim. You ingested a part of its molecular make-up, it just so happens that the acids produced by your digestive system were the other part and so, hence, you gave birth to your own demise. And there's no operation to defend against this beast because it's never, obviously, been seen before.

"However, should you choose to take your own life, the pain would cease. That is why I am here; I will empower and inspire you to take part in this endeavor, if only you utter a word."

"H-h-help me…" he says meagerly, though I don't think it's meant for my ears.

"Say it again…with *feeling*." I lean in close to him, breathing hot and slowly on his face.

"*Help*!" he croaks in a half yell.

"Good enough," I release everything. The nurse completes her motion and Townsmen is blinding fast in tackling her. He bloodies her face and I merely watch in slight amusement. "You see, it takes some twenty, thirty minutes for her to complete these rounds," he's still beating her. "And by the time you've taken your own life, they will have just begun to *wonder* where she is."

He falls over to the side; this is always so exciting, watching someone scramble to take their own life. His hands reach out like an unskilled child trying to grab everything he can. He can't decide which pills to take, but then they start to move in his hands, little grub worms and maggots.

"No," I say. "Just take them all, let them eat away your pain, that's what they're there for."

He stuffs pill after pill down his throat, not actually swallowing but shoving them down into his stomach. He begins to shiver and convulse as he suffocates on his hands and the multitude of pills.

"Just relax, go ahead and lay back, let them do their work."

I find that watching a soul die is very interesting. They all look so different and so fresh compared to the sacks of flesh they have been occupying. But my fascination is shattered.

The soul is recognizable, I know what it is, what it was, and suddenly, realize that this is some terrible trick. A Dark Soul.

"Yes, little one." Lucifer is standing in the door, waiting patiently.

You see, there are some people in this world that are just so downright evil, so controlled by hatred and corruption, that killing them is a *good* thing. Captain Townsmen just happened to be one of those particular souls. Sometimes, demons are made from what's left of these people. Heaven sort of has a bounty on Dark Souls, too. And there's a loophole that Hell tries to use as much as utterly possible.

"Looks like you have a new name, King…"

I'm frozen, I actually feel bad for killing this man, or maybe it's that I feel bad for what's about to happen to me. This loophole, Heaven doesn't much worry about it because most demons are smart enough to avoid it, but me, I was a drunk bastard looking for an easy way home, and now I've found myself in something I never dreamed I would be a part of.

"No…" I'm still frozen. Lucifer comes closer, preparing to rip out the heart that beats in my chest. I can die, just not by your standards or conditions. It takes an Angel's touch. "No," I repeat, finally looking up.

If a demon or monster, or any denizen bound for Hell, is so fortunate to kill a Dark Soul, and then to be murdered by a Fallen (you can see why Heaven doesn't much worry about those kind of circumstances), he is then washed of all sin. Not likely is he to stay in Heaven however, just like any repeat offender, he'll either Fall or Abandon, eventually. When that happens, they are transformed into Armageddon, a living weapon and the reason Hell chooses its planets wisely, there's only a few. And now, I'm on the path to becoming one.

But I know there's another way and it's burning at me to move, to dodge that fucking bastard in front of me. And finally, with all the abilities I was born with, I move, I move away from here, from all of this, from this very spot and put myself in front of a guard who watches the doorway to the mentally ill wing of the hospital. He has a gun, *good*.

He doesn't know to run because his eyes are still trying to register the fact that something has just *appeared* in front of him, and for that matter, something inhuman, though quickly melting into the form of a human.

Lucifer is coming.

I grab the man and smash him into the wall, knocking him unconscious and retrieving his gun. I check it for bullets, *good*. I put it into my mouth and the last thing I hear is the pleading cry of Lucifer and only a barely audible crack. Ten points, plus triple-word-score, plus fifty points for using all my letters. Game's over. I'm outta here.

THW

DESTINY-STAR

Written 2005
PUNCH/PANTS, October 2012
DESTINY-STAR was mostly my writing, but it was also a collaborative effort with my friend and roommate, Francisco Peña, while other friends make cameo appearances. I wanted to write a western. I wanted the bad guy to be truly reprehensible while having a disability the heroes think they can exploit, only to find he's ahead of them regardless. I also wanted the villain to be cut off before he could antagonize the hero one last time. No villainous soliloquy, it happens through the action, but the ending is meant to be definitive. This story still lives and breathes in my head, and I hope to reintroduce these characters someday soon. For now, the first script I wrote.

INT, MORNING, POTTER HOME

It's December 12th, 1863, today is JACK POTTER'S twelfth birthday. His room is rather well kept, with a single window letting in the morning light. Dark wood walls and flooring, a nightstand and a chair in the corner with a piece of wood carved into the shape of a rifle leaning next to it. We see the young boy sleeping in bed, suddenly cringing as a knock breaks his sleep. A little girl's voice erupts from the other side.

GIRL:
JACK! Wake up, you been in bed too long!

Jack screws up his face, disgusted with the admonishment.

JACK:
Go away, SALLY…and it's YOU HAVE!

SALLY:
Mom and Dad said you can't shirk your chores today!

Jack pounds his fists down against the bed, frustrated.

JACK:
But it's my BIRTHDAY!

Eyes still mostly shut, Jack gets out of bed, pouting and stomping while he puts on some clothes. He flings open his door and his eyes snap wide open as something catches his nose.

INT, HALLWAY to DINING ROOM

Following Jack, we enter the dining room where Jack's family is waiting for him at the table; a large breakfast with some of his favorite items is on the table. He brightens and smiles wide, his two younger sisters, SALLY and MAY are snickering with each other over Sally tricking him out of bed. His mother steps away from the stove with a pan in hand.

JACK'S MOTHER:
Good morning, Jack, and happy birthday!

She slides a pancake onto a plate at his spot at the table. He eyes it hungrily and looks up excited to his mother and father. He's nearly speechless.

JACK'S FATHER:
Eat up, son, we DO have some chores today, but I won't work you too hard. Happy birthday!

Jack nods and sits to eat.

CUT TO:

EXT, DAY, POTTER HOME

Snow covers the ground as Jack sets up logs for his father to cut. It's a calm day, however, and quite sunny. Despite the cold conditions, Jack and his father happily converse with each other.

FATHER:
So, have you given any thought to what you want to be when you grow up? You're getting pretty close you know.

Jack sets up another log as he ponders the question.

JACK:
I think I want to be a Ranger, like Uncle Augustus, or a US Marshal; protect the WHOLE United States!

Jack's father laughs slightly.

FATHER:
That's mighty admirable, Jack. Who are you going to protect the United States citizens from?

JACK:
From Indians, foreign invaders and…

A snowball sails through the air and hits Jack in the back of the head, almost sending him falling forward.

JACK (coldly):
…And May.

Jack's father laughs wildly until he, too, is hit with a snowball, right in the chest. A girl laughs hysterically in the distance. Jack and father both stoop low to the ground and prepare to return fire.

FATHER:
Remember, Jack, adjust for the wind and adjust for the sun, but hold on to yourself. You don't have to impress anyone but you.

Jack nods, it's obvious he knows the mantra; it's something his dad has said several times before. Jack balls up a snowball and scans the open field for his target. He catches a glimpse of something flying through the air, another snowball. He rolls out of the way, but this only puts his father directly in its path and the snowball explodes across his shoulders. Jack laughs slightly, but May has given herself away by pointing and laughing loudly. Jack launches the snowball in his hand. May, distracted by her handy work, doesn't see it coming. It smacks her right in the face, instantly silencing her, her jaw hanging open and eyes blinking unbelievingly. Now Jack and his father have their turn to laugh out loud.

EXT, LATER DAY, REAR OF POTTER HOME

Jack and his father are still covered in snow from the snowball fight they partook in with May. They are piling up the wood they had cut.

FATHER:
I've noticed you've been practicing your aiming…

JACK:
Yeah, if I'm gonna be a Marshal, I need to be a marksman. One day I'll get a rifle and I'll patrol the house!

FATHER:
YOU protecting ME? Ha, I have no doubt you'd fight to the last. But what if you ever have to KILL someone, Jack? Being a Marshall means you'll have to hunt down some pretty bad men…are you ready for that?

Jack looks a little shocked at first, having to KILL someone? He cautiously goes back to work. Confidently, he says:

JACK:

If they were really bad, like they were hurting someone or HAD hurt someone, I would have to bring them to justice.

FATHER:
Sometimes justice can be very harsh. But you're very smart, son, I trust you would do what was right in your heart. I'd be afraid to be the man at the other end of YOUR gun, Marshal Jack Potter!

FADE TO:

EXT, NIGHT, POTTER HOME

The sounds of a family gathering fill the air, laughter among children and parents. Outside of the house a posse of eight men ride in on horses and stop some distance from the house.

INT, DINING ROOM

It's a birthday party for Jack. His parents and two sisters have gathered around the table and are sharing in the excitement of his twelfth birthday.

FATHER:
Son, I want you to go out and get some more wood for the fire.

He exchanges a knowing look with Jack's mother.

JACK:
What?! It's my birthday! Why can't May or Sally go out?

MOTHER:
Because they're girls, it's cold, and you're a grown man, now. Do as your father says!

She smiles back to the father.

Jack, defeated, puts on his coat and makes his way for the door.

CUT TO:

EXT, SOME DISTANCE FROM THE HOUSE

Most of the posse has dismounted, two men, a tall well-dressed man wearing a blindfold and an older black man holding the reigns of the prior's horse, look down to the men on the ground.

BLINDFOLDED MAN
(French accent):
Make sure you leave Mr. Potter alive for me, the rest of the family kill immediately. I'll be down to ask him some questions in a moment.

They nod their approval, one saying:

MAN:
"Yes, sir, Mr. Maréchal."

And start towards the house.

CUT TO:

EXT, BEHIND HOUSE

Jack grumbles to himself as he makes his way toward the pile of firewood. Snow has covered the ground and he makes high exaggerated steps. Once he reaches the rack of wood and reaches to gather some in his arms, he notices a rifle sitting on top of the pile.

JACK
(in a whisper):
What…

He picks it up, examining it at first, then tilting it into the moonlight. Engraved on the metal is a large script "12" and a small passage "To my son/Adjust for the wind/Adjust for the sun/But always hold on to yourself." A smile crawls across the boy's face, instantly running for the house to thank his parents.

MOVING TO:

INT, BACK OF HOUSE

Jack comes in and hears voices, then gunshots and the screams of his sisters, silenced by another round of shots. What was joy turns into terror on his face as he hides himself in a closet after slipping into his parents' room.

CUT TO:

INT, DINING ROOM

The six henchmen surround a sobbing man, Jack's father, as Mr. Maréchal enters guided with his hand on the black man's shoulder. The Frenchman draws a pistol from under his long fine coat.

MR. MARÉCHAL:
I am going to ask you this, only once, Mr. Potter; did you tell anyone?

INT, CLOSET

Jack shudders with fear, eyes closed tight as he listens to the brief exchange.

INT, DINING ROOM

Jack's father raises his hands, pleading with the Frenchman.

JACK'S FATHER:
Please, I haven't told anyone, I swear it, I…

Mr. Maréchal raises his gun towards Mr. Potter's head and fires, not allowing him to finish his plea.

MR. MARÉCHAL:
Burn it down, I want it as though this place never existed.

He turns and begins to walk out of the house, but the black man stops him.

BLACK MAN:
JEAN-CLAUDE,

JEAN-CLAUDE:
Yes, SUNDOWNER?

SUNDOWNER:
One is missing…the son. His body isn't here.

Jean-Claude Maréchal whirls on his cohorts.

JEAN-CLAUDE:
Was there a boy? Did you SEE him?

HENCHMAN ONE:
No, sir, Mr. Maréchal, just the man, his wife, and the two girls…

JEAN-CLAUDE:
Find him. Find him NOW!

Jean-Claude storms out of the house, followed by Sundowner.

The henchman who spoke orders two of the men to go out and search in and around the house.

HENCHMAN ONE:
We'll prepare the torches, if he's inside, he'll die by the fire.

Four of them walk out of the house, leaving the two charged with finding Jack to search the interior.

CUT TO:

INT, CLOSET

Jack, distraught and visibly shocked, looks slowly down at his rifle, seeing the engraving again in the light through the closet door. He checks the chamber, unloaded. Frantic, he looks around him, his father's gun is propped on the back of the closet wall with a box of bullets above it on a shelf. He quickly opens the box, loading his own gun.

PULL OUT TO:

INT, PARENT'S ROOM

One of the henchmen comes in through the door, looking cautiously around.

HENCHMAN TWO:
Are you in here, son? Everything's all right, I just want to talk…

A dark sneer curls the man's lip. He looks toward the closet, seeing that it's not fully shut and laughs quietly to himself.

HENCHMAN TWO
(Whispers):
There you are,

He slowly pulls open the door, only to be surprised by a rifle barrel being shoved into his face.

HENCHMAN TWO:
What the…

CUT TO:

INT, KITCHEN

As the second henchman charged with finding the boy searches through cabinets, he hears a rifle blast from the other room. He bolts out of the kitchen, racing to the sound.

MOVING TO:

INT, BEDROOM

Entering the parents' bedroom, he sees the other fellow sprawled on the ground in a pool of blood, looking to the open closet door. Standing just behind it is the boy he's been looking for, aiming a rifle straight at him. He sees a flash of fire and hears a loud boom as he's shot. The bullet hits him in his lower-right side, spinning him into a face-plant on the floor.

Jack coolly walks over the groveling henchman discharging his spent shell that clatters next to the fallen man.

CUT TO:

EXT, POTTER HOME

The four henchmen who have gone outside hear the gunfire inside and all turn to look at the house. They are standing in couples on either side of the house, two of them are preparing a torch. Another gunshot rings out across the quiet night, bursting the top of the torch in the man's hand, sending cinders and sparks all over him and his companion, two more shots ring out and they both fall to the ground, their clothes catching fire.

The other couple, seeing this, cast each other a worried look.

> HENCHMAN ONE
> (Yelling):
> Carl? Lenny? What's going on in there!?

> HENCHMAN THREE
> (Yelling from inside the house):
> It's the damn kid! He shot me and Lenny; he's still in here somewhere!

Another gunshot rings out.

> HENCHMAN ONE:
> Carl? CARL!?

He turns to his associate.

> HENCHMAN ONE:
> Go around the back, I'll take the front, we'll try and flush him out. It's just a kid; we can take care of him.

The other nods and heads around the back of the house. The first henchman draws his pistol from his side and begins to head towards the front of the house but looks to his now dead and burning companions. He ventures toward them and grabs the torch.

CUT TO:

EXT, TOP OF HILL

Sundowner is helping Jean-Claude mount his horse when they hear the gunplay down the hill, Sundowner notices two of the men lying dead in the snow, beginning to burn.

JEAN-CLAUDE:
What's going on?

SUNDOWNER:
They've been ambushed, two are down, but the number of shots?
Maybe more.

JEAN-CLAUDE:
Go down there and see what's happening.

SUNDOWNER:
Might be better if we leave now, the sheriff will be up any minute
what with gunshots and the fire.

JEAN-CLAUDE:
Never trust someone else with something you know you can
complete yourself. Damn fools…let's go.

Sundowner mounts his own horse, grabs the reigns of Jean-Claude's and begins their quiet retreat.

CUT TO:

INT, BACK DOOR OF HOUSE

The henchman ordered to enter through the rear slowly opens the door with his own gun drawn, sweeping the dark kitchen with his eyes. The door swings back shut revealing Jack wielding his gun like a club by the barrel and brings it down over the henchman's head, knocking him unconscious.

Jack kneels beside the fallen body, reloading his rifle as quietly as he can. Looking from the rear of the house he can see that the final henchman, the leader, is walking towards the front door with a torch and gun. The henchman lights the small awning before the entrance with the torch, beginning the blaze to burn down the Potter home. Jack takes aim and shoots the final man in his right leg, toppling him.

MOVING TO:

EXT, FRONT OF HOUSE

The final henchman is crawling on his elbows away from the door, his torch and gun dropped as he was shot.

Jack emerges from the house which is already beginning to burn wildly in the cold night. Puffs of steam escape his mouth as he pants, coming up on the wounded man.

JACK
(In a very dark voice rising to a scream):
Why did you do this? HOW COULD YOU KILL MY FAMILY!?

HENCHMAN ONE:
I was just doin' my job, kid! Your dad was a bad man!

Jack raises his rifle and aims for the man's head.

HENCHMAN ONE
(Groveling):
C'mon kid, I didn't want to kill your family, I was just doin' what I was paid for!

JACK:
Who?

HENCHMAN ONE:

What?

JACK:
WHO PAID YOU?!

HENCHMAN ONE:
Your dad's boss, Jean-Claude Maréchal! He hired us…

Jack seems to let his guard down slightly, thinking about this.

The henchman is still crawling backwards.

Jack raises his gun again.

PULLING BACK TO:

EXT, TOWNSHIP

High above the town we see the Potter home burning, people are emerging from the local saloon looking up the hill to the house. One last shot rings out across the night.

CUT TO BLACK ON GUNSHOT

TITLE SEQUENCE

EXT/INT, DAY, VARIOUS LOCALES

Through the various opening credits, we watch the manufacturing of a single bullet, from raw material all the way to packaging. Inter-cut between these scenes are shots of gunfighters competing in some sort of tournament. We see people that we will later learn their identities. Finally, we see where the bullet is put into a box that when closed gives us the title of our movie, "DESTINY-STAR." The box of ammo is put into a crate with several other like-boxes and the crate is sealed. One gunfighter in particular seems to win the tournament using a

FRUITLESS BODIES

familiar rifle. We then see the crate being put onto a train, and the train departs, and we follow it.

MOVING TO:

EXT, DAY, TRAINSTATION

PORTER, KANSAS, JUNE 28TH, 1876. A passenger train pulls up into the station, after several of the passenger cars are freight cars emblazoned with the Destiny-Star Munitions Company logo.

Several porters walk up to one of these cargo cars, open it, and begin to unload supplies. We're in one of the towns that Destiny-Star is located and nearly runs.

Stepping off of a passenger car and into frame is a young man, mid-twenties, very stern looking, wearing a long yellow duster. He looks towards the men working with the Destiny-Star cargo with quiet disdain.

TRAINMAN:
Welcome to Porter, son, and good luck in the tournament!

YOUNG MAN
(Quietly):
Thank you.

Our young man heads toward the street to make his way into town, we pull back to reveal the lay of the place and see a sprawling township bustling with activity, in the distance is an ominous factory wrapped in oily smoke.

The young man makes his way to an office building, though on his way several people stop to take notice of him, some in awe, some skeptical, some point or do double takes.

CUT TO:

INT, DESTINY-STAR OFFICES

Stepping into the office building, however, no one seems to notice him. He steps up to a desk marked "Registration."

YOUNG MAN:
I'm here to check in for tomorrow's tournament…

REGISTRAR:
Name?

The person sitting at the desk pulls out a tablet with several very well scripted names with signatures next to them about to check in the young man.

YOUNG MAN:
TWELVE.

The registrar stops cold, and slowly looks up to the man.

REGISTRAR
(Sarcastically):
Would that be your first, or last name?

TWELVE:
It's in there…

Exasperated, the clerk looks through the pages, finding a small numerical "12" entry between "Tidwell, Harris" and "Sanders, Cray." He lays the book down and holds out a pen.

Twelve takes it, and signs in flourishing cursive "Twelve." He sets the pen down and turns to leave the office.

REGISTRAR:
Damn young guns and their silly names…

MOVING TO:

EXT, DESTINY-STAR OFFICES

Twelve surveys the street and sees several other gunslingers around a saloon up the street further away from the munitions plant and decides to take in some of the local flavor.

CUT TO:

INT, WESTWARD SALOON & BORDELLO

Twelve walks into the main room of the saloon, a piano player is banging away, and the room is loud with boisterous talking.

Several people turn from card games and conversations to see who has entered, though the sound never drops, and watch him as he crosses to the bar and orders a drink.

The bartender nods his approval and grabs a bottle from the shelf behind him.

Some people looking at him begin to chatter quietly about who it is.

STRANGER 1:
Is that him?

STRANGER 2:
That's the kid who out-shot everyone in Georgia…

STRANGER 3:
I heard he won the tournament with an old beat-up rifle…

We focus in on a table of card players, also talking about him.

CARD PLAYER 1:
I hear his name is "Twelve."

CARD PLAYER 2:
What's that supposed to mean?

One of the players leans into the center of the table.

CARD PLAYER 3:
I heard that a group of bandits attacked him and his family, 12 of
'em to be exact, and he took them all on by himself when he was just
a kid.

An older, bigger, lady sitting with them also leans in.

CARD PLAYING LADY:
That's horseshit…

And she smiles, nods, and leans back.

CARD PLAYER 3:
You think you know why he's called that?

CARD PLAYER 1:
Why don't you, ENLIGHTEN, us.

CARD PLAYING LADY:
He goes by TWELVE because that's his birthday, December twelfth.

CARD PLAYER 2:
And how would you know that? Are you his MAMA?

The other players laugh.

CARD PLAYING LADY:
I asked him…in Crenshaw.

CARD PLAYER 3:
What were you doing there?

CARD PLAYING LADY:
Why I'm SALLY FIRKINS…

The players look at her blankly.

After her smile vanishes and she rolls her eyes, she stands up.

SALLY:
The only woman in the tournament?

The players still just stare at her.

She sighs and grabs her money from the table.

SALLY
(Under her breath):
You would think someone might recognize something important like
that, even a bunch of leathernecks from the sticks.

She walks over to the bar right beside Twelve.

SALLY:
Can you believe that? Bunch of morons…

She continues on about the men and their ignorance.

Twelve sips from his drink and stares down at the bar, seemingly
oblivious to Sally and her ranting.

SALLY:

So where are you staying tonight?

TWELVE:
I'm not interested in going upstairs, thank you.

Sally scoffs, and then begins to laugh.

SALLY:
Now how should I take that? Flattered that you think I'm…

She gestures at herself with her hands.

SALLY:
…A hooker? Or INSULTED that you think I'm a hooker?

Twelve barely turns his head to look at her.

SALLY:
Don't tell me that you don't remember me…

Twelve looks back to his drink.

TWELVE:
I remember you. I beat you in the targeting contest. What do you want?

SALLY:
Well, "Hi, how do you do?" to you, too! I wanted to talk to you…

Sally leans in close, very serious.

SALLY:
I know why you're here…and I know who you are, not that it would matter to them, but it matters to HIM. Or, at least, it will.

She says as she points first to the card players, then out the saloon doors.

Twelve still sits, stern and oblivious. He takes another drink then cranes his neck around to face her.

TWELVE:
If you know, then you'll leave me alone and you'll stay out of my way.

SALLY:
There's no reason to get hostile, boy, I'm trying to offer you some help…

TWELVE:
I don't need…

SALLY:
You don't WANT help. But you do NEED it. You see, I'm in the same situation you are, I'm here, just so I can get close to him, I lost my family, too, because of that French bastard.

Twelve looks at her steadily.

SALLY:
Now as personal as your efforts are, more people…

The bartender walks by, forcing Sally to lower her voice and lean closer to Twelve.

SALLY
(Whispering):
More people gunning for the same target make it a more attainable goal.

Twelve looks at the bartender, then around to the bar, not that anyone has stopped talking or playing, it seems to have gotten quiet to him. He can see people laughing, but nothing comes out of their mouths. Prostitutes play with prospective clients, the piano player plays excitedly and sings away, but all the sound has gone away, and there is only Twelve and his breathing. He takes his final drink, flashes a glare at Sally, the sound comes back, and he walks away.

SALLY:
Where are you going? Don't you even want to talk about this? We can help you!

TWELVE:
I don't know what you're talking about…

Sally stands in front of him, blocking his path.

SALLY:
You know damn well what I'm talking about…REVENGE. And I can help you. We can help each other.

She says the last part forlornly. But Twelve will have nothing to do with it and steps around her towards the door of the saloon, sunlight filters in through the frame and windows next to it when the shadow of a tall man blocks the doorway. Twelve freezes, shock and horror begin to spread across his face.

The tall man steps in out of the light into the saloon and we see it is a black man wearing a long dark coat and a Union cap. It's the same black man who was there when Jack Potter's family was killed.

Twelve pulls his sidearm out quickly and has it squarely aimed at the man. The sounds in the saloon really do stop and everyone's attention is focused on the two men in the doorway.

Sally steps extremely close to Twelve.

SALLY:
What the hell do you think you're doing?

TWELVE:
You say you know who I am, you'll know this man had something to
do with it all.

SUNDOWNER:
That was a long time ago, son…

TWELVE:
That makes little difference, and I'm not your "son."

Twelve pulls the hammer back on his gun as though he's prepared to
shoot.

Sally steps between the men.

SALLY:
You need to calm down, TWELVE…

TWELVE:
I have no qualms with you, Sally; you need to move.

Sundowner's right arm flares out making his coat fly open, a Union
issue Civil War sniper rifle levels out right in Twelve's face over
Sally's right shoulder.

People begin to get up from their tables slowly and making their way
out the back or upstairs to avoid the growing tension.

SUNDOWNER:
We don't need to be doing this here, boy, I'm sorry about your
family…

Twelve begins to lower his gun and slightly bows his head.

Sally and Sundowner both seem to let their shoulders sag in relief, but Twelve, expecting such, lashes out with his left hand and grabs Sundowner's rifle right out of his hand and tosses it aside, clattering to the floor and under a table.

TWELVE:
Sorry doesn't bring them back!

And Twelve raises his pistol again and fires off a shot over Sally's head trying to hit Sundowner between the eyes.

But he is already diving for his rifle across the floor.

Sally screams and claps her hands to her ears.

Twelve tries to train his gun back on Sundowner but notices he's already being aimed at himself; he dives knocking over a table for cover.

TWELVE:
You've only got one shot with that rifle in here…

The sound of a rifle goes off and a hole explodes open mere inches next to Twelve's head. Twelve, seemingly un-phased by this near miss cocks his gun and stands up from behind the table, confident he'll have a clean shot, but finds himself under fire again by Sundowner's own pistol. Twelve drops back under cover and curses himself.

Sally, still rubbing one of her ears, comes over to Twelve's side.

SALLY:
Why are you acting so childish?

Twelve leans out from behind the table and takes a shot in Sundowner's direction.

SALLY:
He said he was sorry, now if you'd just listen to him, you'd find out he wants to help!

Sundowner also exchanges fire, a glass on the bar close to Sally explodes.

SALLY:
God dammit, Sunny, that almost hit me! You both need to grow up and talk to each other like men!

TWELVE:
He helped kill my entire family, I'm not going to sit down and have a round table discussion with him.

Twelve darts toward the back wall of the bar to provide himself with more cover behind all the tables, Sundowner takes another shot. He stands up to take another shot in the direction of Sundowner when all of a sudden, a knife catches the cuff of his sleeve and pins him to the wall.

Sundowner, seeing this, stands up, gun still drawn, he and Twelve exchange leery glances, but Sundowner turns toward the door and fires.

We chase the bullet and see a big Mexican man and two gruff looking men behind him both holding rifles and wearing stars on their lapels. The Mexican has leaned over slightly, as though he dodged the bullet.

MEXICAN
(Thick Spanish accent):

We're all calm down now, sí? The big star from last tournament and you fighting? No, you fight in tournament tomorrow, much more fun, but you go to jail tonight, free place to stay, be happy.

DEPUTY 1:
He shot at you, ALVARO, we should just hang him! Make him an example.

ALVARO:
No, no, he just scared rabbit trying to protect itself…he can no hurt me.

He motions for the deputies to arrest the two men and take their guns.

ALVARO
(In Spanish, subtitled):
Jean-Claude will be happy to know his old friend has come to see him.

The one who apprehends Twelve finds an older rifle hidden under his coat, engraved with a large "12" and a phrase.

TWELVE:
I'd better get that back…

DEPUTY 2:
In the morning, friend, just behave yourself.

SALLY:
I told you two to calm down, now you're going to jail, you're lucky they don't shoot you right now for "disturbing the peace!"

She turns to one of the deputies.

SALLY:

Put them in cells right next to each other, make sure they work out
their differences…

The deputies laugh and shove the two men outside.

CUT TO:

EXT, DUSK, EDGE OF TOWN

Alvaro waits at the edge of town as an ornate, black and purple
carriage pulls in and slows down to meet him. He steps up to one of
the windows and looks inside where he sees only the figure of a man
as a result of the setting sun's light shining through the opposite side
of the cart.

ALVARO
(Subtitled):
Sundowner has arrived, I believe he was traveling with Ms. Firkins, I
found him fighting the champion from the tournament in Crenshaw.
Two of them at least are after you, I am sure of it. Sundowner and
the boy called "Twelve" are in the jail. What shall I do with them?

The shadowy figure bows his head for a moment and brings his hand
to just below his chin. He is manipulating some sort of pouch.

JEAN-CLAUDE:
Many people are after me, Alvaro, this could prove to be
entertaining, but certainly something I will not allow to go very far.
Make sure the three of them place, and I will serve them a banquet in
my local mansion.

ALVARO:
Señor?

JEAN-CLAUDE:

In the meantime, leave the two boys in jail and Ms. Firkins alone, we shall attend to them tomorrow.

FADE TO:

INT, NIGHT, PORTER JAIL

Twelve and Sundowner sit in separate one bunk jail cells positioned next to each other. Twelve is lying down, where Sundowner is sitting on his cot looking into Twelve's cell.

SUNDOWNER:
You're not going to get much sleep if you keep brooding.

Twelve rolls onto his side, putting his back to Sundowner.

SUNDOWNER:
And pouting like a child will be no help, either.

Sundowner stands and walks to the front of his cell to look at the deputy, who is nodding off in the low light of his lamp. Sundowner turns his head towards Twelve's cell again.

SUNDOWNER:
I know you don't want my help; I know you're after me just as much as you're after him. I know that right now you wish you didn't have to listen to the sound of my voice, but I'm gonna keep on talking. Mostly because I don't give a shit about you either.

TWELVE:
Then you won't be offended that I don't take your SPEECH to heart.

SUNDOWNER
(Now quieter):
Jean-Claude was my employer after the war, what I did was a job. I can't even begin to apologize to you for what happened when you

were a kid. Of course, I know who you are, that was also part of my job, to know everyone and where they were. When you popped up in Crenshaw, I knew exactly who you were. Jean-Claude may not realize, not yet, and that gives YOU an advantage. I'm as good as dead right now, that Mexican knows exactly who I am and who Sally is and that we don't have the utmost respect for Jean-Claude. But you, that's why she came to you, and that's why I come to you now, because you can get close to him before he even knows what's going on. Though, you may have jeopardized that with your tantrum today.

Twelve rolls back over and sits up in his bed.

TWELVE:
So you think if you ask real nice I'll just gladly join your little party? Just walk up to him and shoot him?

SUNDOWNER:
For all your schooling you sure are dumb. Going after Jean-Claude is a suicide mission no matter what, no matter how many people in your PARTY. Whole towns will defend him because his company is their livelihood. It's all about this tournament, you know he's opening a third Destiny-Star Munitions plant out west to help the Army fight off the last of the Indian tribes out there. And he's having a huge celebration for the 4th of July.

Twelve ponders it, he can tell where the plan is going, knows that logically joining up with two other people could help, but a weary look furrows his brow.

TWELVE:
Why are you after him? How am I to know you're not still on his side?

Sundowner slinks back to his bunk and sits, head bowed.

158

SUNDOWNER:
I don't expect to earn your trust in just one night; I can just hope you
see how much sense this makes. I've got my own reasons for
wanting him dead…
(Sighs)
…he sent me to kill my own brother. He had adopted a different
name, so I didn't know until I saw him. But Jean-Claude knew all
the time, and I swore I would take his life before I ever killed my
own family.

TWELVE:
Why didn't you just go back and kill him on the spot?

SUNDOWNER:
I walked away; I didn't want anything to do with it at all at first. He
hired that Mexican, ALVARO ALEJANDRO, who was more of a
bodyguard than I ever was. Jean-Claude had him kill my brother.
Then it was a matter of waiting for the opportunity, and now it's
within reach. It'd be real nice to have your help, if you can set your
vendetta with me aside until we both get what we want. After that, if
you're still intent on killing me, we can have it out.

TWELVE:
The enemy of my enemy…

SUNDOWNER:
Is my friend…please, just consider it.

FADE OUT

INT, MORNING, PORTER JAIL

The door to the jailhouse comes open, letting bright morning sunlight
pour in on Twelve and Sundowner who shield their eyes to see who is
there.

FRUITLESS BODIES

It's Sally and she has a wide smile; the jail keeper comes to unlock their cells.

SALLY:
Good morning, fellas, we'd better hurry or we're gonna miss the whole thing!

CUT TO:

EXT, TOURNAMENT FIELD

We see our three moving towards a field filled with onlookers and gunfighters. There's a shooting range and marked off event areas, located just outside of town, special stands and temporary structures have been put up to host the second Destiny-Star Gunslinger's Tournament.

Away from the crowd is an ornate stand set up for Jean-Claude Maréchal and his entourage, who are watching the gunfighters practice on the target range.

Our characters check in and their names are added to a slate board with twenty to thirty other names. Eventually, through the day, these will whittle down to just a few and then finally to a winner.

We now see Jean-Claude talking to Alvaro.

JEAN-CLAUDE:
Our men have been put in?

ALVARO
(Subtitled):
Yes, to your specifications.

JEAN-CLAUDE:
Very good, I like knowing the outcome.

MOVING TO:

EXT, GUNFIGHTER'S REST AREA

Twelve, Sundowner and Sally stand together, checking their guns and conversing with each other.

SUNDOWNER:
Several of Jean-Claude's men are here, something's up.

SALLY:
Yeah, YOU. You two getting into it with each other has raised the very fact that you're still around and now in very close to him. Of course, he's gonna watch you, if not KILL you.

SUNDOWNER:
He doesn't do public executions. He prefers private and quiet, he likes to have control of all of his situations, and it would appear he even has control over this tournament.

An announcer with a large mega-phone begins to call the gunfighters to see the matchups and prepare to compete.

We watch as people begin to compete in the different categories against each other. There are accuracy competitions on the target range, quick draw competitions with special judges to determine who fires first, clay shooting and moving target competitions.

Before the action begins, Jean-Claude comes down from his special stands and greets the crowd.

ANNOUNCER:
And of course, our very special guest and HOST of these events, Mr. Jean-Claud Maréchal!

FRUITLESS BODIES

The crowd cheers.

JEAN-CLAUDE:
Thank you very much, where I may not be able to SEE today's
events…

He gestures to his blindfold.

JEAN-CLAUDE:
…I trust that these are the greatest gunfighters around and will prove
their skills to us all today. This is a friendly competition and
provided by myself to the people who work and live around me as
entertainment in preparation for the nation's centennial. Let the
games begin!

CUT TO:

EXT, TOURNAMENT FIELD

We watch our fighters, and several others compete.

SUNDOWNER
(VO during competition):
He hides behind his blindness but he's as lethal as a rattlesnake. He
lost his sight when he was just a boy, it was his father who owned
and ran Destiny-Star before him. Started the company from the
ground up in Georgia and began supplying munitions to the local
authorities; it was just a gun store at the time. When they got into
actual production, Jean-Claude helped out of course, it was a family
business, but there was a small explosion, it burned his eyes out, he
almost didn't live. He had been learning how to be a marksman and
was apparently devastated by the loss of his sight. To hear him tell it,
he didn't almost die from injuries, but from sadness that he wouldn't
be able to shoot anymore. He became bitter but continued to work
for Destiny-Star where he could, things that he could use his other
senses to complete, and when his father passed, Jean-Claude was a

162

young man ready to take on the world. The War was beginning, too, and he saw opportunity. He began supplying munitions, no charge to soldiers, but many began buying from him on a personal level and the business boomed. He built this second place exactly the same as the first one so that he could still know his way around no matter where he was. He placed them so far apart from each other to benefit the fighting soldiers, but he was also playing both sides. He knew he could get a contract with the winning side no matter what the outcome if he supplied to both from different places. He had control of his future even if the nation didn't. That's what your father found out about, Twelve, the damage had already been done for years, but if the Union found out what Jean-Claude had been doing, he could be deported for war-crimes. I met him right after the War, I had been a marksman fighting for the Union, a young man myself at the time and he needed an assistant and someone to do his dirty work. He paid well and he educated me when neither the North nor South had any place for me. He had already been practicing how to shoot blind, but I helped him with that where I could. He can hear and feel his way around a target and he's amazingly accurate. But he often puts the man-hunting off onto one of his men, I was one, the Mexican came right after me, and I'm sure we're all targets today…

Back in the rest area, Sally and Twelve meet up.

TWELVE:
I know there's a lot of people, but does it look like we're being kept apart from each other in the standings to you? Like we're being herded to the top rankings.

SALLY:
Don't tell me you're WORRIED about winning?

Twelve only stares at her.

SALLY:

Lighten up, son, or your face will stick like that forever. Even if we're gonna die, we might as well have fun before it happens.

Twelve sighs.

CUT TO:

EXT, AFTERNOON, TOURNAMENT FIELD

Most of the gunfighters are now just spectators themselves, Twelve, Sally and Sundowner of course have made it down to themselves and three other men. Down to the final six, none of our three are pitted against each other, but each of the other men.

Jean-Claude has met with these others.

JEAN-CLAUDE:
I want the three of them to win. Do not obviously lose, but make sure that Twelve and Sally are winners today. Sundowner, however…

He turns toward the man that is slated to fight Sundowner as though he can see him clearly.

JEAN-CLAUDE:
Fight with all your might, it will be interesting to see if Sundowner has truly kept up with his skills.

GUNMAN:
What if I beat him?

Jean-Claude laughs to himself and shakes his head.

JEAN-CLAUDE:
You won't.

ANNOUNCER:
Will Sally Firkins and ANTHONY JENKINS please take the field!

One of the men, a tall, lanky fellow with long wavy black hair takes his leave and steps out to meet his opponent.

ANNOUNCER:
In these final games, the gunmen...

SALLY:
AH-HEM!!!

ANNOUNCER:
Uh, and WOMAN…will compete in three events. Accuracy, where the fighters will have six shots, the one with the most hits closest to the bull's-eye will win. A moving target competition where points are on certain boards that travel across the field, whoever has the highest score wins. And, special for these final games, a random clay shoot. Throughout the field are launching devices that will hurl targets at random heights and speeds, whoever can shoot the most wins. Best two out of three will win against their opponent. Now, if the fighters will take their places!

Sally and Anthony take their spots on the target range and ready themselves, both in standing positions.

ANNOUNCER:
Fire when ready.

They each fire all of their bullets at the paper targets and then judges inspect them as Sally and Anthony walk forward to gain their results.

A judge talks to them, then to the announcer.

ANNOUNCER:
The winner is Ms. SALLY FIRKINS!

The crowd cheers as Sally and the other gunfighter go back to their places.

ANNOUNCER:
In this next event, targets will move across the field with points on them, one fighter will play at a time with only six shots to determine points, whoever has the higher amount of points wins. The boards and their points will be rearranged after the first shooter's turn. First up is Sally!

Sally prepares herself, checking her pistol. A whistle blows and being pulled by rope on wheels are large boards with points listed on them in rings. Sally aims carefully and picks her targets, shooting all of her bullets.

The judges again inspect the targets but do not yet announce the points.

Anthony takes his stance and waits for the boards to be reset. When the whistle blows, Anthony takes a more calculated approach and waits for targets to get close to each other and doubles his points by firing through multiples, it's obvious that Anthony has the upper hand in this game. The crowd "ooo's" and "ahh's."

The judges come up with the scoring and the numbers are announced.

ANNOUNCER:
Sally has 125 points, but ANTHONY JENKINS is our winner with 275 points!

Sally throws her hands up in the air, frustrated with herself, but quickly calms back down and starts laughing, even congratulating Anthony who only looks at her smugly.

He looks up and sees a dissatisfied Jean-Claude and Alvaro frowning at him. He quickly changes his demeanor.

ANNOUNCER:
And now the random clay shoot. In this event each fighter will play by themselves again, but they will have access to their very own weapons and will be able to fire as many shots as they choose until the final clay is shot. Twenty will be flung at random places and speed.

Assistants to the tournament carry out tables with each of the fighter's personal arsenal.

Sally and Anthony look over their pistols and rifles.

ANNOUNCER:
The winner of the last event, Anthony, is first up.

Machines to fling the clay discs are set up throughout the field. Anthony holds his rifle at the ready. The first clay is flung lazily into the air, he shoots it easily. He almost laughs to himself and begins to look around as though unimpressed, then four more fly off in different directions, with a surprised look still on his face he is only able to knock two of them out. He stays intent and continues to fire at the discs flying through the air until all of them are gone.

ANNOUNCER:
Now let's see if Sally can beat Anthony's twelve hits.

Sally stands ready with her pistols, one in each hand. She waits patiently, until two are fired in fast arcs intersecting each other, she fires quickly with both of her guns and takes out the two easily. She continues to fire, never missing with her pistols, knocking out 12 consecutive discs herself already matching Anthony. She then grabs her rifle from the table and begins to take aim as the clays continue to fire. She's not as comfortable with her rifle but manages to take out three more, only missing five in total.

ANNOUNCER:
The winner of this round is SALLY FIRKINS!

The crowd cheers and Sally bows to them and laughs it up. She tries to go back over to Anthony to shake his hand, but he ignores her and only walks away. Sally shrugs it off and continues to have a good time of her own.

ANNOUNCER:
Next up is CORT MORRISON and SOL DOWNING! Shooters at your marks!

Sundowner and the man called Cort take their spots on the target range.

Sundowner's arm is already stretched out and aiming when the announcer gives them signal to fire. They each shoot their six bullets and the judges go to inspect.

They actually end up huddling over Sundowner's target.

Cort is the only of the two to approach the judges.

Sundowner only inspects his gun.

One of the judges confers with the announcer for a moment.

ANNOUNCER:
It would appear that Sol has hit ALL SIX BULLETS within the bull's-eye and has won this event with no contest!

Cort looks genuinely shocked as he makes his way back to his standing place.

ANNOUNCER:
Sol will take the first turn in the moving target event.

Again, Sundowner stands with his arm outstretched, aiming even though there is no target yet. The whistle blows and the targets move and like Anthony, Sundowner uses the targets passing over each other to drive a single bullet through multiple targets, but Sundowner's aim is so impeccable that he drives his bullets through the dead center of each of his targets.

Cort, visibly shaken by Sundowner's ability, almost forgets that he has a turn as well. He tries his best to perform the same task but his aiming and shooting abilities are just nowhere near the level of Sundowner.

After the judges make their assessment, the announcer approaches the crowd.

ANNOUNCER:
Sol has won again and has taken the round with a score of 500!

The crowd cheers wildly. Cort skulks off and passes by Jean-Claude's stand.

CORT:
I tried Mr. Maréchal, I did my best…

JEAN-CLAUDE:
I know you did, young sir, the problem is, HE didn't even try. I believe we may have ourselves a winner to the tournament already.

ALVARO
(Subtitled):
There is still the young man, Twelve.

JEAN-CLAUDE:
Yes, we shall see about our stranger-champion.

Twelve is checking his pistol, readying himself. He is confident that he will win as well, if not for his own abilities, then because Jean-Claude seems to have the tournament wrapped around his little finger.

His opponent is also preparing.

ANNOUNCER:
If TWELVE and Mr. JESSE McCREADY could please take the field!

Their paper targets are already set up, ready for the event.

ANNOUNCER:
You may fire at will.

Both of them shoot intensely fast. The crowd gasps at their eagerness to fire all shots and how well it would appear both of them have done.

The judges pour over the targets, the announcer looks over them as well and it would appear that they are stumped as to a winner.

Twelve and McCready step over to the targets and look over them as well.

One of the judges plucks a weed from the ground and uses it as a measuring device. On Twelve's target, one bullet hole is incrementally closer, determining him as a winner of the first event.

ANNOUNCER:
Twelve is the winner by a HAIR!

The crowd cheers for the champion. Twelve shows no elation or satisfaction whatsoever, he only returns to his place and readies himself for the next event.

McCready comes close to Twelve.

McCREADY:
I don't think that I'll LET you win this one, maybe watch you squirm a bit.

And he then walks away. Twelve still shows no emotion. A whistle blows and the targets begin to move across the field. Twelve again is quick on the draw but he manages to use the same tactics as set by the henchman, Jenkins, and racks up an obviously impressive score.

McCready, looking smug, readies himself as the targets are again reset.

ANNOUNCER:
Make yourself ready!

The whistle blows again and McCready fires off his shots, obviously determined to do his absolute best.

When the judges finally tally the scores, the announcer comes close to the crowd.

ANNOUNCER:
And in a second sweep, TWELVE takes the second event and the WIN with a score of 415 to Jesse McCready's 325!

McCready is obviously upset and shouts obscenities but is drowned out by the cheering of the crowd. Twelve has moved on to the final three.

ANNOUNCER:

FRUITLESS BODIES

As our remaining gunslingers take a short break, I'll explain the final round. All three will compete against each other in the same events, best two out of three, should one of the opponents lose twice before the third round they are immediately eliminated and the remaining two will play the last round to determine the grand champion of today's events.

CUT TO:

EXT, LATE AFTERNOON, GUNFIGHTER'S REST AREA

The three of them are standing together as other gunfighters' rest and only watch.

SALLY:
So here we are, the final three and we're all gonna fight each other. Now, I have no doubt in my mind it's gonna be you two fighting it out in the end, but don't turn this into a pissing contest!

SUNDOWNER:
We were let this far into it, we've been made the top three, Jean-Claude doesn't care who the winner is today, but that he has all three of us at the top, no other contest between us. He's assessing the threat AND keeping us in the open.

ANNOUNCER
(From off screen):
Will the fighters please take the field!

TWELVE:
Here we go.

MOVING TO:

EXT, TOURNAMENT FIELD

Three targets are set up this time and our three characters are given their ammo to fire in the event.

They all take aim.

ANNOUNCER:
Fire when ready!

They all aim and fire off their shots.

The judges quickly run out to the targets, of course gathering around Sundowner's first, then checking the other two, they confer with the announcer again.

ANNOUNCER:
Again, Sol has hit every shot within the bull's-eye, next is Twelve, and then Sally, that will also be the order of the next event.

Sundowner prepares himself, calm, hardly a drop of sweat on his brow at all. The whistle blows and the targets move. He shoots as though the targets are stationary before him.

Twelve takes his place and waits for the targets to be reset. This time, when the targets begin to move after their signal, Twelve drops to his knee and begins to fire, then rolls to his left and back to his knee and fires the rest of his shots. The crowd lightly gasps at his change in strategy. In actuality he has hit multiple targets multiple times by forcing them to be in line of his bullets a second time.

Next is Sally, who tries to adopt the same tactic but isn't as quick on her feet and doesn't succeed nearly as well. She gets up, dusts herself off and laughs it off.

The judges reveal the scores to the announcer.

ANNOUNCER:

Sally scored an admirable 315, but has been eliminated from the tournament, let's hear it for her anyway, our third-place victor, Ms. SALLY FIRKINS!

The crowd cheers and applauds.

Sally takes a small bow and heads over to the rest area.

ANNOUNCER:
Scoring next best with 485 points is…

The announcer dramatically pauses.

The crowd leans in, in wonder.

ANNOUNCER:
SOL DOWNING! Which makes the winner of this event, TWELVE with a score of 525 points!

Again, the crowd goes crazy in celebration of the champion.

ANNOUNCER:
This now ties Sol and Twelve at one match a piece.

Tournament assistants again bring out the tables with each fighter's personal equipment.

Twelve has two pistols and a small, older looking rifle. He walks to it, and runs his fingers over the stock, it's the same rifle he received as a boy.

On Sundowner's table is also two pistols, a rifle and a stylized rifle used for marksmanship.

ANNOUNCER:
Of course, Mr. TWELVE is up next.

The launchers have been set, and Twelve takes a deep, calming breath as he holds both of his pistols at his sides.

The clay discs begin to fly and Twelve shoots them effortlessly, his hand/eye coordination surprisingly accurate. He fires all of the bullets from his pistols, knocking twelve discs out of the air and then grabs his rifle and begins shooting them almost before they've taken flight, using all the shots of his rifle, he has taken out all twenty discs.

For a moment, the crowd is silent in awe.

ANNOUNCER
(Stammering):
He-he-he shot all of them!

The crowd, almost as though coming back to life, erupts in elation and cheers wildly again.

Twelve doesn't even look surprised or proud, he merely sets his gun back down and waits patiently for Sundowner to take his turn.

Sundowner takes a similar stance with his two pistols.

When the discs begin to fly, Sundowner is amazingly accurate sometimes seeming to not even look as he shoots one out of the sky. When his pistols are spent, he also grabs his rifle, but towards the end of the firing one manages to slip by and it would seem that Twelve has won. But Sundowner is nonchalant in grabbing his second rifle and taking very careful aim at a disc that would seem too far out of range. He fires only a single shot and for a few seconds the crowd continues to watch, when suddenly, the final disc, coming dangerously close to the ground explodes by Sundowner's single sniper-shot.

FRUITLESS BODIES

The crowd needs no motivation to gasp, then to applaud the cunning display.

CUT TO:

EXT, TOURNAMENT FIELD

Twelve and Sundowner stand together as an announcer bellows to the audience as Jean-Claude and Alvaro come down from their private box.

ANNOUNCER:
It appears as though Mr. Twelve and Mr. Downing have come to a draw, and no winner can be determined! In such an event, a special competition has been set up by Mr. Maréchal, here he is now to explain!

Jean-Claude follows Alvaro to stand before the crowd that has gathered to watch the event. He pulls something from his pocket, a small pouch full of sand that he squeezes between his fingers for a moment, then gently puts it back.

JEAN-CLAUDE:
I must say that I am surprised, a tie! In case of this we do have a special event that young Mr. TWELVE and SOL DOWNING (Jean-Claude says the pseudonym sarcastically and turns his head toward Sundowner as though leering at him) will compete in: a duel.

The crowd gasps and Twelve and Sundowner look at each other blankly.

Sally, with the other gunfighters, stands up quickly, obviously disturbed by this change of events.

JEAN-CLAUDE:

Now, now, I would not have our prized gunmen actually KILL each other, but rather, it gives me a great amount of pleasure to allow them to demonstrate my newest product for the military.

He holds up a bullet for everyone to see.

JEAN-CLAUDE:
Designed for the US Military in an attempt to gain control of chaos in a more civilized and less THREATENING way. It is a special tip constructed of rock-salt. A completely non-lethal yet completely effective material that dissolves within the victim, leaving him only slightly bruised and stinging, but certainly rethinking his actions!

He turns to face in the direction of Alvaro.

JEAN-CLAUDE:
Your pistol…

Alvaro hands it to him, Jean-Claude loads the bullet into one of the chambers. He hands the gun back to Alvaro. He then turns to where he had been seated.

JEAN-CLAUDE
(Shouting):
Jameson? Will you please stand and raise your hand?

The man who had been sitting, not paying attention stands and raises his hand even with his head.

Alvaro smiles.

ALVARO
(Shouting):
Raise it HIGHER!

The man, Jameson, raises his hand all the way up.

Alvaro raises his pistol and shoots the man in the chest.

He falls down, yelping in surprise and pain.

The crowd gasps again.

JEAN-CLAUDE:
As you see, I am confident enough to demonstrate it first on one of my own men, Jameson will be no worse for wear in only a few moments. Now…

Jean-Claude turns in the direction of Twelve and Sundowner.

JEAN-CLAUDE:
Men, YOUR pistols, please…

Reluctant at first, Twelve and Sundowner step forward and pull out their pistols.

Alvaro steps between them and Jean-Claude quickly and holds his hands out for their pistols.

They hand over their pistols and Alvaro loads one special salt-rock bullet into each, rotates the chamber appropriately and hands their guns back to them.

JEAN-CLAUDE:
Now, please take your positions on the field wherever you feel most comfortable, but please, do take the observers into consideration.

Jean-Claude and Alvaro return to their private stands.

Twelve and Sundowner pace out to the field.

TWELVE:

You think he actually put his "special" bullets in there?

SUNDOWNER:
Are you concerned or HOPEFUL?

They take their positions, several meters apart from each other.

ANNOUNCER:
Gunfighters! A whistle will be blown to signal to draw and
fire…may the best man win and good luck!

Both Twelve and Sundowner stare each other down, both at the ready,
arms locked straight down to their sides.

Jean-Claude only bows his head, listening as intently as he can due to
his blindness.

Sally and the other gunfighters in their special area all seem to lean
forward to try and see a little bit better.

The crowd is silent and intent.

Neither Twelve nor Sundowner seem to be phased by the tension, they
only stare at each other from across the field. The wind blows against
the two fighters lightly, blowing their long coats loosely up and away
from them.

A lizard runs between them, as though bothered by the tension and
needing to get away.

The whistle blows and both of them react blindingly fast and shoot,
but Twelve is faster and plants his bullet in Sundowner's chest.

He falls back in a wail but quickly silences himself and only squirms,
grunting occasionally.

The crowd cheers wildly.

ANNOUNCER:
For the second Destiny-Star Tournament, Twelve is the winner!

The crowd continues to cheer and jeer as Jean-Claude along with Alvaro and some other men come down from the stands again to greet the winner.

Twelve comes over to Sundowner to check on him.

TWELVE:
Still alive?

SUNDOWER
(Hissing):
Yes…burns like hell, but I'm alive.

From behind them, Jean-Claude approaches.

JEAN-CLAUDE:
Mr. Twelve! I would personally like to congratulate you, so sorry I wasn't there for your first win, but it is a pleasure AND an honor to meet a consecutive winner in my own tournament. May I shake the hand of the winner?

Jean-Claude extends his hand outward into open space.

Twelve stares blankly at the man, unsure, and un-wanting, of the gesture.

Sundowner manages to sit up behind Twelve and looks between him and Jean-Claude.

Jean-Claude's hand wavers slightly.

JEAN-CLAUDE
(Whispering to Alvaro):
I am facing the right direction…?
(In regular tone)
Please, monsieur…

Hesitant, Twelve steps forward but stalls again.

TWELVE
(Quietly):
My hands are…dirty.

JEAN-CLAUDE:
Nonsense, I have worked around dirt and grime my entire life, your
hands will be no worse than my own have been, besides, I can tell a
lot about a man in his handshake, the more natural the better.

Jean-Claude smiles big below his silk blindfold and extends his hand
in the direction of Twelve's voice.

Twelve sighs quietly to himself and steps forward and loosely takes
Jean-Claude's hand, obviously uncomfortable.

Jean-Claude hesitates himself slightly at first, but then grips firmly
and shakes hard once.

JEAN-CLAUDE:
The pleasure surely is mine. As a special prize to you and the second
and third place winners, I would like to have you all up to my home
for a banquet. I will have my men escort you later this evening so
that you might rest beforehand.

Jean-Claude turns to the crowd.

JEAN-CLAUDE:

As most of you know, these tournaments are leading to the grand opening of my third plant. The third tournament will be held on July the fourth, this great nation's centennial. After a winner has been established and night falls, I will throw a grand party in honor of the nation's birthday and the opening of my newest Destiny-Star company. All residents and guests are welcome!

The crowd cheers again.

Alvaro and Jean-Claude walk away in their own direction, speaking to each other in hushed tones.

JEAN-CLAUDE:
Something bothers me about TWELVE; I can't quite put my finger on it, though…I don't trust this situation at all.

ALVARO
(Subtitled):
What would you have done?

JEAN-CLAUDE:
Find where they are staying, make sure they are left open tonight.

Twelve helps Sundowner all the way up and they walk over to the gunfighter's area.

MOVING TO:

EXT, GUNFIGHTER'S REST AREA

They begin to speak with Sally.

TWELVE:
We've been invited to dinner. I would rather not go, but we might not have a choice. We need to find a place to stay, HIDE even…

SALLY:
I've got just the thing; I ran into an old friend of mine while you two
slept in jail last night.

CUT TO:

EXT, NEAR DUSK, PATTERSON SHEEP FARM

A shepherd guides several sheep through a gate into a paddock after a
day of grazing, their bleating gives way to a conversation between
Sally and RON PATTERSON as they walk past the paddock towards
Ron's house.

Sundowner and Twelve follow closely behind.

SALLY:
I want to thank you again, Ron, for letting me stay again tonight and
letting my friends stay as well.

RON:
Oh, it's my pleasure, Sally, especially now that the three of you are
the most popular people in town…any hotel would have put you up
for the night, though, I think…

Sally looks over her shoulder at the two men.

SALLY:
Let's just say we're trying to avoid the attention.

After saying such she notices a carriage coming towards the ranch.

Twelve and Sundowner both also look.

SUNDOWNER:
Looks like Jean-Claude is adamant about having us to his house.
Avoiding him any longer might make him suspicious.

SALLY:
If he already isn't…

TWELVE:
I have a bad feeling about this…

The carriage catches up to them, straggling sheep dodge the large horses, and the driver looks down onto them.

DRIVER:
Ms. FIRKINS, Mr. DOWNING and Mr. TWELVE, Mr. Maréchal is expecting you at his home to join him for a dinner in celebration of your achievements today.

From behind the carriage on his own horse comes Alvaro, he dismounts.

ALVARO:
He would be very…DISAPPOINTED…if you could not make it.

RON:
Looks like you're being honored tonight, I don't want to hold you up, we'll see you later this evening.

Twelve and Sundowner exchange glances, then both look at Sally.

SALLY
(Quietly to the others):
At least if we die, it'll be on full stomachs.

And then Sally walks up and enters the carriage.

Twelve sighs.

TWELVE:

A VERY bad feeling.

They each enter the carriage.

MOVING TO:

INT, CARRIAGE CABIN

Twelve and Sally sit on one side with Sundowner on the other.

> SALLY
> (To Sundowner):
> What do you think?

> SUNDOWNER:
> It's a trap. Mostly after me, but he knows you as well. Twelve is halfway safe, but even being with us, Jean-Claude will assume the worst, which obviously wouldn't be wrong. We're going into the lion's den.

CUT TO:

EXT, RANCH

Alvaro watches as the carriage begins to pull away and then turns to Ron Patterson.

Ron has almost a look of fear on his face.

> ALVARO:
> Mr. Maréchal thanks you for your help and makes the suggestion that you head into town late this evening by yourself.

Alvaro takes Ron's hand and shoves a large wad of cash into it. He then turns away without allowing the conversation to continue, mounts his horse and follows far behind the carriage.

CUT TO:

EXT, DUSK, JEAN-CLAUDE'S PORTER MANSION

The carriage pulls up to the front of the opulent house and stops, the driver steps down and opens the carriage door. Sally steps out first as Alvaro rides up and dismounts.

Alvaro heads towards the door of the house, blocking their entry, two other men from within join him.

Sally, Twelve and Sundowner stand at the bottom of the steps, all side by side.

DOORMAN:
I'm sure I speak for Mr. Maréchal when I say thank you for taking the time to visit us this evening. However, as a matter of courtesy, I must ask that you leave your firearms with us.

None of our characters seem fazed by this.

Twelve takes the first step forward, taking off his sidearm and emptying it of its bullets and putting them into his pocket, handing the gun forward handle-first, then repeating the same process with his rifle tucked into the length of his duster.

The man looks almost offended.

Sally and Sundowner follow suit.

ALVARO:
You will follow me.

He steps into the house, followed by Twelve, Sundowner, and Sally, in turn followed by the other two men from inside the house.

CUT TO:

INT, FOYER OF MANSION

Jean-Claude stands at the top of the stairs leading to the second story of the house, his hand is held firmly on the railing. He is dressed as though he might be at a ball with a purple, silk bandanna folded over and covering his eyes. He is carefully taking each step as he comes down the stairs to greet them.

JEAN-CLAUDE:
I was afraid you had decided against coming to my home; allow me to express how happy I am that you are here. I have had my chef prepare an especially delectable banquet for us this evening. If you will join me in the dining room?

Alvaro leads them through the foyer and into another room occupied by a long dining table.

Jean-Claude descends the rest of the stairs and follows them.

MOVING TO:

INT, DINING ROOM

The table is already set with fine dishes and silverware.

Jean-Claude comes around the small group with his hand outstretched until he makes contact with a chair. He turns his head slightly as though trying to gauge where he is in the room, then pulls the chair out from the table.

JEAN-CLAUDE:
Madam?

Sally sits in the chair silently then pulls herself closer to the table.

Jean-Claude traces his hands along the chairs until coming to the edge of the table where he feels his way to the head chair. He stands tall and straight, facing the three men.

JEAN-CLAUDE:
Alvaro, please make sure that drinks and bread are brought to us and please let the chef know our guests have arrived and the main course should be delivered directly.
(To his guests)
Mr. Downing, young Mr. Twelve, please, make yourselves comfortable, I trust that everyone here will appreciate a good glass of wine.

Alvaro had left when asked while Sundowner and Twelve cautiously took their seats.

Jean-Claude, after hearing the chairs settle, also relaxes into his own chair.

A servant enters with a large dark bottle and a basket of bread. He pours wine into each of the guest's glasses, then into Jean-Claude's who thanks the servant in his native French.

JEAN-CLAUDE:
I must say that I am quite impressed with all of your displays today. Especially Ms. Firkins, very astounding, pulling third place at the very last.

He says this with a sneer, obviously being sarcastic. He sips lightly from his wine.

JEAN-CLAUDE:
Twelve, I must truly commend you, it would appear that we have a champion on our hands, winning my special little tournament two

times now. I say, I might have to hire you as a spokesman if you can
pull off three in a row!

Twelve, obviously disgusted drinks his entire glass of wine.

TWELVE
(Hissing):
Thank you, sir.

Then, as though he can see as well as anyone with sight, Jean-Claude
faces Sundowner.

JEAN-CLAUDE:
And SUNDOWNER…my old friend Sundowner.

Sundowner only looks straight forward, not meeting Jean-Claude's
blind gaze, nor acknowledging the man at all. Twelve and Sally
exchange shocked glances at Jean-Claude's revelation.

Jean-Claude's demeanor changes to one of sincerity.

JEAN-CLAUDE:
It has been a long time, ten years, I believe. I must say I had assumed
the worst; thank GOD, that you are safe.

The last part sounds almost as though Jean-Claude is telling
Sundowner to give thanks, rather than himself. Jean-Claude continues
to "stare" Sundowner down making even Sally and Twelve
uncomfortable.

SUNDOWNER:
I have only YOU to thank for the life that I have lived.

JEAN-CLAUDE:
So where HAVE you been? What ADVENTURES have you had?
Run into any old FAMILY?

Sally rises to her feet, but at the exact same time that the doors of the dining room burst open.

A chef and other servants come in carrying serving trays.

Sundowner puts his hand on Sally's hand, and she slowly sits.

JEAN-CLAUDE:
Ah! Dinner is served.

FADE OUT

EXT, NIGHT, PATTERSON RANCH HOUSE

The grounds and house are barely lit by moonlight.

JEAN-CLAUDE
(VO):
Kill them.

We see several men on horse riding up to the front of the house.

TWELVE
(VO):
How long have you known Sundowner?

SALLY
(VO):
Oh, probably about four or five years now.

The men dismount, four of them, and slowly approach the house.

SALLY
(VO):

When my son was killed, Sundowner had already left JOHN, so I never associated him with the BAD GUYS like you do.

Two more men ride up, but they do not dismount. It's Alvaro and Jean-Claude.

SALLY
(VO):
When Samuel was killed, I went right after John, but it was a waste of time. I became a wreck, lost my home in Crenshaw, then happened across Sundowner, but it had been a LONG time since I had ever seen him.

The thugs going towards the house enter, there is no light, it's very late at night.

SALLY
(VO):
I had lived in Crenshaw all my life, JOHN-CLAWED inherited Destiny-Star from his father and provided munitions to soldiers during the War. Sundowner had joined him after the war was declared over. After that Destiny-Star became a big private dealer and John started becoming the person in charge. I remember Sundowner was with him all the time…

MOVING TO:

INT, PATTERSON HOME

The men skulk about the house, drawing their firearms.

TWELVE
(VO):
Then Jean-Claude and Sundowner went their separate ways, he told me about that, having to walk away…

SALLY
(VO):
I never thought anything of it when he disappeared, at the same time
I didn't have anything against what was going on, didn't KNOW
what was going on…

The men start searching rooms…

SALLY
(VO):
When I ran into Sundowner, we opened up to each other, shared our
stories and tried to put it behind us, John was un-reachable.

They finally come to the bedrooms…

TWELVE
(VO):
So, you had a common bond…

SALLY
(VO):
…And more. We became good friends…

But no one is to be found.

CUT TO:

ON THE RUN

EXT, OPEN FIELD

Ron Patterson, Twelve and Sally stand next to their horses.

Sundowner is riding quickly up to them.

SUNDOWNER:

We'd better get moving, they're in the house, they'll know we're gone soon, and they'll start looking.

Sally turns to Ron, urgently, and grabs his hand.

SALLY:
Thank you so much for this, Ron…

RON:
Don't think anything of it, just get going…

Sally and Twelve get onto their horses and they immediately ride off.

Ron mounts his horse as well and heads back towards his home.

CUT TO:

EXT, FRONT OF PATTERSON HOME

One of the thugs walks up to Jean-Claude and Alvaro, still sitting on their horses.

THUG:
Not a soul in that house.

Jean-Claude's light grip on the reigns of his horse tightens into a hard fist.

JEAN-CLAUDE
(Quietly):
I want every man to scour this town.

THUG:
I think they might be gone, sir…

Jean-Claude kicks out, connecting with the man's jaw, who falls sprawling to the ground.

JEAN-CLAUDE:
Do it for my peace of mind.

ALVARO
(Subtitled):
He's right, they won't be here…

The sound of a horse riding in along the road that leads to the Patterson ranch catches their attention.

When Alvaro turns to see who it is, he dismounts.

It's Ron Patterson. Ron also sees that he has been noticed, and rather than trying to run, he swallows hard and turns towards the men. Once he reaches them, he also dismounts and looks around nervously.

RON:
It's an honor to have you here, Mr. Maréchal…

Alvaro grabs him.

ALVARO:
Did you send them off? Where are they?

Jean-Claude dismounts as Ron begins to stammer in fear. Jean-Claude shoves Alvaro aside as Ron falls to the ground after losing his balance.

He looks up but finds himself face to face with the barrel of a pistol in Jean-Claude's hand. He has no time to react, Jean-Claude shoots him.

JEAN-CLAUDE:
Destroy everything, blame it on them.

Jean-Claude and Alvaro mount their horses and ride off.

The thug is left still rubbing his jaw and looking at the dead body, a black pool spreading out in the moon light.

FADE OUT

INT/EXT, MANY LOCATIONS

We see Twelve, Sally and Sundowner all riding their horses across fields as the sun rises.

We see a variety of locations as they make their way further from Porter and to the next town.

We also catch glimpses of Jean-Claude and his men as they prepare to leave for the next town as well. Before end of collage:

TWELVE
(VO):
It happened on my birthday, I was catatonic, couldn't speak, didn't for a year. The sheriff knew my family was pretty well off, gathered the funds from the bank and sent me to school in New York. The name stuck only because I never corrected anyone. It was always in my mind to find Jean-Claude…

CUT TO:

EXT, NIGHT, CAMP

The three of them are sitting around a fire.

TWELVE:
And you.

Acknowledging Sundowner.

TWELVE:
But I guess people can change over time…

SUNDOWNER:
Betrayal helped.

SALLY:
…And friends.

Sundowner smiles slightly.

TWELVE:
So, I was properly educated, learned how to read and write, but always kept up my shooting. Traveled a bit and then, here, years later, learn that Jean-Claude and his company are going to celebrate the nation's one hundredth anniversary. I didn't care if I lived after he was dead, I had nothing to live for, but, yesterday, when I was standing there in front of him, when we were IN his HOUSE…

Twelve shakes his head as though he doesn't even understand his own actions.

SALLY:
I felt like that for a while. When my son was murdered. I had nothing to lose and even tried to go after John-Clawed, but his men stopped me, beat me, and had a laugh. I gave up. I left town, found myself somewhere else in a bar, drinking myself to death and then THE Sundowner came in. Everyone was paralyzed with fear, but when I saw him, it was just a sad old man who wanted a drink. So, I bought him one and we haven't left each other's side since.

TWELVE:
What about your son? What happened?

Sally stays silent.

TWELVE:
I'm sorry, I won't force…

SALLY:
No, it's all right. He was barely 16, my husband had died and there was no one working for us, I stayed at home, tending our land, someone had to go earn money, though, so I sent him down to the same place his father worked, got him a job. But my son, he…FOUND, something… He swore to keep quiet about it, but he lived in fear for several months. He never told me what, but I assume it had something to do with shady business because that's all John-Clawed conducts. My boy worked for the shippers, he stayed away from the actual plant, but there was an explosion, he was the only one killed, not a single other person was even injured. I knew it wasn't an accident…especially when John came to my house, asked me if Samuel and I had ever discussed his work, and offered me money — as an apology. It was SILENCE money.

Sally begins to look furious.

Twelve notices and tries to quickly change the subject.

TWELVE:
We should rest now, we're just outside of Nash, we'll try and find someplace to stay that doesn't have Jean-Claude's men all over it yet.

Sally sighs heavily and lies down, muttering to herself.

Twelve and Sundowner glance at each other, then lie down themselves.

FADE OUT

EXT, NIGHT, TWELVE'S DREAM

Twelve stands outside his boyhood home, it's night and winter, realizing he's in a dream he begins to head toward the house. As he's moving the rest of the world moves in a very slow motion, the henchman are going into the house looking for his younger self. But he slides past them as though they're standing still.

MOVING TO:

INT, INSIDE HOUSE DURING TWELVE'S DREAM

He knows where he had hid, and goes straight toward the kitchen, hoping to see himself as a child. When the henchman who had come through the back door enters Twelve sees his younger self raise the gun, but rather than fire a look of terror washes over his face in this super slow motion.

Twelve turns to look at the henchman but instead sees Jean-Claude Maréchal, aiming directly at him.

Jean-Claude, despite his blindness, has a gun leveled right at his chest, and fires.

CUT ON GUNSHOT TO:

EXT, MORNING, OPEN FIELD

Twelve bolts upright out of his dream. The sound of gunshots in the distance brings him to his senses, he quickly looks around and sees that Sally and her horse are gone.

TWELVE:
Oh, no…

Twelve shoves Sundowner awake and quickly mounts his horse, riding off before Sundowner even has an opportunity to ask what's going on.

Though, he sees Sally is gone and quickly bolts into action as well.

CUT TO:

EXT, GATES TO TOWN

Sally is riding towards the arriving carriage belonging to Jean-Claude outside of town. Her gun is drawn, and she easily shoots the shotgun passenger, the driver is already dead.

Dismounting before the horse has even come to a complete stop, Sally hits the ground running, gun still held out in front of her, an almost animal yell rises from within her as she blasts a man exiting the carriage.

One more leaps out of the carriage trying to take a shot but misses, Sally easily shoots him down before he can take another shot. She stops well away from the carriage.

SALLY:
You got any more goons in there, John, or are you gonna come out here and die like a man?

CUT TO:

INT, JEAN-CLAUDE'S CARRIAGE

Jean-Claude and the Mexican are sitting across from each other; Jean-Claude has something of a smirk on his face as he maneuvers his small pouch through his fingers.

JEAN-CLAUDE:

It would appear I have an admirer.

ALVARO
(Subtitled):
I'll take care of it.

Alvaro begins to stand, but Jean-Claude halts him.

JEAN-CLAUDE:
No, I believe I will.

CUT TO:

EXT, GATES TO TOWN

Jean-Claude stands up and faces out from the door of his carriage, he carefully places his feet and comes to the ground with no assistance.

Sally is pointing her gun at him, but shaking slightly, she has waited for this for so long, she knows she needs to shoot and begins to walk towards him menacingly.

JEAN-CLAUDE:
Who, may I ask, is calling?

SALLY:
You arrogant sonuva…

Sally closes the gap and hits Jean-Claude hard over the head with her pistol.

Jean-Claude falls hard to the ground but seems to be chuckling. He reaches to his face, feeling where he had been hit, right above the cheek, a small amount of blood is there, he yawns his jaw and laughs lightly.

SALLY:
You had my son killed, he was just a boy and you had him killed for seeing something he wouldn't have understood anyway!

JEAN-CLAUDE:
Sally Firkins…

SALLY:
The one and only…

JEAN-CLAUDE:
You all but sold your boy to me, Sally, you put him in that dangerous position that no boy should face…wouldn't that then make you partly responsible for him?

SALLY:
Just because I put him to work doesn't give you any right to put him to death. I don't give a shit about your cheating business but when you killed my boy…

JEAN-CLAUDE:
I did the world a service?

Sally's eyes flare open, and she lunges forward, cocking her gun ready to fire.

But Jean-Claude, who has gathered dirt in his hand, throws it in a sweeping arc. It hits Sally across the face and chest, making her flinch.

Jean-Claude quickly stands and draws his gun.

CUT TO:

EXT, TOP OF HILL JUST BEYOND TOWN GATE

Twelve and Sundowner come over the hill just in time to see Jean-Claude ready his gun, aim, and kill Sally Firkins.

Twelve's eyes shut and his head slowly sinks to his chest.

Sundowner's jaw falls open, he dismounts, awe and grief crawling across his face. He takes a few steps and then falls to his knees.

CUT TO:

INT, JEAN-CLAUDE'S CARRIAGE

Jean-Claude is sitting back down, wiping his hands off.

ALVARO
(Subtitled):
What of the woman's body?

JEAN-CLAUDE:
Hang her. Whoever tries to take her down was with her.

Alvaro nods, exits the cab.

MOVING TO:

EXT, JEAN-CLAUDE'S CARRIAGE

Alvaro climbs to the driver's seat and takes the reigns to drive the carriage into town.

EXT, LATE MORNING, MIDDLE OF TOWN

NASH, COLORADO, JULY 4TH 1876. The body of Sally hangs still from a noose on a gallows in the middle of town, several people stop to look at the body, a sign is hanging from her neck, it reads: "SHOT

AND HANGED FOR MURDER OF INNOCENT MEN AND THE ATTEMPTED MURDER OF JEAN-CLAUDE MARÉCHAL".

Two guards stand around the gallows.

Within the crowd we see a couple of men with hats pulled low and collars up.

SUNDOWNER:
We can't just leave her there…

TWELVE:
It's a trap and you know it. We'll wait until later, we can talk to the undertaker here in town, make him believe we're part of DESTINY-STAR and we'll bring him her body later tonight, he'll make sure she's taken care of.

They walk away. Beyond them, the third tournament is gearing up.

We see Twelve and Sundowner approach the local funerary place and speak to a man dressed all in black, he nods his approval after checking his watch and looking over their shoulders to the hanging body of Sally Firkins.

Next Twelve and Sundowner approach a stable called ANKS & BROW close to the edge of town. They meet with the stable manager and his assistant.

TWELVE:
It would appear we've gotten in a little late and all the hotels are filled, and we have no friends we can stay with. We'll pay handsomely if you'll just let us sleep in your loft this evening after the celebration.

STABLE MANAGER:

FRUITLESS BODIES

I'd need something up-front; I'm not opposed to letting you stay, but I can't rightly let you without some compensation, I charge for horses to stay, I'll need to charge you as well.

Sundowner steps into the conversation.

SUNDOWNER:
Sir, I was a soldier for the Union in the war, I can pay you some now and then have a significant amount wired to you at a later date once we reach a town that has a government office.

He pulls out a one-hundred-dollar bill. The manager's eyes light up and go wide.

STABLE MANAGER:
I think that can be agreeable. My name is Jarod Henderson! This is Kedrick.

He extends his hand towards Twelve who takes it and shakes firmly.

TWELVE:
Jack Potter.

Jarod then reaches towards Sundowner. Sundowner shakes it.

SUNDOWNER:
You can just call me SD; we'd prefer it if no one knew we were staying here.

KEDRICK:
That shouldn't be a problem sir.

Kedrick also extends his hand and Sundowner slides him the hundred while shaking his hand.

CUT TO:

EXT, AFTERNOON, TOURNAMENT FIELD

We see several gunfighters, some new, some from the previous tournament, all competing as they had before.

Again Jean-Claude and his entourage are all watching.

Crowds cheer at certain displays, every once and a while we catch a glimpse of either or both Twelve and Sundowner within the crowd, examining their surroundings.

Eventually the tournament winds down and a winner is announced to much fanfare and Jean-Claude again personally congratulates the winner. He then turns to the crowd.

JEAN-CLAUDE:
Many of you may be wondering where our grand champion from the previous two tournaments has disappeared to. It is my sad duty to inform that he was tragically killed before arriving into town. DESTINY-STAR, along with local officials, is seriously investigating this heinous and unsolved act.

The crowd gasps at the news, but then claps apologetic and appreciatively.

Twelve stares blankly from within the crowd.

Sundowner leans into him.

SUNDOWNER:
You're dead now. If you survive this then you can go on and start a whole new life, none of this will come back to haunt you, not if you don't let it.

Twelve seems genuinely un-phased.

JEAN-CLAUDE:
Not to cast a somber mood, today is a day of celebration! It is our
fine nation's one hundredth birthday and the opening of my newest
plant, and as a special treat for those of you have joined me today…

He pulls out two pistols from under his coat.

JEAN-CLAUDE:
My own brand of marksmanship.

The crowd murmurs in wonder and awe.

Jean-Claude turns around and faces the field where the clay disc
launchers have been reset.

JEAN-CLAUDE:
Now if I may ask for the utmost of silence until all the discs have
been fired.

The crowd complies, and the first disc launches.

Jean-Claude is stone-faced and concentrating intensely on the sound
of the object flying through the air. He fires and the disc explodes in
the air as though he could see it perfectly to shoot at it.

The crowd gasps, but Jean-Claude turns slightly and makes a "shush"
motion with his mouth and the barrel of one of his guns.

He continues to fire them out of the air, just through listening, at one
point, more than just one disc flies through the air and he fires them
all out of the sky in succession.

He goes to reload his guns, but a disc fires off as he is doing so. His
ears twitch and he concentrates both on reloading and where the disc
is going.

He aims very carefully and fires. As he does so a slight wind picks up and Jean-Claude notices it immediately, he quickly fires off another shot.

The first bullet only clips the disc, setting it flipping through the air as the second bullet obliterates it.

The crowd cheers at his display and Jean-Claude turns around and bows to them.

JEAN-CLAUDE:
Thank you so much, I must admit, however, I very nearly missed that last one…it would appear that a storm may be on its way this evening. But that will not stop our celebration this evening, to which you are all invited as my guests!

The crowd applauds and cheers for Jean-Claude's display and invitation.

CUT TO:

EXT, NIGHT, MIDDLE OF TOWN

A fireworks blast brings us into scene.

Jean-Claude and his entourage watch from their private area while crowds of people sit in the grass at the edge of town.

Large fiery displays light up the night sky.

In the distance nature is putting on its own display with lightning bolts within thunderhead clouds.

A lone guard leans against one of the polls supporting the gallows Sally is hanged from.

CUT TO:

INT, ANKS & BROW STABLES

We get a glimpse of Sundowner with his sniping rifle propped between two barrels.

CUT TO:

EXT, GALLOWS

The guard looks up slightly to catch the fireworks, one goes off and he jolts as if surprised by the boom, but then slides down the poll, leaving a trail of blood, almost black in the low, night light.

CUT TO:

INT, ANKS & BROW STABLES

Sundowner gets up and walks towards the ladder that will lead to the lower level.

Twelve is already down there, they nod to each other, and head towards the gallows.

CUT TO:

EXT, GALLOWS

Twelve and Sundowner climb the gallows and cut down Sally and carry her body down the street as quickly as they can, but no one is around on account of the fireworks display still going on in the sky above.

MOVING TO:

EXT, FUNERERY OFFICE

They reach the undertaker's office, and he is there waiting for them. There's a brief exchange and Twelve hands him a wad of money.

SUNDOWNER:
Please take care of her as best you can.

UNDERTAKER:
Of course, sir, she is in good hands.

Twelve and Sundowner now head back to the stables to regain their hiding spot.

TWELVE:
How can we be sure we'll even see him?

SUNDOWNER:
The temperature is nice, it's about to rain, he'll stand outside at some point and that stable loft gives me view of pretty much the entire main street. We'll see him.

They continue on as we see a few drops of rain start to spot the ground. It turns slowly into a full rain as the last of the fireworks display finale go off.

People run to their homes covering their heads.

Jean-Claude's crew takes off for their respective places, but Jean-Claude himself and Alvaro walk casually through the downpour.

CUT TO:

EXT, DESTINY-STAR BUSINESS OFFICE BUILDING

Jean-Claude Maréchal and Alvaro Alejandro are standing together outside the town office of the newest Destiny-Star Munitions plant, privately conversing as it storms around them.

Maréchal is barely visible in the shadows of the awning above them while Alvaro stands just in out of the rain.

ALVARO
(Subtitled):
That woman today…that was too close, your making appearances is becoming dangerous, you should not even be here.

JEAN-CLAUDE:
Did I not deal with her accordingly? So, she killed a few hired men, you drove the coach just fine and you are all I need to PROTECT me.

Alvaro grumbles and casts leery sideways glances down the length of the building.

ALVARO
(Subtitled):
You KNOW she wasn't alone; her body has been taken down…they are here.

Our vision changes to looking through a measured scope looking down at the two men as Jean-Claude lights a cigarette and inhales deeply off of it staring at Alvaro but hidden by a pillar.

CUT TO:

INT, ANKS & BROW STABLES

Sundowner is lying on his stomach aiming his sniper rifle out a propped open loft-door of the upper floor. He is stone-faced, as his eye is pressed firm against his scope.

SUNDOWNER:
No shot on Jean-Claude, but the Mexican is in the open.

From behind him we hear someone moving.

TWELVE
(From off screen):
Take the shot; I'll deal with Jean-Claude myself.

There are the sounds of precise footsteps trailing away as Twelve goes down the ladder.

Sundowner has barely even moved the entire time.

SUNDOWNER:
Dodge this.

CUT TO:

EXT, OFFICE BUILDING

Lightning flashes followed shortly by the loud clapping of thunder. Jean-Claude doesn't even wince at the sudden sound.

Alvaro, however, shudders, then topples backward slamming to the muddy street behind him. Blood begins to darken and mix with the rainwater beneath his head, there is only a look of shock on his face.

Jean-Claude pauses just before taking another drag off of his cigarette and leans forward to spit.

JEAN-CLAUDE:
Merde.

FRUITLESS BODIES

We begin to pull away from Jean-Claude as he draws both of his pistols and aims them down the opposite lengths of the building, he keeps his head level and tries desperately to listen beyond the pouring rain. We stay very level to the ground pulling still further, even beyond the body of Alvaro until suddenly a boot steps into the mud, taking up nearly all our vision with the exception of the very focused Jean-Claude slightly turning his head from left to right and back again, listening for anything. The boot continues forward to reveal Twelve's back and he steps very quietly all the way up to the wood flooring below the awning of the building.

He stays very quiet, letting the rain hide him from Jean-Claude's ears and never steps onto the planks, he leans in out of the rain, right in front of Jean-Claude.

TWELVE:
You're all alone.

Jean-Claude whips his guns forward and fires them both but hits nothing, Twelve has already moved, though we have not seen where.

Pressed against the outer wall of the building, Jean-Claude realizes he's against a window, leaning forward again then suddenly slamming his body backwards, Jean-Claude enters the building by breaking through the window.

MOVING TO:

INT, OFFICE BUILDING

Jean-Claude rights himself, but stays stooped low to the floor, he holsters one of his guns and pulls out the small silk bag of sand we have seen him fumble in his hands before, though this time it is not a stress-reliever. He pulls it open and throws a handful of sand in an arc, he listens carefully to everything it hits and instantly knows the lay of the furniture and what paths are safe for him to take, he knows this building. Plans he had designed while he still had sight come to him in his imagination, plans he uses at every installation of Destiny-Star so that he can make his way around without so much as a walking stick.

TWELVE
(From outside):
Die like a man, Jean-Claude!

JEAN-CLAUDE:
Surely! But first you must FIGHT like one!

And Jean-Claude begins to maneuver through the office without even his hand in front of him.

CUT TO:

EXT, OFFICE BUILDING

Twelve draws a pistol from his side and approaches the window, sidling along the wall, he barely even peaks through the broken window but sees that Jean-Claude is already gone, or at least, not visible. Lightning strikes give a very brief vision of what the front room looks like.

Several desks take up the center of the room. Twelve puts his hand to the sill and quietly removes a remaining piece of glass and tosses it into the room a short distance, gunfire is heard and close to where the glass had fallen is where the bullet shatters wood paneling.

Twelve looks in again quickly but cannot see where the shot had come from. It is just too dark. He tries a second time but there is no gunfire.

JEAN-CLAUDE
(From within):

Fool me once, shame on you…I will not go wasting ammunition on petty baiting noises…

Twelve turns his whole body into the window and begins to shoot in the direction of the voice.

Twelve rolls into the office and fires another shot as he comes up.

MOVING TO:

INT, OFFICE BUILDING

It is quiet, with the exception of the rain outside and the low rumble of thunder. Lightning flashes again, Twelve now has a feel for the room and can also see a doorway, now scarred by bullets.

JEAN-CLAUDE
(To himself, grimacing, subtitled):
Fool me twice…

Jean-Claude pushes himself farther down the hall so that echoes will hide his exact place.

JEAN-CLAUDE:
I see my penchant for conversation precedes me, who is it that wishes me dead?

Twelve does not respond, there is only the sound of the storm.

JEAN-CLAUDE:
Yes, I suppose you wouldn't answer, why fall for your own tricks, eh?

Gunfire rips through the silence as Twelve begins shooting through the wall in two-foot intervals.

Jean-Claude curses wildly in French and drops to the floor as he begins to crawl towards the interior of the building.

Twelve can hear the scurrying and rounds the hall, taking a final shot at disappearing feet through a doorway.

CUT TO:

EXT, OFFICE BUILDING

Sundowner makes his way towards the building but stops in the middle of the street when he realizes that there is no longer a body lying dead before the building. He pulls his gun to the ready, but all he has is his rifle, he's been here before and long-range weapons are cumbersome in a close-quarters fight. Exactly what the Mexican wants. A look of confusion crawls across Sundowner's face, it was a headshot, how could the Mexican still be alive?

ALVARO
(Roaring):
SUNDOWNER!

Sundowner turns to see the Mexican standing in the middle of the street, his right arm hanging like a dead thing, blood has soaked almost his entire body.

It appears that the shot had been just a few inches shy of his skull and had ripped out a large portion of the backside of his neck. It also appears to have done a severe amount of damage to his motor skills; it seems as though nothing on the right side of his body works.

In his left hand glints a large bowie knife.

ALVARO
(Subtitled):
You and I, man to man, we end this…now!

Sundowner raises his rifle, he doesn't even have to aim, he knows his gun well enough, but the Mexican knows he only has one shot.

Sundowner fires.

Alvaro throws his blade.

The bullet smashes into the Mexican's face, a cloud of blood erupting from the back of his head as he finally does fall down and die.

The knife sails through the air slamming into Sundowner's midsection. He does not scream, but drops his rifle, and falls himself backwards, staring into the sky.

CUT TO:

INT, OFFICE BUILDING

Jean-Claude is making his way upstairs, but not before turning over tables and slamming out of the way doors before he does, he is trying to throw his pursuer off the trail, if even for a moment.

Twelve, knowing this full-well, cannot just pass rooms by, he must investigate every noise, for his safety if not to find Jean-Claude. He curses under his breath as he finds another empty storage room.

Jean-Claude will only speak in places that cast echoes, and since he built the building, he knows every angle.

JEAN-CLAUDE:
You must be getting tired of this by now, just leave the building, leave the town…OBVIOUSLY I haven't seen your face. You've killed the only other person who could help me to find you out, we'll call it a mystery, something to ponder in bed before falling asleep!

TWELVE:
There will be no mystery; tonight, you'll sleep in Hell.

JEAN-CLAUDE:
And if you lose, where will you sleep? You seem intent on faceless
murder, I don't recall any psalms about that.

Another door slams as Jean-Claude darts his way to the stairs.

Twelve bolts in that direction, too far away from where he is for Jean-
Claude to be hiding nearby.

TWELVE:
I may not be Heaven-bound, but when YOU die, at least all those
you murdered will be able to rest in peace.

Jean-Claude begins to grin, as he quietly ascends the stairs. He doesn't
speak until he reaches the top, the echo here resounds throughout
almost the entire lower floor.

JEAN-CLAUDE:
That lady today. You were with her, but her heart got the best of her,
and she tried to take me alone. Sally Firkins. She damn near sold her
son to me, after her husband she needed someone to bring food to
the table so she offered up her son at half wages, if I would just take
him in. But he was sloppy, not the first child I've had to kill, but
certainly the least remorse I've felt for it, got himself into the wrong
place at the wrong time. Just like his mama…just like you. I built
this town, boy, I know every inch, and where I may be blind, you
can't see past your rage. You'll still be turning over tables when I'm
long gone.

The last door Jean-Claude had slammed slowly creaks open.

Twelve winces at the noise.

FRUITLESS BODIES

CUT TO:

INT, UPSTAIRS OF OFFICE BUILDING

Jean-Claude only smiles again, he doesn't have a shot to take from here, but he has time. He begins to walk down the hall, silent as a cat until suddenly he bumps into the edge of a doorway. He stops, a look of sheer disbelief on his face.

> JEAN-CLAUDE
> (Whispers):
> I must have that new carpenter shot.

CUT TO:

INT, DOWNSTAIRS OF OFFICE BUILDING

Twelve hears the bump and instantly runs up the stairs just after the room he had entered.

CUT TO:

INT, UPSTAIRS OF OFFICE BUILDING

Jean-Claude makes a break for the door that leads to the outside stairs on the back of the building but stops short.

MOVING TO:

INT, MAIN OFFICE

He realizes he is in his private office; he distinctly has the advantage especially in here. To go back outside will put him in danger, it is still storming, but in here he has a customized wall safe hidden behind a bookcase set on hinges. He opens it quickly, quietly; the door to the safe actually opens inward so as to not cause any protrusions in the wall. He hides in the alcove shutting only the bookcase behind him.

Twelve finds the doorway to the private office, he sees the shadow of Jean-Claude enter the room, but he himself stops. He knows this HAS to be a trap.

TWELVE
(To himself):
Where are you?

Seeing a small space between the floor and the large desk in the center of the room, Twelve sinks to the ground as quiet as he can and waits for a flash of lightning. What he gets is weak, but the large windows behind the desk reveal just enough, Jean-Claude is not under the desk. He curses under his breath, his gun still drawn, he advances. He can see there is a door built between the two massive windows, perhaps he went out onto the balcony? There are only a few more chairs in the middle of the room, their high backs to him. Feeling cautious, Twelve shoots towards the lumbar of each chair, nothing but cloth and feather down erupts, no body. The room, for all its appearances, is empty. Twelve walks slowly forward, perhaps Jean-Claude did go outside, maybe he's standing just on the opposite side of the door, gun aimed at the middle of it waiting to be bumped so he can shoot. So Twelve rounds the desk to see what he can see through the window.

Behind Twelve one of the seemingly stationary bookcases swings open without a sound. As quiet as Twelve had tried to be, Jean-Claude's hearing is just so precise he could tell when the man had passed him by, gone around the desk, and paused, since there was no sound, not even a change in the young man's breathing, Jean-Claude had not yet been detected. Knowing it was too dangerous to fully come out of the safe, Jean-Claude aims his pistol from through the opened bookcase. He knows precisely where to aim and pulls the hammer of the gun back so gently as to not make the distinct click.

But Twelve has keen senses of his own, and through sheer luck, sees the reflection of a gun six feet away aimed at his back when lightning flashes bright enough to light the room. He drops just slightly when the gun fires and shatters the window, thinking and moving as quickly as he can he goes through the broken window out to a place he has the advantage.

Jean-Claude, not sure if he has shot his pursuer or not listens as careful as he can. There is nothing but the sound of rain and the low imposing roll of thunder. Surely if the man was still alive, he would have shot in retaliation by now? Jean-Claude steps out from his hiding place, hesitantly at first, then finding himself not under attack strides quickly to where a body should be. But there is none, and quickly smug arrogance becomes frightened apprehension as two hands grab the front of Jean-Claude's shirt and drag him onto the balcony.

MOVING TO:

EXT, REAR BALCONY OF OFFICE BUILDING

Not to be outdone, Jean-Claude realizes another thing: he is now very close to his aggressor with his own pistol still in hand. He shoots, and his movement is brought to a halt, and he finds himself clambering to the floor of the balcony. He hears the distinct thud of a body hitting wood and a smile of satisfaction crawls its way across Jean-Claude's lips.

TWELVE
(Rising to a yell):
You son of a BITCH!

Jean-Claude is hit squarely across the jaw, the shock of which makes him drop his gun, NOW he is defenseless. He is hit again and again, but each hit is from the left side. Something is wrong with the man's own left side, forcing himself to focus, Jean-Claude lashes out and grabs the man's left arm which is hanging limply, and bores his thumb into the bullet hole through the inner bicep.

Twelve cries out in pain and goes weak.

Jean-Claude buries his thumb further into the hole.

JEAN-CLAUDE:
How is it? How does it feel to be made feeble, that you are about to lose your life to a sightless old man? Who are you, TWELVE? What are you fighting for?

Jean-Claude reaches down and takes Twelve's two pistols and throws them over the balcony edge.

TWELVE:
My name is Jack Potter. You stole my life, my freedom…I want them back.

Jean-Claude seems to ponder this for a moment before a look of realization crawls across his face.

JEAN-CLAUDE:
Twelve is the lone survivor of a family massacre…little Jack Potter. I knew it was a mistake to leave you alive. And what about your freedom? I've given you purpose, a goal in life. You should THANK me. If I hadn't killed your family, you'd be another bumpkin living off a farm. Because of me the state gave you an education, and this is how you repay your benefactor? Through murder and treason? I AM your life, to kill me would destroy your great objective! What life do you know beyond revenge? What would you have done if you had won, boy?

Twelve, despite being in great pain now no longer worries, for he can see Sundowner in the street behind Jean-Claude, walking towards them.

TWELVE:
I'd learn to live again.

Jean-Claude furrows his brow in a look of anger and dissatisfaction.

CUT TO:

EXT, ALLEY STREET

Sundowner is forcing himself closer to the building's edge, holding the knife he had been hit with in one hand and holding the wound of it in his other. He raises the knife to throw it and calls out:

SUNDOWNER:
JEAN-CLAUDE!

CUT TO:

EXT, BALCONY

Jean-Claude looks as though he has been shocked, and begins to trace his head back and forth, listening closely to whatever he can. But he never hears the large bowie knife sailing through the air. It slams into his leg, carving out a decent chunk of flesh and he brings his hands to his upper thigh, letting go of Twelve.

Twelve stands amazingly fast and pulls from underneath his coat the old rifle he had received on his twelfth birthday. He doesn't say a word, just shoots, blasting a hole into Jean-Claude's mid-section and sending him over the balcony. Twelve lets the barrel of the rifle fall to the floor and he leans on it. It's over. He climbs down the stairs at the edge of the balcony to make sure Jean-Claude is dead.

MOVING TO:

EXT, BEHIND OFFICE BUILDING

Jean-Claude writhes in the mud, rain and blood-soaked. His bandana that covers the scars over his eyes has come loose, at this point he looks very pathetic. Twelve comes up to him, sees one of his own pistols not far and picks it up.

Jean-Claude can hear that Twelve is approaching.

JEAN-CLAUDE:
I bet you've always wondered why I killed your family. Let me tell you something about your father…

Twelve aims the pistol at Jean-Claude's head and fires, not even giving him the chance to speak. Twelve stands for a long time over the body of Jean-Claude before going to Sundowner.

MOVING TO:

EXT, ALLEY STREET
Sundowner is lying in the mud himself, very close to death from blood loss.

When Twelve reaches him, Sundowner smiles slightly.

SUNDOWNER:
It's over, even I'm dying, looks like you got your revenge.

Twelve only shakes his head.

SUNDOWNER
(Intermittently coughing):
You lived through it, now it's up to you to keep on living. Not just for yourself, but for me, for Sally, for your family, and I AM sorry about them. I hope you forgive me, but I understand if you don't. Now you need to run away, far from this place, and pray you never

raise a gun to another man ever again, start a family, and live the life that was taken from you. If you don't mind, I'm going to close my eyes now.

Twelve nods his approval and pulls Sundowner's head up onto his lap and begins to rock gently back and forth as Sundowner tries to hum some old tune interrupted by painful coughs and eventually a long sigh. Twelve is alone in the rain.

FADE OUT

INT, ANKS & BROW STABLES

Kedrick and Jarod read over a note pinned to one of the horse pens:

"Thank you for letting us use the loft, I have taken one of your horses, I'm sorry I will not return it. I have left what I hope is enough for it. My friend, The Sundowner, thanks you as well. —Twelve"

Opening the pen gate, they see an open chest filled with bank notes; the front of the chest is emblazoned with the Destiny-Star logo.

CUT TO:

EXT, TRAINSTATION

Two men are unloading a cargo car of Destiny-Star materials.

MAN 1:
Did you hear they found Mr. Maréchal dead outside of his office?

MAN 2:
Are you serious? Did they catch anyone?

MAN 1:

I don't think so, I heard that man they call Sundowner was in town, though, and Twelve, too. Lotta people saying they worked together and killed him then got outta town. Stole a buncha money from Mr. Maréchal's personal office.

MAN 2:
Wonder what'll happen to the plant?

MAN 1:
This is the third one Maréchal built, someone'll take over, no doubt, probably run it into the ground, though. That Frenchman was a great businessman.

MAN 2:
Gun shows certainly won't be as good.

We pull up and away over the train station, looking east at a rising sun, we can see someone riding a horse in that direction.

CUT TO:

EXT, OPEN COUNTRY

Twelve is riding as fast as his newly bought horse can run; for the first time, we see him smiling.

ST

DOWN IN IT
Written 2006
PUNCH/PANTS, October 2012
I was staying with my now wife, lying in bed one early morning, trying to think of some way to pull something heavy up into the attic without hurting myself. Then our cat, Devo, started meowing outside our bedroom door for his breakfast. It culminated in a thriller of man vs nature vs man. This one is just a story about a tiger in a hole, and a photography who just wants to help. This story is also the inspiration for the cover art of both PUNCH/PANTS and this collection. A friend in the Army read it for me to give me pointers on a realistic gun and its usage if someone carried one into the wilderness to protect themselves. Fortunately, he enjoyed the story and really only had a model of handgun to suggest.

The hunter heaved a great sigh of relief when his prey fell in the deep hole he and his party had dug. He was the only one here, on sentry duty, and would be here for three more weeks before the rest of the party returned to check their progress. He loaded his rifle and checked his surroundings making sure no others were around. The prey roared its anger and confusion from the deep pit, the sound of it frightening, but the hunter was glad they had finally acquired their goal.

He walked over, intending to deliver a killing blast and cover the trap again, but something rustled close behind him. He was quick to turn, swinging his rifle, ready to shoot, but the prey's mate had been close by, too close. She leaped out at him filling his entire field of vision, his only reaction to pull the trigger, no time to aim. The last thing he would hear would be that sound of his rifle blast. The beast fell upon him, ripping out his throat, the shear shock of its great weight upon him knocked him unconscious before he ever felt any pain.

*　　*　　*

I had left Katka early in the morning, my guides offering prayers, warnings *against* and well-wishes *for* my journey. I was to take a boat down one of the rivers flowing through the Sundarbans, loaded down with camouflaged gear and essentials, so that I could grab some photos of the wild life in its natural state. I would be a week out from any civilization and four days gone to find as much as I could to photograph. I had studied and talked to locals, the part of the forest I was to venture into supposedly had very little predator presence. To tell the truth, I wouldn't mind coming across a Royal Bengal Tiger or two to capture those brilliant orange coats among the dark green foliage.

I took several great shots on the way in, spotted deer, several birds and an abundance of crocodiles sunning in the morning brilliance.

"Are you sure you want to do this by yourself, there are many guides who know the dangers of the forest!" my boatman pleaded as we neared my drop off point.

"The more people I have with me, the fewer animals there will be to see! You know well enough I was in the United States Marines, I can fend for myself." I assured him.

"Take care, George, I have prayed to Bonbibi for you, I suggest you keep him in your heart while in the forest, perhaps he shall protect you!"

I placed my hand upon his shoulder and smiled. I unloaded my gear, a very large backpack with all my rations and necessities. I pulled from the holster at my hip the Smith & Wesson Model 500 I had brought in case of predators.

"Bonbibi can watch over me, I hope he may guide me and Dirty Harry here if need be." I said waving.

My guides down the river bade farewell and I turned to look at the thick forest, cut open here only by the river. I groaned as I lifted my pack, but I was excited more than anything. I slid the pistol back into the holster and swung around my camera. The only thing I wanted to shoot was fantastic pictures. I was due to return back to Katka well before the rainy season set in, but out here it seemed as though the rain had never stopped. Wet and muddy, dark, humid and musty, I would come out of this place looking worse than a monster. I couldn't be happier.

My camera found all kinds of brightly colored birds, insects, reptiles, and amphibians. I had been sanctioned by a nature magazine to capture the wild settings of the Sundarbans well away from the fishing villages and populated areas. The reason for the length of my stay here was to absorb it, an article was to accompany the photos and I didn't mind taking a sabbatical after my stint in the military anyway. Work gave way to mystery very quickly, however, when I heard a pitiful moan emanate from the recesses of the forest.

I expected to hear all manner of oddities while in the wild, but this sounded like something genuinely depressed, hurt and lonely, an injured boar? I tried to track the source of the sound, intermittently snapping pictures, but the low guttural moan seemed to echo from all angles, and it was night of my first day before I knew it. The dense forest crowded out sunlight a great deal in areas, but when it had become almost pitch, I gave up and erected my small tent.

Barely big enough to hold me and my things, it mostly served to guard against mosquitoes and other vermin. I had a certain amount of clean water with me and several MRE's that had no need of heating, but I also had butane to light torches in case I needed to purify water or start a fire. I snacked this evening and only sipped at the water. Sleep came quickly.

I slept only about seven hours before the cacophony of birds and animals woke me at daybreak. Folding the tent, I could see all around me beams of sunlight piercing the forest ceiling, the flittering of birds and the evident rustle of floor creatures. There were no growls or moans this morning and I found the touch of concern gone as my eye became that of a photographer's again.

So many birds befell my lens, white ibis, black-necked stork, swamp francolin, white-collared kingfisher, brown-winged kingfisher, Asian dowitcher, too many to name, I think if I shot all day long for the entire week, I could not capture the abundance. Lizards, too, from geckos to monitors, pythons coiling along tree branches trying to put as much of their skin to sunlight as possible. I half-feared I would run out of digital storage before my time in the forest was done!

Then the animal-moan returned. It startled me at first because of how close it sounded now. I had kept good track of where I had been and how to return to the river, but something drove me to find the mysterious source of the cry. I stilled myself, steadied my breathing and waited to hear it again amid all the chirping and movement among the foliage. When it came, it was quieter now, which I believe made it easier to find since it did not echo throughout the trees.

What I finally found was disturbing; a macabre scene of man versus nature, yet here there was no decided victor. A clearing revealed a man, mauled by a tiger, a rifle lying well away from his body, clearly decomposing and the corpse of his assailant in not much better shape suffering from the same rate of rot. I judged it must have been weeks since the event transpired. I deduced the man must have dealt a killing shot on the attacking tiger, but the tiger had had enough strength and life to kill him as well. Just beyond them, where the clearing re-met the forest was a hole covered with dried foliage.

Careful and quiet, I set down my pack and stepped to the edge of the pit and pulled away the debris. Within, a living tiger, cramped with only enough room to lie down slightly curled. His ribs were showing, and he breathed heavily, obviously weak. The man must have been a poacher who had dug the trap. When he went to retrieve his prey, its mate must have ambushed him. The tiger looked up wearily and moaned again. It was one of the most pitiful things I have ever seen and the vision of gore just behind me paled by comparison.

It coincided with the entrance of two more people, more poachers from the looks of them. We all stared each other down, one raised his rifle, leveling it with my chest and motioning me away from the pit. He followed me, keeping the gun trained at my midsection as the other one approached the hole and pulled out a pistol. My captor glanced away from me to watch as his partner was going to kill the defenseless tiger.

I let out a loud "No!"

Survival instincts and Marine training kicked in, I grabbed the rifle and holding it away from me pulled my own gun from underneath my shirt, shooting the would-be tiger killer. His body fell forward into the hole, briefly I wondered if it would be sufficient to feed the tiger, if he was even strong enough to eat. The remaining poacher tried to wrestle his gun back, I turned my eyes back onto him and instead of the anger that had been in his face I saw an incredible fear. The Model

500 can fire a 0.8 oz. bullet at 1,975 feet per second, generating muzzle-energy of over 3,030 foot-pounds of force; at three inches, nothing much of his face was left as it exploded through the back of his skull.

I looked around making sure there were no more of them hanging back and after determining they were the only ones, I returned to check on the tiger. He had started into the fallen poacher, ravenous. I had heard the Bengalis were man-eaters, but to see it, firsthand? Suddenly there was a spark of wondering if I had done the right thing. Then the tiger turned his head to look up out of his prison and we locked eyes. Whatever guilt had sprouted melted immediately; this may have been a wild animal, but I saw *gratitude*.

Surely there wasn't enough there to bring the tiger back to full strength, and for how long it was to get in and out of this place, I couldn't just leave him. The poachers must have wanted the pelt, and I was sure for how deep in the jungle they were that was just what they were after. I had no qualms taking their lives. These might be a dangerous predator in their own world, but no man had the right to take their lives in this way. The tiger in the hole continued eating the body. I pulled out my camera but couldn't bring myself to take the pictures.

I set out to find more for the tiger to eat, I wanted him to be strong and able to survive another two weeks in the hole, it would be that long before I could come back with a crew to save him. Obviously, the hole was too deep and small for the tiger to maneuver to jump or climb out. I made my way back to the river to hopefully find some spotted deer. Despite hope I was surprised to come upon a small herd of the illusive creatures watering along the banks, they were jumpy and leery, though, due to a couple of crocs hanging out, sunning along the opposite bank. Fortunately, the deer were on my side of the river.

I got as close as I could without being noticed and readied my pistol. As I was about to shoot the closest one to me, a crocodile neither I nor the deer had seen exploded out of the water dragging and rolling one of the deer into the water, the other deer scattered away. I sighed heavily and put my gun away, sitting down where I was, impressed with what I had seen but wondering how else I could feed the tiger.

Coming back into the clearing I had heard something both familiar and wholly alien at the same time. I approached the hole and there, resting from his meal, the tiger had curled back to a laying position and was *purring*. Not quite like a domestic housecat, the vibrations only seemed to come as he exhaled, but recognizable. It was the first time I had ever heard a big cat purr and for the situation, it was the most beautiful sound I could hear in this dark atmosphere.

It had been a long day and I could tell from the dwindling light evening was coming. I wanted to set camp in the clearing but I could barely tolerate the smell of the two long dead corpses and I knew my victims would start to smell soon. With concentrated effort I pulled them into some dense foliage. I doubted anyone would come looking for them any time soon. The dead tiger, despite an accelerated rate of decomposition was still close to three hundred pounds and getting it away from the clearing took far more strength and energy. Once I got it several yards out, I returned to the clearing and sat on the edge of the hole.

"Hello, Tiger, my name is George. I'm gonna try and help you as best I can."

The tiger didn't seem to pay attention to me.

"There's a beachfront resort town in Greece, it's called Skala. I've always thought it was extremely beautiful there; you're a very pretty cat, Tiger, and I think I'm going to call *you* Skala. It's a human thing, we like to name stuff."

The tiger let out a grunt. He may have belched, but to me it sounded as though he didn't care for me talking to him.

"All right, Skala, I understand. You're saying, 'I don't need some stinking human helping me or calling me names!' But here I am, and there you are in a hole. I'm going to make sure you live through this. I just want to make sure you're fed full enough you can make it another two weeks. I'm sure I can get a crew with a crane or a helicopter to pull you out of their and set you back where you belong."

Night fell and I set up my tent. Again, Skala began to purr. I went to sleep to his sounds; surely, to his thanks.

Day three, I went back to the river to look for something to bring back to Skala, his belly looked fuller, but he would need more. When I had left him, he had been licking and gnawing on a bone. There was a certain terror to the sight in the hole, but I felt I had become a part of nature now, and where animals like this might not truly help each other out, I could not just leave the tiger to die a slow agonizing death at the bottom of a pit.

I did bring my camera and took several pictures as I was waiting for some sort of prey to come close. At one point I had sat so still for so long that a small deer came out from the foliage literally two feet from me, I could reach out and touch it. At first, I thought of letting it go, it being so innocent and awesome. But thoughts of Skala, of the crocodiles in the water, of predators in general sprang to mind. They don't kill for the sport or thrill, this is food, the cycle of life.

I let the deer go closer to the water, removed my gun from its holster, took careful aim and squeezed the trigger. The deer fell dead at the edge of the water, several birds took flight and further down from me I could hear the startled splash into the water of a crocodile. I stood, replacing my gun and stepped out to drag the deer back to the clearing.

Transporting it through the forest in a fireman's carry I caught the curious gaze of several monkeys, birds and lizards. Finally making it back, I found the tiger sniffing at the air, sitting at the bottom of his pit.

"Lunch time, Skala!" I said cheerily.

I let the deer's body down near the edge of the hole and briefly saw Skala's pupils dilate in anticipation. All the effort of last evening and this morning made me quite hungry as well. I broke into an MRE and sat at the edge of the hole and the two of us ate together.

"Tomorrow my friends will be returning to retrieve me; I hope that what you've eaten will fill you enough. I'll rush them of course and be back as soon as possible."

Skala was purring again, listening to me idly chat.

"You must want some water."

I took out a pot and poured out a bottle of water, rigging some twine to keep the pot upright as I lowered it into the pit. Skala watched curiously, shaking his head once to get some flies out of his ears. When it was to him, he sniffed furtively, lapped once, and then looked at me.

"I'm not one of them, Skala, I want to help you, you may want to eat me, but you can't help that, it's what you are. But I'm going to do my best to make sure you live through this."

He drank the rest of the water and then started playing with the pot. I pulled on the twine to move the pot and he lit up just like a housecat. I moved it around to play with him and he batted and bit, huffing as he did. I laughed and he looked at me curiously, I looked down at him and blinked with a very light smile. He blinked slowly back and then began to chew on the pot again.

The day wore on and I tried to take more photos, but I began to prefer the company of Skala. He may not let me pet him, I may not even have his trust, but I felt he realized he'd be dead if not for my presence, so he tolerated it. When I came back, I was surprised to see him stretching within the hole, his paws were only inches from the edge of the hole. He stopped stretching and stared at me, still standing with his paws outstretched. They were massive and I took a very dangerous chance and reached into the hole, he stared at my hand, but didn't back away. I touched his paw which was much larger than my own hand, he never moved, I scratched lightly where his "fingers" met the paw.

He blinked at me again and slowly descended back into the hole to curl up and lay down.

As evening came so did a storm. With the storm came a very heavy rain that inundated the forest floor. Darkness came very early thanks to the clouds high above. I checked on Skala and to my horror saw that the hole was retaining water, already covering his paws. If it continued to rain like this, he could be drowned easily with so little space, there was no way he could tread water and make it out on his own.

There was no way I was going to be able to leave him in there for two weeks if a rain could come in and wipe him out like this, I had to get him out and now. I pulled from my pack a trench shovel which I had been using to cover my own waste but now I was going to put it to full use. I began digging a foot wide swath at the edge of the hole in hopes to give a hold for Skala to grab and pull himself out of the hole on his own.

Mud and clumps of earth fell into the hole on Skala's head, he flashed his teeth and rumbled, annoyed, but watched with great interest at what I was doing. As I got a great amount of earth moved, the rain came even harder, making it very slick where I was, I had to take great care not to fall in the hole myself and become Skala's next meal. He actually stood again, testing his paws at where I was digging, then, like a cat who knows there's something just below the surface, started digging as well. He made grunting noises; I think a desperate fear mixed with exertion in the hope of escape was driving his intuition. He could tell what I was doing and wanted to expedite his own escape.

Eventually I had a very small ramp built at the edge of the hole that the tiger reached up and gripped, his massive claws digging deep into dark thick mud. He moaned as he kicked with his hind legs, dragging and pushing himself up.

"Come on, Skala, just a little more!" I shouted excitedly.

But Skala slid back, unable to get sufficient grip. I cursed wildly and Skala himself let out his own frustration in a roar.

Driven by mad frustration I started digging deeper at the edges making a large V even deeper into the edge of the pit. This time Skala gave a hop with all the strength he could muster and slammed his front paws into the earth, kicking with his back legs and forcing himself up and out. There were grunts and moans and heavy breathing, from both of us, I backed away as it looked like Skala was well on his way out.

Then Skala was horizontal, low to the ground, no doubt exhausted, using all the energy he had gained in the last day and a half in this one effort. He stood, breathing heavy, his mouth wide and tongue hanging slightly. The rain fell all around us, the tiger was free.

Skala swung his massive head around to see me, still panting; we stared at each other for what seemed an age. He blinked at me, slow and heavy, then walked out of the clearing, leaving me be. Snapping to my senses I grabbed up my camera and set the aperture wide open in hopes of gaining just enough light, fortunately for me, lightning flashed as I took the shot. I hoped I would get something out of it.

Not wanting to lose my trail because of the rain, I made my way back to the river, the same place I had been hunting, and traveled along the shore to where my meeting place would be. I watched in the brief instance of light from the lightning as the river rose and knew I had done the right thing.

When morning broke, the rain had stopped. I exited my small tent and was greeted with sunlight and guns in my face. Two more poachers, their boat just down shore; obviously checking after the first three. They began talking rapid fire, I couldn't understand them; I stood slowly, raising my hands. Now they chattered among themselves, and one pointed his pistol at me, pulled its hammer and what happened next I never expected.

A flash of orange and black knocked them both down; the tiger had jumped out of the forest from just behind me. It crunched one of the poacher's heads in its powerful jaws. The second poacher scrambled to gain his bearings, unsure of what had just occurred. I stood transfixed. The tiger whirled on his hind legs, slashing out with claws extended. The second poacher was slashed across the back and barely had time to let out a scream before the tiger bit onto, and through, his neck. The tiger looked at me while still holding his prey.

"Skala?" I whispered.

He continued to stare at me, the look was menacing, but it said to me quite clearly, *We are even.*

Skala dragged the one poacher into the brush, and I was quick to gather my things. I walked down the riverbank in the direction my boat would be returning. There was no way I could convince anyone of my story, I could show them the dead bodies and explain what had happened, and I did, but people gave me a questioning glance at the thought of a bond between myself and the Bengali. No charges were pressed against me, nor was I to be held for any amount of time, it was deemed the men I had killed, were shot down in self-defense. Quietly, my embassy representative said it was most likely because I had killed poachers, loathed it would seem, across the world.

My boatman, however, before I was gone from Katka, told me he believed my story. "Bonbibi watched over you and over the tiger, too. You were blessings upon each other!"

Having gone through my pictures, I had come across one that was a dense and very dark green, with a swath of orange, black, and white. The picture had a smeared appearance, but at the same time an oil painting quality, such was the bright contrast of Skala and his surroundings. I gave a copy to him and bade him farewell.

ATG

CTRL+V

Written 2006
PUNCH/PANTS, October 2012

*In the wake of the Human Cloning Prohibition Act of 2005, I thought
of some Frankenstein-ian scientists doing it anyway in an offshore
lab—for giggles really, just to do it. There is a twist, that cloning is
either the end of all things or what we're meant to do.*

The young man entered into the room from one door, on the wall
opposite him was another door, though it had no handle. When he
turned to see his own door hissing shut, there was no handle on the
inside of this one either. The room itself was quite nondescript, off-
white with some florescent lights interspersed between drab ceiling
tiles. In the middle of the room were a very simple table and two chairs
that didn't look like they would be comfortable for very long. The wall
to his left featured a very large mirror, which would be a two-way
mirror that the guards and psychiatric doctors would be monitoring
through from the other side. The floor was a boring beige Berber.

He stood there just inside the room, nervous, waiting, until a
heavy magnetic click signaled that the other door was opening now.
Another man, much older, walked in. They stared at each other for
what seemed a good long while. There were many stark similarities
between them, they were the same height, same-colored eyes, the
older man was definitely graying but one could tell that, at one time,
they had the same color hair as well. There was an odd, shared
sensation between them, that of one looking at himself in a mirror in
the future and one in the past.

"Victor," the older man said with recognition. "I admit I was
curious who would come to see me, I've had no visitors since being
incarcerated."

Victor swallowed hard; introductions would not be necessary.

"One hour, gentleman." A non-descript voice said from an unseen
audio system.

"Shall we sit?" the older man asked.

He moved to the table in the middle of the room. He was wearing
a loose-fitting gray jumpsuit, "COLORADO DEPARTMENT OF

CORECTIONS" in block letters on the right breast, and as he turned, a randomized serial number emblazoned across the back shoulders. Around both his ankles and wrists were small silver bracelets with alternating red and green lights, currently they remained on green. These were nerve restraint shackles, should he, or any prisoner wearing them, attempt something out of bounds, they could paralyze and restrict movement.

Victor doubted they would be put to use, this prison was for non-violent offenders, and the older man was quite eager at a chance to speak with him.

Victor stepped forward, pulling out his own chair, he felt an excited nausea come over him, took a deep breath, and sat. He croaked, choking on lost words, but the old man already knew.

"Where to start?"

Victor sighed and smiled. "How?"

"Of course, you would ask that question, it's legitimate, but it would take me longer than our allotted time..."

"Of course, I'm sorry, Dr. Mickelson—"

"Call me Tracy, it's only fair." He said cutting off the formality.

"Are you sure you don't want me to call you *Dad*?" Victor suddenly snapped.

Tracy looked stunned, then bowed his head. "I didn't think you would be so venomous, though I can understand that; I suppose I deserve it."

It was Victor's turn to bow his head, for an instant, they held the exact same pose.

Tracy took a large breath, looked back up at the bowed head of the younger man. "How did you find out?"

"It was only recently." Victor said his head still low. "I had been asking who my real parents were, why I was in such private studies when I knew other kids went to school in groups, why people I never knew seemed to recognize me."

"Did they ever say anything to you, those who knew you?"

"No, but I could tell they saw me as though I was; I don't know...a celebrity?"

"But they finally told you?"

"Yes, when I turned sixteen, I had a party, was allowed to have over the very few friends I had, and after the party had gone down and my friends were off home, my foster-mother brought in a large box, with several articles and videos. She also let down the firewall on my internet connection so that I could seek anything additional out on my own. I didn't sleep for three days."

"That's understandable; I bet you felt like a completely different person."

"I didn't feel like a person at all, I was a thing, I understood why people gawked and why I was never allowed a lot of access to the outside world. Here I was no longer human, but…"

"You are human, Victor, if anything you're more human than anyone else."

"What do you mean?"

"A lot of technical jargon that would no doubt waste our time, let's just say, we made sure you were *perfect*."

Anger flashed though Victor's eyes, but he let it pass without saying anything. The silence began to draw long, but before Tracy could continue on, Victor spoke. "Why 'Victor?'"

"Oh, several reasons, any one of them as good as another." Tracy smiled, musing on past memory.

"Don't tell me 'Frankenstein's Monster,' I don't think I can handle that."

Tracy let out a laugh. "No, coincidence on that count, I assure you. No, you're not a monster, nor did we try to be Frankenstein, you were one of five, so there was the Roman-numeral 'V,' a lot of the process was actually handled in computers, I'm sure you're well aware of keyboard shortcuts; control-V? That was one that stuck with me the most, and Victor happened to be the first strong name that came to mind."

"Why did you do it; why am I here?"

Tracy suddenly felt a rush, elation and terror at the same time. It was the age-old questions that Victor was asking, though in this case there were answers that could be given. "Why am I here," "Who am I," "What is my purpose?" Could he sufficiently answer these questions to this young man; was he fit to answer them? Was Victor fit to hear them? He stared at Victor eye to eye for another long moment. Decidedly so, this young man could handle it.

"Curiosity; a desire to prove to the world it could be done and that there was nothing wrong with it. We were thinking of the scientific advancements that could be made through it."

"That's a disgusting answer." Victor looked reviled.

Tracy leaned back in his chair, setting his hands in his lap. "Why did you come here?"

Victor shook his head. "You said I was one of five, where are the other four?"

"You're the only one, the others failed."

"You terminated them?"

"No, they failed, they never held on, they didn't make it, it was a trial-and-error procedure. We do everything in batches to allow for chance, variance, to see what happens different between subject 1 and subject 3."

"Subjects!"

"Victor, I don't expect you to understand or agree, but you are here, we succeeded!"

Victor stood from the table and paced on his side of the room. He looked at the mirror, did he want their help? No, he was looking at his own reflection, and he could see the old man, watching him, there was a look of concern. Victor faced him.

"And had you not been caught? What then?"

"You were to be revealed to the world, we knew what we were doing was illegal, we knew that once you were revealed we would go to prison. I think the main difference is you would have grown up knowing, rather than having it crash down on you like it has. You would have asked all these questions at a much younger age and been able to grapple with it, and when you were released into the world, you would know your significance, rather than trying to find significance for your life."

"I'm a clone. That's my significance! That would have been it; that *is* it; that's *all* it will ever be. No matter what I achieve in my own life, that is it. I am a clone."

"There's more to it than that!" Tracy pleaded.

"What? I can be your body-in-reserve? When your heart goes bad you can take mine? You succeeded in *body farming*? What about *me*? Don't *I* count?"

"Of course, you count; you count for something far greater than some science fiction horror story! You are human, made by a human; you give this race hope of survival in a world destroyed *by* humans. You are a son of science, insuring man's continued existence, why leave it to nature to evolve into a hotter world with less fresh water when we can take destiny into our own hands!"

"Now I can see why you are in prison, you're stark-raving mad! Do you really believe that?"

Tracy realized he was leaning forward in his seat, on the verge of jumping forward. "I-I'm sorry. Yes, I get excited. But that is the truth of it, of the entire experiment. We wanted to make a perfect human, one who could continue on, immune to the death we wrought upon the Earth. Have you ever been sick?"

Victor thought about it. He had had colds, which should prove Tracy wrong! "I've been sick; I've had colds several times!"

"That lasted any longer than a week out of an entire year, and not every year? And when you feel those symptoms, you can almost gauge how long you're going to be sick?"

Victor thought about it, and it was true, his immune system had always been referred to as very strong, and he had never had anything worse than a cold. He had never even suffered allergies when he saw those around him congested and red-eyed in the spring or early fall.

He wanted to rally against Tracy for trying to play God, but something held him back. Something almost wanted to thank Tracy for giving him a life without suffering, though he suffered mentally now.

Why am I here? The question danced and danced throughout Victor's mind, but he knew, had known for quite some time, and that was the reason he was here.

"I sought you out in a matter of days after finding out whom and what I am. I needed to speak with you, needed to convey a…message."

Tracy looked puzzled now, but Victor continued on.

"It's never struck me or anyone else as odd, I am, for all intents and purposes, a human being, but it should probably mean a great deal to you; I dream."

Tracy's confusion shifted, now there was steeped curiosity.

"I have dreamt as long as I can remember. I read that they found your facility on a remote island, not far from Cuba, you and several other scientists, building up a lab with your own funds. I saw pictures of the lab and knew them from dreams. I saw pictures of you and the other scientists and already knew your faces.

"Before I ever knew my true past, I had spoken to you, though, obviously not for real."

Where Victor was only a few weeks older than sixteen, he suddenly looked identical to Tracy, the doctor who had volunteered his own blood and tissue to the experiment due to a very healthy family and personal medical history. Victor swallowed hard and moved forward to the table again, leaning in to speak to Tracy in more hushed tones.

Tracy imagined the people on the other side of the mirror all leaning forward in anticipation as well. Though, Tracy realized things had grown quite silent, there had been a faint electric hum of the light bulbs, of just the static noise of the world around them, now all of it was gone. Victor had him locked in his gaze and where Tracy felt a need to be suddenly afraid, he trusted Victor, knew that everything was going as it should, and that he just needed to relax and hear what was coming next.

"The night before my birthday, you were in a dream, in a white room, but it only looked like you, it was someone else. He told me to tell you, that what you did was not wrong."

Tracy's eyes squinted. "What is this?"

But it was as though Victor did not hear him. "That what you did was according to design; that humans had faltered a long time ago and stayed dumb despite themselves. You are persecuted now, but one day, you, Tracy Mickelson, will be viewed as the man who freed humans from their own self-inflicted bondage.

"God put restrictions on Humans, but to deny the abilities one is capable of, is to slap God in the face and spit on his…" he trailed off.

242

"Plan." Tracy finished.

"You see?"

Tracy thought about it long and hard. He had touched on it in his own thoughts before; the whole reason for their experiment, to *help* humanity, to make sure humanity lived, and lived as best they could."

"You, sir, the man who created me, *spoke the language of God*, and I for one, have the great privilege to say, I have met my *Maker*."

When Victor leaned away, the room seemed to swirl and suddenly Victor was standing much farther away without seeming to have ever taken any steps. They stood in a verdant field, bright and warm. Despite Victor was standing several paces away, he was radiant, but was not surrounded by the tranquil environment in which Tracy found himself. Rather, Victor stood in the room still, on the opposite side of the table, a bizarre diorama placed in an equally bizarre and detached beautiful world.

"Is this…?" Tracy asked, almost afraid of the answer.

"It is whatever you want it to be," said Victor, though it was from very far away now. "I have a message to convey."

Tracy turned and was enveloped by his new world.

The door behind Victor opened quickly, and forcibly, a doctor and guard rushed past him to check on the body of Dr. Mickelson, who was wheezing uncontrollably and clutching at his chest. His eyes stared blankly at the table. Another doctor tugged at Victor's arm, urging the boy away from the gruesome scene.

"You don't need to see this; we'll take care of him."

"What's going on?" Victor feigned concern.

"Most likely a stroke, he should be fine, there's a fantastic medical facility here, he should make it; he's been healthy up until now."

Victor smiled. "Yes, he'll be fine, I'm sure of it, and will live happily ever after!"

THW

VEIL
Written 2008
PUNCH/PANTS, October 2012
I have written a number of female protagonists, often from their point of view, and I often wonder if I'm not trying to see the world the way my mom did. I had my mother and my aunts in my earliest days. I had as many female friends as male. Writing to inhabit another point of view, I believe, helps me stay open-minded, and open-hearted. The protagonist of VEIL is not based on anyone, and the conceit is a bit Twilight Zone, but I can understand being angry with a box and no one letting you out. This is a gaslight mystery with some science fiction thrown in to make you wonder just how much gas is actually in the room.

Janelle awoke to see the white ceiling above her. The ceiling connected in imperceptible corners with the white walls and again to the white floor. She stifled a yawn and threw back the white comforter and white sheets. As she sat up and slid her legs over the edge of the bed, she was reminded at the sight of her knees that not everything could be so clean. Out of her periphery she saw the one contrasting thing in the room, herself. The mirror, it could be argued, was not white, either. But so long as she was not standing in front of it, it only reflected white surfaces. She was Caucasian, and quite pale, but the pink pigments and the short blonde hair, was starkly not white.

Moving across the small space she stared disgusted at her naked, *contaminated*, reflection. She knew that she was not unsightly, the nurses tried to convince her regularly that she was, in fact, beautiful. She pinched one of her nipples between her index finger and thumb and lifted up until pain shot through her breast. She watched the flesh bounce back into place as she let go and sighed. She picked at herself as though her own body was a loathsome specimen better left in a lab. Some might see a lovely woman, but she only saw this impure shell.

Grabbing the white robe from the white hook next to the mirror, she stepped out of her reflection's view. Approaching a small panel three feet from the floor, she spoke aloud, "Tea, Earl Grey, hot." She could hear the synthesizer producing the clean white cup that would soon contain her beverage. Her monthly government credits would deplete by only two points for the cup of tea. She tried to keep breakfast small and often only drank a cup of tea or coffee without actually eating anything. Once the amalgamation was complete, the protective panel slid open revealing her tea. She grabbed it and the small saucer it was placed on and sat in the plush white chair at the foot of her bed.

Balancing the saucer on her knee while sipping her Earl Grey, she could see the first headlines appear within the imaging membrane on the wall. Stills and video proclaimed the day's interplanetary news: the now five-year-old construction effort of new apartment complexes on Mare Crisium had been halted again due to finding more and more consumable ores beneath the Moon's surface. Earth-type mosses were acclimating well to the south polar region of Mars and the Terra Secondus Group proclaimed the Martian atmosphere would be breathable in the not-too-distant future of several hundred human generations. Which of course lead to the headline regarding the Earth.

"Equatorial Zones Showing Promise of Rehabilitation."

Scientists had been hypothesizing for years that Earth would right itself after the firestorm that had sent humans scattering throughout the solar system. Janelle gritted her teeth, Dr. Purcell would definitely make mention of this.

As though on cue, the seal of her lone door hissed and in strode Dr. Thomas Purcell, with his *off*-white lab coat and distressing black hair. Perfectly quaffed and shining as though it were wet, Janelle couldn't recall a single hair ever being out of place.

"Good morning, Janelle!" he said so cheerily.

"Have you been implanted with a telepathic probe, Doctor?" she asked.

"Were you thinking about me?"

"I saw the headline regarding the Equatorial Zones…Earth is becoming habitable again…you're always trying to discuss the surface. I figured either you planted that headline today or maybe you *heard* me reading it."

He looked at the wall absent-mindedly, "I hadn't seen that. And no, no *telepathic* implants for me; trying to stay true to my human heritage."

"So, are you here to *screw* me then?"

Purcell scoffed. "Feeling bullish this morning, eh?"

Janelle gave him a blank stare, sipping at her tea.

"Listen, I've been assigned to you for close to a year now, I see no more affects to your brief exposure--"

Janelle finally engaged, "Are you telling me we're through, Doctor?"

There was an edge of worry to her voice. She had been locked away from society for so long that Dr. Purcell and a handful of nurses were her only connection, beyond the interplanetary network, to the outside world. Purcell putting in his notice and releasing her from his care was both exhilarating and terrifying.

Purcell smiled. "No, ma'am, I've requested from the Agency to take you to the surface."

"The Sea of Tranquility? It's just miners and scaffolding," she frowned; she would rather he was releasing her from his care.

"Earth."

Janelle very slowly placed her cup of tea back on the saucer balanced on her knee. "I think you did have that story planted, Doctor."

"I've gained special permissions from the Agency and Senator Clarence Dill to take you to a Clean Zone, there's green vegetation and clean air and drinkable water--"

"I've never set foot on Earth, Doctor…this is coming as a shock, and I must admit a bit frightening."

Dr. Purcell sat on the end of the bed close to Janelle's chair. "It's time for you to get away from all of *this*." He said gesturing to his surroundings.

"But the Earth was contaminated; I was contaminated…"

Janelle thought of the incidents that very nearly destroyed all life on the Earth. A massive solar flare had shot a wave of radiation that had reached out across the distance and licked at the atmosphere. Breaking through the Earth's natural protective layers it had destroyed life in only a matter of weeks. She, on the other hand, found herself in a reactor room, exposed to the open core without a protective suit. She found herself quarantined and put into decontamination for a week with little human contact. The psychological ramifications matched the extinction event on the planet: they had each been wiped barren. Disgusted by anything that was not clean, including her body, she had broken down into a husk of her former self and hadn't even left this room since coming under Dr. Purcell's care.

"I can't go to the surface." she said.

"It's time to get you out of here, Janelle, you have to get away from all this sterility, you need to get away from this information overload," he said waving his hand at the wall she had been reading from. "The *Moon* is no place for you to get well."

"Neither is the Earth."

"It's a *Clean* Zone."

She sighed, burying her face in her free hand.

"We can provide a sedative, once you've relaxed, we can put you in--" he searched as though he had forgotten the right word. "*Stasis*. We'll make the trip down and by the time you wake up, you'll be in the Clean Zone; you say the News even discussed it this morning."

"Where is it?"

"As if it matters, Janelle, it's the surface." He said with a frustrated laugh.

"I mean is it one of the equatorial zones or one of the scientific communities under the domes?"

"Domes?" Purcell asked confused, then shook his head. "No, the *domed* communities are for study and aren't fit for what we're looking for. Senator Dill cleared us for an open area; prestigious, really. Private homes on acres of land, away from the hubbub of society."

"*Homes*?" she asked disbelieving. "Plural?"

"Portions of the Earth are safe to live in now. Nature found a way, I suppose."

"And you singled me out for this, addressed a Senator on my behalf?"

"The Agency feels you're an acceptable subject to test an environmental therapy, perhaps all this seclusion has done more harm than even your initial event. We want to see you well, Janelle."

"I don't really have a choice then do I?"

"Do you really want to stay in your white room forever?"

"It's clean…" she said sullen.

"Nurse Baxter will be in with the sedative momentarily."

Janelle's eyes widened just about as wide as the saucer on her knee. "We're going now?"

"If it were a week from now, or even *tomorrow*, you would fret about it. I know it's a terrible trick on my part, but it's for your own benefit. You'll be away from all of this, reintegrate yourself into some sort of *normalcy*."

Unhinged by the sudden demand put upon her, the cup and saucer toppled to the floor, shattering and spilling tea as she stood up abruptly.

"This is unacceptable! I do not *feel* well enough to do such a thing, Doctor--"

"But *I* feel it's time, and the Agency agrees, we need to get you out of this room if you're going to start getting any better."

Seething, Janelle stared at him. The door opened and Nurse Baxter entered with a silver platter with two small cups, one presumably with the sedative pills and the other with water. The urge struck Janelle to send the platter against the floor as well, but she stayed her hand as she examined the nurse. Miriam Baxter wore a white dress uniform that went to just above her knee and wore a matching white cap pinned into the tight bun of her red hair. Nurse Baxter and Dr. Purcell went home at night, maybe to family, went out on the weekend with friends. They didn't care about the air or how clean a surface was. They could stare out at the stars from the surface and see the Earthrise.

She looked at Purcell. "I'm scared."

He stood and came to Nurse Baxter's side. "That's fine, that's why I suggested you sleep for the trip. You'll wake up at the cottage and we'll get you acclimated before we start getting you into society. It's a small community, but a good jumping off point for you."

248

Janelle reached uneasily for the two small cups Miriam held out. She took the pills and downed the water.

Purcell smiled warmly. "Now go ahead and lie back down; once you've fallen asleep, we'll take care of the rest."

Janelle nodded and lay back down on the bed, clutching her robe at her chest, and stared at the white ceiling.

*　　*　　*

Janelle awoke to see a white ceiling. This wasn't her room, though. The ceiling was only inches from her face and dusty. The room was darkened, and the air stank like something she had never smelled before. Had she woken up in her stasis pod? She tried to move but found herself bound. It must be the pod; she had woken up in the middle of the flight. Surely a doctor would notice her vitals change and come and check on her.

"Hello?" she cried.

Nothing; only the low rumbling of the ship's engines humming through the cabin.

Claustrophobic fear gripped her and she thrashed in her limited space, pulling her right arm free. Looking down she saw that she was actually strapped to a board that lay askew in a large compartment she couldn't recognize. She used her free arm to undo the straps holding her to the board.

Flopping to her side as she freed herself, she noticed that the board was leaning on something. Realizing her compartment was much larger than she first thought she moved the board and saw the body of Dr. Purcell; his neck dark and bent at a disturbing angle. His eyes were half open, but it was obvious he was no longer looking through them. She looked around and saw the foul odor was accompanied by thick smoke filling the strange cabin. Seeing two small, square windows at the back of her cramped space, she crawled in search of some sort of release mechanism. A small handle twisted in her hand and popped a door open and bright light flooded in.

Stumbling out of the enclosure, her hands and knees scraped against a gravel surface. Looking down at herself she was wearing a dingy hospital gown and had no shoes. Turning to see what container she had just been in, her mind struggled with what she saw. It looked like an antique van, lying on its side, black smoke billowing into the sky from the front. She came around the side and saw an acrid liquid had spilled on the ground from the vehicle's guts and bright orange flame danced across its surface. What she thought was the thrum of engines was actually fire burning. Also, the crashed vehicle had *rubberized* tires. Rubber! Rubber hadn't been used in tires for centuries.

She gripped her head, trying to come to terms with what she was seeing. Where was the hove? Where were the directional spires to guide the hoves? Why was there rubber and combustible fuel in this thing? A driver and an attendant were sprawled on the ground in front of the truck, dead. Another black car with its front-end demolished, also on fire, didn't seem to promise any survivors either. Looking around she saw tall trees and a curve in the road. There had been an accident and she was the only survivor…but where was she? Was this the Clean Zone? Why the archaic vehicles? That hardly seemed the technology to use in a *Clean* Zone.

The most important thing now was to find help. Looking at the direction they had been going, she decided to travel down the road the way they had been headed. Before leaving the scene, she checked the bodies for communicators of any kind and was disturbed to find nothing.

Walking only a few yards down she saw a side road with a box on a post. In hand painted letters was familiar writing spelling "Purcell." "A real *mailbox*?" she queried.

It was not so surprising the doctor might own a house on the Earth's surface. But that a mailbox was there, that it looked *old*, that the road looked well-used, and that antique vehicles had wrecked killing their passengers with no way to signal for help began to make Janelle feel sick. She traveled down a side road which turned out to be a long driveway surrounded by tall, verdant trees. This did not look like a world ravaged by solar radiation and blanketed by years of nuclear winter. Nothing was fitting her preconceptions.

The house she came upon was blue and gray, two stories tall and surrounded by a wide veranda. It was as ancient in appearance as the cars on the road. She began to reason that perhaps the Earth had been really wiped clean and these crude constructions were either make-shift or salvaged. She walked up the wooden steps, startled to hear their creaking protest of her weight. Instead of a security scanner at the entryway there was an old-fashioned handle and a hole for a key. She tested the lever and found it to be open.

She called "hello" into the doorway before stepping in, but the cavernous front room revealed no one home. The walls were painted white, but every surface she laid her eyes on appeared to have some sort of decoration; paintings, *photographs* in frames, and decorative shelves pressed against the walls. There was no clear surface for the interplanetary network output. Lights hanging from the ceiling appeared to be wired and covered in a layer of dust. No air-reclamation. Did the doctor sacrifice technology to have a home on the Earth? Did he really forsake such standard conveniences as automatic lighting and the interplanetary network?

Something that caught her eye was a large wooden cabinet that appeared to have a dial and a meter of some sort. Examining the device, she turned knobs until it finally came blaring to life. A light behind the numbered meter flickered on with a voice calling out "--*the formation of any political party other than the Nazi party in Germany has been deemed illegal, further straining ties with their European neighbors.*"

She stared in wide-eyed wonder at the device. A radio? *Nazis*? It had to be a joke, or a "this day in history" broadcast. But who was still broadcasting radio waves? She let the device continue its loud announcements as she explored the house further, looking for any way to call for help.

Happening upon an office with a large desk, she saw stacks of paper and small leather-bound books. "Not very eco-friendly, Doctor," she said as she came around the desk. She thought of Purcell lying dead at the accident and apologized silently. She riffled through the papers and books and came to a file with a large stamp reading

Eastern Washington State Hospital and her name written prominently on its identification tab.

Janelle Marie Specter/Admitted August 8th, 1932.

"1932?" she said aloud, astonished.

Her mind swam with confusion as she opened the file and began reading Dr. Purcell's notes.

"Ms. Specter was brought in today after awaking from a week-long coma she suffered after a car accident. She was admitted to the sanitarium due to delusional behavior and the hospital staff's inability to calm her down. She believes the year is 2432 and that she lives on the Moon in a mining facility she calls 'Tranquility Base!' She is to be sedated regularly and kept in solitary confinement until she finally comes to her senses. We've placed her in with the other catatonics."

She dropped the file to the desk and clutched her temples. As the folder hit the surface, loose, smaller pieces of paper revealed their edges, more photographs, grainy black and white images she recognized as herself but did not remember being taken. Her head was nearly completely shaved, stitches holding large flaps of ragged skin together across her scalp.

She eased herself into the large red, leather chair at the desk and stared at the photo for a long time before continuing on with the doctor's notes.

"After gaining Ms. Specters records, we have found that she has no living relatives, husband, nor anyone that can claim her. Police notes from the scene of her accident indicate that, despite her young age, Ms. Specter is a shut-in they have been called to check up on by worried neighbors. With her current wild condition, I'm afraid the accident may have caused her to crack up in her already delicate condition."

Purcell didn't seem to really care at all, even put off by the fact his staff now had to put up with a ward of the state. Why would Purcell fabricate such a story? Was this an elaborate hoax gone terribly wrong?

"When she is left alone, she seems to quiet down. I've talked with Ms. Specter several times, indulging this fantasy world for the moment in hopes of reaching her and gaining her trust. Instead of

remembering a car accident, she instead recalls being exposed to a 'nuclear reactor' that powers the base she believes she lives in. She is afraid of developing cancer due to 'radiation poisoning.' I have convinced her we are keeping her in isolation to monitor her, that she shouldn't worry about the radiation. This has calmed her down significantly and she has opened up a little more and revealed much more about this world she has created."

She skimmed several notes discussing different ways they had accommodated her in her room, including the special construction they had put into the room based on her belief that food and drink could be "*synthesized*" upon request. Over and over, they discussed that the closer she came to actually being in a familiar setting, the calmer and more compliant she became.

Purcell mentioned several times that he believed she is not so much delusional, but actually *believes* she is in this future-society, how her mind could develop all these details and retain them as memory versus imaginings was beyond him.

"Ms. Specter is simply astounding. I have kept notes to ensure I do not shatter the fairy tale she has created for herself. To my surprise, these notes are becoming like a history that hasn't happened yet. She has remained consistent, not changing any aspect, explaining technologies and events the like of which remind me of Edgar Rice Burroughs' stories I read as a child, but for her are mundane daily experience."

Purcell's notes went from excited to cautionary, however. Janelle's mind fought against what she was reading, events he saw as fantastical were her life.

"I may have been wrong in indulging Janelle's fantasy. She has begun to hallucinate something she refers to as an 'interplanetary network.' Coaxing information from her on the subject proved difficult as I have now inserted myself as a character in her illusion. This network appears to be something like a newspaper or a stock-ticker that updates constantly and can gauge her interest in a particular subject based on body and eye-movement."

All the papers and folders across the desk seemed to be this on-going catalogue, including a paper he wrote to compare the differences between the rising Nazi party in Germany and her notion of the Asteroidal Mining Union that tried to monopolize the most precious resource in her *fictitious* world, water.

"I've spoken with the hospital administrators and board of doctors, which I refer to as 'the Agency' with Janelle, and they have agreed to allow me to take her to a residential care facility. I intend to convince her that portions of the Earth have redeveloped. The home is in a wooded area of Spokane. The lack of technology she will no doubt question and I can explain as due to the re-growth process, that there is no infrastructure yet. I will slowly introduce our modern day world to her, and re-introduce her to the world she actually exists in. I plan to present the evidence of her car-wreck to her in due-time, hopefully easing into this will allow her to abandon her future-world and rejoin society."

Hyperventilating, she tried to remember ancient history about the Earth. Purcell seemed fascinated by the nuclear reactor powering the mining facility. When was nuclear power realized? Fighting through the stress she tried to remember her school days before she worked in the plant. It was a Hungarian, right? Something about a *stop light*. She looked at the tab of the folder, Purcell had just said they had been together about a year, if this was right, it would be 1933. This had to be a joke…

She looked at the pictures of her head again, and let her fingers run along her scalp, searching for evidence. She found the jagged lines where stitches had held the skin together to heal. Her stomach lurched and she vomited on the floor to her side with only water coming up. The pain was far beyond physical. In the other room, the radio continued to belch its signal, out of time for her.

She *remembered* growing up in Tranquility Base. She remembered getting the job monitoring cooling pools in the reactor zone. She remembered the klaxon alarms ringing the emergency venting process and the shielding dropping on the core. She remembered not making it to the exit before it was sealed. There were others, she recalled all of their terrified faces as nothing seemed to happen, but they knew they had been exposed to massive amounts of radiation.

A particularly large stack of papers caught her interest. It appeared that Dr. Thomas Purcell was beginning to write a book about his experiences with Janelle. *The Girl from the Future*. He must have requested to stop by his home to gather these papers to continue his work wherever he intended to deliver her.

"Janelle Specter was born on January 23rd, 1902, in Kent, Washington, though when I met her for the first time and asked her to tell me when and where she had been born, she said without pause, 'January 23rd, 2402 in the Tranquility Base.' I asked her where Tranquility Base was, at which she became very offended and spoke to me as though I was a child, 'on the Sea of Tranquility basin, the Lunar Surface.'"

She backed away from the desk, doubling forward, wanting to vomit again, but nothing came. She let her head hang between her knees, trying to come to terms with what she was being presented with. Was her whole life a lie? A lie that she told *herself*?

Weak with fret, she looked around the room with its visible layers of dust and the musty smell of old paper and wood. Hanging on a wall was a large paper calendar with a painting of a boy above the dates and emblazoned with a bold "1933." Had she been transported through time? The doctor's notes indicated she had always been in this ancient decade. Could her mind have been transported into this other woman? Did the reactor meltdown fling her across the centuries to the dawn of the nuclear age? Or was she really a sad, lonely individual who had fabricated whole histories to make up for a life never lived?

She noticed a siren above the radio transmission. Someone alive could tell her, maybe Purcell was the crazy one!

She ran down the long driveway, hoping to run right back into the time she belonged in. Two black cars with air horns winding down sat a few feet away from a red truck with men trying to douse the burning cars. A man in a black uniform turned to see her running down the road and caught her as she ran into him.

"Hey there, missy, do you know what happened here? Are you alright?" he asked, holding her at arm's length. "Someone saw the smoke and called it in—"

"What year is it, where are we?" she frantically asked, cutting him off.

"Now, ma'am, I'm sure you're rattled let's slow down…"

"*What year is it?*" she screamed in his face.

The other officer looked at her like he might be looking at something disgusting. The same way she often had looked at herself in the mirror. "Sweetheart, it's 1933…just like it was this morning and yesterday."

The one holding her chuckled and asked her again if she knew what had happened.

She fell to her knees, her stomach churning, but again nothing was there. She *knew* she had been on the Moon; that was the only life she had lived, not as this nobody woman with nothing from the twentieth century. But here she was, surrounded by a wholly alien world out of history. Her unfamiliar scars told her she was in this strange place. She even yearned to be back in her windowless white room, yet there was nothing she could do, the veil had been dropped. Tears began to stream down her face as she felt like an abandoned child.

Looking up at the officers, she saw the confusion on their faces, but they could never understand. They would rush her right back to the hospital. She recognized a gun on one of the men's hips, but she shook away the thought before it could fully form.

"Ma'am," he said leaning over to her, "do you need a doctor? Can you tell us what happened?"

"I don't know," she said, pulling herself together and sounding far away. "I just woke up. And it was *today*."

THW

J.D. Buffington

THE ALIEN AND THE LAST MAN OF GOD

Written 2008
PUNCH/PANTS, October 2012

Not another War in Heaven entry, this is more maintaining one's faith in the face of absence by the thing you have faith in. A church's attendance is dwindling, but coincidentally, an affluent race of aliens believe a genetic disorder in their species may be explainable by a human experience rooted in the church. Miracle or coincidence? Does it matter if it gives you something to work toward, to look forward to, to make sure your faith, and livelihood, survive? This may be where I start trying to work into my stories that even our worst events can result in some sort of positivity. There's always a silver lining; death comes for us all, but for the mortician, it's job security. I'm a humanist, I believe all faiths are just as real to their believers as any other. But I'm a white American from the United States, Christianity is a default. Imagine this with a Rabbi, an Imam, any faith leader and a quirk of physical manifestation of the divine and my intent is the same—having something you believe in, and having it bolstered or restored, can be life-affirming.

What Humans call the Galactic Council began to debate whether or not Humanity would be invited into their organization when we finally left the planet Earth, what they had labeled Ersus Milia X-97c. Fortunately they accepted "Earth" as the planet's name when they finally did approach us. The first time we entered orbit gained their attention, finally traveling to the moon piqued their interest, then all we sent were probes and cameras and radios into space and the Council felt we had fallen short, even no longer returning to the moon for so very long. But about twenty years after the beginning of the 21st Century Human interest once again turned to the skies. We returned to the moon and after many years of research finally broke the Earth's orbit and visited Mars, or Ersus Milia X-97d, again "Mars" stuck fortunately.

Visiting Mars was a great point for the Council to consider. Humans had finally taken their first step into becoming a space-faring race and like our ancient ancestors who finally took to the seas and oceans we began to discover new and great things in our explorations. Energy sources, new answers to old questions, evidence of ancient life, nothing so advanced as our Human civilization, but our eyes were being opened and the Council was taking that into consideration. We would later find that the one thing keeping the majority of the Council apprehensive about approaching Earth and its inhabitants was religion.

When they finally approached, religious extremists reacted just as the Council had feared, war threatened to destroy our chances at entering into a galactic neighborhood. Fortunately, through a meeting of Earth governments, Council representatives (I would name them, but there were about thirty different species there and all so unique describing them would waste a great deal of time), and leaders of the significant churches publicly discussed Earth's place in the galaxy, what we could provide and what we could gain. The transition from the only life in the universe to next to insignificant puzzle piece or cog was drastic and devastating. *Apocolypticists* continued their ignorant fight, and slowly, the public at large began to see the faults in religion compared to the environment they now lived in.

Religion began to die, giving way to secularism, life simply fitting in. Church attendance severely declined, even in theocracies, and churches began to close their doors, unable to continue operating when donations from parishioners diminished and ultimately stopped. All of this came about not necessarily due to the introduction of superiorly intelligent extraterrestrials, but the discovery of a previously unknown form of life right here on Earth.

Kecksies were revealed to be present on the planet Earth, a form of life that permeating several worlds. They exist at a different dimensional plain than most complex life and had once been considered a paranormal phenomenon; ghosts. Instead, they were insect-like creatures, an infestation at the nth level.

The alien race known as Prexians could actually see them and just as our own cameras are built like our eyes, so are theirs and Kecksies were proven to be a xeno-entomology. If what was once thought to be hauntings was actually an insect infestation, what else did we have so severely wrong?

I am a priest at one of the last open churches in the United States. I've been able to remain in operation due to my rather radical ideas that just because the environment has changed, it doesn't mean God has gone away. But even those people who still want to believe find it more difficult to continue coming to church when there's nothing new coming out of religion, just different interpretations of the same old stories. Of course, when it comes to the Bible, there aren't exactly new chapters being written. So even I am faced with shutting my doors for the final time.

Today though, I was greeted by an unexpected visitor, an Alfoon, particularly scary looking individuals, though very kind once you get past their appearance. They look like spiders about the size of a typical cow; however, they have ten "legs" with several knobs at intervals along their spindly extensions making them look like long fingers with far too many knuckles. Their bodies were about the same size as a Human torso though not as recognizable. Their head, as though their bodies weren't unsettling enough, were a shape similar to a pterodactyl; however, they had six orbs forming their visual matrix, three along each side of their head, which sat on a much shorter knuckled extension making their neck. Alfoons, quite aware of their appearance when compared to other species, could mimic the basic shape of many different species, including humans by closing together six of their legs to form two trunk-like legs at the bottom of their body and forming the other four into two arms. In this formation, they could wear human clothes. The Alfoon standing in the doors of my church wore a nice suit, including a neck tie that fit more like a necklace on its loose-fitting collar. The underside of the Alfoon's jaw has two air sacks with several filters like gills; they can breathe in almost any environment including liquid environments. By vibrating the filters at varying speeds and breathing in and out, Alfoons can speak almost any language.

"Charles Battaglia?" the Alfoon asks in a voice that sounds like a cross between crickets chirping and a child's high-pitched timbre.

I had been locking the doors to the sanctuary, however until I leave in the evening, the doors to the entry foyer remain unlocked. Of course, I was startled, it's odd enough to have a visitor outside of regular worship hours, but an alien?

"I'm sorry, I wasn't expecting anyone," I said explaining my slight jump at the sound of its voice.

It's hard to tell the sex of an Alfoon, especially considering they all like wearing men's clothing. A xeno-biologist friend of mine tried to explain it to me once and I still can't tell until they introduce themselves.

"I am Arsauxis," he said, names beginning with a consonant sound among the Alfoon are male, where his name may have begun with a vowel in our spelling, the "r" sound was the key. "I wrote you several weeks ago, making sure your church was not closing any time soon…?"

I thought for a moment, and finally the name came back to me. "Yes, I'm sorry, I thought you may have been wanting to study or observe I wasn't expecting a private meeting."

"Let me apologize also for being so unclear. I did not want to convey any concerns or cause you any undue stress by explaining my visit beforehand. To be honest, I did not want my message intercepted, I would much rather speak with you in private."

I look around; no one has been in the church for nearly an hour. The office workers had taken off shortly after the congregation. "I'm free now; did you want to go to lunch?"

Arsauxis shakes his long head, his eyes blinking in succession as to convey appreciation but denial. "No, as I said, the more private the better."

At this point I have to admit a little bit of fear envelopes me. As far as xenotypes go, none are more amicable and peaceful than the Alfoon; however, they are also some of the most disturbing creatures produced by the Galactic Council. My same xeno-biologist friend said that Alfoons evolved in similar ways as Humanity in that they could manipulate their environment with tools, except with the Alfoon, their entire body was equivalent to our two hands.

I point to a short hallway. "My office is right back here." I said.

Arsauxis nods and follows, staying at a comfortable distance, which all at once makes me uncomfortable because I realize I must be exhibiting my nerves much clearer than I believe. I turn to him. "I'm very sorry, Arsauxis, for being nervous, I don't get many…*alien* visitors."

"If it helps you any, Mr. Battaglia, Humans freak me out, too."

I laugh, surprising myself. "I forget that *we're* the aliens to you." I say excusing my laughter.

I show him into my office, and he stands waiting for a moment as I come around my desk. I point to one of the chairs opposite me and Arsauxis carefully manipulates his legs to bend as though he had knees and "sits" in the chair. The action is slower than a human would do it, showing a certain level of concentration.

"I know I keep apologizing, but is that uncomfortable to you, Arsauxis?" I ask concerned.

"No, I can rest in this position; it is just an abnormal way to reach this point of relaxation." He says nodding, the body within the suit seeming to finally relax and loosen up.

"So, how can I be of assistance, friend?"

Facial expressions are very different among the myriad species introduced through the Galactic Council. Arsauxis pulled back his very thin lips revealing the double rows of fine needle like teeth, it could be confused for a snarl, revealing teeth is a universal image for expressing a threat. For the Alfoon though, baring the teeth in this way is non-threatening, rather more a display of confusion.

"You have considered closing your doors permanently have you not?" Arsauxis asked.

"Sadly, people aren't coming as much anymore. I cannot extend my credit any further, most people that still study the Bible study from their own homes, they are either disenchanted or embarrassed to continue going to church."

"Disheartening," Arsauxis said.

"I'm surprised to hear you say that, Arsauxis, I was not aware the Alfoon were interested in theology."

"Precisely the reason I wanted to speak to you in private, Charles; I'm willing to offer you 275,000 Dacteri to keep your church open."

I almost choke. Dacteri is the galactic trade medium, money accepted by every member world of the Council. Due to its wide use, its value has never fallen since its inception according to the Council. At latest closing, the Dacteri was equal to 7,272.73 US Dollars.

"That's over two billion dollars, Arsauxis!" I say, forcing my words out, after calculating with a small desk calculator and checking my answer several times.

"Is that sufficient?" he asks, clearly unaware of the conversion.

I start rubbing my head, the offer sounds like winning some sort of Galactic lottery. I look at Arsauxis, is he playing a joke on me? "If I played my cards right, I could run the church for the rest of my life *and* live comfortably."

"Then you agree to the terms?" he asks.

"Wait, Arsauxis, this is out of nowhere to me, why would you offer me such a significant amount just to keep the church open?"

The air sacks on the underside of his jaw inflate and make a flatulent sound, their sound of a sigh. "Short of boring you with thousands of years of Alfoonian medical history, I will get straight to the point." Arsauxis said. "I suffer from a condition called Weeping Fore-node. It's painless, more annoying than anything and requires very little treatment outside of perhaps bandages when flare-ups occur. It is not contagious and does not appear to be genetic either, striking its victims quite at random. In very rare cases this weeping can occur around the cranial back plate. In even rarer cases my people will even suffer from this weeping in their midsection."

"So, you want me to keep the church open for people who suffer from this condition?"

"For thousands of years Alfoons have thought nothing of this condition, but with the introduction of Humans to the Council, I came across a condition that has struck Humans seemingly at random as well, it is also how I came across you."

Something at the back of my mind begins to tingle, old memories I hadn't thought of for many years.

"You are certainly familiar with *Stigmata*?" he asks, leaning forward.

I lean back in my chair, feeling nearly about to vomit. I suffered Stigmata as a child, I was lauded as a sign by many extremists that joining the Council was a sin in the eyes of God, despite the fact we had been in the Council for several years by then. It was never explained how I had bled from my wrists and ankles with no visible wounds. In one event only did I bleed from my forehead, supposedly mirroring the Christ's crown of thorns. After the episodes finally passed, I became disillusioned myself, not returning to the faith for nearly twenty years.

"Arsauxis, I don't think your Weeping Fore-node and Stigmata have anything to do with each other. Human's do have genetic conditions that seem to strike at random as well, like Multiple Sclerosis, but just because something doesn't have an answer…"

"You wouldn't jump to religion. I understand that. And no one among the Alfoon has ever considered turning to theological study to make up answers. My consideration comes from the fact that people who suffer from the Weeping all see a startlingly similar comparison to our condition and Human Stigmata, when we assume a bipedal form. Alfoonian blood is a very dark purple in our natural environment, however the substance that oozes from the skin in Weeping outbreaks is always crimson, like Human blood."

He does not stand but does stretch his "arm" appendages out like a crucifix, and bows his head slightly, where I can see staining from his condition looking like scratches. The similarities are frightening and goose-bumps rise on my arms and a shutter fills my body.

"I do not know your God, Charles," he says. "Nor anything more than the name of this Jesus Christ, but the truth is, I want to, and so do many other Afloonians. I brought these similarities to my own government and procured the amount I have offered you today."

I began to speculate, could it be possible that God had known this day would come? Did He inflict me with Stigmata and gently usher me back into the church so that I could one day act in assistance with this alien race and perhaps help them find answers they had never considered before? In my church I began to try and teach that God did not act so directly, that you had to find Him in the details, open your eyes to the wider scope of things and see how everything fits together. A message that I hoped would appeal to the secularist society around me. But even those who believed passionately began to fade away.

And then today, of all people, an Alfoon, an *alien*, offers me the chance to keep spreading the Word.

"I can't take your offer, Arsauxis." I say shaking my head and looking at my desk.

He sighs again. "I can request a larger amount, Mr. Battaglia…"

"It's not the offer itself. I can't profit from teaching, I don't feel right about it. What I would like to do is invite you and any other Alfoons currently planetside to come to mass. If you appreciate the message, then you can make an offering of any amount you choose to help me keep the lights on."

He made a slight cooing in the back of his throat, the sound of appreciative acceptance.

I suppose it doesn't matter who comes to hear the message, a sanctuary full of Alfoons might take some time getting used to; just as long as the light is always on.

ATG

J.D. Buffington

THE AWAKENED

Written 2009
PUNCH/PANTS, October 2012

I set out to write a cosmically weird monster, an incident, and a warning. Lovecraft's Cthulhu and Yithians in one fell-swoop. Three perspectives on what should be a world-ending event, an impossible beast, and a message about doing better by our planet; it is fragile and the universe is hostile.

I am the deluge.
I am the current that drives the flood.
I am the awakened who forces your eyes open from eternal slumber.
Know that your fear is not of the destruction I have caused, but that it is I that has caused it.
Die now and be reborn enlightened by the stars that you have ignored.

PAUL

Blessed are those that cannot see the horrors to which the rest of us had to bear witness. What once was the sound of thunder, now recalls the hammer-strike footfalls of that terrible spawn. I shall never sleep in peace again as a result of that unimaginable behemoth that strode across the surface of our Earth. Its destruction visible from orbit is all anyone can see anymore. But I was there, I saw the thing as it came from nowhere and vanished into nothing, leaving behind a ruined world I cannot fathom being rebuilt. I daresay I long for the days of unawareness.

It was at dusk in the middle of September, the 14th, as no one shall forget, when the wandering monstrosity appeared just beyond the hills north of Grand Marais. It had been a fairly decent day until a loathsome and chilling fog rolled in with the distant rumblings of a storm that threatened from over the hillsides; a disappointing, though not unexpected end to the warm days of summer. But these rolling banks of fog carried something far more sinister than early snow.

FRUITLESS BODIES

In the clouds hanging high in the stratosphere people claimed to see lightning like no other. Bright hues of red and orange lit up the roiling thunderheads. I had gone outside on my front stoop to take in the surprise storm. Feeling the chill of coming cold I made to step back inside and grab a jacket before enjoying nature's fireworks, but something in the skies caught my eye. The lightning was not caused by the interchange of positive and negative ions, but by flashes of faraway structures succumbing to explosive destruction. Black smoke was filling the grays and whites of the natural fog and clouds.

I stared in awestruck wonder, trying to fathom what terrible attack was coming our way. Terrorists? Some long forgotten volcano? Then it reared its hideous head. Fifteen unblinking eyes stared ominously skyward, devoid of iris or pupil, glittering with the reflections of the terror it wrought on the ground at its feet. Someone screamed, but I could not pull my own eyes away to see what the matter was; surely, they had seen the unfathomable features break through the clouds as well.

The head was enormous and all that could be seen high among the clouds. It was rounded with fleshy nodes upon both sides and a wrinkled, squat snout that at first appeared to suggest a mouth would lie under. But as it slowly lumbered forward, the proboscis was revealed to cover rigid looking tentacles. It was all we could see for the longest time, and it only grew larger as its unseen feet continued its unrepentant destruction of the earth below. The tentacles rigidity was exposed as knuckled segments like repugnant fingers reaching from the monster's maw. These appendages swayed like immense trees with each forward step, revealing still more knuckled tentacles of varying lengths which could only lead to the thing's mouth.

Families began to spread in panic whereas I could not move, stricken with dread and planted firmly to my stoop. I could hear cars screeching out of driveways, children crying, the barking and baying of dogs as they all tried to escape the onslaught of the horror that drove toward us. Then came a sound I had not expected and broke my alarmed state, gunfire. The fools, that the fog had not broken to reveal the monstrosity's entire form suggested it was still nowhere near us,

266

and still yet larger than what could be seen. Guns of any caliber would be like throwing eyelashes at the moon.

The bullets, unsurprisingly, did nothing to gain its attention. As it moved ever forward, it suddenly bellowed a low, though deafening, trumpet blast. Its proboscis swelled and the nodes upon the sides of its head vibrated with the thrum. The sound was indescribable, disorganized, and only further perpetuated the creature's horrific presence. I wanted to cover my ears, but something made me listen, though I could not understand then.

Once the length of its tentacles finally broke the bank of clouds and smoke, I was looking nearly straight up. I could see now that its skin was scaled, not like a reptile, but like a tropical plant, and diverse shades of green. Behind the head came impossibly tall towers of more finger-like appendages folded backwards and connected by immense fleshy sails like those of a bat's wings or the extinct avian pterosaurs. These wings were so enormous it would be physically impossible to spread them, as it no doubt would have scraped the upper-atmosphere if not breaking into orbital space.

What was this thing doing here? My mind could not comprehend the awfulness which my eyes delivered. Despite their spindly appearance, the wings supported the girth of the creature's upper body, digging canyon-like trenches and tearing apart the hills as it lumbered forward. Four hind legs looking like the unsightly, stilted legs of elephants from Salvador Dali's surreal paintings supported the rest of the thing's...*body*. The immensity of its form could be compared to the underbelly of a roach or beetle. Though, it could also be mistaken for the carcass of a whale. Was this thing some giant (there is no word *big* enough to describe its size) insect from another world?

The trenches that it dug with the hooked, bent ends of its wings were nothing to the effects produced by its clawed elephantine feet. Craters would be an understatement, followed by such massive weight that the earth actually caramelized and glazed into gooey volcanic glass. One footfall destroyed a house three doors down from my own, the shattering of wood and glass sounded as though a bomb had gone off. The vibrations that issued were like an earthquake, rolling the ground like a wave. More glass, including on my own house, shattered. A gas line busted and the heat from the creature's intense pressure upon the ground ignited the spewing fumes.

The fireball was extreme, and I could feel the superheated air rush past me. Much to my surprise, though, I saw the fire continue to crawl up the alien beast. Its sweat, or whatever secretion it was producing, was like kerosene and lit in waves like the burning edges of thin paper, but the monster paid it no mind.

As it passed in its slow unwieldy way, no doubt sinking its claws into the bay of Lake Superior, I found myself walking out into the cracked, debris strewn street. I stared, aghast, yet intensely interested. I could not break my gaze, nor could I cover my ears as it bellowed its strange song again. Night had come and the power had been destroyed for miles. I stared up, even when it was gone, and all I could see left were the stars in the sky, occasionally blocked by passing clouds or wisps of smoke.

There I stood, continuing to stare, for how long I do not recall. A military vehicle happened to pass down my street looking to regain the path of the thing after the hills. An officer called out, I could hear him, but not answer. He walked up, shining his flashlight on me, asking me mundane questions concerning my physical well-being or what I had seen. But I had seen everything I would ever need to see, our lives were forever changed by what I had *seen*. No explanation would be sufficient, no words in any human language could describe the visitor, and no amount of time could pass to heal the wounds this thing had inflicted.

I felt my eyes drift down, though this progeny of some other place that surely was more horrendous than any conjuring of Hell or its denizens was all I could visualize.

"Sir?" the man before me asked.

"I am the deluge…" was all that I uttered, ever again.

MAGGY

Streaks of red and black mixed in with the muddy brown. I stare, scared near to the point of tears as the ripples subside in the soiled water, my face's reflection coming clear. I hyperventilate, feeling another heaving urge, my forehead and neck cold with sweat and my entire body aching, wanting to explode from fear. I wretch, but nothing comes up…thankfully, but also painfully. I reach up weakly and find the handle to flush the toilet, the water swirling quickly away, blasting a wretched, acrid stink, but the small burst of rushing air is also morbidly soothing. I fall back, staring up at the ceiling, hands on my stomach as though I might be able to calm it down.

"Chrisss d'ulcère…" I whisper to myself. No one else is here. No one else to talk to.

As I sit trying to regain my composure, I'm torn between trying to shut my eyes and resting or to look again back at the television set. It was there that I had seen what I had seen to make me so nauseous, my ulcer erupting in flaming convulsions. I'd seen blood in my vomit before, I've done enough heroin on an empty stomach, but none of that compared to what had just been displayed on the little 9" monitor in the corner of my cell.

Curiosity got the better of me. There on the set was the disturbing image of…well, whatever the hell it is. The bastard of an octopus, bat, whale, and elephant with a hundred fingers sticking out of its mouth walking due south from the foothills and mountains of northern Minnesota. It had destroyed forests, towns, cities, everything in its path. The grotesque nature of the thing terrified me like nothing I had ever seen before. No Ridley Scott Xenomorph, or Clive Barker Cenobite could prepare me for something that was real and tearing apart the American landscape.

One might think I was safe in the Joliette, but the entire world shook, if not physically, then from cold terror. The thing itself was a fright to see, but its wanton destruction, unedited scenes coming through as they were captured on every single channel showing death and devastation, did not sit well with an already weak stomach. A hospital, not warned, unaware and scrambling for what they thought was an earthquake, was ripped in half, the bodies of patients, nurses, doctors, families…*men, women, children* decimated, torn apart, their bodies hanging lifeless and bloodied from the iron and masonry.

As the creature marched forward on whatever mission it saw fit, it destroyed infrastructure, cell-towers, electrical hard lines, telephone poles; warnings were difficult to get out, so it was several hours before people were notified that something dangerous was headed right for them. There were reports that people with guns had shot at the creature's feet but that proved fruitless. American officials made a national announcement to not attack or provoke the thing; neither would any military action be taken. It was deemed more suitable to deal with the damage than to try and kill the beast estimated to be over a hundred thousand feet tall and have its body wipe out half a country.

A hundred thousand feet tall! How impossible, how unfathomable, my brain hurt to even think about it. Helicopters couldn't get anywhere near the monster's height, only able to observe its legs. The thing couldn't even be seen except from very far away. It had showed up at dusk and as it destroyed electrical light in its path and the sun set, it could only be seen as a black void high above, according to witnesses. All it did was walk, but as it did so it annihilated the Earth.

News programs on every channel tried to make sense of it:

"Impossible que ce ai présenté une menace, tout ce que c'a faisait c'est marcher!"

Change the channel.

"C'a a peine virer de sa trajectoire on dirait que c'était programmé…"

Change the channel.

"Il y'a même des rapports que ca à souffleter l'atmosphère avec son apparition soudaine…"

Change the channel.

"C'est une uncursion extra-terrestre, ils ont envoyé cet *affaire* pour montrer leur puissance!"

And there we go. This thing is going to cause insanity. Maybe that's what it was trying to do…

Slick video game style graphics display a path over North America through the United States, pinpointing major places of destruction: hospitals, capital buildings, areas of dense population, stadiums, natural and manmade landmarks. It walked basically a straight line from upper Minnesota to the border of Mississippi and Louisiana right into the Gulf. Now, the news was diligent enough to explain that the Gulf of Mexico is not deep enough to compensate the thing's size in the same breath as explaining the tidal waves causing even more destruction along the coast. But it was in the Gulf the thing vanished, like an impossible stairway opened up to the creature and it submerged itself out of sight and seemingly out of existence.

Submarines launched searching for anything. Through the kicked up silt they saw only craters like the ones it had created on land. It was gone, the "footprints" simply ceasing before they even reached the Sigsbee Abyssal Plain. I'd never even heard of that until now.

Where did it come from? Why was it here? Where the hell did it go?

My stomach churns, I know there's nothing left, but I lean over the toilet anyway, suddenly seeing spots. There's a dizzying rush…

LT. BRULEY

"I want to know everything, I want every possible explanation!" The General screamed at the room full of personnel.

"Well, sir," a timid bespectacled man ventured, "the major consensus is that the creature was a wild animal from, well, *another dimension*, that somehow slipped into our realm of existence."

The General stared the man down. "*That's* the major consensus? Is this fucking *Star Trek*? We spend a billion dollars a year on scientific research, and you give me the McGuffin of a weak science fiction movie?"

The man squirmed.

The General looked around. "*I don't know* would be a better response than that. When I say I want every possible explanation, I don't want *consensus*, I want an *answer* that can be backed up with substance."

He raises his hand to his forehead, massaging his temples as the crush of people sit silent.

"Anything, anything concrete, what…do…we…know?"

Someone took in a sharp breath to say something, but then thought better of it.

I guess I had to go ahead and speak up. "We have some information gathered, mostly about the creature's effects on the environment."

The General stared at me now, waiting for me to continue.

"Obviously the physical destruction it caused is beyond calculable at this time and could take decades to repair." I say. "But it's sudden appearance, the space it occupied, changed air pressure instantly, threw off established air currents with its immense size, it actually even affected temperature by a half of a degree."

"And those could be serious?" asked the General.

"Immensely. It could take several years for everything to get back to normal, but as the planet tries to reboot itself from this obviously unnatural event, more changes will occur in the wake of the initial changes. There's also the matter of the air it consumed and expelled with those noises it made."

The General began rooting through some paperwork in front of him on the table. "I'm sorry, before you go on, what's your name? I don't have my glasses; I can't see your credentials…"

"Lt Brian Bruley with NASA, sir, I serve as CAPCOM supporting the ISS and was on duty when the event occurred. Data from weather and communication satellites pours in all the time, but with its appearance we, well *NASA*, began getting erratic readings. We can't say much about the creature itself, but we've got plenty on what it affected while it was here."

The General nodded. "And about its breathing and the noises it made?"

"Well, there's two major points; it goes without saying that this thing was quite large, we can only assume that it naturally required the same gas mixture as most Earthling creatures, so by breathing it actually increased CO_2 levels…incrementally but measurably. It would be safe to assume plants of the world could compensate, but with environmental changes already impacting most flora, their intake levels of CO_2 has actually declined. So increased CO_2 gas levels could lead to a warmer than normal winter for much of the United States-”

“And a hotter summer as well for who knows how long.” The General completed. “Leading more to the continual changes you mentioned.”

The General began to shake his head and I could hear him mumbling, probably cursing under his breath. This was a severe bit of information, but not what I had been sent to deliver. “There’s the other point about the *noises* it made, and why I was actually sent to this meeting, sir.”

The General looked up; weary of any further distressing news.

“As I said I’m in CAPCOM and I was talking with a couple of astronauts who were setting up a continuous experiment to gain information in regard to a manned flight to Mars in the near future. One of our big concerns is the astronauts being bombarded with solar radiation outside of the Earth’s protective ionosphere.”

“I hope you’re getting to a point…”

“I am…this experiment involves wearing a helmet that monitors known radiation particles and simultaneously monitoring brain activity to determine interactivity…anyway…when the event began it was dusk over the mid-North American continent and they saw it, it just sort of popped into existence. Its sudden appearance buffeted clouds, stirred up dust, caused destruction on the ground, they could see this all, but its own body heat created a fog that emanated from it for quite a while until the air pressure adjusted to its presence. About that same time was when it first made its, well, we’ve been calling it its ‘call,’ and something happened to Jensen who was wearing the BRAA,” I stopped short realizing that was going to gain some quick questioning glances, which of course it did.

“Brainwave/Radiation Acceptance Apparatus…the astronauts nicknamed it that,” I say sheepishly.

Some people smirk, but the General continues to stare, patiently awaiting the point of my revelation. I clear my throat.

“Jensen was wearing the *helmet* when the creature made its first call, and Jensen suddenly started speaking very rhythmically, apparently going into a trancelike state. Somehow, the creature’s call tapped into Jensen's brain through the helmet, and since Jensen speaks English, that was the translation we got."

"So, the creature brought a message?" the General asked.

"The, um, *consensus*, that it was a wild animal that wandered into our dimension? NASA officials, with the message we've received, are afraid that it was purposefully sent here, as a messenger…through from where or by whom we don't know."

The General appeared to be losing his patience. "And that message would *be*…"

I look down at Captain Jensen's trance quote. *"I am the deluge."* I begin. *"I am the current that drives the flood. I am the awakened who forces your eyes open from eternal slumber. Know that your fear is not of the destruction I have caused, but that it is I that has caused it.*

"There seems to be an emphasis on 'I,' in that the destruction is belittled by the fact that this *thing* is what caused the destruction." I explain.

The General nods, considering what I have just delivered. Then a spark of recognition crosses his face.

"What was that, 'I am the deluge,' I have that somewhere…" he says rooting through his stack of documents.

Someone from the press corp. speaks up, "A *Paul Verner* from Minnesota is quoted as only being able to say that phrase after the creature actually tore through his neighborhood. He can still write and communicate, but he can only *vocalize* 'I am the deluge' now."

Someone else chimes in, "There's been several reports of people being stricken catatonic, even people nowhere near the incident path,"

"Right," someone else still, "the Joliette Women's Institute in Quebec reported the inmates of an entire cellblock blacking out at the same, about three hours after the creature disappeared."

The General takes in all the information, slowly nodding, but also giving these people a disappointed look for not sharing earlier. To be fair, though, I understand…where do you even start?

"Is that all it said…or what the astronaut said anyway?" he asks me.

"Um…there was one more statement…"

All eyes in the room seem to turn to me and my heart races with nerves, but I don't have any choice but to continue. *"Die now and be reborn enlightened by the stars that you have ignored."*

Fearful murmurs begin to build in the room.

"Is it a threat, a warning?" the General asks.

"We only have what we have, sir…but, if I had to hazard a guess…" I cut myself off, realizing this isn't friendly conversation but an official matter that should be devoid of editorial viewpoints. "I'm sorry, sir, it's just my opinion."

"No, go ahead. I don't think anything can be dismissed at this time." He says shooting an apologetic look to the inter-dimensional animal theorist.

"All of the changes, the destruction, the eventual changes that will occur in this event's wake…everyone's going to have to pull together to fix and overcome this situation. Every day from this day forward, that thing and what it did is going to be in our thoughts, considerations, and concerns."

"That goes without saying," someone quips.

"Be reborn enlightened, is what it said, like maybe something out there thinks we haven't been paying attention to what matters. Now we have no choice but to pay attention to our environment."

"Something out there?" the General asks. "Like *God*?"

"Or *nature* or maybe some cosmic police force, it did mention *stars* that we've *ignored*. Humans used to plot courses and plan events around the stars. But to be honest, *I don't know*, sir. One thing for certain is that we are now being forced to attend to issues that were largely being ignored for decades and now it's going to take decades to repair and to come to terms with."

The room sits quiet for what seems like an eternity as everyone digests the possibilities.

"So…*something* has told us to take care of our environment…" the General says rhetorically.

"And each other," I say, feeling the urgency of the alien messenger, "we are after all a product of our environment."

ATG

STUMBLE
Written 2013
Self-published March 2015
This story is based on seeing a grave marker with my name, and a birthday one day, and many years, off from mine. What I write in here begins to outline the rules of time travel I place both on myself and the world it exists in. The inciting event, mentioned in this story, is a major event between the many universes I write in. A wrinkle and fracturing of space-time that ripples through multiple stories—conveniently so that I can even take my older writing and affix it to one of my timelines.

Rick fell down. Not in the sense that one might stumble and roll a few feet, or even down a hill. Not even like falling into a hole you hadn't seen and ending up in a cave or sewer. No, Rick fell down on a sidewalk in front of a quaint flower shop in Clearwater. He saw the wooden flower cart shift, catching his foot and tripping him up. He heard the girl yelp and start to apologize. On the way down he started to laugh, but when he got up, he wasn't where he had been: Florida in the year 2137.

When he stood up, he was on the side of a dirt road. He was shocked, horrified even. The disorientation was nauseating, the smell was different, air pressure was off. One moment he was among shoppers on a sunny day, where the next he was by himself relatively in the middle of nowhere under an overcast sky. He had stumbled. Now, to him, that meant nothing, not yet. If it had been a year later in his time, he'd know what it was, but still be stuck. Twenty years later and he would have been able to go back home, but, that's when he fell, and this is where he was, and that's how it'd be.

Unfortunately, no one was around, and panic started to set in. In either direction there was only road and open fields. A few trees here and there, but not even a fence post to guide him in the right direction. One way would send him on a day's walk over the border into another state, the other actually into town. He had a fifty percent chance of being really screwed. From his pants pocket he pulled out a thin, clear film. By manipulating the surface, he pulled up icons, the date and time (they were wrong), and applications that might help him find his way. With no service signal they didn't work. Short of what media he had stored to its memory, it was useless. He couldn't call for help. His maps wouldn't pinpoint where he was. He had to make a blind decision. By luck alone, he headed into town.

It was quiet when Rick came upon a set of buildings where a lady with her daughter wearing unusual, full length and heavy looking cotton dresses despite the heat. Though they returned the same look he gave them at first, they were kind and cordial.

"Hi," he said to them, "I seem to be lost, like, really lost, can you tell me where I am?"

The little girl gave a nervous smile, and the woman eyed his unusual attire: a black kevlarachnid silk jacket, red fabrique shirt, and denemp jeans. Her look changed from mild curiosity to disgusted and fearful disdain. "Williams Street."

Before he could inquire further the woman grabbed her daughter's hand and hurried on past.

Okay, he thought, I'd probably think I was a weirdo, too.

Ducking into the first door he came across, he appeared to be in some kind of supply store, empty of people save for the old man standing behind a counter. He was dressed oddly as well, wearing coveralls, but the look the old man gave to Rick was just as perplexed as the ladies outside. Rick took a deep breath, smelling all sorts of musty and dusty odors he couldn't identify. He saw almost random items on the shelves around him and asked the first thing that came to mind. "Is this, like, a theme park, or something? Augmented reality?"

"Excuse me?" the old man said in a gravelly voice.

"Look," Rick said brushing it off, "I don't know what's happened. I tripped walking through Peridot Market…uh, in front of Astrid's, and when I got up, I seemed to be someplace completely different."

He pulled out the clear film again, "My phone's not working, I've got no service, I'm not seeing any Info-Surfs, and I'm really afraid maybe somebody's pranking me with a virtual or augmented reality display."

The old man had that same confused, albeit perturbed, look about him as the woman on the street did. "Public telephone's on the wall there," he said pointing behind Rick.

Rick looked over his shoulder to see a wooden box with some black pipes and cables sticking out of it. "A-ha," Rick chuckled. "Okay, yes, um…thanks, I guess."

A young man with tan skin and dark brown hair stepped out from a door leading to a back office or storeroom. Wiping his dusty hands on a rag he said, "You said your phone's not working?"

Rick waved the film again before putting it back in his pocket. "Yeah…I'm, uh…I don't even know what to say, I feel stupid trying to explain it."

The young man shook his head, "No, no, no, don't worry about it." He looked to the shop keeper. "I'm gonna take a break, John; I'm gonna go down to Sue's and pick up a sandwich, you want me to bring you anything back?"

The old man, John, just shook his head no, still staring at Rick as if he was truly bothered just by his standing there.

"What's your name?" the young man asked coming around the counter.

"Uh, Rick," he said.

"Come with me, Rick, I bet you could do with a meal."

Rick shook his head. "Not really hungry, I just want to find out where I am, if it's real, and what the hell is going on."

The young man stopped right in front of Rick. With a very serious face and tone said, "Come with me."

Rick, taken aback, loosely shook his head trying to process how serious this guy looked and sounded. "Okay…?"

The man nodded toward the door and in a lighter tone said, "Come on."

They stepped out into the street. The young man shut the door behind them. "My name's Parker," he said. "You have no idea where you are, and that's okay. I'm going to tell you, but first thing's first: no attitude, no freaking out."

"Are you a cop or something?" Rick asked.

"No attitude."

278

Parker walked down the street, further into town, obviously expecting Rick just to follow. Partly offended, but mostly curious, Rick followed, letting off a huff and a shrug.

Parker said nothing until they reached a little diner four buildings down. When he did finally start to talk again, it was to a tall, skinny, black lady behind a service counter. "Can I get two ham sandwiches, Sue? And, uh, two bottles of Coca-Cola."

"Fancy, Parker!" she said with a smile. "What's the occasion?

"I've got a new friend in from out of town," Parker said. The emphasis on "out of town" cued a knowing nod from the woman.

"I said I wasn't hungry," Rick complained.

"You are," Parker said. "You just don't know it, the smells are all off, your disorientation is taking up all your attention. Trust me, you smell the ham, your stomach will set to growling."

Rick sighed and walked into the diner. There was a couple of old men on one side just sitting at a table, playing a game of dominos with actual pieces, not with a display on the table. Parker pointed to a table on the opposite side and Rick sat down with him.

"This is some period piece—a game, right?" Rick asked.

"No, it's real. It's Tuesday afternoon, you're in Westville, Oklahoma, and the year is 1912." Parker said quite assured. "What year are you from?"

"From?"

Parker shrugged, "Sorry. What year is it, for you? If someone asked you the year, as strange as that might be, what would you say?"

It was Rick's turn to give someone the apprehensive glance. "Uh, 2137."

Parker nodded. "Damn...so you don't know about this...just missed it, too."

"What's it? This?"

Parker scratched the side of his head and sighed. He looked at his fingers a moment. Upon hearing footsteps and a floorboard creak, he looked over his shoulder to Sue, carrying two plates with sandwiches and pickles.

"I'll be right back with your soda-pops." She said.

The smell of the ham slammed Rick in the face, and sure as Parker had predicted, his stomach gave a little rumble and he realized he was absolutely famished. "I ate just an hour ago…"

"Time travel does that to you." Parker said. "Doesn't seem to matter how far or long, stepping out of your time into another completely wastes you."

When Sue arrived with the sodas in frosty bottles, Parker asked, "Can you bring Rick a glass of water, too?"

Sue smiled and nodded. "Welcome to Westville, Rick." She said directly to him.

Rick smiled back at her and prepared to pick up his sandwich.

"Now," Parker said, raising his hand and pointing at the sandwich. "Hang on a minute. You're not going to like that. You're just not, no matter how good it smells right now, the bread is going to be awful, the cheese all wrong, the ham all wrong. You'll get used to it. You might even be able to finish your sandwich, but it's going to take you a few weeks to really get used to how things taste and smell. There's been a lot of change in air quality, sanitation, water filtrating, and food processing in two hundred and thirty years."

Rick frowned and took a bite anyway as Sue came back with a glass of water. Again, Parker was right. The ham and cheese were intensely rich, and the bread tasted like raw vegetation. Even the texture was confusing. He wanted to immediately spit it out, but he was so hungry. Chewing quickly, he tried to swallow it down with a gulp of the soda.

Parker just shook his head.

The soda wasn't right either, it tasted nothing like Coke; he couldn't even begin to describe it. His eyes watered as he tried to force himself to swallow the awful mess he had just piled into his mouth with careful sips of water.

After finally getting just that one bite down, he let out an exasperated sigh. "Okay, what the hell is going on? All of this," he said waving his hands around indicating his surroundings, "I can see how you might fake it, but why? Why me? Is this some experiment?"

Parker gave a sad smile. He looked over his shoulder to a calendar hanging on the wall behind the counter. "2137 right? About two years ago, for you, do you recall hearing about an incident at the Chicxulub Crater Collider? Fears that they had actually blown through the collider and maybe even breached the underwater facility?"

Rick thought for a moment. "The Phantom Hole."

Parker nodded. "Pretty intense scare, but it looked like it was just sensor errors setting off alarms. Everything was in perfect condition and working order; except it wasn't. At your point in time, it's an interesting mystery, but a fluke. In a year from your time, they discover they did blow a hole through the facility, but not in physical space. They blew a hole in time, the very fabric of the fourth dimension. As the Earth moves around the Sun, the facility immediately moved away from the hole, but space and time are affected by gravity. That hole remained; but like putty or dough that has a hole in it, if you stretch and knead it, it changes shape, or might compromise other portions, making soft spots. More holes might form from this, or get longer or wider, but eventually the holes will work themselves out. The initial hole stretched out along Earth's orbit, spread, wobbled, and caused a lot of havoc."

The look of disbelief and frustration on Rick's face wasn't anything new to Parker. There weren't a lot of people that fell back in time, not in the grand scheme of things. However, he'd met enough to read their faces, and he had experienced the disbelieving once before himself.

"In the last six month period," Parker continued, "actually maybe about a month ago, you may have heard of an unusually high number of missing persons reports, no clues, no foul play. People just disappearing?"

"Oh God, I've been kidnapped." Rick said leaning back in his chair.

"I wish that were the case," Parker said nodding. "You'd have a chance to go home. Like I said, in a year they figure it out, they take measures to make sure people don't fall through time, but also inform the public on how to act if they do fall through time. It becomes a natural hazard, but fewer people dropped through.

"The holes worked themselves out in a number of years, but not without being scrutinized. We learned how to actually safely travel through time. As per the Württemberg Convention, time travel cannot set destinations prior to the invention of the Stable Event, the first occurrence of intentional time travel. An unfortunate aspect of that is, since you are from the year 2137, you are not eligible for extraction."

Rick's eyebrows pointed down into a "V" between his eyes. "You're serious?"

"Unfortunately." Parker said. "You are stuck in 1912. You're welcome to move, but small towns are your best bet. The fewer people you interact with the better, mostly for health reasons, but this world is a lot different from ours. The smaller the contact, the less abrasive customs and society will feel."

"You say 'we' and 'our world,'" Rick asked. "You're from the…future?" he said the last rolling his eyes.

"Further ahead of you, I knew what happened immediately. But I'm not eligible for extraction, either."

"So, a lot of people have fallen through time?"

"A fair number all over the world have stumbled. It's thought that perhaps there's an instance of quantum entanglement. Somehow, some amount of particle matter is in both periods of time right where the soft spot is. It could be a part of your own matter, or dirt from here and concrete from there."

Parker shrugged. "There's a network of time fugitives—those who stumble; we call them the Stumbled or Stumblers. Most of us are from within twenty years of each other's original times, yet we can be separated by many years here. Somebody who stumbled yesterday in your time, could have fallen fifty years prior in this time, or even fifty years from now. It's terribly alienating to be here but coming across people from our own time helps."

Rick's expressions ranged from disdain, to confusion, to questioning, right to the edge of believing, then back to finding the whole thing humorous, though frustrating. "If so many people have gone back in time, wouldn't somebody have messed it up? Prevented the World Wars or the Great Depression, or 9/11, the 2020 Schism, the Three Day Night, the Pacific War…" he counted off atrocities on his fingers. He knew his history, and like every single other Stumbler, he thought knowing what was coming could be stopped by knowing it.

Parker held up his hand. "You know you're going to die one day, right?"

Rick looked shocked and perhaps even scared. Was that a threat?

"Can you stop it?" Parker continued. "If you tell me I'm going to die one day, can you stop that? Does my knowing help me to stop it? Some things are just inevitable, and history is like that.

"We have rules for the Stumbled—no waving your flashy technology around; like your phone you had out in the store, for instance. No telling or showing people what it can do. We have no problem with you keeping it; I'm sure it's bio-charged, right? Having it means nothing; it's so advanced that not even Albert Einstein would know what to do with it. The machines to make the machines to make a single part of that are nowhere near existing today. It might plant an idea, but if I gave you or somebody else from the 22nd century a butter-churn, for example, without telling them what it's for or how to work it? There's no context, no modern analog. It just becomes junk. Same thing for that phone or anything else you happen to have on you. You might as well destroy it, for all the good it'll do you; burn it and separate as much of it as you can.

"You can scream from the rooftops that World War I is coming, or to hide everybody's cash, the banks are going to crash, but I wouldn't suggest it. I would, however, get a job and start hoarding cash and supplies. You can protect yourself against what you know is coming, but everyone else will look at you like a nut."

Parker paused and took a drink of his soda and a bite of his sandwich. Rick watched a moment. He decided he was still hungry and took another bite of his sandwich as well. It was still awful, the bread tasted raw, like he could actually taste the wheat and flour individually. The ham tasted almost uncooked; there was an earthy flavor to it, as though he could tell what the pig had eaten. Then it dawned on him. The food didn't taste wrong, it tasted like it should. That's what these things were made out of—raw handmade ingredients and meat from an animal that had been alive.

"What about the wars? Could I end up fighting in them?" Rick asked.

Parker thought about pressing him; seeing if he had accepted he had fallen back in time, but it never came that quickly. This was idle conversation, and a good way to spread more ground rules. "You can volunteer, if you want. Military is a good way to see the world for free, but you could die of course. However, that could be reason enough to join I suppose; easy ticket out of here without having to do the dirty work yourself."

"You mean suicide?" Rick asked, disgusted.

Parker nodded. "Suicide is a very serious issue. It's not cowardice by any means. It can be born out of fear or irrationality and removing yourself from your 'sane' surroundings can easily drive you to the brink. We've lost a number of Stumblers that way."

"How do you make sure people behave?"

"Oh, it's not like we police anybody, we only support. Police of the day can take care of anyone acting a damn fool in the streets."

Parker took another bite and continued to talk between the chomps of his jaw. "We can provide you with a current ID, social security, and birth certificate. We can put you up for a few weeks, if necessary, but you are ultimately responsible for finding a job and getting on with your life. You are stuck here."

Rick got a sudden twinkle in his eye. "Can I buy stock? Can I make my family rich?"

"Was your family rich?" Parker asked.

"No."

"Then no." Parker shrugged.

"I thought you said it didn't really matter what we did—that history was inevitable?"

"Trying to start or stop things will just annoy people for the most part. But things like inventions, acting in movies, being an artist or a writer, trying to play the stock market, these are all traceable. There's a recorded history. If your name isn't part of that history, then you're just not part of that history. Even if you got around us—and like I said, enough people have fallen back in time that there's a network, and even further ahead of us in the future there is indeed time travel—

somehow history would work itself out that your family wasn't rich. So, you're not going to finagle some magic to alter your own family's history. Oh, and speaking of family, don't count on making babies, you're sterile now."

"What?" Rick said, leaning back.

"And if you don't pass away before it occurs, you will definitely develop cancer with significant age."

"Don't give it to me easy or anything, Doc." Rick huffed.

"It's from passing through the tear in space/time. You stepped out of your three dimensions, and even though you didn't see or feel anything, you were wholly exposed to a dimension outside of your own environment. That includes all its energies and rays and radiation. Apparently, time is just chock-full of radiation."

Parker finished his sandwich and pickle and washed it all down with the rest of his Coke. "Listen, I've got to get back to the store. You're welcome to hang out here for the afternoon. Sue makes great company. Also, Daryl and Darrel there have all kinds of stories. Darrel even remembers the Civil War, but I don't remember which one of them is which."

Of the two, the old man closer to the counter reached up and flipped off Parker but didn't look at him.

Parker chuckled. "That's Darrel."

Parker headed for the door. "I'll be back later on. We can get you set up in the motel on the other side of town. Making you a new identity isn't too difficult. And look, Rick, it's really not that bad once you get used to it. It's nice here and Westville is quiet."

With that, Parker made his exit, leaving Rick with strangers in a strange diner and the idea that he had stumbled through time.

Sue didn't let him sit alone too long, though. "When's your birthday? What year were you born?"

Rick looked at her, she was older than him, but not unattractive. The look wasn't one of curiosity—not like seeing a foreigner you'd like to learn more about. Instead, it was of someone interested, maybe trying to find some avenue of conversation.

"I, uh…" Rick faltered. How should he answer that? If he was really in the past, he'd have to try and count back and make up a year…

"Just answer honestly," she said as though reading his thoughts. "We know you stumbled, we'll help you adjust."

He sighed. "August 7th, 2107."

She smiled. "You look so young."

Rick smiled awkwardly back. He wasn't sure how to respond.

"You're fifteen years older than me," Sue said.

The man who had flipped off Parker looked up from his dominos. "I was born in 2126, stumbled when I was 10, fell into 1861. I can only thank God the policeman I was brought to when that young couple found me was also a Stumbler."

As Rick examined the old men, he realized they looked incredibly old and tired, especially Darrell if he should only be around 60. Then what Parker had said about cancer struck him.

"I was born in 2139," said the other Daryl. "I stumbled in a freak soft spot the day before the Stable Event. But rules is rules and I'm stuck here too."

The two old men continued their game, and Sue had written down Rick's birthday on her order pad and had done some simple math. "Get used to the number 1883, that's your birth year. If you happen to have any history type stuff on your phone, an encyclopedia or something, brush up on it, but we have reading material, too."

She continued to rattle on about technical details, how the doctor should see him, but it was all just background noise. What he thought was a fluke, a scam, wasn't clearing up—it was just getting more and more complicated. He was really two hundred years in the past in a small town in middle-America, surrounded by other fugitives both younger and older than himself, but their ages were all messed up. He couldn't do anything about it. He could feel the chair, smell the food, hear the voices and sounds, but nothing was what he had been seeing, smelling, and hearing just over an hour ago. He could feel himself starting to lose it. His breathing was growing shallow, his hands and feet were getting cold, and even the edge of his vision was getting fuzzy and dark.

He looked down at the sandwich. His hands were on either side of the plate and he reached over and rubbed a dab of mayonnaise from the edge of it. Sue's hand reached across and grabbed his wrist. When he looked up, she didn't say anything. She just smiled, that same welcoming smile from before.

THW

SHE SPEAKS TO ME

Written 2014

Self-published March 2015

New and increasingly enhanced methods of archeology have opened windows onto pasts we thought we had learned all we could from. Hell, just digging up old parking lots reveal things about our past we chose to forget. What is buried is not always buried forever, and what lingers with the missing, is not always meant to be found. A little Lord Carnarvon fucking around and finding out, but with much more present and gruesome effects.

Lair was really the best word for it. In the wilderness west of Staiti and north of Pietrapennata, deep in the toe of Italy, the lair had been discovered by digital explorers pouring over high resolution satellite imagery. The structure wasn't natural, no cave structure existed there. However, whoever had excavated the site initially certainly attempted to make it look like one.

At first, considering the number of large blocks of stone found within, it was believed to be a small query. Perhaps a landowner at one time had discovered exposed bedrock and dug it out through his own means. But it was when one of the blocks was being moved that the place began to divulge its secrets.

Quite unexpected, and through no excessive action, a corner of one of the stones crumbled away, revealing something within. Once exposed, the rest of the casing, which had been carved to appear as rock, gave up a pristine statue of a well-muscled man. Posed in a stand with his fists at his side and his head held high, it appeared to be something out of the Archaic Period of Greek sculpture.

Out of ten blocks, only three seemed to be hiding statues. In addition to the rigid man was another Archaic style modeled after the Egyptian god Anubis. The jackal head, though, was more realistic than in Egyptian portrayals and more akin to the half man, half beast creatures of Greek mythology. The third statue, however, garnered the most attention.

A female form in Hellenistic style, more detailed and lifelike than the other two, it had the unique feature of being encased twice. The outer layer gave way easily as the others did, but the statue was slathered with a concrete mixture that required delicate removal. The marble was rough, unpolished, indicating the piece was incomplete, but as the concrete gave way it became apparent the surface had been intentionally damaged.

I had been there when the female was finally cleaned. For the effort that had gone into hiding these statues, speculation arose that these pieces were being smuggled. But the female form seemed to be hidden in a way as though no one wanted it found. Why not just destroy it?

"Maybe they couldn't." Postulated Olivia Cartright.

The pieces had been moved to Rome. We were cleaning them, assisting in the cataloguing, trying to glean some history. The faux stone casing was a brittle plaster, but the concrete was a pozzolanic cement. Stronger than modern material and messily smeared over chiseled scars, it was an ordeal to remove it without further damaging the statue. This wasn't a patch-job, someone was trying to hide it. The face had it the worst, great effort had gone into destroying the surface and layering globs of concrete.

"I think they tried." Olivia said, pointing to the random gashes in the stone. "It's like someone took hammers, picks, the largest tools they could get their hands on to try and smash it. Yet, all they could do was scratch it."

"It looks no different than any other marble statue I've seen." I argued. "I guarantee if we took a hammer to it, we would break it. I think the artist wasn't happy with the work and they were going to renovate the piece in order to save the larger portion."

She shrugged. "I don't know, Ryan. I just get a feeling of malice. Someone was angry, but they couldn't destroy it. So, they hid it."

"And the other two?"

She chewed on her bottom lip. "I don't know."

The female statue stood straight up, its hands folded in front, palms up. The hip was popped out to one side just slightly, a relaxed figure of an average woman of the day.

"I can see someone being terrified of Anubis, Olivia," I pressed, "but this...how could someone hate this?"

She shrugged and said not much more.

Our small team had the facilities for a week. Cleaning the statues, determining when and where they were carved, potentially by whom, and trying to piece together the available clues as to their origins was exhaustive. But Olivia grew tireless. Through the days she was earliest to arrive and the last to leave, often shooed away by campus security.

For every note we made, she wrote ten. For our frustrations at the mystery, she was fascinated and more enamored with the marred female form. Finally forcing her away for lunch in the cafeteria midway through the week, I tried to take her mind off the work and statue, if only for half an hour.

"Did you call your husband last night?" I asked her. "I could hear you talking through the wall last night…I hope everything's okay. I only ask because it sounded…"

She stared at me, a dual look in her eyes. At once she looked afraid of what I might have heard, but also there was confusion, as though I had asked something absurd.

"No," she shook her head firmly. "I did not speak with my husband, I do not have time. She needs me, I was talking with her."

I made the connection, but it was so sudden I was caught off guard. "She? Who?"

Olivia leaned over the table, her chest nearly dipping into her plate of untouched food. "The others only whisper, but she speaks clearly…urgently. She tells me answers to questions I didn't know to ask."

"Who speaks, Olivia?"

She scowled and leaned back into her chair, pushing her plate signaling no desire to eat. "If you do not know then she must not want you to know."

I pressed, but she only stared silently a moment more before getting up and returning to the workroom. A few heads turned awkwardly back to their own meals as I looked around, catching gawkers of the scene. I would have ogled as well. Olivia was not herself in the slightest; even those who did not know her could see something was wrong.

290

Approaching our last day of study, chemical analysis on what was thought to be paint on the head of Anubis proved to be blood. Sacrifice wasn't unusual for Greeks, Egyptians, or any others from the period, but it was unsettling, nonetheless. Especially given Olivia's growing obsession. She was unfazed by the news and rather seemed annoyed we had only just figured something out.

In the middle of the night just before our last day, Olivia began moving about her room, speaking franticly. My bed was against the wall between us, and the sounds gave me a start. As I tried to listen, words were not clear, though it did sound like two distinct voices. When I heard her door open and slam, I jumped up and dressed quickly to pursue her.

Few pedestrians or cars were about the streets of Rome at 3 A.M., fortunate since Olivia meandered down the middle of the road. I found it unusual she was alone when I was certain I had heard a second voice from her room. I considered perhaps she had had her speakerphone on. I kept my distance, but it was no surprise when she approached the university.

She gave the main entrance a pass and headed round to an unlocked window that looked in on our workroom. She must have been anticipating this midnight sojourn and left herself access. I watched as she clambered through, all the while muttering loudly, though I could make out no discernable subject.

She did not turn on the room's lights, but instead I saw only the faint glow of a desk lamp. I considered calling authorities, but curiosity got the better of me as I approached the window.

Peering in, I could only see her back. She was kneeling at the foot of the female statue, but the light was poor, I could see nothing more. Again, I heard two voices, but could see only Olivia.

I called to her in an elevated whisper. Her shoulder twitched as though she would turn, but the second voice hissed, and she remained. Fearing for her safety I jumped through the window, again foregoing better judgment.

When Olivia spoke, it was difficult to understand. "She s'oke to ee. Told ee what she needed. Only I could gith it to her."

Her voice was full of air, and I could hear the gnashing of her teeth. It was strange that the second voice still sounded so far away as I approached Olivia. It was a whisper, soft, but earnest. There were no words I could understand, but it was incessant. Meanwhile, I could hear ragged breathing from Olivia.

"Who's here with you, Olivia?" I begged. "Are you in danger?"

I was nearly on Olivia when she finally turned. What I saw sent me reeling backwards, I hit the desk with the lamp, casting the light higher and wider into the room. Before me, Olivia was drenched in blood, her eyes bugging, and her teeth exposed. When I realized she had cut off her face I nearly fainted.

"She can s'eak now!" Olivia said without the benefit of lips, her teeth and tongue clicking loudly. "Can't you hear her?"

Now angry the whispering elevated. I realized it came from above. When I looked up to the statue, I was horrified again to see that Olivia had affixed her face to the scoured surface of the statue's head. I screamed a sound I did not think I could make when I saw the lips moving, the culprit behind the menacing second voice.

I don't remember finding the hammer, but it was in my hand as I smashed at the thing's face. Hindsight suggested that the horror of Olivia's visage perhaps caused me to hallucinate; that I should have removed the face to possibly save it. But I remember hearing that voice, speaking in some other language I did not recognize. Not Greek or Roman, but something inherently ancient, something that awoke a savagery in me necessary to destroy stone.

Despite my failure to alert authorities, they arrived on the scene shortly, silent alarms no doubt tripped by our presence. I was dragged away, still thrashing and attempting to put an end to the reborn monster. I can remember hearing Olivia explain as I tried to kill the unliving thing that the others were merely guardians that posed no threat, but it was her, the statue, who needed a face to enter our world.

The statue was removed, moved to a place no one on our team knew. To protect it, or to protect us, I can't be sure. Olivia lived, she was given a face transplant and her husband never left her side, but she was never the same. Though neither was I. I speak to him sometimes, to see how Olivia is doing, but it's always the same. She laments endlessly and sometimes I hear her over the phone. In those instances, all I can see is her face on the statue, eagerly begging for life.

THW

EATING CROW
Written 2014
Self-published, March 2015
EATING CROW was one of those near-misses. Accepted, rescinded, alternative route from the same publisher, then silence to the tune of nothing happening at all. Sometimes a publisher folds. At least it wasn't stolen. This story was written on lunch breaks while I worked for a furniture store. I sat on some benches next to a high school's running track. Usually, it was empty. Occasionally, students actually took to the track and I had paranoid fears a teacher would approach me. But I left them alone and they did the same. Eventually I went the other direction for lunch breaks and did my writing in a cemetery. The protagonist isn't identified in any way, this is your, the reader's, point of view, and the final question is yours to ponder.

I could hear the scuffling; another victim. My eyes burn like sandpaper is being dragged across them, yet there are no tears left. I think my last drink of water was last night. Maybe it's been about a day. We'll go through this again, he'll get frustrated, but he'll succumb. Only after another victim, though.

There's a startling jar as he grabs the wheelchair's handles and leans over me to unlock the wheels. He doesn't say anything, yet. I'm carefully wheeled out of the room, through the hall, and back down the steps. It bothers me how delicate he is with me versus the victims. We're back on the tile, turn to the right, turn to the left, I can hear her gasping for air. Dammit, it's a woman.

He takes the hood off, but not the cloth covering my mouth. Just a bandana folded over, not even a gag.

"We have a young one, tonight," he says with no remorse. "Maybe the right kind of temptation."

She's been beaten pretty bad, fresh bruises cover her arms and body, she's undressed and awfully thin; most likely a homeless girl. Her face is fine, though, he doesn't hit them in the face. She looks scared and confused, but far away. God! I recognize this girl, a vagrant that hangs out outside of my regular supermarket asking for change or cigarettes. She can't be any more than 15.

"You have to stop this…" I plead, muffled by the bandana.

I can't see his face, he never lets me see his face, but I can hear him sigh with disappointment. "Not until you admit what you are. I'll find what you desire, it's just a matter of time…or you'll die of starvation and the world is less one more monster anyway."

"This is bullshit, you're fucking crazy!" I scream rattling in the chair.

"Careful, now, you'll fall in." He says.

I look to my left, right on the edge of the pool.

The girl isn't even aware of what she's looking at and isn't coming around. Her eyes are searching, but she looks like she's in shock, she must have been clobbered. She's not bound at all, just dragged back here and laid at the edge of the pool so I can see her.

He comes around from behind me with his hood on as always. He shows me the box-cutter, as always. He stands over her for just a moment.

"Get up! Wake up!" I scream.

No response, just gasping for air and eyes lolling about like a fish out of water.

He bends over and slices her neck so deep I hear the pop of air as her throat opens up. Blood gushes out over the tile. Awareness suddenly comes back, but her scream only results in a hideous gurgle as the air finds the new hole instead of her mouth, the blood bubbles and foams as she tries to struggle. But the sudden loss of blood and the last of her energy cause her simply to faint.

I shut my eyes tight, refusing to look, but I can still hear and smell, knowing yet another victim has died.

"Why…" is all I can whimper as I want to cry myself to sleep, again.

I hear him move. Then his hand is on my face, wiping blood all over the bandana covering my mouth. I can smell it, his initial force slipping cloth through my lips, and I can taste it. I choke but have nothing to vomit up.

"This is why. Show me; show me what you are, just once. Let yourself feed!"

Just like always.

"I am not a fucking vampire!" I scream with such vehemence that I startle even myself.

He gets in my face, his breath stinking through his mask and the blood, "Quit lying, just do it, just feed on her blood, admit what you are…just show me."

I have no strength to scream or yell anymore.

He makes a disgusted sound and walks away, leaving me alone with the poor young girl. He'll be back soon. He'll continue to "tempt" me as he puts it, and finally give up and hose me off where I'll finally get some fresh water.

Four nights now, I'm starving, he hand feeds me undercooked meat and the only liquid I get is when he hoses me off. Four nights and this girl, probably a runaway living on the streets, parents wondering where she is, is his fourth victim. Every night he accuses me of being a monster, a vampire, he's going to reveal to the world. But he's the monster, murdering these people in front of me. Sometimes I wish I was the monster he thinks I am…I would gladly tear him apart.

There's a clattering sound, followed by running water, as he washes his hands and the box knife. I hear the rustling of cloth, either drying his hands or removing his hood to get some air. He dares to sigh.

Somehow, I manage tears and flutter my eyelids, I don't want to see the girl, but the tears sting my eyes. Her mouth is hanging open and the eyes stare blankly at the end of the pool. It doesn't look like the blood is pumping so strongly from her neck wound anymore, but the blood has spread out over so much of the tile it's actually under the wheelchair. I can smell it, which reminds me I can taste it, and despite my eyes being so swollen and irritated, the tears manage to flow.

The chair shakes, startling me, he's moving me out of the way, treating me as a thing, just an object that's currently in his way. He does the same to the girl, shoving her into the pool where she floats for a moment, but the water begins to rush in to the wound and she slowly sinks to the bottom, to rest with the other three bodies. I can't take it anymore. I begin to rock the chair, I want to fall into the water,

I'll take big gasping breaths when I hit and drown myself. But without a word, he comes over and pulls me clear of the pool's edge.

I'm stuck, still his prisoner, but now just a piece of furniture. This is nowhere near as bad as seeing him murder people trying to tempt me to eat them, but seeing him mop the tile, then clean the pool filter and kick on the pump system and check chemicals, it frightens me. What depths his depravity that he can pick a victim, beat them into submission, bring them here only to kill them while accusing me, a stranger to him as well, of being a monster, and then go about his chores in some macabre routine? Is that his purpose? Is he a serial killer that needs an audience and placing the blame on me makes it okay for him to kill these people?

I don't know where we are, but it must be his house, and the pool must be in some interior basement. There are no windows, reminding me of the practice pool my high school swim team had in the basement at the center of the school. But it's not a school, here the walls are blank, white or beige, the soft yellow lights in the ceiling make it hard to discern color. I don't know if he's white or black or whatever, but he's got to be wealthy. He's never gone long so I can only assume we're mid-town. Nice houses with access to unsavory areas. He's got to have a regular area he cases, too, if he picked me and his last victim from the same area. Regardless, if it's a pool in the basement sitting under a mansion, no one would hear me anyhow.

"Hey…" I say, almost surprised with myself.

He stops mopping, thin, bright red streaks smearing across the tile.

"You say I'll die anyway, that I'll starve if I don't 'feed;' why do you keep feeding me meat and letting me drink water?"

"Anything that suffers long enough will reveal its true nature." He says in a gravelly huff.

"A dog will snap at anything if it's hungry enough, what makes you think turning me into a desperate animal will prove I'm a dangerous monster?" I ask trying to reason with someone clearly unreachable.

He begins to swirl the mop in a figure-8. "We are all dangerous monsters, but sometimes even the hunter needs a predator."

Oh, God. This is the part in the movie or TV special where you figure out the bad guy is really acting out like this because he's trying to bring about justice against himself. Like he knows what he's doing is wrong, and knows I'm no vampire, but is waiting for something horrendous to happen to him so that he can pay for his crimes in some twisted justice of his own design.

"Has it occurred to you that if I were a vampire, I wouldn't have allowed you to catch me? That maybe I would be strong enough to break through duct tape? Why haven't I changed shape to escape you?"

I'm nauseated to even feign conversation with him, but if I can appeal to any sort of reason or logic within his mind…

"We live in the real world." He says continuing to clean the girl's blood. "Shape-shifting is a matter of context, you cannot exceed or dismiss your current amount of mass, whatever you would change into, if you could change at all, would be the same general size and mass you currently have. I imagine the process wouldn't be fast or comfortable either and more akin to a rat shifting its bones to fit through a tight spot versus actually changing the physical makeup of your anatomy.

"You also have no leverage to gain momentum, so regardless of how strong you might be—which vampires aren't typically very strong since they are in near starvation-mode on a constant basis due to the shame of their lifestyle, but I digress—you simply cannot break your bonds because you can't move against them."

He stops and leans on the mop, looking at me through the black sack that is his hood. He's not terribly big, but obviously strong. He clocks his victims from behind then singlehandedly transports them from the scene to this place. That's what happened to me as I was leaving a grocery store in the early AM, and I'm sure that's what happened to the victims in the pool.

"If you could do the things you claim, you would have done it." He says, turning my logic back on me. "No; vampires are vicious predators, yes, but they are still bound by the laws of nature. In an ideal environment in full health, I would suspect a vampire to be on par, if not having the edge over, say, an Olympian; superior to their prey, but only enough so to satisfy their needs. If nature was handing out super-powers, we'd all have learned to fly by now."

He believes his own stuff, believes it in a way that it's not a matter of belief or faith, it is a matter of fact not to be argued.

My eyelids suddenly grow very heavy, and I maybe doze off for just a second, my head teetering on my neck. "Why me," I say abruptly, maybe loudly, trying to stay awake. "What makes you think that I'm a vampire?"

He drops the mop on the floor, walks over to the hose coiled up on the wall and unravels it. Turning the spigot, he grabs the sprayer and washes the blood into the pool off the tile, making quick work of his chores. Maybe I struck a chord? Then he turns the hose on me, the water is frigid, but I begin to suck on the bandana on my face, this is the only moisture I get.

The bandana still has her blood on it. I'm drinking her blood; he's turned me into a desperate animal. Probably his intention anyway.

After he's done pelting me with cold water he comes over and leans into me, in the bad light I can't even make out the shape of his head or what kind of hairstyle he might have. Finally, he answers my question.

"You stink. Vampires all stink of death."

He reaches behind me and pulls out the hood and blinds me. I expect to feel the chair go back the way we came, but instead he wheels me forward until the front wheels hit the raised lip of the pool. He pushes forward, tipping the chair up onto its front wheels and gravity starts to pull me down, toward the water.

"A vampire wouldn't die under water, not in the same way a human would. You'd bide your time, waiting like a crocodile. But if you were stuck to a chair…maybe that would be a better way to keep you."

Oh, God, he's going to drown me. The adrenaline surges, I try to use my taped limbs to hold me up and, in the chair, to push my center of gravity back against him. I can hear myself begin to hyperventilate.

Without a word, he lowers me back down, and we go the way we came.

Back in the empty room he keeps me in, I can thankfully no longer smell the blood, bleach, and chlorine of the pool, however this room stinks of urine, my own urine; hardly a consolation. He removes my hood again.

He comes from behind the chair with a dirty plate that has small slices of raw-looking meat. I don't know where he gets it from, but this looks like the same plate and even the same meat he has been feeding me. It's dried out and perhaps even beginning to rot. He pulls down the bandana and shoves his fingers with a piece of meat into my mouth, down my throat. He doesn't feed me so much as shoves food into me. He covers my mouth so I can't spit it out and natural impulse causes me to swallow, especially as starved as I am.

I can only barely maneuver in the chair thanks to his restraints, so there's no way I can dodge his feeding ritual. I think to ask him that if I were a vampire, why not just bite off his fingers? But I know his answer, with that lack of mobility I'd be stuck forever and unable to defend myself.

With no more conversation, he finishes feeding me four thumb-sized pieces of meat, covers my head again, and shuts off the light. I have no choice but to sit and wait for the next victim he'll offer up to sacrifice to me. I'll cry and piss myself. It doesn't matter where this house is on Earth; I'm currently in Hell.

In the dark, I have no choice but to reflect on the series of events that have occurred. A middle-aged woman who screamed uncontrollably, unable to move since he broke all of her limbs, and my captor spoke in normal tones, directly into my ear that first night. I had only been bound for a few hours before that happened, and I thought I was going to die from sheer terror. He cut her wrists until she bled out, the screaming slowly fading to whimpers until she was silent. Then he "bathed" me and force-fed me for the first time.

The next two nights it was older men, possibly vagrants as well. One he cut all over the man's body turning him into a bloody mess before slashing his throat. The second he tortured for an extended amount of time, fileting the man's arms and legs, exposing muscle tissue; he either died or passed out and when I didn't react, he was dumped in the pool.

Then this evening, a beaten girl, unceremoniously murdered in an effort to entice his monster quarry with a lot of blood all at once. This evening was the first time he tried to force feed me the victim's blood.

Nausea strikes me hard and I vomit in my hood, mostly stomach acid and water, but it feels like I coughed up the meat as well. Just as well. Waves of hot and cold wrack my body, I begin to weep, and just pray sleep comes quickly.

*　　*　　*

Out of the room, through a door, carpet to smooth floor, next will be the steps, then tile. But it seems like I only just fell asleep. Has it already been another day? I haven't seen a clock or outside light in the last four days. Or is it five? It may not have even been four days yet…he may be just waiting for me to pass out then starting the process over again. I have no idea. In fact, I feel especially fuzzy right now.

He closes one door, opens the other to the pool room. The smells hit me hard, chlorine and bleach; I can still smell blood, a tangy, raw iron smell. He moves me down the stairs, each of the three steps feeling like a free fall. In fact, I lose track of the movements after the last step, I wretch and cough up bile and blood.

He speaks, but his voice seems far away, "You are dying. Perhaps tonight you'll finally give yourself up."

"I'm not a vampire," I whisper. "I'm starving and sick and stressed. You're feeding me rotting scraps of meat and barely letting me drink and making me sit in my own filth."

He pulls off my hood and his hooded face is in front of mine. "I'll kill you, set you free; but you're going to show me what you are first."

"I thought you said I wouldn't be able to shape shift? Mass or whatever…"

"A lion is magnificent and beautiful sitting still on the Serengeti, but a horrifying beast on the hunt, despite being exactly the same animal."

He goes behind me. I can hear and feel him manipulating some sort of device, affixing it to the back of the chair. He gently grabs my forehead and pulls my head back against a rounded headrest and then fastens a leather belt around my forehead to hold my head in place. I see a couple of metal wire frame…things, come into view. He pushes them to my eyes and slips uncomfortable polished metal pads under my eyelids forcing them open. I cannot shut my eyes to even blink. He intends to force me to watch.

If there's a victim I can't hear them, but I then focus on a rope hanging from the ceiling to the floor, though I cannot see the floor directly in front of me.

He steps away, soft footfalls on the tile as he goes to my side, I hear metal clanking and the rope slapping the floor. The rope in front of me goes taught, then pulls up and I hear plastic sliding against the tile. A black, makeshift body bag rises with each pull of the rope, the new victim is tightly wrapped in plastic, tied at the ankles and swaying now completely lifted off of the floor. I cannot tell their sex or age, but most likely an adult male.

"You've refused to react to the offerings I've made so far," he says from out of view.

Offerings? "I'm not a fucking vampire!"

Did I yell that? Or was it a whimper?

"So, we'll treat this as cattle, blood only, but fresh. That's how you see us anyway."

I can see the person is moving against their bonds within the bag. Small slits are cut to allow for breathing, but they're gagged within the bag, and I can only hear the smallest of grunts. I still can't tell if it's a man or woman.

He finally steps into view. In his hand he has an ice pick rigged with some sort of plastic, tapered drain plug affixed to the hilt. Without a word he jams the pick into the person's neck, and the plug holds open the wound and lets the blood pour freely onto the floor. It's forceful and spurting, I can feel drops hit my ankles.

I contemplate putting on a charade, maybe if I act like I want a drink of the blood, give him a show, he'll finally kill me. He's going to kill me anyway, through starvation or infection, one. The body in the bag jerks violently and I hear a murmur past a gag. This person is dying, blind and scared, and for absolutely no reason and I can't shut my eyes, I can barely look away.

The man is standing to the side, his arms folded, waiting for a reaction. I can't scream or yell. I can't cry; my eyes are already drying out from being held open. I can't even act like I want out. I've gone catatonic and I can feel myself slipping away. Is this shock? Am I fainting with my eyes held open?

He steps in front of me, thankfully blocking my view of the weakly thrashing body hanging there, dying. He doesn't care. He's taken at least five lives now, and he doesn't give two shits. He's trying to coax out a non-existent monster.

"Maybe you have gotten weak," he says. "Just ask, just show me that you need it, and this can all be over."

I stare into where his eyes should be with little alternative, until something catches my attention to the left, in the water. I must be losing it, hallucinating, something is moving in the water. Did this fucker put a shark in the pool? The oddity of it pulls me into focus, he notices, and looks.

I figure he'll tell me something seriously messed up, like when he feeds the shark this next victim, the feeding frenzy will remind me of what I am or some shit.

"What the fuck?" he says instead.

And with that, the water explodes, splashing and soaking me entirely, the chlorinated water burning my exposed eyes, which brings the offhand realization a shark couldn't live in chemically treated water. The force of the splash sets the hanging body to swinging to and fro. And I realize my captor is no longer in front of me. Trying to focus and turn my head the little bit I can, I look to my right, where I can see two bodies struggling, but I can't tell what's happening. There's no sound other than that of a struggle against wet tile.

Then with an exceptionally wet sounding tear there's a scream, a man's scream. They move violently now, whatever came out of the water is on top of him, pinning him. It's moving too much or I'm too shocked to comprehend, but I can tell it's naked, thrashing against the man.

He gags and gasps, then he starts saying "No" over and over in a scared, childish whimper. It becomes strained and the sound of his voice grows almost alien, just a weird guttural exultation, no words, just sound. Suddenly there's a loud crack.

It's quiet, save for the sound of the wake subsiding in the pool, splashing against the edges and the sound of blood pouring out of the hanging body. And a wet sucking sound. I can't see far enough to the right, I can only tell there are two bodies, one naked on top of my captor. The crack must have come from him, there are no more sounds of pain or fear; he must be dead. Whatever was in the water just erupted from absolutely nowhere and killed him. And now I'm stuck to a wheel chair with my eyes held open, burning from chlorine, in front of a dead or dying hanged body pouring its blood all over the floor in a house I have no idea where is.

I am fucked.

I realize I can feel adrenaline surging through my body, it actually burns, and since I can't move, it's really making me nauseous…or maybe that's the reality of the situation.

The naked thing lifts up and moves in such an abnormal way I could only liken it to a crippled spider. Seeing small breasts hanging from its chest, I realize it's a person, but it doesn't look at me and its dark wet hair is obscuring its face. Watery blood is dripping from its hair onto the floor before it reaches the hanging body and tears out the ice pick and drinks from the gaping hole. The body shutters a couple of times, most likely death spasms. The thing from the water sits, but not in any ordinary fashion, it sits like it doesn't know how to sit. This thing looks human, but clearly is only mimicking.

"I'm sorry," it says in a deep, manly voice. I would almost think it was from someone else if I hadn't seen the back heave with the breath and vocalization.

"There's no reason you should have been here, to see any of this. What's happening shouldn't be happening to you."

As it spoke, the voice began to soften, like someone was changing the pitch on a dial, going from an earthy James Earl Jones to a sultry Marilyn Monroe.

"Do you feel sick?" it asks, now sounding completely female.

I can't answer, I'm shaking, and I've probably soiled myself.

It turns in that unfamiliar movement, looking under its left armpit at me, eyes huge and questioning, but upside down. Somehow it turns itself entirely around passing through the arch of its arm. Its face and the center of its chest are completely covered in blood.

"It's because you're already changing."

It wipes its mouth with one arm, smearing the blood, but exposing enough color that I realize, much to my horror, it is the girl from last night; the homeless girl from the supermarket. Her throat is still slashed but healed significantly.

"You had no choice, no way of knowing, and I am sorry." She says.

I can see the throat, muscle, and tendons move within the slit. I had heard her throat pop open.

"How…?" I manage to ask.

She gives me an apologetic smile. "He had the wrong one, he thought you were me, or what I am anyway…"

"Vamp—"

"It doesn't matter," she interrupts. "What's happened here is a crime, not just against innocent people, or even you, but against nature; the way of things. You're changing through no choice or fault of your own or even by design. He was stupid, and I cannot apologize to you enough, I can only offer you a separate choice."

"What…?"

But I realize I know exactly what she's talking about.

She reaches up delicately, making sure not to actually contact me skin to skin, and pulls out the retractors holding my eyes open. I blink rapidly, which hurts at first, but begins to soothe my eyes.

She points at her neck, then points at my mouth. "He didn't know and put you in danger, exposed you to something you never should have dealt with."

She stands up and stretches, the movements finally looking more human.

Bending back down, she begins to delicately remove my restraints and the tape holding me in place. "You are changing. But I can offer you a choice. You can let it happen, and become something more than human, but it will hurt. The change will hurt, the existence will hurt, but you will live…I don't know, forever is cliché, we can die, but if you survive and take care, you can live a long time. Or…I can kill you; that will hurt, too, but that pain will end."

"I-I…"

She's set me completely free. She brings her face right in front of mine, her eyes are so big. "Choose."

ATG

J.D. Buffington

THE HOUSE WITH NO DOORS

Written 2014

Self-published, February 2015

I love this story. It originated with the single image of a person being hanged, barely off the ground, their toes able to touch ground, but not gain purchase or alleviate the strangling. The house built up around this image, then the world and trio of friends, based on me and my real friends. One of my friend's brother is even a cop. There is a single line spoken by Matthew McConaughey's Rustin Cole from True Detective, "This place looks like someone's memory of a town, and the memory is fading." I wanted to spin that line out into the whole town that's being forgotten, and why.

"The story goes, an old couple, a pair of writers, built a little house away from town." Bram said to his two young daughters. "Their driveway was a mile long and the only road to it was the only road back to town. When the town grew and made their driveway a city street, the old couple demanded they get to name the roads: Soliloquy and Cellar Door. They liked the sound of those words. But they didn't really want to be a part of the town. So, the old man sealed him and his wife up in the house; in a living tomb!"

The girls' eyes went wide and one asked, "Wouldn't they die?"

Bram sneered as he spoke, "They were never seen again. Though if you go to the house, they say you can hear them knocking from inside…"

As they listened, he moved his arm to the table next to him and rapped on it firmly. The girls jumped and Bram's friends sitting in the living room with them laughed. The girls giggled in return.

"Don't worry too much, girls," Craig chimed in. "When they named the street Cellar Door, the husband thought it would be funny to hide the doors to the house."

Bram shook his head and looked at his girls. "That's what chickens say so they won't be scared."

"That's funny…" Sean mocked.

"Don't start." Bram moaned.

Sean leaned forward to catch Bram's daughters' attention. He pointed his thumb at Bram, "Your dad is the one who very first told me that line."

The girls giggled at their dad while he shot withering glares at his two old friends. "Come on, girls, that'll be enough."

"Aww, the sun is still up!" one of them whined.

"It's still 8 o'clock, and that's still bedtime." Bram countered.

They reluctantly marched to their shared room as their father followed to tuck them in.

Bram came back into the living room a few minutes later carrying a new round of beers. He handed one to Craig then started to hand one to Sean, but pulled back as Sean almost grabbed it. "Fuck you, buddy; I'm not gonna hear the end of that for a week!"

Sean laughed. "Hey, you're the one trying to terrify your girls before bedtime."

"They asked and I tried to give the closest thing to the truth." Bram shrugged.

He handed the beer to Sean then sat back down.

Craig took a long drink then said, "There is no closest thing to the truth. Soliloquy and Cellar Door were there before the house, but I've heard the story of the writers before."

"Hell," Sean said, "it's not even close to that intersection; that's just where you leave the beaten path."

"I remember." Craig said. "God, what's it been? Fifteen years?"

"Heck no," Bram shook his head. "I'm not heading out there"

Sean leaned forward with a devilish grin on his face. "Craig, I think that's the best idea you've had in a year!"

Bram took a drink and just stared at the two of them.

"Come on, Bram." Craig begged. "It is still light out."

"For now!" Bram whined.

"Bok! Bok bok bok!" Sean teased.

Bram sighed. "Fine…"

Sean hissed out, "Yes."

Bram pointed at Sean. "You're lucky this is strong beer."

Bram went to his wife to let her know he and the boys were going for a joyride. More interested in her program, she barely raised her cheek for him to kiss with her eyes glued to the television. He laughed, they exchanged I love you's, and he grabbed his keys.

Craig shot up. "Huh-unh! You just commented on strong beer. I've only had one; I'll drive."

"Fine." Bram said. "I like your car better anyway."

"No, you cannot mess with the power windows in the center console." Craig chastised.

Sean shot around them as they headed out through Bram's front door. "Shotgun!"

"You're such a child." Bram said. "I don't care anyway. If I'm in the back seat I can reach the power windows without Craig knowing."

"Don't." Craig ordered. "I will rip that shit out of my own car. I gotta deal with my kid doing that every day, I don't need a grown man wearing it out, too."

Bram shoved his shoulder. "Just get in the car."

"Hey, you didn't even want to go!"

Sean laughed and hopped in the front passenger seat as he heard the automatic lock open. Craig and Bram piled in as well and they were off.

* * *

The house took twenty minutes to reach and the closer they got, the more skeletal the town became. Affluent neighborhoods gave way to poorer sections and cultural sectors. Once thriving shopping centers stood mostly empty; cars in the parking lot just as likely to be broken down as belonging to a customer. The mall they used to go see movies at as kids was a closed off business headquarters that never seemed to have anyone working.

Soliloquy ran north and south. Pulling onto it was like crossing into another world. It marked the county line, but of all the disrepair, this road seemed to suffer the most. On one side was suburban sprawl, the other lonely fields untended by whoever owned them.

"This town is so bipolar." Sean said.

Cellar Door turned east, framed by overgrown trees. Like the legend said, a mile down was an unmarked drive to a simple, abandoned house. Cellar Door continued east for several miles, an access road for farmers.

Despite sitting on someone's land, the house still stood, surrounded by a simple post and wire fence. It was barely tended, a tree growing so close to one wall a person couldn't fit between them. Also true to the legend there were no doors, neither were there windows.

The sun was very low, casting a warm, orange glow. There frankly wasn't even anything creepy about it, just a sad abandoned house.

"I remember being a lot more scared as a kid." Bram said.

"I remember being here much later with cheap beer." Sean lamented.

Bram asked Sean, "Didn't we bring a girlfriend of yours once?"

"I don't remember." Sean shrugged.

Craig took the first steps towards the platform that served as a porch. "It's just boarded up." He muttered.

The other two approached as well, inspecting the large panels. Outside of the curiosity of an empty house, there was nothing extraordinary.

Bram saw an edge warped away from the wall, the wood water damaged. In the gap he could see a glint of glass. "Aha," he mused, "a window."

Pulling at the panel, he found it loose and easy to pull down. At first, the glare of the setting sun made it impossible to see inside. He pressed his face to the glass, shielding his eyes.

When his eyes adjusted, he could feel his skin begin to crawl and his insides go cold. Chalking it up to his own imagination he continued to stare, to try and verify to himself what he saw. The impulse to call out to his friends was strong, but he couldn't tear his eyes away.

In a doorway just outside of the light it looked like a stretched out figure, either dangling or tiptoeing. Or it could be a curtain just out of view. Something caused it to shamble. Pulling out his cellphone he turned on the flash and pressed it against the window.

In a dusty slip, her skin sickly pale, a woman hung by her neck with her toes just barely scraping the floor. Her arms stretched forward towards him, and he could see the words on her lips: "Help…help."

Without a thought he stepped back and pitched his phone as hard as he could through the window. The old single-pane glass shattered easily, and he scrambled through with little regard for the stings and scratches his mind told him he would need to get checked out for how dusty this place was. Rushing for the woman, his mind also told him it was incredibly cold in here despite the summer heat.

He could hear Sean outside, ignorant of the situation and ever so crass, "What the fuck is going on over there?"

Craig went around the other side of the house and saw the panel on the ground and broken window. He couldn't believe Bram would break in.

Before he could investigate, he heard a loud whoop and honk. Turning around, a highway patrol car had pulled up behind his car. The officer stepped out and called to them.

"Are you gentlemen aware this is private property?"

Craig laughed out loud as he approached and recognized the officer. "This town is entirely too small!"

"Excuse me?" the officer said.

Sean rushed to Craig's side and hissed, "What are you doing?"

Craig looked between them, sure they were playing a joke on him. "It's Bertram, Bram's brother."

They both looked confused.

"Bertram," he continued. "It's us, Craig and Sean! We were at you and your brother's house, like, every weekend…"

The officer clicked into the radio on his shoulder. "I'm going to need backup, one mile down Cellar Door from Soliloquy; possible burg…"

"Shit." Sean groaned.

"Hey, hey!" Craig nervously chuckled. "That's not necessary."

The officer looked directly at Craig. "I can see you recognize me, but I'm afraid I don't know you and I don't have a brother. I don't know how you know my name, maybe we went to the same school, but I'm going to need you to afford me the proper respect; we are not friends."

Craig flashed his palms in surrender. "Ooo-kay."

"Is there anyone else with you?" the officer asked.

Sean said "no" while Craig said "yes."

Sean looked at Craig like he was ready to strangle him.

Craig in turn wondered why these two were acting so strange.

"Yes." Craig pronounced. "Bram; who I know as your brother, Officer. We heard glass shatter and I think he did break into the house…"

The officer leered at the house.

Sean hissed at Craig again. "Who the hell is Bram and why are you pestering this cop; what the fuck has gotten into you?"

Craig shook his head and turned to lead the officer to the side of the house. "We just came here from Bram's house, I don't know what the heck he's doing, I don't know what the heck either of you are doing; but if this is some elaborate trick on all of your parts, I'm punching you all square in the face."

The sun was now all the way down, but the dusk light was still sufficient to see inside of the broken window. Chills ran through his extremities as he saw something just outside the reach of the light inside of the house.

"What did you say your friend's name was again?" the officer asked as he walked up to look in as well.

Craig tore his eyes away to spit the name at the officer, tired of the joke. But the name wouldn't come. A completely different fear washed over him as he realized he suddenly couldn't remember his friend's name. He looked up into the officer's face and struggled to even remember why he felt the slightest bit upset to begin with.

He looked up at the broken window again and saw a morose looking man covered in scratches. The change of view shocked him, causing him to jump. The officer didn't seem to notice as he tried to reposition the displaced panel.

"You look like you've seen a ghost…" the officer noted of Craig's face.

Craig motioned toward the window but said nothing. The officer removed the panel again to look for himself, but there was only an empty room. He shrugged and hung the panel back on rusty nails.

"I'll let the landowner know you all were just sightseeing." The officer assured.

312

Craig nodded, though he was still unsure of the situation or even how he'd gotten to this point.

"I think your friend should drive, though." The officer chastised.

Sean quickly agreed. "Of course; thank you, sir."

The officer canceled his backup call over his radio as they all walked back towards their cars.

"You know," the officer said before the two piled into Craig's car. "A lot of weird calls come up over this house. Nothing ever comes of it, though. I don't know why it hasn't been torn down by now. Hell, I don't know why it hasn't fallen down by now."

He shrugged. "You be safe tonight, we'll forget this happened."

They pulled back out onto Cellar Door and headed back into town as the stars started to poke through the maroon sky.

ATG

EVEN IF AS GHOSTS

Written 2015
Self-published March 2015
A number of my pieces are based on nightmares and night terrors. The wild animal in this story, and how the two protagonists deal with it, was the dream. The rest, was world-building. I wrote this short story while still working on IN THE HOUSE OF IN BETWEEN, so if the title seems familiar, it was a line of my own writing that inspired an entirely separate and different story. I just hope I'm wrong about the use of nuclear weapons to the north of the United States in any future.

Inside was no different from outside; gray, drab, trash everywhere…was it refuse or debris? It took three days to get from the last town to here. Here looked no different than the last town or the road along the way. Everything was wrecked. There was no telling if it was abandoned, left to nature, or bombed out. Nothing grew to help differentiate it. Time marched on, though all it did was rot everything.

The most interesting thing along the way had been where the road had buckled and caved in on an old sewer. Just a hole. But holes were worth paying attention to, especially when they lead someplace you couldn't see into. The building had a hole, too, but no windows. It was dangerous to go in, especially not knowing the area too well.

Perkus and Dardet had walked around the perimeter; only the one hole in the wall. Some large bay doors, rusted shut, and regular doors, locked from inside. They probably wouldn't budge anyway. So, the one entry it was. A defensible building might have plenty to salvage. Perkus made hand signs to Dardet to keep his eyes open and check every corner they encountered.

Inside there was very little light. Turning on flashlights could harm them as much as help. They sidled along the wall and away from the soft light outside, trying to allow their eyes to adjust. Perkus tripped on something that Dardet had managed to miss, though Dardet was quick to catch him. Neither of them made much sound with the incident, but something had noticed them.

Through a smaller sequential hole on an interior wall, opposite where they had entered, a large, sickly looking animal emerged. It was a mammal with just a little hair along its spine. Its skin was exposed with a melted look from severe burns that had healed. It walked on four legs standing about five feet high at the shoulders with spindly front legs. An oversized black and cataract-infected eye stared out at them from the left side of its head.

"Shit." Perkus hissed. "It's a bleach-rat. I wouldn't be surprised if it's what busted through the walls."

"I don't think I've ever seen one of those; are we safe?" Dardet asked.

"It looks like its ears are fucked up, so it may not have even noticed us, and it might be blind judging by that eye; at least on this side." Perkus explained. "This far down from the Snowfields? I bet it's a male and we're best just to stay away from it. They don't eat meat, but males are violent, they charge anything. It's probably looking to stake out new territory. Judging from its scars, it's survived a lot. They aren't good for anything; not meat, not work, not even the females produce milk we can drink. Just mutant cows. After Autumn people herded them to eat trash. Their piss smells like bleach—hence the name."

Autumn. Perkus hadn't talked about that for ages. A hundred and fifty years ago nuclear war happened. It only lasted a few days, but the targets that were hit, that's all it took. Now 37% of the Earth's habitable regions were irradiated, so older folks said. Humans slowly, carefully probed areas closer and closer to contaminated epicenters. Like the Snowfields, where the sun hadn't shone for decades. The animals that survived couldn't very well tell the difference between hot or safe zones. Thus, bovine as living trash compactors, adapting to eat almost anything just to survive.

"You'll have to shoot it in the eye." Perkus told Dardet. "With how that's bulging, it's probably got a tumor pressing it out. Put it out of its misery and keep us safe."

"Why do I have to kill it?" Dardet complained. "That's a waste of a shot."

"I'm not wasting an hour—or God forbid, a whole fucking day—waiting for a bleach-rat to mosey out of a warehouse that could have a treasure trove."

Dardet sighed and pulled out his pistol. "It could be full of rolls of paper growing black mold like the last warehouse we explored."

He checked the magazine and chamber, then knelt to steady his aim. Despite their entire conversation, the act of kneeling seemed to finally catch the creature's attention. Dardet cursed in his mind, it sensed the vibrations in the floor.

The bleach-rat bellowed a horrible mewling sound then charged at them from only three yards away. Dardet took a shot and caught the shell as it popped out. Even in danger, his scavenging instincts dictated his actions. Having his left arm crossed over to catch the shell probably saved his life. The bleach-rat lowered its head to ram him and caught his crossed arm first. Unwittingly shielding himself and relaxed from rote movement, Dardet was just bowled over as the beast fell after ramming him.

The shot had connected. Mercifully killing the beast in one shot, it saved Dardet from having to use another bullet. Hopefully this place had some scrap to make more.

"Perkus?" Dardet called out.

He was nowhere to be seen. He had dove along the wall in the direction the bleach-rat had come from, but now Dardet found he was alone.

"Mister?" asked a small voice from where the bleach-rat had emerged.

Making his way over, Dardet carefully looked around the edge of the hole. Standing just inside the little bit of daylight shining in was a young boy.

"Your friend was hurt, he's back here," the boy said. "You should come help him."

"Perkus?" Dardet called into the darkness.

"You have to come help him, he was knocked out..." the boy continued.

Dardet stared at the boy. Every instinct was telling him to get out and fast. Before he could make the decision to back away, a shadowy figure grew out of the darkness and seemed to snatch the boy back.

The boy screamed and called out for help. "It's my uncle, he's crazy! He'll hurt us all!"

But there was no sound of struggling and the mysterious man said nothing nor made any sound.

"Perkus?" Dardet called again, more forcefully.

Then the sounds of a violent struggle broke out, and a grunting voice sounding like Perkus came out of the darkness. Dardet reacted before he could think, he stepped through the threshold.

Surprised and knocked down again, Dardet felt the gun clatter out of his hand. The boy was on top of him and directly behind him was a man, but he had no color, he was just sooty gray. Dardet was so confused by what he saw he couldn't think on how to defend himself or get away. Fortunately, Perkus had managed to free his mouth, wherever he was, and called out.

"It's a bandol! You'll have to shoot both heads!"

Then there were sounds of another fight erupting in the darkness. Dardet hoped Perkus could take care of himself.

Dardet, knowing what he was up against now, was able to act appropriately. A bandol, technically a human, was a predator, especially out in uncivilized areas. They often had a parasitic twin they would use in some way to lure or disarm victims. The main body of the thing had covered itself in ash to hide in plain sight while its childlike twin, attached to its hips, tried to coax people into the darkness where it would attack.

This is why holes were so dangerous; bleach-rats and bandols and any other number of monsters from a hundred years of radiation, chemicals, and infections—or other people. It sounded like Perkus was in a much more conventional fight.

Dardet was able to push against the bulk of the bandol, forcing the thing up and off of him. He grabbed the "boy's" head. Twisting hard, he felt a snap. Both parts of the creature screamed in pain and fell to the side. Dardet scrambled to grab his gun, but the bandol was back up and charging him before he could take aim.

Lowering his right shoulder, Dardet charged as well. The bandol just so slightly hesitated in surprise giving Dardet the opportunity to knock the thing down again. As it struggled to get back up, Dardet wasted no time grabbing the gun and fired two quick shots into each of the thing's heads.

If one brain in a bandol was left alive, it would heal the other. Dardet had to force its childlike qualities out of his mind. In a better equipped township, a bandol might be operated on at birth and live a normal life if the parasitic twin could be completely removed. Out here, though, if they survived, it was by preying on other people.

Perkus was still fighting. Dardet, fully exposed now, had two choices: run and save his own life or enter a fight he didn't know the parameters of and try and save his friend.

"Perkus, I have four shots left, tell me where to shoot…"

"I can't see!" Perkus cried.

"Tell me where to shoot from my voice!"

"Your right, three feet up!"

After taking the first shot, there was a scattering of feet, multiple bodies running away. Perkus came running out from the shadows—far left of where Dardet had shot, thankfully.

"Come on, you know they'll be back." Perkus said, barely slowing up on his way out of the building.

After making it about a mile further down the road, Perkus finally stopped and sat down, pulling out a map and making some marks.

"We'll need to come and clear that out," he said. "If they're set up to lure in passersby with a bandol, ain't nobody gonna miss 'em. Probably a lot of great supplies, too, if they've holed up there for a good long while."

He wrote "ghosts" in a circle on the map; murderers, bandits, and thieves out on the road.

"Not much of a living…" Perkus complained.

"Living's living," Dardet countered. "That's just what they know. It's what we all know."

"Even if as ghosts?" Perkus asked.

Dardet checked his pistol. "We should head back to the scouting party; let them know what we've found."

Perkus smirked. "Even if as ghosts."

ABOUT THE AUTHOR

J.D. Buffington lives in Tulsa, Oklahoma with his wife, daughter, a capricious cat and two devious dogs. He seamlessly weaves vivid nightmares and haunting anxiety together to immerse readers into a state of fright and wonder.

MORE BY J.D. BUFFINGTON

Nothing But The Willows & Other Things That Are Not There
Come Hither No Malice
In the House of In Between
The Light Across the Street
Red Clouds